Perchance to Dream
and Other Stories

Perchance to Dream
and Other Stories

Michael A. Stackpole

Five Star • Waterville, Maine

First Edition
First Printing: April 2005

Published in 2005 in conjunction with Tekno Books
and Ed Gorman.

Set in 11 pt. Plantin.

Printed in the United States on permanent paper.

Library of Congress Cataloging-in-Publication Data

Stackpole, Michael A., 1957–
    Perchance to dream, and other stories / by Michael A.
Stackpole.—1st ed.
        p. cm.
    ISBN 1-59414-149-5 (hc : alk. paper)
    1. Science fiction, American.   2. Fantasy fiction,
American.   I. Title.
    PS3569.T137P47 2005
    813'.54—dc22   2004029573

Dedication

To Dr. Jack Murray
In fond recollection of Irish whisky, Republican songs
and lots and lots of laughs.

Table of Contents

Introduction

I'll keep this introduction fairly brief since I've written small introductory pieces for each story. I realize writing them and even this is a bit of a narcissistic indulgence. I always find pieces where writers talk about their stories fun and fascinating, and I hope others do too. If you don't, turn the page fast.

When I was growing up, the paradigm for getting published and having a career was simple. You started by writing short stories and getting them published. Once you had enough out, someone would offer you a contract to collect them. If the collection sold at all well, you'd get a contract to write a novel—probably set in the world described by some of your short stories. Once the novels started selling, you were set. It all seemed fairly straightforward, even if there was a lot of work involved in it.

That all changed in the mid-80s, when it became easier to have a novel published in SF/F than a short story. Readers wanted longer work, magazine sales fell off, so the market for shorter work just dried up. And this book, which would have been the prelude to a novel career, suddenly became something possible only *after* a string of novels.

The thing I love the most about writing short stories is that they provide a window on a variety of worlds. The work is as demanding as writing a novel, just shorter in duration. Roger Zelazny used to say that writing a short story was really just writing the last chapter of a novel. He's right in that all the drama has to be packed into this one small space, and to do that, you have to put all the set-up and characterization in there as well.

I attended a literary conference where one speaker noted that if a story went beyond 25 pages or so (roughly 4,000 words), "the reader really expects a payoff." I admit to snorting out loud—to me *all* writing is about the payoff, regardless of length. The stories here range from 2,000 words to over 10,000, and every one of them pays off. They might pay off in different ways, but they pay off nonetheless.

That's the other thing that is fun about short stories. In shorter pieces you can write humor and sustain it, which is all but impossible to do in an entire novel. Drama becomes focused as well. All your energy gets delivered on one point, for a single purpose, which makes short stories the espresso of fiction.

I hope you enjoy what follows. It's a mixed bag culled from throughout my career. I picked each of these tales because there is something about them I love. I think you'll love them, too.

Michael A. Stackpole
Scottsdale, Arizona
21 June 2004

"**Perchance to Dream**" is a story written especially for this collection. In the DragonCrown War novels, we learn that among the exile community of people from Okrannel, there has arisen the custom of returning to their native soil to spend one night and dream. The dreams are given prophetic import. This tale concerns Alexia's Dream Raid and all that flows from it. The events herein have been alluded to in the novels, but never before explored.

Perchance to Dream

A Story of the DragonCrown War

I

"No, cousin, I am quite firm in my conviction. No matter how much I am begged, I shall not marry you."

Princess Alexia turned in the saddle and looked at Mikhail through a shower of raindrops. "You won't marry me?"

He shook his head and stringy black locks flicked water from their ends. "No. No reflection on you, of course. You are tall and quite comely, even beautiful, and shall become more so. And there are those who say your manner is odd, you having been raised by the Gyrkyme, but this matters not to me. You're really not that strange."

Alexia frowned and almost flicked her right fist out at him. She'd have caught him square in the chest. Mikhail, even when he wasn't astride a horse, was not nearly as agile as Perrine and her other Gyrkyme companions. They would have dodged the blow without so much as a fleck of down left behind, whereas Mikhail would topple in the saddle and land in the mud.

"Then, cousin, there is this whole warrior business, which some like but some think is just odd. It may have been your father's desire for you to become a warrior, and Great Grandaunt Tatyana sees this as our salvation, but were I to marry you, it would be so you could bear children for the future of Okrannel."

"Our nation will not have a future if I do not liberate it."

Mikhail's brown eyes sparkled mischievously. "Ah, you've pierced the center of the conundrum which besets the elders."

They both glanced back along the road. Mikhail's father, Grand Duke Valery, rode proudly in the saddle, his head held high, despite the rain and his small stature. Like Mikhail, in accord with a decree from the Crown Circle, Valery wore his hair long in mourning for the death of Prince Kirill, his brother and Alyx's father. White hair peppered the grey on his head and beard, and water glistened at the ends of his whiskers. The man smiled when they looked back at him, the pride he felt in them and his mission undaunted by the weather.

As they turned back, Alyx caught her cousin's eye. "Mischa, you've told me all the reasons why you would not mind marrying me. You haven't said why you wouldn't."

"Two reasons." He grinned at her and stroked the wispy beginnings of his goatee and moustaches as if they were already long and luxurious. "First, there is quite enough inbreeding going on within the Okrans exiles in Yslin. The Crown Circle sometimes acts positively like herdsmen, comparing pedigrees and matching temperaments. Gods forbid anyone fall in love. 'You marry for the love of Okrannel, not yourself,' is the order—and infidelities within and without the community are dismissed as misplaced expressions of grief for our lost nation.

"Second is the fact that Aunt Tatyana *wants* me to marry you." Mikhail's expression soured. "That just won't do. I will admit I almost did agree when I heard about you biting her. She must have tasted foul."

14

Alyx snorted. "Like gall gone to vinegar, then boiled with brine to stew a toad."

Mikhail groaned. "You could have just said she was bitter."

"But that goes without saying." Alyx allowed herself a little smile. Before the nation of Okrannel had fallen to the Nor'witch's forces, her father had sent her south with Preyknosery, a brave Gyrkyme warrior who had long been his friend. Alyx had been a mere baby at the time. Her father died soon after, and the Gyrkyme raised her to be a great warrior. Until she was fifteen she had not left the mountains of Gyrvirgul and the only humans she had seen were those who came to instruct her in history and the arts of war.

The Crown Circle, led by Grand Duchess Tatyana, controlled the life of all Okrans exiles. Tatyana had a reputation of being a mystic and had made the first Dream Raid into Okrannel over a dozen years before. She slipped into the conquered nation, spent the night sleeping on her native soil, and had a prophetic dream.

From that point forward she decreed that every exile should return to Okrannel and similarly dream. Many did—including seasoned warriors like Valery—though the practice quickly became focused on the children of nobility or others who showed signs of promise. In their fifteenth year they would be presented to the Crown Circle, then sent on their Dream Raid. Once they had completed it, they would return to Yslin and report the results to the Crown Circle. The dream would be recorded in the Book of Dreams. Everyone knew those dreams would come true, and events big and small were pointed to as having been predicted by one dream or another.

As per custom, Alyx had been taken to Yslin. Tatyana

had sought to inspect her, prying her mouth open to examine her teeth. Alyx, resenting the rough handling and violation, bit the old woman. She'd been dismissed from her presence and it had been two years before Alyx had been allowed to go on her Dream Raid.

I wonder, Mikhail, if you know that the only reason I'm here is because I am traveling with you. The Crown Circle was indeed in the habit of matchmaking, and Preyknosery had warned Alyx of their intent. Fortunately Valery had not approved of the Circle's plan, and while Alyx sensed no interference or influence from Valery in what Mischa said, she was fairly certain he could have intervened.

Mischa, of course, showed no sign of knowing what was unfolding around him. Alyx didn't think he was stupid, however. In fact, it struck her that he was purposely playing stupid so others would underestimate him—specifically Count Serjei.

While all the others on the trip came from Valery's household, Serjei represented Tatyana. He served to ensure the procedure for a successful Dream Raid was followed to the letter. Alyx found him to be obsequious to the point of making her want to kick him. Though a young man, he was skilled beyond his years in flattery and subservience, which doubtless stood him in good stead with the Crown Circle. In Okrannel his family had been minor nobles in the city of Svoin, but in Yslin he had risen to importance a southern lord would never have known.

Through the years the whole ritual of Dream Raids had become a small industry. Ships usually took the youths from Yslin to Ooriz, a small town on the Jeranese coast. From there the pilgrims picked their way through the mountains that formed the Okrannel-Jerana border. They could have entered almost immediately, but that would have put them on the Zhusk plateau. While the Zhusk had no love for Chytrine and her Aurolani hordes, they had less for Okrans nobles who had continually waged war against them.

Jeranese forces led by General Markus Adrogans maintained order in the border region and tolerated the pilgrims. The Jeranese did nothing to clear the Aurolani from the area the pilgrims would enter. They assumed the Okrans nobility were addled, and if they wanted to camp out in a dangerous area, that was their problem.

Valery had made the trip more than once and had chosen their route with care. They had not shipped in through Ooriz, but instead had sailed all the way to the Jeranese capital of Lakaslin. After having paid their respects to the king, they headed due north and now, a day shy of Okrannel, entered the mountains. For the most of the trip, both on the sea and road, the weather had been miserable. Alyx was fairly certain she would never be dry again.

Valery's scouts rode back to the main party, then led the way to a large cave complex that travelers had clearly used for centuries. Alyx and Mischa helped stable the horses in the cave's lower chamber, brushing them down and making sure each got a healthy serving of oats. Others gathered firewood and set up camp in the cave's upper chambers. In fairly short order, pots had been set to boiling and the scent of stew filled the air.

Alyx lingered behind the blanket that screened an alcove from the main cavern. She was supposed to be changing out of wet clothes, and she was more than willing to do that, but she needed the time alone. She had been raised among the Gyrkyme—a people born of an unholy union between elves and monstrous bird-women. The Gyrkyme themselves were tall and slender, covered with feathers and blessed with wonderful wings that let them fly. Her foster-family had all been of the warrior caste, so had the plumage of raptors, and a fierce love of life that allowed compromise in little. Secrets were seldom tolerated among the Gyrkyme and it was with that ethic she had been raised.

Among men, however, secrets abounded. Even the Dream Raid had at the core of it a secret. Whatever you dreamed you were supposed to reveal to no one save the Crown Circle. This made no sense to her, for if the dreams were truly prophetic, wouldn't it be best to let others be forewarned? And if sharing these visions would allow others to act to change them, then of what value were they in the first place?

The whole phenomenon struck her as silly, but Prey-knosery had impressed upon her the need for her to undertake the journey when the time came. "You are your father's daughter, and Okrannel's Crown Princess. You are a leader and that means you have some obligations. Abide until you have power; then you can change things."

She shivered. So much about humans was alien to her. Some of it was comical. Men made funny noises, belching and farting, grunting and groaning. Other things were disgusting, like how much they were willing to drink. Among the Gyrkyme intoxicants were tolerated, but only in tiny doses. Anyone who became drunk could take wing and end up seriously hurting himself. Some men seemed to revel in the experience of drinking themselves into unconsciousness. It made no sense to her, so she watched and tried to understand.

Mischa, at the very least, had been a joy. He took himself just a trifle too seriously, but she suspected this was to further annoy Count Serjei. He moderated his behavior when his father frowned at him, which Alyx took as a very good sign. Clearly father and son loved each other very much. While that warmed her heart, it also caused a pang of longing in her.

She had been told by many that her father had loved her fiercely. She believed it because the first time she'd heard it, Preyknosery had told her of how she had been entrusted to him. " 'She is your daughter now,' your father told me." The Gyrkyme had bobbed his head a couple of times. "He is very proud of you." ˙

Alyx had accepted that from Preyknosery and had clung to it. The knowledge of her father's love had been a rock throughout her life. Her father had wanted her to be with the Gyrkyme. He had wanted her to grow to be a warrior like him. Her father had ordered her to be taken away while Svarskya was still in Okrans hands. Some day she would return and take it back, just the way her father wanted.

That much she knew of her father and his love for her. Preyknosery had also told her tales of him and their adventures before either of them had married. Those stories made her father very real for her, because Preyknosery did not romanticize things. He let her see her father as he truly was: not the epic hero he became in the minds of others. She had seen the truth behind the legend, and emulating the truth had been a daunting task.

She rose, pulled down the blanket and replaced it with wet clothes. Alyx wrung water from her long, white-blonde tresses, then began to braid her hair. She'd almost finished by the time she crossed to the large fire where her uncle and cousin sat with others.

"Oh, Princess, I'm afraid you can't do that." Count Serjei stood and offered her a prime spot near the fire. "The Crown Circle has stated that any fixing of hair, any decoration, will interfere with the Dream Raid. You see, the hair is for the mind what roots are for a plant. For you to draw in the correct sense of Okrannel, your roots must be spread far and wide."

Mischa snorted. "This would explain why bald men are not required to make a Dream Raid."

Serjei turned quickly and snapped at him. "Men of an age to be bald can still remember our nation—or they died in its defense."

"Not all of them died, Count Serjei." Alyx knotted a small piece of leather around the end of her braid. "Uncle Valery is still quite alive."

The older man poked at the fire with a stick. "I'm certain the Count did not mean to imply that those who survived had fled or otherwise dishonored themselves."

"No, no, of course not, I meant nothing of the sort." Serjei smiled almost innocently. "If I seem a bit over-wrought, it is just that I wish this Dream Raid to be perfect."

"Aunt Tatyana would want nothing else." Mischa's eyes twinkled. "I do believe she is expecting great things from us, Alexia, great portents for the future."

Serjei began to sputter, but Valery's quiet, warm voice cut him off. "I know you are teasing the good Count, Mikhail, but he is correct. One can learn many things by examining the dreams had on a raid. There are private things, and public things, and sorting one from the other can be tricky. Still, dreams can come true—because the gods will it, or we work to make them come true."

Serjei frowned. "Would you then, my lord, be calling into question the veracity of the dreams?"

Valery stirred coals a bit more. "I am a simple warrior, Count Serjei, and there are wiser people than I who interpret the dreams from Dream Raids. The fact that dreams

20

require interpretation leads me to believe there could be errors or cause to question things."

Alyx sat next to her uncle. "How do you mean that?"

"It's simple. Let us say, Alexia, you have a dream in which you take your sword and cleave a gibberer in two. It could be that this dream predicts an encounter where you will do just that. The dream could also be taken as allegory. You will be seen as destroying half the gibberer armies Chytrine has amassed. Or it might indicate that at a critical moment in a battle you will split a gibberer formation, which leads to its destruction. All three readings of the dream are equally valid, but the question is: Which is correct?"

Serjei clapped his hands. "I'm certain, given the Princess' importance, it shall be taken as her destroying all the gibberers she faces, leading to the liberation of our nation."

Valery looked up. "I would hope your interpretation is correct as well, Count Serjei, but who can tell?"

"Why, the Crown Circle, my lord, they can tell." Serjei nodded confidently. "And I shall make certain everything is prepared perfectly. The omens from Princess Alexia's Dream Raid will be clear to read by all."

II

Conversation lagged as the cooks announced the stew was ready for serving. Made from what few fresh provisions they had been able to trade for on the road and a lot of dried meat which had been boiled soft again, it was not the finest cuisine. On a rainy night in a cave, on the other hand, it seemed the best meal Alyx had ever eaten. It certainly was one of the more exotic meals, for men used a great deal of spice. The Gyrkyme, who ate their food fresh and even raw, had little use for spice.

Once they had finished eating, Alyx retreated to her small alcove, recovered her sword and a small pouch and returned to the fire. The blade she bore had a hilt long enough for her to wrap both hands around it, and a curved blade just over a yard long. The blade tapered to a sharp point which could be used for thrusting, but the weapon had primarily been designed for slashing. The forte had been reinforced and the crossguard was long enough to protect her hands from a blade sliding down along hers.

She unsheathed the sword and pulled a small bottle of oil from her pouch. Along with it came a whetstone and a cloth. She splashed some oil on the blade, then began to wipe it down.

Count Serjei smiled at her indulgently. "You are such a creature of habit, Princess. Every night you see to your sword."

"You have your rituals, I have mine."

"Yes, well, tomorrow night you may have to abandon yours, for the Dream Raid is very specific."

Alexia looked away from him and to her uncle. "Did you abandon your blade for your Dream Raid, uncle?"

"I did mine a long time ago, before things were much formalized. Such a prohibition had not yet been established." He smiled. "The route we are taking is the one I took. I'd been in Lakaslin when Tatyana returned from her Dream Raid. She was full of wonders and visions and, well, I found it a bit intoxicating."

Mikhail looked at his father curiously. "You've not told me this."

"You were very young and back in Yslin with your mother."

"But how did you find what the crone said so interesting?" Mikhail frowned. "You've never seemed that enthused with anything she has said when I've been around."

The older man sighed. "You have to understand the situation. It was a dozen years ago or so. I had been one of those who had fled south from our country during the invasion. I didn't want to go, but my brother ordered me to lead many people to safety—Tatyana included. When Prince Augustus fought his way down through Okrannel, I led a force north as far as Svoin. We linked up and were driven out, driven south. While many more of our people were saved in that campaign, I had hoped for liberation, but we were defeated again.

"Five years later I was in Lakaslin, hoping to influence the Jeranese crown to let us stage in Jerana and conduct more raids. The king refused and wisely so. Unbeknownst to either of us, Tatyana entered Okrannel—not the first time, nor the last—and returned full of visions of a free Okrannel. She had dreamed it, this master vision of a free nation, but it had come to her as a mosaic. She determined that the dreams of others would be the tiles in that mosaic."

He smiled wistfully. "I asked neither her permission or the King's leave and sped north. Alone I entered Okrannel and spent the night on a mountainside. Down in the distance I could see Lake Vriyn and Svoin. Somewhere out there, further than I could see, lay the graves of your older brothers—the twins—Mikhail. They died as we retreated, not yet five years old, and looking at my nation I felt my heart crushed again as it had been the day it died.

"My heart heavy, yet pounding with the hope Tatyana spoke about, I lay down to dream. Mine was a long night, but one full of portent."

Mikhail's eyes widened. "What did you dream, father?"

Count Serjei raised a hand in objection. "He cannot tell you. It is not allowed. You must tell no one of your dream."

Alyx arched an eyebrow. "Except the Crown Circle."

"Do you think that is wrong, Princess?"

"Your conclusion is unwarranted given what I said, Count Serjei." Alyx narrowed her violet eyes. "Your statement was wrong. I corrected you."

Valery smiled slowly. "The way I undertook my Dream Raid has little in common with what you will be doing. There were no procedures. When I returned Tatyana did ask me what happened, and I explained. I've told no one else, but this is not because of any prohibition. I keep my own counsel and, truth be told, do not put much stock in dreams."

"But you would agree, my lord, that the dreams of the Dream Raid are very special."

"As you say, Count Serjei, they are certainly seen as such by our people. I do not think this is a bad thing."

"Why not, uncle?"

"It is simple, Alexia. We are an exile people. Though you did not see many of them in Yslin, the Vorquelves are in the same position. They have been for a century, since their homeland was overrun by the Nor'witch's forces. If you look at them, you see what being homeless can do to a people. Some of them cannot stand the pain and seek oblivion through drink and herb. Others are reduced to being criminals, for they have no purpose. Some seek favor with the powers that might be able to liberate their homeland and yet others, the brave few, carry on a war against their enemies.

"The dreams, the Crown Circle, the Book of Dreams, all of these things provide us with hope. Just as the world has the Norrington prophecy to show us that Chytrine will be slain, so the Okrans have our dreams—dreams which will restore our nation. They keep us united, even if only one of a thousand were to have the least bit of truth to it, the dreams would have served a great purpose."

Alyx slowly nodded. She understood what her uncle was saying and could even agree with it. What she did not like was the way the Crown Circle wrapped everything in secrecy. It gave them a great power. While the Crown Circle might order exile life and provide it focus, it also stole freedom from the Okrans people. Just as Alyx had found happiness among the Gyrkyme, so others might find happiness outside the strictures of the exile community.

Count Serjei nodded solemnly. "The dreams do much more, my lord, as well you know. To maximize their import and validity, we do have procedures. The system has developed through the years. I have led many a journey here— none as important as yours, but some nearly so—and the results have been highly successful. I trust it will be so with you as well."

Mikhail frowned. "Procedures? This won't be painful, will it?"

"Oh my no!" Serjei laughed lightly, but the echoes sounded false on their return. "In my kit I have robes for the both of you to wear, special pillows for you to sleep on and wine for you to drink."

He glanced at Alexia. "Tomorrow evening you'll need not tend to your sword, Princess. Having such things with you in the Dream Pavilion will not do."

Irritation flashed over her face. "I would have thought having me feel comfortable would be important. I am a warrior and quite uncomfortable when unarmed."

Valery reached over and laid a hand on her shoulder. "I shall see to your sword, niece. You need not fret after it.

Besides, we have a full company of men here who will see to your safety."

"The Grand Duke is quite correct. The raids are usually led by myself and perhaps two other family members. We rely on stealth to protect us—that and the sanctity of our mission. The two of you are far too important to take chances."

Alyx's uncle looked around. "Those here who are not blood kin have been sworn to the House of Svarskya for generations. We have nothing to fear here."

Alyx remained silent as Serjei prattled on about what they would do and when, with everything measured in its relationship to sunset. On one level, it all struck her as exceedingly silly. They were marching into hostile territory to set up the equivalent of some springtime idyll so two children could get a good night's sleep. The absurdity of it assaulted her, but she also recognized it was basically harmless.

And a huge waste of time.

She almost stopped there in her consideration of it, letting that judgment be enough to dismiss the whole procedure as stupid. There was something else going on, however, that made her feel uncomfortable. She refused to take the easy way out, and a glance at Mikhail's dreamy expression provided the key to what she was feeling.

Alexia shivered. The reason she wanted to dismiss everything was because the Dream Raid was something at which she could fail. Her uncle pointed out that the dreams provided a sense of hope for the Okrans people, and she was seen by many as the embodiment of that hope. What if she had a banal dream? What if she had no dream at all? Worse yet, what if her dream was one of disaster and defeat? What if she, the hope of her nation, served only to dash hopes?

She watched Serjei speaking, seeing that his mouth smiled but his eyes did not, and wondered how the Crown Circle would handle a disaster dream. Would they suppress it? The easiest avenue would be for them to interpret it as prophetic of a worst case and initiate changes in Okrans society that would work against its coming true. If she saw herself being defeated while fighting beneath the wing-horse rampant banner, they could change that or any of a million other details so her dream would not come true.

But what if it came true anyway? Either one believed in the validity of the dreams or one realized they were just night-fancies and worth only the story one could spin out of them. While Alyx tended not to remember very many dreams, half of those she did were mixed up and odd—of little or no relationship to the world. The others often gave vent to anxieties. Those types of dreams she'd always used as a means to examine how she felt and find a way around troubles, but the gods alone knew what the Crown Circle might do with such a thing.

Ultimately she rebelled against the exercise because she would be judged based on her dreams, and she had absolutely no control over them. It was the equivalent to being allowed to live or being put to death based on the toss of a coin. She would not be judged for who she was or what she could accomplish, but for how easily her dreams fit into the mosaic Tatyana had dreamed years before.

Part of her wanted to stand up and announce she was going back to Gyrvirgul, but that impulse died almost as quickly as it was born. Mikhail, though she hardly knew him, set great store by her presence. While he doubtlessly would have seen his Dream Raid as very important, it became so much more so in her company. For her to leave would hurt him, and she had no desire to do that.

27

And her uncle, there was something about him that stopped her from open rebellion. Everyone else in the company took their duty solemnly, but betrayed a nervousness that grew as they came closer to Okrannel. Valery exuded a confidence that became the quiet at the core of a storm. As much as she might feel the turmoil in her heart, when she looked at him it seemed insignificant and, oddly, a necessary part of the exercise.

Alexia let herself yawn. "My apologies, but I feel very tired. I think I will retire for the night. I assume we'll want to start early and make good time?"

Valery nodded. "Before you sleep, I have something I would share with you. If you will excuse us."

"Of course. Sleep well, cousin."

"And you, Mischa."

"Good night, Highness."

"Sleep well, my lord."

Valery stood and waved her toward the front of the cavern. They walked down past the horses and to the mouth of the cave. The rain had stopped, and streaks clawed through the clouds allowed them to see a sprinkling of stars. Alyx couldn't quite see enough to identify the constellations, but their mere presence suggested the weather would break for the last day's travel.

Valery took her hands in both of his and squeezed. "I know that much of this seems like nonsense for you. Mischa was not yet born when Okrannel fell, and Serjei was a child, so he barely remembers his homeland. For them, rituals like this are what allow them to feel they truly are of Okrannel."

"I understand that."

"You're a smart girl, so I have no doubt you do, but perhaps not in the ways you should." Her uncle chuckled lightly. "Tatyana would never confirm it, but I think the

idea of the Dream Raid came from the ritual the elves use
to bind them to their homeland. The Dream Raid is the
first time our exiles have touched Okrans soil. It is their introduction to their home. This experience binds them to it,
just as their dreams are bound into its future. They and our
nation are woven together through this act.

"You don't need this, for you already feel that obligation. You are truly my brother's daughter. Preyknosery has
been true to Kirill in raising you. Others might see it as
ironic that you, raised outside our community, are the true
daughter of Okrannel, but not me. The purpose then of
your ritual is not to bind you to Okrannel, but to bind the
Okrans people to you."

"I'm not sure I understand, uncle."

"You will. Think on this very simply, Alexia. The Crown
Circle, in assuming a leadership role in our society, provides hope for our people." His eyes narrowed. "In their interpretation of dreams, some might say they even
manufacture hope."

"Manufacture?"

The older man smiled slyly and lowered his voice.
"While Serjei is correct, that no one should share their
dreams, you must know that they have been shared. You
might be able to imagine, then, that if one heard about a
dream before it was told to the Crown Circle, and then
heard after what the Crown Circle told the dreamer they
had really dreamed, you would be amused."

She closed her eyes for a moment, lost in thought. "I
could take that to mean that what I dream is not important."

"Not true. What you dream will be very important. I fer-
vently believe some of these dreams come true." He held a
finger up. "What is more important, however, is that you,

Princess Alexia, *dream*. That you have dreamed makes valid the dreams and hopes of all the others. You, like the Crown Circle, must lead; and if that means you manufacture hope, that you must do. It could be argued that manufacturing hope is the true essence of leadership, for hope inspires, and inspired people act."

Alexia nodded, then met Valery's gaze. "I think our people would be better served following you instead of the Crown Circle."

"An immaterial point. The Crown Circle is ascendant and I am not. That's not a problem. It frees me to act in ways that will help you and your generation win back what the rest of us lost."

He reached up with both hands, drew her head down and kissed her on the forehead. "Sleep well, Alexia, and save your dreams for tomorrow night."

III

"Can you feel it, cousin? I can." Mischa rose in the stirrups and threw his arms wide. The sun shined brightly on his face and huge smile. "We are *home*."

Alexia said nothing, but turned inside, waiting for some sort of magic tickle, some sensation that told her she was once again in the land of her birth. The trail through the mountains had wended east and west as it inched north. They forded a small river, then came up a short slope to look down into Okrannel. They rode past small stone pylons officially marking the border, and many of those who rode with them sighed or cheered.

Alexia felt nothing, and instantly a blackness clutched at her heart. Down below she could see the waters of Lake

Vriyn shining silver and could make out the city of Svoin beside it some fifty miles distant. Dark smoke smudged the city's outline. Something about it struck her as very wrong, and she would be happy when the trail sank back into forests and hid the city.

Is there something wrong with me that I feel nothing on my return? She shifted her shoulders uneasily. *Or is it that such magic only works for those who enter the land for the first time? I was born here and taken away. Perhaps it is as Uncle Valery said—I already have a bond with Okrannel.*

She mirrored Mischa's smile. "I think, cousin, you feel it enough for the whole of us."

"Oh, I can, I can, Alyx." His eyes narrowed. "I can feel the land crying out to be liberated. I'll help you do that, you know. I will be here when we drive them out. No quarter asked or given, no retreat allowed."

"No, of course not, Mischa." Alyx glanced to her right as Count Serjei rode up. "And you, my lord, what do you feel when you look upon Svoin?"

"Fury, Highness. Impatience." The intensity in his expression broke, shattered by a forced smile. "I, too, shall see my home free. But that is the future, a future your dreams shall guide us into. It won't be much farther now."

Valery, who had crossed into Okrannel ahead of the two youngsters, reined his horse about on the narrow trail. "Oh, yes, Count Serjei, there has been a shift in planning. I know you intended we use the grove at Splitrock, but I wish to remain a bit higher on the mountain. About a mile above it is a meadow where I made my Dream Raid. I wish my son to have that experience there."

Serjei's face darkened. "But I was given very specific instructions, my lord. Indulging you in coming north from Lakaslin as opposed to moving through the mountains was

one thing, but this, I cannot countenance it. The Grand
Duchess was very specific in her wishes. The grove at
Splitrock has been very successful."

"I am aware of that, my lord." Valery smiled softly. "I
appealed to my father and he granted me leave to bring my
son there."

"But that will put you far from where we are with the
Princess."

Alyx shook her head. "I shall go to the meadow as well. I
would be honored to share such a special spot."

The Count opened his mouth, then snapped it shut
again. He nodded slowly. "Of course, Highness. Higher up
the mountain, the closer you are to the gods, the better your
dreams will be."

The meadow did prove to be a wonderful spot for
making camp. It lay a hundred feet above the tree line, so at
the very northern edge one could look out and see a carpet
of evergreens. A stream running through it provided fresh
water, and the summer grasses gave them plenty of fodder
for the horses. Trails down to the forest made the gathering
of firewood simple, and by early afternoon the various pa-
vilions had been erected and Serjei had set about brewing
up whatever odd concoctions were needed to begin the
ritual.

Alexia and Mikhail were allowed to do nothing as
others set things up. Serjei handed them both silken robes
which Alexia found as soft as a Gyrkyme's down. Had the
foul weather continued, they would have been scant proof
against rain or cold, but for sleeping garments they would
do well. Once their tent was set up at the northern edge
of the camp, they were bid to change clothes and sit in it.
Serjei circled it with a burning bunch of herbs that gave
off a pungent smoke; then he entered and similarly

blessed the interior with smoke.

Alexia didn't like the scent of it, but kept her face placid. Mikhail smiled the whole while, breathing deeply. She didn't think there was anything narcotic in the smoke, but Mikhail relaxed and began to hum to himself.

When Serjei left them, he nodded to her. "Do you know the song?"

"No."

"It's a lullaby, one my mother used to sing to me. It will help me sleep." The set of his features became serious. "It is very important we compose our minds to be receptive. We should be thinking on our nation, our future, and how best we can serve it."

She arched an eyebrow. "This is what the Crown Circle has told you?"

"No. They say nothing, but I have spoken with others who had very important dreams. They said that was how to do it."

Alyx gave her cousin a short nod. "This is very important to you, isn't it?"

"Of course it is." Mischa glanced down at the blue and gold, star-strewn carpet. "I know I am not as important as you to our nation, but I also know a few other things. I know I *will* be part of our nation's future. I will do anything I am called upon to do to free Okrannel, and my dream will show me what I need to do."

He lowered his voice so only she could hear. "My father was very proud of my older brothers. They were just children when they died, not even five years old. While he says nothing, I can see in his eyes that I am carrying their future, too. I don't mind. I am proud to do it. This dream, its import, will prove I am worthy of that burden."

She reached out and squeezed his shoulder. "I have no

doubt you are, Mischa."

Valery appeared and flipped a tent flap back. "It's almost sunset. It's time."

The two of them emerged and took their places in camp chairs with their backs to the setting sun. Before them a large fire had been lit and a stewpot bubbled above it. Another sat on the ground, near the coals, and fluid steams in it. Serjei acknowledged them both with a nod, then began ladling the aromatic stew into bowls. One each went to the assembled exiles, with only Serjei and the two dreamers not being given any. Valery set his bowl down untouched and filled cups with mulled wine and distributed them, for which Serjei thanked him.

Valery came to the two dreamers last, giving each one a small cup. "Save yours until you are in the tent. That's right, isn't it, my lord?"

"Yes, Grand Duke. We drink, we eat, we salute them, then they will drink, sleep and dream."

Valery lowered his voice. "It is seldom this much of a production, but everyone plays a part."

Once the company had eaten, they rose and circled the two dreamers. Serjei led them in the singing of traditional Okrans songs. They might once have been gay airs, but their tempo had been slowed and lyrics adjusted to express the grand lament of the Okrans people. What might once have sparked a smile and quickened the heart, now tugged down the corners of the mouth and tore at the heart.

Alexia had felt no magic as she entered Okrannel, but the doleful voices and sad expressions on the faces of the men surrounding her puckered her flesh. Each singer used the voice to share with her his pain and loss. Though the words did not touch upon it, she heard Valery singing for his lost sons, his dead brother. Though they kept their voices soft and even, they must have carried, for Alyx could feel ghosts rising to join them. She sensed the presence of others, and the responsibility that came with her blood settled firmly on her shoulders.

Mischa is dreaming to serve his father and prove himself worthy of his family's sacrifice. I will be dreaming for so many other people. The cure to their pain is hope, and that is what I must bring them.

The voices slowly trailed off, then each of the attendants filed past. They kissed the dreamers on both cheeks and whispered, "Sweet dreams, strong dreams," before passing on. They melted away into the night, some to take up picket positions, others to sleep until called for their watch. Finally Serjei bid them both to take up their wine cups and go to the pavilion.

He stopped short of it. "Once you enter, your tent will be closed until dawn. Drink your wine, the wine you share with us all, and then lay your head on your pillows. Be at ease, no danger awaits you, just your future. I bid you both the most fortunate of dreams."

Alexia followed Mischa into the tent. Her cousin seated himself immediately and tossed off the cup of wine. He shivered, then licked his lips and stretched himself out. "I am going to dream the most glorious dreams."

"I'm certain you will." Alexia took a token sip of her wine. She'd assumed that the wine the two of them had been given might have been drugged, since the pressure of the Dream Raid would be enough to keep anyone awake. Having been raised by the Gyrkyme, she didn't feel comfortable resorting to intoxicants, so she set her cup at the edge of the blanket and tried to make herself comfortable.

That effort failed, and Mischa's light snores did nothing to make her feel at ease. The ground seemed inordinately lumpy beneath her, so she peeled the carpet up and found her riding leathers and sword tucked into a small depression there. She pulled them out and smiled.

Uncle Valery said he would take care of these things for me. He must have known I would not be comfortable and, given the nature of my destiny, dreaming while girt for war would be appropriate.

She quickly pulled her leathers on, even donning her boots, and let her sword lay beside her. Feeling much more comfortable, she settled back and caught the faint scent of herbs as her head hit the pillow. They smelled vaguely like the smoke from before. She tried to identify the various components, but before she could make much headway on the problem, sleep claimed her.

At first she didn't think she was dreaming, for what unfolded was anything but epic or prophetic. She found herself in bed, naked, laying beside a man she did not know. From the corner of her eye she saw his long white hair, his white beard, yet the hand she held in hers was not old and infirm. She wanted to turn her head and study him more closely, for the bond she felt with him burned intensely, but she could do nothing. She could not move.

That paralysis did not startle her because she'd felt it before. What did surprise her was the appearance of a glowing woman, tall and slender, lithe and strong. Her eyes had no pupils and the tips of pointed ears poking up through long hair revealed her to be an elf. *But not a normal elf: a Vorquelf, or something else.*

The elf slipped a pillow from beneath the man's head and thrust it down over his face. The man convulsed, ripping his hand from Alyx's grip. The elf spoke, looking directly at her, but Alyx heard nothing. She just knew this man was dying and she was powerless to stop his murder.

Then a shadowed figure appeared at the end of the bed. His mailed fist whipped out, smashing the elf in the head. The blow knocked her from the bed and into the wall. The pillow came off the man's face and he gasped loudly for air.

Alyx saw the shadowed figure resolve into something more solid. His face took on features she found familiar, but it was a face she could not summon from memory. In a heartbeat she identified him from countless statues and paintings. *My father!* He had saved her and yet, in the moment it took her to recognize him, he vanished.

Alexia jerked awake and sat up, her chest heaving, sweat pasting platinum locks to her forehead. She blinked, disoriented; then Mischa's snores anchored her. She was in her dream pavilion, in Okrannel. She'd woken from a bad dream.

But it wasn't just from the bad dream. Something else lurked at the edges of her consciousness. She listened between the gaps in Mikhail's snoring, hoping to catch the normal sounds of nighttime, but heard nothing. The crickets remained silent and no night-birds called.

She did, however, hear the snap of a twig, the rustle of some grasses and a mild oath carried in whispers in the breeze. Something was not right. She rose into a crouch and buckled her sword belt on.

Tonight might be the night for dreaming, but I've done enough of that. She slipped from her pavilion and into the night. *Others have long dreamed and often with evil intent. I want to make certain their dreams do not come true.*

IV

Moving silently through the darkness, Alexia was again in her element. Her night vision was not good enough to identify the person she was following by his tracks, but the course he took through the long blades of summer grass could have been followed by a blind man. The man's mutterings, which presaged Alyx's finding a spot where he'd fallen, did give her a clue as to who she pursued, but then there had been little choice in the matter.

Aside from Count Serjei, everyone present had served the House of Svarskya directly for generations. Serjei had not drunk any of the wine—which now Alyx was certain contained a soporific. As nearly as she knew, everyone else in the group slept deeply in a narcotic haze, so only she stood between Serjei and whatever deviltry he intended.

Her quarry made his way down one of the paths that led down into the forest, then picked his way through the trees. His route evidenced no knowledge of woodcraft or the means of stealth. Alyx found a game trail that roughly paralleled his route and allowed her to travel in silence.

It matters little since he makes enough noise to cover an army's advance. She had little doubt that his cloak had left threads on dozens of bushes, and his trousers were black and wet from the number of times he tripped over roots. Onward he went, however, and Alexia shadowed him. He had a fifty-foot lead, so she could not see him, but that wasn't necessary.

Alexia focused on making certain she passed noiselessly. This was something she had learned to do very well in Gyrvirgul. The Gyrkyme were able to fly very quietly and had acute hearing. In games she often found herself the mouse seeking safety while her companions played the hawk. Their sharp eyesight doomed her in the day, and their hearing did the same at night.

Up ahead Count Serjei's crashing-about stopped abruptly with a yelp. Two voices came from a spot off to the left and a bit downslope—his being shrill and the other almost barked. She couldn't make out the words; then the sound of travel began anew—albeit more quietly. She resumed her tracking and quickly found a spot in the trail where the man who intercepted Serjei had been waiting. Catching an odd scent in the area, Alexia quickly amended her conclusion.

Whatever had waited there was not human.

And if it wasn't human, it's working for Chytrine. That realization lent urgency to her. She hurried on down the game trail, chancing that nothing had yet been sent to take that position back up.

After roughly a quarter mile she stepped off the trail and moved into the underbrush. A hundred yards ahead, a trio of small fires burned at the center of a grove. The tall trees were enough to dissipate the smoke so it'd not have been noticed even at high noon. As she crept closer, more of the camp's details became clear and she was able to hear the conversation between Serjei and another man.

"This is a fine and merry chase you've led us on, Serjei."

"It's not my fault, Nikolas. Duke Valery has made changes as we went. I wanted the party taken in the mountains near the Zhusk Plateau so we could blame things on them. Valery determined we should go to Lakaslin. It turns out we've been repeating his Dream Raid step by step."

Nikolas, who stood taller and had a heavier build than Serjei, waved his excuse away. "You know how important this is. Our sale of Princess Alexia to the Nor'witch will put us back in control of Svoin. The territory around it will become a free state and we will once again rule."

"I know, brother, I know. The exiles will rally to us and we can win our way free . . . I mean, we can share with others the glory of Chytrine's leadership."

Serjei's voice had become tight before he shifted what he was saying. Alyx had drawn close enough to the camp to know why he had shifted his comments. A musky odor permeated the camp—the same scent she'd caught on the trail. It emanated from a quartet of gibberers huddled to the south. Bestial creatures that resembled men in general shape, they had a motley fur covering them, jutting muzzles full of teeth, sharpened ears, clawed fingers and large black eyes that glowed dully. The one that had brought Serjei into the camp snapped at another and settled into a crouch.

Nikolas flicked a hand out, cuffing Serjei none too gently. "Idiot. They barely understand our tongue, and are quite stupid. They could not plumb the import of your comments—and if they could, they'd already be ripping you apart. City life has made you far too soft, Serjei, but you were always too soft."

"That's not true."

"It is. If you had a spine, you'd be camped below us, at Splitrock. Now we have to mount an assault up a narrow stone path which is easily defended. We might not be able to do it."

"Fear not, brother. I managed to slip a sleeping draught into the wine—normally it just goes into the sleeper's cup, but I planned ahead and was able to dose everyone. Valery himself served the wine, so no one refused. They all slumber above, waiting for you to slaughter them. We can no longer blame the Zhusk, but it hardly matters. Chytrine will be pleased enough to rid the world of their filth."

"Good." Nikolas clapped his hands, then looked at the gibberers. "We go now. Quietly. Quietly."

The knot of gibberers bobbed their heads, then moved into the darkness.

Serjei glanced at his brother—a man whose face had been lined by life in a city owned by Chytrine. "What of the Duke and his whelp? Will you kill them or ransom them?"

Nikolas shrugged. "Duke Valery convinced Augustus that Svoin could not hold, so I would just as soon see him dead. Still, Chytrine might want the old man. We'll see when the time comes."

His comment, which passed with nonchalant airs, shook Alexia. The idea that Nikolas would use her to ransom his city she could almost understand. For Svoin he had passion. His comment about her uncle had no emotion involved whatsoever. Valery was a thing of no consequence to him. All the things she had learned to like and admire about him on the journey had been reduced to nothing.

Just as he will. Alexia slid her sword from the scabbard. *As he will be if I do nothing.*

She parted the brush at the edge of the clearing and stepped into the firelight. "Worrying about pleasing Chytrine is premature."

Serjei spun about, eclipsing his brother, and stared at her. His face was a mask etched with fear. "Highness, you cannot be here."

"But I am."

Serjei's mouth hung open for a moment; then his body shook. Blood poured black from his mouth as easily as honeyed words once had. He pitched forward with a dagger standing erect from his back.

Nikolas lifted his head. "His intent was to betray you to me. He thought I worked for Chytrine."

41

"I've heard everything. Do you think I'm as stupid as he was?"

"You're here, alone, so I have cause to wonder." Nikolas drew his sword. "If you surrender to me, I'm certain Chytrine will treat you well."

Alexia shrugged. "You'd still kill my uncle and the others."

"They'll die even if you do kill me."

"I'm not afraid of you and four gibberers."

"Confident, good. Just what our nation needs." Nikolas raised his blade in a salute. "It's not four gibberers. Those were the company commanders."

A hundred and twenty of them? Saliva turned sour in her mouth, but she shrugged. "It doesn't matter. You'll be dead."

"Oh, you *are* of House Svarskya, no doubt about it." He brought his sword back down again. "I would prefer you alive, but dead will do."

Nikolas darted forward, feinting a slash. Alyx pulled back to let the slash slip past, then parried Nikolas' thrust. Her parry carried his blade wide, but he slipped his beneath her sword and prepared for her backhanded slash. Alyx retreated a step, leaving him frozen for the moment in anticipation.

Leaving him looking like a timid fool.

Embarrassment flushed his face and he came at her again. He slashed high, but she blocked his cut. Though he could not imagine how it was possible, she did not falter or withdraw. As his body pressed in toward hers and their swords locked crossguards, her left hand came around and smashed him in the temple.

He staggered back a step and Alexia advanced. Her sword came up and around, poised for a high slash. She feinted and his blade came up to block. Already having anticipated that tactic, Alyx pivoted on her back leg and kicked Nikolas full in the chest. She left a muddy boot print in the center of his dark green tabard, splashing mud over the white griffon emblazoned there.

Nikolas stumbled back and caught his heels on Serjei's corpse. His arms flailed as he tried to stay upright, but without success. He landed hard on his tailbone, crying out in pain, but managed to retain his grip on his sword.

He started to roll to his left to get back to his feet, but Alyx gave him no chance. A sweeping slash knocked his sword flying into the underbrush. He stared at his empty hand for a second, then raised it to ward off any other blow.

"Mercy?"

"You plotted to murder sleeping men." Her sword whistled down and would have split him crown to jaw, but she twisted her wrists at the last moment. The flat of her blade cracked him on the top of his head. His eyes fluttered, then rolled up in his head as he collapsed.

Before she had a chance to wonder why she'd not killed him—for she had fully intended to—gibberers came boiling out of the darkness. Most bore single-edged long knives which surrendered nearly a foot in length to her sword, but a few brandished clubs and a third of them bore shields in their off hands. Snarls and hooting laughter filled the night, and nary a hint of mercy lit their flat eyes.

Alexia knew in an instant that she would not survive the night. There were too many of them. Perhaps if she could retreat to the trail she might be able to hold them off, but they were coming too fast to let her do that. In the darkness she would trip, they would pounce, and their weapons would shred her back.

No wounds on my back. I will not run. She tightened both

hands on her sword and offered them a snarl of her own. She bared her teeth and as the first of them reached her, she struck with the anger and outrage she'd felt at Serjei's action. She battered the first longknife down, then brought her sword up in a backhanded slash that cleanly beheaded the gibberer.

The head, with lolling tongue flapping from the left side of its mouth, sailed past her shoulder. She parried another blade wide, then stabbed its owner through the guts. As it folded around the wound, she jumped back. A gibberer leaped over its two comrades, but went down as his foot rolled on the first's head. Alexia's cut crushed its skull and it flopped in the dust.

Her mind cataloged the fluid chaos. The fires restricted certain paths to her and she could use that. She recalled tales where heroes had the dead laying so thickly about them that they formed natural breastworks, but she could not slay enough fast enough to pile them that high. All she could do was match the gibberers in their wild ferocity, though that tactic would only help her so much.

It was the only tactic she had, however, so she employed it with fervor. She shrieked as she struck, using Gyrkyme curses and war-cries that did not come easily from a human throat. She doubted the gibberers understood the words, but the fury in her voice did cause some to shy. Their own bestial snapping and snarling could not match her and, just for a heartbeat, the gibberers nearest her faltered.

Alexia did not. Her blade flashed in the firelight. Slashes severed paws, leaving them spasming in the sand, or opened bellies. Savage blows bit deep into skulls. One cut clove a shield and the arm to which it was bound, leaving that warrior reeling back and howling.

On they came, relentless even if daunted. Longknives

thrust at her. Some she parried, but others slid past. Some nicked her, barely slicing through her leathers, others pierced her flesh, but never deeply. The owners feared her blade's lethal arc, but the little cuts began to add up. She might dispatch ten or even twenty, but at some point a leg would falter, a dodge would fail. A blade would stab into her vitals. She'd kill that gibberer and perhaps a half-dozen more, but finally they would overwhelm her.

Alexia kept moving, doing all she could to drive back any attempt to flank her. She'd been successful, but then heard crashing through the brush behind her. Somehow a knot of them had circled all the way around and would burst out to kill her. She couldn't turn to face them, so she did the only thing that made sense. Snarling viciously, she drove forward and slashed her way into the gibberers.

"Svarskya Eternal!"

Gibberers shrieked as from the brush boiled Duke Valery and the company of men he'd brought with him. Many throats echoed his war cry. The mews of wounded and dying gibberers underscored it, as swords rose silver and swept down in arcs that splashed crimson in the dust.

The knowledge that she had allies with her did buoy her heart, but inspired no desire to sink back into their midst and safety. She hacked through the shoulder of one gibberer, kicked another in the stomach and slapped aside a third's longknife. She stabbed that gibberer, then appropriated its weapon to parry other thrusts. A quick slash to the right opened a neck that sprayed her with hot blood. Her longknife stabbed another gibberer in the chest and was ripped from her grasp as the body fell away.

Gibberers turned to run, clawing their ways back over corpses. Men hamstrung them, then dispatched them. Some did so gleefully, but most with an emotionless

economy that spoke more of need than mercy. The people
Valery had brought with him were as hard-eyed now as they
had been wistful before. They swept past her as the
gibberers broke, and disappeared into the shadows beyond
the fire's light.

Valery, too, raced past her, then held a hand out to stop
her. "You've done enough; your part ends here."

"No, uncle, there are more to kill."

"I know, but it's not our place to hunt them down." He
faced her with blood trickling from a wound in his forehead.
"You stop now."

"Uncle."

"Alexia, this is the third and final time I will tell you."

He had a queer tone in his voice, and that stopped her
more than did his command. "How are you here? The wine
was drugged."

Valery regarded her openly for a moment, then bent to
wipe the blood from his sword on a gibberer's pelt. "I think
you know how."

She hesitated, but only for a heartbeat. "You dreamed
this. You dreamed this all?"

"Just this part, including the questions, including you
telling me the wine was drugged." He swiped at the blood
on his face. "Once Tatyana told me who would be leading
us, I had him watched. In Yslin he purchased certain supplies and I purchased the antidotes. He thought the wine
would eliminate us, but my people simply feigned being
asleep."

"But in your dream you didn't see Serjei and Nikolas. I
think they are brothers."

"I didn't see Serjei's face, and did not recognize
Nikolas'. The years have not been kind to him." Valery
waved her over to where the two brothers lay. Serjei's body

now covered his brother's, and a slender boot dagger had been slid between Nikolas' ribs. "Brother slays brother."

"So they *were* brothers?"

"Half-brothers. Nikolas refused to join Augustus and remained behind in Svoin. Most believed he was dead, and we should let them believe he died long since. In fact, of this entire incident we will say nothing."

"But . . ."

"There are too many who know to allow it to remain a secret?"

"Yes."

"Not these people. They will remain silent about what happened here until you give them leave to speak. That is why I chose them." Valery wiped at the blood trickling down his face again. "I dreamed coming to your rescue here. I dreamed being struck in the face, and I wish I'd dreamed staunching the wound. I knew all this would happen, and it pained me to let it happen, but I had to."

Alexia frowned. "Why? I could have been slain. Others could die."

"Three will have, and one more will never walk again. It's a frightful price, but one that has to be paid."

"I don't understand."

"Your having undertaken a Dream Raid makes you one of us, Alexia, not in your mind or mine, for you are already there as far as we are concerned. In the minds of our people, you have now joined us. And, in the minds of these men, you have shown all the promise of being a warrior-queen. This we need if we are to liberate our homeland."

She nodded, slowly comprehending. Even though the battle's survivors would say nothing of the battle itself, they would communicate to others, by words and deeds, that they trusted her and would follow her. Others would follow them, and when the time came to free Okrannel, her people would join her.

"You didn't tell Tatyana your dream, did you?"

"No. If she had known what Serjei was plotting, she would never have allowed things to unfold as they did."

"If you believe that all Dream Raid dreams come true, then she would have been constrained to let them go forward."

Valery smiled. "It was my dream, and my slice of fate to control. I did what was necessary."

Alexia nodded.

He looked at her carefully. "Did you dream?"

"Yes, uncle. Shall I tell you?"

"Is your dream one that will give our people hope?"

"Only if interpreters work very hard on it." She smiled slowly. "I think I may have to lie to the Crown Circle. Is that permissible?"

"If it will save lives, it is a duty." Valery shrugged. "You'll have to make that decision yourself. And soon."

"Soon?"

He nodded. "We're returning to our camp. Mikhail slumbers there and when you reenter the tent, he will waken and tell you about his dream. He's dreaming of his twin brothers and together they are the Three Brothers. His dream will inspire great hope. I know, for I overheard him telling it to you."

"And what did I tell him in return?"

"I don't know. I stopped listening." He smiled. "It's not much help, I know, but you can inspire him. Do that, and you will inspire all of us. That's what leaders do."

"Inspire, and make dreams come true."

"Exactly, Alexia." Valery sheathed his blade and started back toward their camp. "You are the hope and dream of our people. Many will take counsel of your dream, but I think the portents here are more proper. We need not a dreamer, but one who can face a living nightmare and not shy from it. Through such a woman we will be returned to our home."

Alexia stood there for a moment, looking at the corpses, then nodded. She started after Valery, intent on finishing his dream, and starting down the road to completing so many others.

"The Krells of Tancras Moor" is a story that I wrote just for the heck of it. I was working at Flying Buffalo and the title kept repeating itself in my head. It also felt good in the mouth. I finished it in 1989, but never could find a home for it until *Dragon* Magazine took it in 2003. Jesse Decker asked me to expand it, adding 700 words to bring it up to 7,000 words total. In it, you can probably catch hints of Robert E. Howard and his Solomon Kane character.

The Krells of Tancras Moor

Colder than the coins on a dead-man's eyes was that black night. The wet breeze licking up from the sodden moors ignored my woolen cloak and thick winter clothing. It twisted and snaked between flesh and cloth, and soaked deep into my bones. The cold crystallized in my marrow. All silver and agate, the hollow rot of it waited to erupt and take all of me.

I can make you warm again, said the voice within my skull.

"No." I indulged myself and reveled in the prickly numbness in my fingers and face. "You will have much to do tonight. Better you save yourself for that."

It did not like my refusal, but there was nothing it could do about it. I could feel anger coiling in it the same way its slender body writhed within the arteries of my brain. It wanted to consume me just like the cold did, but I held it at bay. I would not let myself become like the others.

The stars hung like flakes of mica in the sky. The moon, a white ball of cotton succumbing to a grey fungus, made the night all that much colder for its warmthless light. It deepened the shadows of the hills and hollows, and hid the stones that might trip a traveler or shatter a wagon's wheel.

As if it sensed my anger with it, the moon gathered a halo around itself to protest its innocence.

I walked on. I crested a low hill, but could not yet spy out my goal. Still, off to the right, in a hollow that sheltered the fire from the wind, I saw five men and heard the sound of laughter and song.

Kill them, kill them all.

I smiled. "No." *It* never gives up trying. Even at *its* most insistent, though, my hand never strays toward the sword I wear. Never again, by my hand, will it be bloodied.

I would have shouted a greeting and waited to be welcomed to the fire, but one of them was strumming out a tune on his lute. He was long of limb and youthful looking, but the edges of his eyes and the touches of grey in his hair bespoke experience and some years of living. His fingers, though, they were lean and quick. They flew across the silver strings with the speed of a kitten at play and the music they coaxed from the lute sounded clear and bittersweet in the frigid night.

Your favorite song, my lord.

My nostrils flared for a red second. *Be silent!*

If that is your wish . . . it hissed sarcastically. To annoy me, *it* wove a minor spell to augment my hearing.

I ignored it. *It* took on the quiet of an abandoned crypt. *It* knew the song tormented me more than *it* ever could.

Outside the firelight, the shadows hid me from discovery, but they did nothing to shield me from the man's full voice and passion as he sang.

> *Not long ago and to the East,*
> *Sung of in battle and in feast,*
> *Was a warrior tall and strong*
> *Aught for battle did he long,*

Until he met the Lady,
Until he met the Lady.

Hers was a throne on unsteady ground,
Plotters and enemies did surround
Her nation so weak and small
Quite certain now soon to fall,

Until she met Black Morgan,
Until she met Black Morgan.

A deal was struck, a bargain made.
Blood's the task and love was paid.
Morgan shattered the enemy host,
Then was heard to loudly boast,

T'was done all for the Lady,
T'was done all for the Lady.

Aldare freed was a nation proud.
The ale was cool, the songs were loud.
To Morgan their queen they quickly wed,
And Morgan took her to his bed,

And then they both were happy,
And then they both were happy.

But enemies scattered are not foes dead,
And all of them wanted Morgan's head.
So with the sorcerers they did plan,
The death-in-life of one man,

Morgan was to be broken,

Morgan was to be broken.

Morgan was called with army to field,
Foe after foe he forced to yield.
Rumors of his wife came to his ears,
And played upon his worst fears,

Black Morgan sped home angry,
Black Morgan sped home angry.

Morgan found her with another man,
One of her nation and of her clan.
In a fit of rage he could not contain,
She and her brother both were slain,

Morgan had killed his Lady,
Morgan had killed his Lady.

Time there was for him to cry,
Time there was for him to fly,
Time for his glory has gone by,
But time's not yet for him to die,

'Cause Morgan's revenge is brewing,
'Cause Morgan's revenge is brewing.

'Tis said he stalks the sorcerous host
Caused him to slay the one he loved most,
He tracks them down and hunts 'em dead,
Cuts out the heart, burns the head.

Morgan's revenge is final,
Morgan's revenge is final.

The last note rang off into the night and burned there like a star. The men in the hollow breathed steam and laughed and clapped. They congratulated the singer and he smiled. He took a proffered flask and drank.

Over the flask's heel he caught sight of me and choked.

That's not the first time I've had that effect on men.

The singer lowered the flask. Firelight flickered and flashed from the silver binding the leather to the bottle and made the flask appear to writhe in his grasp. He put it down by releasing it from his hand nearly a foot above the ground. A comrade cried out and righted it, but the singer—brandishing his lute as if its silver strings or golden notes were a bane to me—never heard his protest.

"Who be ye? Or better to ask, on a night belike this, what be ye?" His voice, as when he sang, was easy and elegant. He tried for courage and authority—the elements his training as a bard would have given him—but the tremor of fear betrayed him.

I smiled easily and opened my cloak slowly. He saw my gloved hands were empty and that I wore clothing not so different from his own. The longsword at my left hip seemed to unsettle him, then he noticed the leather thong wrapped over the crossguard to keep the blade sheathed. "I am merely a man."

Not anymore.

". . . A traveler who heard your song and whose bones long for any warmth you can spare from the fire." I moved closer and kept my voice friendly and even. Still, the fire's light stripped the shadows away from me quickly enough and they saw a man who dwarfed even the largest of their number.

The fire warmed my face and encouraged color back into the frozen flesh stretched taut across high cheekbones. I am certain my eyes remained hidden in pockets of shadow, but that mattered little as few men like holding my stare long. My eyes are dark enough to seem all pupil until an argent fork of *magefire* shoots through them. I doubt the fire lent any color at all to my long white hair.

A rotund, jocular man—the one who recovered the flask before too much of the precious liquid in it quenched the earth's thirst—laughed aloud and slapped the singer on the back. "Come now, Patrick, 'tis not a night to be jumping at all the shadows. You've gone and scared yourself with your playing of 'Black Morgan,' and it's naught but the Krells that ought to be afeared of that lay."

The man turned to me. "Be ye welcome to our fire. I am Andrew Mac Alistair, and the one with the golden voice is Patrick Mac Fergus. He's my nephew; his talent and the ease of scaring gotten on my sister by his father. The fire's for your outsides and this is for your insides." He passed me the flask.

I raised it to my lips and let the liquid course across my tongue. It tasted neither sour or sweet; it was more dry and warm than possessed of any actual flavor. Then it turned bitter and biting on my tongue even as it spread fire and warmth into my throat and chest. The taste lingered on the edges of my tongue, then drained off like the day's heat at sundown. My eyes narrowed and I resisted both spitting it out or draining the flask.

How many years has it been? Have more. Do not worry, I will care for you. I will handle everything.

I returned the flask to Andrew. "Very good, just the thing for a fierce night like this. Do you make it?"

"Being that you're a stranger he'd try and tell you he did, but that's not the truth." A sandy-haired man to Andrew's right gave me an open-faced smile. He stood almost as tall as me—making him remarkable for a moorsman—but was as gaunt as a battlefield scavenger or a plague-ridden starveling. "I'm Edward Mac Robert and this is my brother, Logan. We make the whiskey." He glanced at Andrew. "He just drinks most of it."

All five of the men laughed at Edward's joke—Andrew the loudest of them all. Logan, standing across the fire from me, was shorter than his brother and lean like a hungry wolf. He wore a smile on his face, but something in Patrick's song had touched him and he viewed me with suspicion.

Suspicion likewise masked the face of the last man. Old, grizzled, and bony, he wore his clothes as if his body were nothing more than broomsticks and kindling. His cold eyes—narrowed so he could see what I truly was—were the color of his pipe-smoke. "Where be ye heading a' this time o' night, Stranger?" He rolled his R's lovingly and long and turned the word *stranger* into a sinister accusation.

Our gazes met and instantly we reached an understanding. He had the answer to his question, and all the others he wanted to ask. I had his assurance that no one, save perhaps his grandchildren on a cold night later in the winter, would have those answers, or would believe them in the way he told them.

"Beyond Tancras Moor. I have business to the north."

Andrew rubbed his hands and held them out to the fire. "Be ye going to Richardston?"

I nodded. The old man knew it for a lie, but the others accepted it as the truth.

Edward shook his head. "This is not the night to be crossing the moors. Hugh Krell will be about."

I inclined my head slightly and raised my left eyebrow. "I've heard tales. Is that why you are out here?"

Andrew laughed aloud. "Sure it's not because we like the cold, my friend. Aye, 'tis because of Hugh Krell and his moonsickness that we come out here. And he's the reason we have Patrick sing 'Black Morgan' a time or two in the night. Werewolf or not, no Krell's going to come within a mile of a man who dares sing of Black Morgan of Aldare. The mention of his name's enough to have all those God-cursed witches and warlocks cowering in their pentagrams."

"Even Remington Krell?" My eyes tightened slightly. "I would have thought him of sterner stuff."

"He's na a problem, Stranger. After his son, Neil, went off with Morgan, and Liam died, he has na to do outside his keep. N'er one to dirty his hands, and Hugh makes for a poor servant. He'll be home on a night like this."

The rotund smiled as the flask reached him again. "You'd be welcome to stand watch with us. Fire enough for all."

I shook my head solemnly. "I'm afraid, Andrew Mac Alistair, I have to press on. I've word an uncle is dying in Richardston."

Andrew smirked, the liquor having brought a rosy tint to his cheeks. "Who is it? I have kin in Richardston. I might know him."

"Na, Andrew, ye would na know his uncle." The old man's voice caused Logan to stiffen and urged a frown onto Edward's face. He looked at me. "Sorry to keep ye from your journey, Stranger. Shame ye won't be passing this way again."

I nodded to the old man. "Thank you for the fire and drink and song. God be with you."

"God speed ye, Stranger, and steady your hand."

I walked away from the fire and surrendered to the night the warmth I'd taken in. Behind me I heard a confusion of voices, but only one had any strength or edge to it. It belonged to the old man.

"Again, Patrick, play 'Black Morgan' again. Sing it loud. Remind the Krells of Tancras Moor o' what they brought on their house when they plotted against Morgan of Aldare."

You should have killed them all.

I shook my head, a movement it did not like very much. I heard my long hair brush against my cheeks, but I could not feel it. I reached a hand up and touched the frost-deadened flesh. It felt thick and stiff. "There was no reason to kill them."

The old one, he knew who you were.

"Yes, but he did not know what I have become. They are no danger."

It lapsed into silence. I drew my cloak more closely about me and lengthened my stride. If not for the cold I might have given myself time to enjoy the walk. While the moors are not beautiful in the way that a high mountain valley or thick green forest might be, especially in the dark, they have their own charm. Added to that was the splendor of the night sky, despite the mocking moon and ice-chip stars, and the vast emptiness of the moors. When I tire of the crowds I can dream of being alone in the grey-green expanses of moor.

We are not alone.

It gathered the power needed so I could see through the darkness. I knew the spell well. It would gather the light from the stars and moon and let me see as if it was noon in the far Sand Sea. My sight would pierce the fog like sunlight through thunderheads. I stopped it.

She broke from the fog and stumbled down a small hillock. Her yellow-gold hair cloaked her face as she fell.

Her sleeping gown would have been ill-suited to a night like this even before the wear and wetness of a mad flight through the moors shredded and stained it. At the hill's base she rolled to her bleeding, bare feet and froze when she saw me.

Her hair slid like a veil from her face. I thought I caught a flash of blue in her wild eyes, but it might have been nothing more than the spark of terror. The moon bleached all color from her fair complexion—her skin tone, like her eyes and hair, were her mother's legacy to her. Only her straight nose and the way she squinted at me bespoke the Krell blood in her veins.

"Quickly, he's coming. You must run!" She pointed back at the hilltop. She pleaded urgently with me to leave, yet her voice betrayed no fear.

"To me, girl. Your uncle will not harm me, or you."

She ran to me and grabbed my right arm. Gold hair lashed my shoulder as she shook her head and tried to pull me along with her. "Don't be a fool or try to be a hero. Just run, please, just run!"

I ignored her cries. I spun my cloak off and settled it round her shivering body. The cold air attacked me with renewed vengeance as I foolishly left myself open to it. It sliced through to my flesh like a headsman's ax, but now I welcomed its nip. It chopped away the weariness of the day's travel and sharpened my senses.

"Where?"

The girl, thinking I addressed the question to her, mumbled something unintelligible as she hugged the cloak tighter around herself. Waiting for an answer, I listened to *it* communicate with the *other*. Though I could not understand the hisses and barks that *it* used with others of its kind, the challenge *it* issued was clear.

"Where, damn you, where is he?"

Be calm, my lord. It should be at the hilltop just about now.

The mist folded in on itself like a curtain behind which a person poked and prodded to find an opening, then it parted. Silhouetted by the moon, Hugh Krell crouched on the hill. He stopped and croaked out a low laugh. He sniffed the air once, then raised his grey muzzle to the moon and howled out his delight.

He took two hopping steps down the hill, then leaped to the level ground below. He landed on all fours, his hands and feet digging sharp claws into the soft, loamy soil. His clothing, once fine and undoubtedly tailored, had been rent and soiled by the transformation of his muscular body. Tufts of grey fur protruded from every split seam and tear. The upper parts of his riding boots still graced his calves, but below the ankle they had been clawed away for running.

His ears pricked up as more barks and hisses echoed within my head. He dropped his jaw in a canine grin. "Come, sweet Trista, come to your uncle." His voice warbled and whined around human words—all of the R's were growled. "Come away from him so his blood will not stain your beauty."

The other says its master is powerful. There was a sharp hiss and a whipcrack, then cold quiet. *I said you would eat the Krell's heart.*

I saw Hugh's nose twitch as the breeze rose behind me. His feral eyes grew wider and he tilted his head in an all-too-canine attitude of confusion. He pulled his head up and twisted his lips back in a snarl. His fangs were the color of desert-bleached bone.

He snapped his words. "Long time waiting. Now you will die!"

He sprang from his crouch. He came fast, but I had expected his attack ever since my *chacael* had warned his *chacael* of my abilities. Clawed hands forward, Hugh reached for me, but I dropped to my knees and ducked beneath his diving lunge. He sailed over me and landed face-first in the peat.

I turned and he rose, spitting out mud and moss. Bog water dripped from his muzzle and whiskers to mat his chest pelt. "Once only. Now I kill you," he smiled, "I eat you alive."

The blade. Use it. I will make it kill him!

Hugh's enraged rush gave me no time to reply with words, but I fought *its* urgings to draw my sword. Clawed paws sliced through the leather of my jerkin as I stepped back and to the side. I felt fire ignite in the bloody furrows he raked across my ribs, but I forced myself to concentrate—for to lose control would mean *it* would be free to act and that I could not allow.

If I did, I would become one of *them*.

I slammed my left fist into the side of Hugh's head as he swept past. Werewolf or not, he felt the blow as if it were delivered with a hammer. He whipped his head back toward me just in time for my right hand to smash into his jaw from below. His teeth snapped shut with a sharp click, then another blow from my left hand dropped him to the ground.

Trista looked down at the twitching form of her uncle, then raised her eyes to look at me. "Is he . . . ?"

"Dead?" I shook my head. "No. The *chacael* rides him in this state. It lives within his brain and wields great power, but it is somewhat fragile itself." I lifted my bruised and bleeding knuckles into the moonlight. "It cannot tolerate much abuse. It has withdrawn its power from Hugh Krell and he is exhausted—the transformation will do that."

I draped my arm over her shoulder and steered her back

toward the clan keep of the Krells. "Come, I need you to lead me to your grandfather. We have business to decide."

Trista glanced back at Hugh's body. "You're not going to leave him out here, are you?"

"He'll live. For now."

I felt a shiver run through her body and knew it did not come from the cold. "You're him, aren't you? You're Black Morgan of Aldare."

I hugged her tighter to my chest to reassure her. "I am an old friend of your father. I've come to fulfill a promise I made to him."

Remington Krell, seated on his grey-veined, white marble throne, did not appear surprised at my entry into the keep's grand hall. To my left, blazing in a hearth the size of a peasant's hovel, a fire blasted heat into the room. Still, because the hearth had been fashioned after the head of a dragon, only the light spilling from between jagged teeth or glowing in amber eyes did anything to dispel the dim gloom. What it did illuminate reminded me of nothing so much as dusty grave relics falling to decay in a sepulcher long forgotten.

Remington leaned forward in his chair and steepled his fingers. "Well, well, you have come at last."

I caught a strange note in his voice. "Is that pique I hear, Krell? Are you upset that I did not come for you first in my crusade, or does it surprise you that I did not save you for last? Neil would have been amused by your reaction."

The elder Krell's eyes narrowed at the mention of his son's name. "Trista, leave us. You need not be privy to this conversation."

Trista brought her head up questioningly. "But he speaks of my father!"

I laid a hand on her left shoulder. "Do as your grandfather asks. Go to your room and pack a light bag for traveling. Dress yourself in your warmest clothes. You are leaving here tonight."

Magefire arced ebony bolts through Krell's steely eyes. "Oh, you are a bold one, Morgan. Do you actually think, in the last twenty years, you learned enough to deal with the likes of me? I have known the *chacael* since before you were born. I have harnessed its power. I will use it to destroy you."

My eyes hardened. "As you destroyed your own son?"

He snarled and clenched his fists, then returned to me as good as I had given. "Better a killing with just cause than a slaughter of innocents . . ."

The image of my beloved Atlante surfaced in my mind. I saw her as I had first seen her—young and eager, yet possessed of a wisdom that belied her years and made me feel as if she knew all I had ever been and would ever be. Auburn hair cascades hung over her shoulders and framed a face that could make the gods jealous. Her green eyes had a spark of life in them that sizzled no matter how tired or worried she might have been. It was there always, until . . .

"You murdered your own wife in a fit of rage. What a fool you were!"

Remington's ridicule lashed me like a molten whip. I snarled and heard the popping hiss of my *chacael* challenging his to a battle of wills. For a half-second I toyed with letting my *chacael* loose and letting it wield the power we both possessed without regard to anything but making Remington Krell's last seconds seem like years of agony. Then, as the rage built, the sense of caution and control I'd forced myself to develop sliced through it and choked the fury back.

"Succinctly put, Krell." I forced my racing heart to slow. "There was a time when I did blame you and the cabal of sorcerers of which you are but a minor part for her death. You started the foul rumors of my having been cuckolded. You laced them with bits of truth you'd gathered with your dark arts, and I believed them. I reacted in the violent manner that had been the source of my strength for my whole life. I acted in a way that I will regret for all time."

The mocking expression of sympathy Krell settled over his features leered at me like a clown poking fun at a hapless circus patron. "I heard that you rode your horse into her chambers. You saw her there with her brother, drinking wine and laughing over a game of chess . . ."

When she saw me, my wife looked surprised at first, then smiled with all the innocence in the world. She stood quickly and rushed to me as I vaulted from my mount. As her arms enfolded me, I shoved a dagger through her heart, then cast her body aside with less feeling than I would have shown an enemy on the battlefield. Her brother stood and drew his sword, but he was no match for me. A quick parry and a thrust through the stomach. I knew the wound was fatal, but I'd struck him there because I knew it was a painful and hideous way to die.

I was not wrong. Somehow, though, he mastered the pain enough to tell me that he was my wife's brother—the one who had been off traveling when she and I were wed. He said he had come because she shared with him a secret—the secret that she had conceived my child. Lying there on the floor, he tried to raise himself up enough to look at her.

He could not.

Biting back tears, I told him she would live.

He died happily. I died as well.

You can have me bring her back, you know. I have the power to return her from beyond the grave. Just let me handle it.

The whispers of the *chacael*'s seductive suggestion evaporated as I choked down the lump in my throat. "You should thank your son, Neil, for your having survived this long, Krell. After I buried Atlante, I wanted to storm your keep here."

The elder sorcerer laughed derisively. "What you wanted to do and what you could have done are two entirely different things. These moors are mine! With my power they would have swallowed your army whole."

I smiled coldly. "Nothing you could have done would have stopped me from destroying you. But that is something that might have happened another time, in another reality. Your son pointed out to me that there was only one way to fight against sorcerers. He convinced me of the truth of his idea and I pursued it. I have succeeded."

I saw the fear flash in Krell's eyes. He knew the stories of dozens of sorcerers whose reigns of terror had ended abruptly. From places all throughout the Valaksanian Isles, the stories of great magical combats won by a stranger had filtered even as far as the Krell Keep. The song sung by the men warding the moors was just one of many, and they had not escaped Krell's attention.

Remington ignored the fact that his granddaughter had not yet left the room. "Neil died for having betrayed our secrets to you. For the longest time we had hoped he had been dealt with before he could make the final secret known to you."

I shook my head gently. "No, he survived long enough to train me in what I had to know to become a sorcerer." I glanced at the girl. "He made me promise I would come for his daughter and take her away before you could do to her what we have done to ourselves."

Trista blinked twice, then stared blankly at her grand-father. Remington waved off her forlorn gaze. "Do not listen to him, Trista. He is a heretic, like your father. He will not take you away from here. You are right in your desire to become a sorceress, and so you shall become one."

I reached out and turned her to face me. "Have they told you what it means to become a sorcerer?" I tugged at the collar of my tunic and pulled it down enough to reveal a small scar over my carotid artery. "They must have told you how the *chacael* will come to be part of you. It will slip into your brain and know what you know. It will allow you to wield incredible magical powers. It will give you wealth and pleasure and anything else you desire."

I gripped her firmly by her upper arms and held tight until she struggled against the pain. "Have they told you the cost of this power? Have they told you that when you go to the place where the *chacael* dwell that you have to beg for one of them to come to you? Have they told you that you must strike a bargain with them? The *chacael* want more than the mobility you give them and the dreams you share with them. They are perverse creatures that feed on hatred and greed and misery. This is what you must give them to have the power they offer."

I pointed back toward the moors. "Hugh Krell struck a particularly poor bargain. Desperate to be out from under the shadow of his father and his brother, he offered far more than he ever should have. The *chacael* that chose him uses him like a lump of clay thrown on a potter's wheel. Your uncle chased you through the moors tonight so his *chacael* could revel in Hugh's whimperings and fears concerning what he might be forced to do if he caught up with you."

An unseen force ripped her from my grasp as Remington Krell shot to his feet. "Enough, Black Morgan! She belongs to *us*. *We* shall decide her fate after *we* have dealt with you!"

With a half-murmured counterspell I deflected the fireball shooting at me into the hearth. It exploded into a great licking tongue of flame that blacked the dragon's snout and cracked one of the eyes. Burning embers scattered themselves across the grey floor to define a no-man's land between us. The lurid red glow painted Remington's madness on his face in bold relief.

I will crush him. I will crush him!

"No!" Draining some of its power, I fashioned a spell that roared through the hall like a gale. The heavy winds buffeted Remington Krell and threatened to topple him back into his throne. Grey and black strands of his hair whipped across his face, half-blinding him. He clawed at the wind as if grappling with a physical foe, then sheets of ice flew from his hands. They formed themselves into a sphere that captured the wind, then shrank down to compress and kill it. Finally the iceball dropped to the marble floor and shattered amid the coals.

Krell brushed hair from his eyes. "You have learned much, but you do not allow yourself the *chacael*'s full power!" Krell gestured at me and suddenly the floor flowed like water. The fluid stone surged upward and encased me up to my waist in marble. "This is not a battle, Black Morgan, in which you can hold back."

Part of me, a piece distant, bristled at his telling me what I could and could not do. Of the foes I'd faced, he was hardly the most powerful, but the others had not expected me to be able to oppose them at all. The counterspell for the fireball came easily since I had used it so often against my foes' first gambit. My windstorm likewise surprised many for they guarded against lethal assaults, which mine was not.

What the elder Krell lacked in pure power, he made up for in guile. Spells sprang from his fingers spawning hell-born bats flapping at me with leathery wings and mouths full of razored teeth. They swooped and snapped, their piercing cries barely audible. My jerkin blunted some assaults, but with my feet bound, I could not escape them.

Panic began to nibble at me as the stone crept higher. Nips at shoulders and ears drew blood. Those fiery bites burned and fever began to spread through me. The stone rose over my belly and back, pressing in, making it hard to breathe.

Yet, even with all these things, had I faced Remington Krell alone, I could have defeated him.

He was not alone. He had an ally.

My *chacael*.

Free me! Free me!

"No!" I fought panic down. I fought to put aside the pain and concentrate. I fought with my *chacael*, twisting it to power the spell I needed to escape my prison. *It* fought all the harder, reigniting the pains I sought to quench, encouraging the panic.

Free me, or we are done! He's fashioned a trap!

My mind reeled for a moment and then I realized that Remington Krell was likewise holding back. A half dozen bats nipping could have been one huge bat gorging. A stone sheath could have been a sepulcher. He could have killed me himself, but Neil and the old man had agreed: he never got his hands dirty. He was waiting for something, but what?

Before I could trigger a spell to free myself, Trista screamed. In the corner of my right eye I saw a hulking, furred form crawling through an arched window, but who it was did not register in my brain until too late. Her scream, my pain and my rising panic about being trapped, broke my grip on the incredible powers I constantly controlled. In an eyeblink the *chacael* was free to act, and act it did.

A searing silver ball of lightning launched itself from the fingertips of my right hand. It flew unerringly at the window, then dropped down as the werewolf landed on the floor. The lightning hit Hugh Krell on the right side of his chest and exploded in a thunderclap. It sprayed flesh and blood back against the wall and spattered it across the floor. I saw ivory ribs for a half-second before the fire blackened them.

The lightning turned Hugh Krell into a living, screaming torch. His howls sounded like those of a tortured dog, then died in a rasped gurgle as he breathed fire into his lungs. His pelt ignited like tinder, wreathing him in golden glory. He fell to the ground, thrashing, until the flames dwindled and became a column of sickly-sweet smoke.

Anger flared anew within my breast, but it was not directed at Remington Krell or his dying son. I directed it at the demon living within me and used it to regain control. Wordlessly, precluding any protest on its part, I grabbed its power firmly and bent all the *chacael* was to *my* will.

The stone encasing my body whirled away in a dervish of marble fragments that ripped the bats to pieces. I extended my left hand toward Remington Krell and balled my fist. I did not hold back. The air around him hardened to a stone consistency and crumpled him. I kept my fist closed for long enough to insure his unconsciousness, then opened it and let his body slump at the base of his throne.

It is a mistake to let a foe like this one live. You will regret it.

"So you have told me with all the others." Scorn laced

my words. "You thought he might be my master. You hoped he would win and in victory allow you to do with me as you will."

Ever the hope of a slave!

"You, a slave? You have forgotten much. You will have to remember." My anger remained unabated and I stabbed it like a spear into the *chacael*. "You acted without my leave." I looked at the smoldering body of Hugh Krell staring blindly at the ceiling. "You killed him."

It was a trap. I had to defend us. You even allow that of the others.

"You acted without my leave."

It twisted and writhed within my mind. *The others act without leave of their hosts . . .*

I shook my head. "Remember, you and I are not like the others, are we? Hosts come to the Joining Place after a few years of study. They are young and they believe, in their youth, that they can command all you offer. They believe the sacrifices they have to make are worth the prize and they believe the debts they incur will never be collected. That is how the others succeed and why the others can act without the leave of their host.

"This is not the bargain we struck. I came to the Joining Place but I offered no concessions. You have not forgotten how you battled and vied with others for the honor of becoming my *chacael*. You knew that I'd studied longer than most, and you sensed in me the pain and despair I carried with me for my past deeds. You hungered after the revenge I harbored in my heart and the power you knew I could command. You made a concession to me, remember?"

I promised not to act without your leave.

"And you have violated this promise. You will atone."

How?

73

"You have boasted that you can defeat even death." I pointed at Hugh Krell's body. "Fix him. Cure him of the things your compatriot has done to him."

It wanted to balk and rebel, but my anger gave it no release. Energy flowed from my body and wrapped the charred corpse in an azure cocoon. Sparks and dark blue threads spun through it, obscuring the body and the reconstruction process. The blood and bits of flesh on the walls and floor vanished, then the cocoon split open to reveal the sleeping visage of a naked clean-limbed youth no longer warped by the form of his other self.

You said nothing of his clothing, it reminded me.

"You do not deflect me that easily." I looked back over at where Remington Krell lay sleeping. "Both of their *chacaels* have acknowledged us their master?"

Yes. It hesitated, then added a plea. *Not again, Morgan. Do not force me to do it again.*

I laughed low and cruelly. "What? You would not have me keep my part of the bargain we struck so many years ago? You promised you would not act without my leave and I promised to make you the master of your race within my world. I would not go back on my part of the agreement. I have honor." I exhaled slowly. "Bind them. You know the formula. Bind them forever."

I heard the hissing, crackled speech of the *chacaels* and easily recognized the outrage in their replies to my demon. It had charged them with never using magic except in self-defense, or in a case where it helped another with no chance of remuneration or compensation reaching their host. By virtue of their defeat, the Krells' *chacaels* became bound to help those who had struck no bargains with them.

They complain they will starve to death.

"Tell them to feed on their own misery."

Trista Krell crossed to me and returned my cloak. "Am I to leave with you, my lord?"

I looked down into her cerulean eyes and saw the same lifespark I had extinguished in my wife's eyes. "Do you understand what it means to become a sorcerer?"

She nodded. "I will not pay that price." She looked over at her uncle and her grandfather. "You have stopped their magic, haven't you?"

I nodded solemnly. "Except in certain cases, yes, they will have magic no more."

Trista tucked a strand of golden hair behind her left ear. "Then they will have to become accustomed to living without it. They are my kin . . ."

I pressed a finger to her lips. "Say nothing more. Your father, my friend, wanted me to come and take you away before you could become a sorceress. He did not want you to labor under the burden he had taken on, and he did not want you to become like your uncle. That being the case, he would want you to be happy. I pray that in caring for these two you do find happiness."

Back on the road, heading toward Richardston, the night sucked heat from me like a leech. The clawmarks on my chest and the bites elsewhere stung but neither they nor the cold bothered me. I walked along locked in memories of far-away places and times when I knew joy.

Host, you felt the power. You felt how easy it was to defeat both Krells. Why do you deny yourself the exhilaration of that power? There is nothing and no one in this world that could stand against the power we possess.

Again Atlante's angelic face blossomed before my mind's-eye. "You are wrong. *I* stand between us and what the power could give us."

Why?

Atlante's face blurred and dissolved into Hugh Krell's smoking body. "Because I know that the power, no matter how much is used, can never give me what I desire."

But I can give her back to you, just as I did with Hugh Krell.

I shook my head, gently this time. "No. If I allowed you to talk me into that, I would allow you to talk me into all manner of hideous crimes—with you justifying it all because everything could be made right later. I would once again become the bloody-handed monster that slew his own wife. No matter what your power, Black Morgan of Aldare is one creature I will never allow you to resurrect."

The *chacael* fell silent—once again considering me impossible—and I lengthened my stride. Using just a bit of magic, I summoned a slight breeze at my back. I cared less that it sped me on my way than for the strains of song it carried to my ears. Humming along to myself, I walked on into the night.

"Let Me Call You Sweetheart" was written in the mid-1980s to parody political correctness and all of the laws being passed to save folks from their own stupidity. It also had elements of cyberpunk stuff in it, though Lawrence Watt-Evans, who bought it for the anthology **Newer York**, cautioned me against using the "C-word" to describe it.

I recall having just finished the story when a friend, Scott Wareing, came over to give me a lift to soccer. I handed him the story to read while I changed for the game. I was hoping to hear laughter, since I thought it was funny, but there was dead silence from the living room. He got through six pages; then we left. On the drive, after about twenty minutes, he said gently, "Um, did you mean for that story to be funny?" I said, "Yes, but you didn't laugh." Then Scott *did* laugh. He'd been fighting back laughter because he thought I was trying to write a straight story.

Let Me Call You Sweetheart

The languid drizzle steamed off the alley's brick wall and unraveled the streetlight's glare into a thousand rainbow threads. Hidden deep in the shadows that lurked beyond the light's sphere of influence, I reached up and adjusted the microphone by my mouth. Gloved fingers traced the line back to the jack behind my left ear. I snapped it out and back in—the check signal said the full radio system functioned—then ground my teeth with impatience.

I flexed my right hand and tightened my grip on the Smith and Wesson M-19 Multi-cart pistol. My thumb caressed the selector lever, but I resisted the impulse to flick it from Tefjac to Blender shells. The M-107 T-plas attachment slung under the barrel, with the two fanglike electrode-tangs flaring out on each side, glowed green in the charging coils. I smiled; no hardware problem here.

I looked over at the dark door sunk into the alley wall opposite my position. The streetlight couldn't reach it, but did glow brightly enough from the wet pathway cleared of debris by the shuffling feet of lost souls drifting into the place to point up its hidden location. I glanced at the menu bar at the base of my shooting glasses' right lens and let the IR vision program paint the door itself in shades of gold and red against the darker maroon of the bricks themselves. It even outlined, in yellow, the handprint of the last man granted entry through the metal-core door.

Before I could lose myself in ruminations about the evils enjoyed beyond that door, the call crackled into the speaker sunk in my left mastoid bone. "Sewer detail in position. Sorry, hadda kill two 'gators. Ready."

"Gimme a three-count," I growled into the mike, "then shut everything down!"

I stalked boldly from the shadows, my left hand stripping my grey trenchcoat open. It flapped back around my legs and the star it revealed on the chest of my shirt clearly identified me as a government agent, one of the elite of the elite. The people huddled in the smoke-easy would never forget their first meeting with an agent of Alcohol, Tobacco, and Confections.

The M-19's muzzle flame blackened the door as the first burst splashed through the door's lock. Patrons reeled away from the spray of metal fragments as I stepped through the doorway and glanced at "seek" on my glasses' menu bar. My shooting glasses instantly cycled through different modes and settled on Starlight targeting as appropriate for the smoky, low-light environment I scanned. Red lines blazed to life over my right eye in a crosshair pattern, and a red dot flared up whenever my pistol pointed at a viable target.

I wheeled to the left where a mutant giant, the stub of a Cuban Corona hanging from his thick lower lip, rose up to loom over me like a tidal wave. He reached for me with hands the size of shovel-blades and the half-light glinted from the razor talons capping both fingers on each hand. I triggered a three-shot burst but only realized I'd unconsciously downshifted to Blender shells when his chest flew back and his legs fell in the doorway.

The clonekin at the bar—an Einstein model—raised its four hands in surrender, but the vat-thug guarding the back door sprang off the stool it'd occupied and raised a pre-war model shotgun. The patrons between us dove for cover, upsetting ash-laden tables and boosting cigarettes into the air like missiles. I almost laughed at the nico-freaks—whose "recreational" addiction was killing them anyway—as they clawed for the smoke-easy's scant cover. I was tempted, for a moment, to let the genegineered hoodlum blast away blindly, but the idea of letting it get a shot off before I killed it was as repulsive as pushers selling candy-canes to unsuspecting school children.

The red dot ignited over my right eye and my thumb clicked the pistol back to Tefjacs as I tightened up on the trigger. The friction-resistant bullets blew through the bouncer's body armor. The thug flattened back against the wall, then slid down and settled in a rumpled, bloody heap over his toppled stool.

I raised my gun toward the ceiling and the targeting light shut off on the lens over my right eye. That, and the smile creeping across my features, drained some of the anxiety from the room and lowered stress to lawful levels. "You're all under arrest for violations of the self-protection statutes." Ignoring their complaints and pleas, I nodded purposefully in the direction of one overturned table. "That includes you, too, Councilman Foster."

I laughed at his groan, then smiled even more broadly as the radio crackled and reported the warehouse annex to the smoke-easy had been sealed off. The city's tactical unit—dressed in their smoke-grey, chocolate brown urban camouflage—streamed in through the open door and started to round up prisoners as I looked over at the biotank-baby at the bar. "Buzz me into the back."

It did and I stepped over the Councilman on my way through the doorway. The scent hit me immediately and my nostrils shut down in protest. Crates of various sizes and shapes filled the long, low, dark warehouse to bursting. Lists of contents boldly stenciled in black stood out on the crates' sides, but I knew instantly they lied. This place reeked of chocolate.

I holstered the M-19 and shut the T-plas off as my newest partner brought a man to me. The suspect struggled fruitlessly, as if his corpulent bulk could possibly prevail against a healthy, young, dedicated patriot. The suspect disgusted me, and not just because he peddled confections to children. Greed I could understand, but stupidity revolted me. One look at his darkened fingers and the stains smeared along his grey suit and I knew he'd not been smart enough to resist the lure of his product.

He sniffed the red and white carnation boutonniere on his lapel and sneered at me over it. "Well, if it isn't Elliot Nestle!"

I slapped him once, hard, before I regained my composure. "Insults won't help you now, Cadbury!" I looked beyond him at my deputy, Raul Danton, and saw, in his electric, hawk-eyed stare, he'd deny I'd ever struck the suspect.

I fished the worn card from inside my coat pocket. "You have the right to remain silent for as long as you can. Anything you say or think can and will be used against you in a court of law. You have the right to have an attorney cyberlinked during mindscan. If you so desire but cannot afford one, the court will give you a Rom-based legal Expert-system for immediate interface." I stared into his blank, chocolate-brown eyes. "Do you understand these rights as I have explained them?"

Cadbury smiled, revealing yellowed teeth. "It'll take more than your interrogators to work through the cognitive jungle they've mesmered into my brain."

I shrugged. "So we can't break you, big deal." I pointed at the crates surrounding us. "You're going away for a long time, Victor. This is serious dealer weight."

Victor Cadbury laughed and his thick jowls bounced to echo his derision. "This? Ha!" His dark eyes flickered from crate to crate. "As your men will soon tell you, this is just milk chocolate. You've got nothing!"

"Take him away!" I snorted furiously. Once again the Coryza, the smugglers' underworld, had anticipated a raid it took three months to plan. All that work and all I got was milk chocolate. Without getting the harder stuff, like Brazilian Stinger or, better yet, Swiss White, even I began to doubt my ability to protect Americans from themselves.

My boss, Inspector Harris Martin, set aside the bureau's affairs in the Mobo sector just to listen to me rant and rave. "I don't know, Harry," I heard myself whining, "nothing works. We have men everywhere working to smash the smugglers bringing the stuff into the country, but the more we do, the stronger the damned Coryza gets. It spreads like an infection!"

Harry nodded his white-maned head and a serious expression slipped over his face like a mask. "Insidious, that's the word for it. All we can do is try our best to keep things under control."

I shook my head. "How can we do our best when everyone winks at the first flirtations with confection addiction? Think about it, Harry." I turned toward the office's darkened window. "When it gets really cold up here,

mothers from Montreal to the Boston hub make 'hot chocolate' for their children to ward off the cold. No kid will take
candy from a stranger, but how can anyone think of chocolate as evil when their mothers give it to them?"

Harry's voice became gravelly as the gravity of the situation once again battered him. "You're right, Mark, we've
got a double standard. I can remember an uncle shaving
strips of dark, bittersweet chocolate—Brazilian Stinger, I
think—into the first cup of coffee I ever had. It didn't seem
bad then."

I snorted. "Tell me about it. I grew up in Hershey,
Pennsylvania Military District. I lived in the shadow of the
old factory and I can still remember days when the vile,
sweet smoke from the factory would fill the valley. Oh, I
saw the evils of chocolate early on." I gritted my teeth and
pounded my right fist into my left hand. "I saw the disease
get my older brother and have its way with him."

Harry leaned forward. "Acne?"

I nodded solemnly. "The worst, Harry, all over his face
and back. His friends tried to tell him it wasn't the chocolate, and he believed them. He kept drowning his sorrow
and shame in it and he ballooned. For a while he dealt—
selling kisses and bars to kids at school—and could afford
the good stuff: Swiss White. But his empire melted like
chocolate held too long in the hand." My voice broke. "He
died a candy mess."

Harry shook his head sympathetically, giving me time to
recover myself. "You couldn't get him into a carob treat-
ment program?"

I sighed heavily. "He was too far gone for that. I remember the last time I saw him, Harry. The boys in Boston
Vice called me in when they found him. There he lay, deep
in an alley, ready-to-spread frosting smeared over his face

and on his index finger. I don't know where he got it, but the double-Dutch chocolate was too much for him."

Harry shivered. "An overdose is never pretty." He picked up one of the gold-foil wrapped bunnies we'd liberated from the warehouse and examined it closely. "It's hard to believe, sometimes, that something so innocent looking could be so dangerous."

I watched the sugary lagomorph slowly spin in his grasp. The foil clung to it like a negligee and revealed, in a flash of golden highlights, only the benign physical characteristics of an animal lauded in stories and folktales. It did look innocent, but that made it fouler, to my mind, because it snared the unwary and propelled them into a life of crime and degradation that few successfully escaped.

I stood. "Innocent it looks, Inspector, but I know better. I look at the flag, those thirteen stripes and sixty-seven stars, and I feel proud. Then I look at that rabbit and I know it, and those who bring it to these shores, just want to undermine the last bastion of true freedom on the Earth."

I leaned forward over his desk and said smugly, "And I'll tell you something else, Harry. *She's* behind this."

The rabbit stopped spinning and Harry's brown eyes locked onto my gaze. "Andrea Tobler! How do you know that?"

I shrugged. "Heard a rumor she'd gobbled up the Cadbury family holdings last year. Besides," I nodded at the rabbit, "you must have noticed, Inspector, the rabbits are light. They're hollow. How better to bleed more money out of those who crave her foul wares?"

Harry's dark eyes narrowed cautiously and he regarded the rabbit anew. "Perhaps, Mark, you've stumbled onto something." He looked up at me. "I'll follow up on it, and let you know what's happening. Given your history with her, though, I think you should take a few days off. Don't want anyone thinking you've gone round the bend over this."

"Gotcha, sir," I smiled easily. "I wanted to spend some time out on my ichthyoculture plantation anyway. Good hunting."

Raul looked as disheveled as his apartment when I woke him at midnight. He raked fingers back through his thick, black hair and stared at me. One of his contacts had slipped, making his right eye look like a brown moon being eclipsed by a blue shadow, but he did not notice. "Gosh, Lieutenant Glace, what are you doing here? I thought you were on your fish farm in Jersey."

I shook my head sharply. "That's just what I wanted people to think. You are I are heading out to Montreal tonight. She's there, and I mean to get her."

"What, how?" Danton asked as he sprang from bed and pulled his combat jumpsuit on.

As he strapped his H & K MP-47's belt around his waist and tied the holster down on his right leg, I explained. "You remember that flower Cadbury had on his jacket? It was a Peppermint Carnation, and it's only grown in Surrey. Coryza buy them in Holland at the flower market, then smuggle them into Montreal. She gave us Cadbury because he was eating up the profits."

Muscles twitched at the corners of Danton's lantern jaw. "Andrea Tobler. I never thought I'd get the chance." His right hand caressed the butt of his gun.

I shook my head. "Anyone else, including even Fred Whitman, you can have, but Andrea, she's mine."

Images frozen by the engine's backlight strobed past the

rain-streaked window as the train slashed through a night darker than bakers' chocolate. I stared at my reflection until Danton set a hot cup of chicken soup in front of me and the steam erased my features.

"Earth to Lieutenant Glace, are you OK, sir?"

I lightened the dour expression on my face and turned toward him. "Yeah, sure, Raul, I'm fine. Call me Mark, OK?"

He nodded and sipped gingerly at his soup. "Do you mind if I ask you a personal question?"

I shook my head. "No, go ahead." I expected what was coming; all my new partners eventually asked. None of them could believe the rumors until I confirmed them.

"You were over there, weren't you, sir, um, Mark?" I saw a light flash in his eyes—a light I'd seen in my own reflection long ago. "What's it like in Europe anyway?"

I sipped my soup and got a moment's taste of salt before the liquid torched my tastebuds. "Well, it's not as bad as some would make out, Raul, because it can be very pretty. I mean, yes, it's a decadent place, a hedonistic heaven for those who have a fortune built on kisses and bars of chocolate, but culture is not restricted to their yogurt."

I smiled at a recollection. "I almost blew my cover the first night in Switzerland. The maid had turned my bed down and left a chocolate on my pillow! That threw me off for a moment, but I managed to give it as a gift to a friend. Needless to say, it was close."

Raul nodded solemnly. "Working undercover for the CEA must have been a challenge."

I sighed heavily. "It was that, and so much more. When you spend so much time in the company of confectioners, you begin to lose your perspective. They accepted me quickly because I pretended to be an ex-patriot avoiding the draft in the latest round of Russo-American martial games in The People's Republic of Columbia, and then they discovered I grew up in Hershey. Within a month I was thick with them, and they sent me to Switzerland because they thought I could do great things there."

Raul swallowed hard and timidly approached the question he'd wanted to ask all along. "You knew her, didn't you?"

I nodded silently, unable to speak past the lump in my throat. I raised my cup of soup and took just enough in to force the lump back down. "Yeah, I knew Andrea. A couple of the Cadburys recommended me to her father, Herr Helmut Tobler, and he saw something in me he liked. He brought me to his home in Zurich and started to teach me the business. He appointed Andrea to help refine my German."

My voice dropped off as I pictured her as I first saw her. She'd been riding, so a helmet capped her head, but when she removed it, black cascades of hair swept down to frame her angelic face. Blue eyes—naturally blue—regarded me carefully as she strode across the white-marble expanse of her father's ballroom. Halfway to us she graced me with a smile and I felt a blush rise to my cheeks. Slender and petite, she had a strength of character that burned like a fusion-generator and suffused her entirely.

Raul cleared his throat. "They say you even loved her . . ."

I nodded. "I'm sure they do, and they think of it as a great conquest for me to have slept with the Queen of confections. But," I said, staring at him harshly, "I don't think of it that way." My voice lost its edge. "I actually did love her."

Raul watched me with sympathy in his eyes, and an unspoken plea for an explanation on his lips. He knew he couldn't ask and he recognized he'd never heard this part of the story from any of his locker-room buddies.

I forced a smile. "I know it sounds like treason, Raul, and that's why I've not said anything about it before. I spent weeks and months working with her. My mission had been to work myself into the Tobler empire, and her father smiled upon our romance. At first I thought I could control things, but I soon fell for her as hard as she fell for me."

Raul shook his head ruefully. "I'm sorry, Mark."

"You shouldn't be, really. I was happy then and I savored every moment we had together. Life is to be lived, within the law, and we really did love each other." I chuckled lightly. "In fact, if not for one word, you might be riding this train with Inspector Martin, coming after me!"

"One word?" Raul's surprise at my admission succumbed to his probing sense of curiosity. "What could she say that would drive you two apart?"

I gulped some soup and used the burning sensation to fortify me. "Sweetheart."

"What?"

I nodded sagely and stared past the cup's rim at him. "You heard me. Sweetheart. You know I don't often use profanity, but she called me her sweetheart. In that instant I realized I'd almost been seduced by a society and lifestyle so perverted that they could consider an utterly obscene word a term of endearment."

Raul rode the rest of the way to Montreal in stunned and horrified silence.

The hoodlum screamed as the azure T-plas ball expanded and engulfed him. The blue lightning skittered over him like a fishnet on acid, firing muscles and singeing hair as it tightened about him. Energy tendrils drifted down his legs and finally reached the earth. They flared argent, then drained down and dropped him like a marionette with cut strings.

I crouched and nodded unconsciously as Raul's voice burst into my head. "Roger, Raul, one is down, but I can't find his partner. That sniveling candyman better not have lied to us about the Coryza's security precautions."

"The sentries are right where he told me they'd be." Static crackled through Raul's reply, but I couldn't hear the sounds of gunfire or the hissing of a plasma bolt. "I'm going in, Mark. See you at the rear of the flower warehouse."

Afraid that his transmission may have hidden any sounds in the alley, I turned my head and scanned for Coryza, but no targeting dot appeared. I glanced at the menu bar on my right lens and switched the glasses over to IR, but the downed thug's smoldering body and the dissipating golden signature of his footsteps were all I could see. I looked up, to cover the roof edges and the rusty fire escape, and nearly made as bad a mistake as the man above me.

I saw his red-purple form and the growing white fire in his hand. I screwed my eyes shut against the argent burst of light on my glasses, and blindly clawed them from my face. I turned and ducked, twisting away from the first burst of tungsten needles from his Colt, but even the hand over my eyes could not keep out the magnesium flare's harsh nova-glare.

Had I been a second or two slower, the flare would have burned my eyes out with its intensity or his initial burst would have torn through my body. I slitted my eyes open but could see almost nothing in the flare's unwavering blaze beyond the gunman's bloated shadow. The flare, held high in the gunman's left fist, drenched the alley with pure light and carved him into a silhouette with a Mohawk and the ragtag body armor favored by Montreal's gangs. The Colt looked like it had grown at the end of his arm and, from his position on the fire escape, he triggered another burst that sprayed metal slivers—half of which ricocheted from the fire escape's railing—that drove me back behind the burned-out hulk of an Iacocca wagon.

The gunman laughed and taunted me with accented English. "I play with you like a dog plays with a blind squirrel, eh, *couchon?*"

"You stupid Goober," I swore at him. "Even a blind squirrel finds an acorn now and then." I pointed my pistol at the fire escape and triggered the M-107.

His scream filled the brick canyon as the first ball of energy sizzled to life on the electrodes and greedily launched itself at the iron parasite clinging to the old brick building. A tornado of blue fire whirled around the metal structure and sparks exploded where paint combusted, or clothesline remnants burned away. The cyclone sucked up the second and third plasma bursts, then raced skyward like a rocket on a jet of azure thrust.

High above me the gunman danced a jerky, spasmodic tarantella. The energy wrapping him like a cloak detonated his pistol's propellant in a ball of red and green flames and consumed the flare like a nico-freak's first cigarette of the day. Then blue fingers of electricity reached up and tickled a response from the low clouds above.

The lethal bolt of silver lightning crashed down and fired the entire fire escape to a cherry red an eternity before its thundered report blasted me to the gritty alley floor. Energy rippled out from the fire escape and flowed across the rain-slicked alley like fire over a sea of gasoline. It swept up over the wagon's blackened skeleton and flooded its bones with a crimson glow. I rolled to my feet, making the best of the protection my insulated combat boots offered. Deafened by the thunder, and nightblind without my glasses, I turned toward the warehouse and froze. I saw the scarlet crosshairs on a third gunman—one I'd not been warned about—and tried to dodge, but the street detritus gave way beneath my feet. I saw the crosshair's flash for a second, then felt the narc-dart's sting in my throat.

A black storm stole my sight, and the ground rose up to club me into unconsciousness.

Awakening, I heard a laugh I hoped was the last trace of a nightmare evaporating. I identified it instantly and bitter fear rose in my throat. If I was not waking from a nightmare, I was surely drifting into one.

I opened my eyes and swallowed hard past the pain in my throat. Seated, securely bound to a metal chair by rope and leather straps, I found myself center stage in a small enclosure with walls built from packing crates. The wooden boxes, marked similarly to those I'd seen earlier in the evening, rose to a height of twelve feet and nearly touched the fluorescent lights hanging down from the ceiling on long chains. In their backlight I could see a second, crate-laden level and a narrow catwalk passing through the darkness.

Danton sat in a chair beside me. His bruised and battered head lolled to the side as if they'd broken his neck, but his chest rose and fell with a strength and regularity that told me he still lived. Crumbs of chocolate dappled the thick cords of rope binding him to his chair and I smiled. He'd resisted eating chocolate despite their torture. With a couple more like him . . .

Fred Whitman's cackled laugh sliced through my private thoughts and sank jagged talons into my brain. I flicked my eyes over at him and stared hard at his face. I lowered my gaze to his cheek, then snickered, "Never did fix that, did they?"

Fred, fear flooding his eyes, recoiled. He reached unconsciously up and touched the broad, twisted scar that scored his right cheek the way cow-paths mar hillsides. Then the fingers gently probing the wound hooked into claws and balled into a fist which he shook in my face. "This time, Glace, you will pay!"

The small cortege at his back nodded, but I could read the pity for him on their faces. Fred Whitman had decided, back when I worked in Europe, that he should be Andrea Tobler's consort. Known then as "Handsome Fred," he was very popular with ladies and assumed he had only to eliminate me and Andrea would fall into his bed. While his campaign against me did result in my cover collapsing, our final battle left him broken and, because his flesh did not readily culture, scarred for life.

Fred turned back toward a table behind him and picked up a clear, fluid-filled bottle with a thick glass stopper. He gingerly teased the stopper loose and a very light vapor rose from the colorless liquid. Holding the bottle in his right hand, he sank a glass pipette into the liquid and capped the cylinder with his left thumb. He pulled the pipette up enough to let liquid drain from its exterior, then held it up so I could see a single drop glistening at its tip.

"Hydrochloric acid, Glace." Fred smiled cruelly and flicked the droplet down onto my knee. The uniform smoked and the acid ate the fabric away. "The surgeons will never be able to reconstruct your face . . ."

I saw the flicker of motion and the glow from above as Fred raised the pipette toward my face. The blue energy globe smashed him on his left shoulder and blasted him against the crates to his right. The pipette clattered to the ground and fragmented into a dozen pieces as the full bottle of acid exploded against one of the crates. The blue plasma spun a cocoon around Whitman and lifted him into the air, then dissipated like fog and dropped his limp body to the warehouse floor.

I looked up toward the catwalk and, in the backglow of her T-plas projector, I caught the hint of a smile on her face. The greenish glow lit her face softly and reminded me of many dawns when I'd risen early and just stared at her beautiful face while she slept. Our gazes met for half a second, and my heart burned with an emotional fire I'd long since hoped I'd utterly smothered.

She turned from me and stared down at her henchmen. "Haul Fred out to the gyrojet, then stay well clear of this warehouse." Amid a chorus of affirmations they jumped into action and quickly left Danton and me alone with Andrea Tobler.

I looked over at the crate the acid had eaten through. Floating in the acid lake bubbling with the last remnants of packing material, I saw a dozen golden bunnies. I smiled and nodded to her. "I congratulate you on discovering a way to gouge more profits from your clients. Hollow instead of solid, brilliant."

She returned my praise with a salute. "And I congratulate you on discovering this warehouse. I instructed Victor to remove the flower before he traveled down to your sector, but Fred taunted him, hoping you'd backtrack and fall into his clutches." She pointed up toward the street-level flower warehouse. "The flowers help hide the scent of our product and keep the CEA's silicurs from sniffing us out. In fact, the only mistake you made was in leaving your informant alive. He sold us to you, then sold you to us, and we picked you up as soon as the two of you started conversing on your radios."

I acknowledged my mistake with a grimace, then I smiled and decided to gamble. "This place is blown, Andrea. I left a program running on the department's computer that will inform Inspector Martin of my location by dawn." I slowly scanned the warehouse. "You can't move all of this by then. I win."

She shook her head and fixed me with a reproving stare—the one she reserved for when she felt I was spinning a story. "I doubt that, Mark. You could not lie to me then, and you cannot lie to me now. Besides," she added, raising her T-plas gun, "it does not matter, really."

She triggered a burst of energy that arced off across the warehouse and hit something that promptly exploded and flickered firelight up to the ceiling. The gold and red flames illuminated Andrea and slithered highlights onto her raven hair. "You, Mark Glace, and your aide will die heroically in a fire that consumes the largest stash of illegal chocolate ever discovered in North America."

I stared at her, speechless. Smoke already brought the scent of wood and burning chocolate to me. I swallowed and looked up one last time. "Isn't this a bit much just for two ATC agents?"

"Expensive, perhaps," she mused, "but even the Swiss White bunnies and the bittersweet chickens are hollow—no great loss." Then she smiled at me. "I think 'spectacular' is a better word. But, then, I couldn't do less for the man I love, could I, Sweetheart?"

A burning undercurrent of pain coursed up and down my acid-gnawed left arm—despite the dressings, unguents, salves, anesthetics and doctors' assurances—and held my fatigue at bay. The wooden chair creaked beneath my tired body and the scent of fire and hospitals rose up in a thick cloud that forced Inspector Martin to lean back as he read the transcript of the report I'd dictated in the ambulance.

He laid the last page down on the pile centered on his blotter, then removed his glasses and used them as a paperweight. He stared at me with red-rimmed eyes. "My God, Mark, that's an amazing piece of work. Playing a hunch, you uncover a massive storehouse of chocolate. You escape a flaming deathtrap and carry your unconscious partner to a nearby hospital." Jerking a thumb at the picture of the President hanging behind him, he smiled wryly. "When the news broke I had a call from the Old Man, and he's going to give you a medal."

Harry shook his head, but not a single lock of his white hair fell out of place. "You played it close to the vest. I wish you'd told me your plan so I could have helped."

"That's OK, Harry, because Andrea didn't need your help this time." The stunned look on his face, and the pain coursing through his eyes, gave birth to the beginning of a stuttered denial, but I cut it off with a snarl. "I wondered how the hell Andrea knew where we were going to hit; then I realized she had someone inside our bureau."

Indignation flushed Harry's skin and chased off his deathly grey pallor. "What do you mean, accusing me of taking bribes? How dare you!"

I snorted derisively. "Save it, Harry." I stared at him and he dared not move. "I told her I'd left a message for you with my location and that didn't concern her in the least. The big trick, though, was figuring how she managed to pay you. You're too smart to trust money held in an account abroad for you, but you also know you can't hide money in your bank account here."

I smiled and licked my lips. "I should have seen it sooner, but I didn't until the warehouse was burning down around me." I leaned forward and gestured carefully with my bandaged arm. "You see, the only way I could get out of my ropes was to tip my chair over and inch my way to the acid pool draining from one of the contraband crates. The acid took its time, eating into my flesh while it consumed the ropes. I had plenty of time to stare at the golden forms of chocolate bunnies, and I finally figured out how she got money to you."

I nodded solemnly. "It was a good plan, Harry."

I reached up and pointed my left hand at the golden bunny still sitting on Harry's desk. "As Andrea noted, the loss of hollow rabbits was insignificant in terms of chocolate weight, hence there had to be something of greater value connected to them. Because we use a chemical bath to destroy all the chocolate we confiscate, the foil must be stripped off each rabbit before it's tossed into the vat."

I pulled my pistol and pointed it at Harry's chest. "The acid didn't eat through the foil, Harry! It burned the ropes and burned me, but not the pure gold foil. I'm sure the trashmen who collect the foil for you will betray you when they learn how much it was really worth."

I rose and Harry opened his hands in supplication. "Come on, Mark, be reasonable. There's plenty to split. I can make you a honey of a deal."

The backhanded blow with my pistol snapped Harry's head around. I watched blood dribble down his cheek from where a tang had cut him; then I holstered my pistol and picked up the bunny. "You played me for a sucker, Harry, but now you're the one who's been licked."

Two Federal Marshals opened the office door and came to take Harry away. As he passed by me, I crushed the rabbit's hollow head and tossed the candy carelessly into his hands.

"Hey, Harry," I called after him.

He turned wearily, the gold icon clutched to his chest. "Yes?"

"While you're in prison, think of me," I smiled cruelly, "think of me and have sweet dreams."

"**Tip-Off**" is a story I wrote for Roger Zelazny's *Wheel of Fortune* anthology. Roger had asked if I would contribute a tale for this book of gambling stories. I originally thought I would complete and send him one of my **ShadowRun**® stories—I figured FASA would let me use their world— which eventually was published as "Designated Hitter" in the *Wolf and Raven* book. If you compare the openings of the two stories, you will see similarities in setting, though the two tales wildly diverge after that. Knowledge of the America West arena where the Suns play came courtesy of Tom Ambrose, a VP with the team, who gave a tour of the facility to six writers from Phoenix.

Tip-Off

"Hey, Killian, how come you're wasting time reading that book when you could be returning some of these calls or helping me or something?" Hank's question surprised me, not in its content, but in that he had waited all the way to Thursday to ask it this week. Normally he took his responsibilities as the president of the local "Save Killian Sloane from antisocial behavior" club more seriously. "C'mon, you could pop a wafer and have it all in an instant, so why spend the time reading it?"

I carefully punched the "Mark Current" button on the ScanReader and placed the device on the bar. "I'm reading the book because that action improves my mind." Looking over at him, I focused on his good left eye, not the glowing red replacement in the other socket. "*Knowing* the stuff is better than being able to tap it. You told me that in Lhasa, remember, Sarge?" I let him chew on that for a second, then shrugged. "So, what is it you need help with?"

He grinned at me with yellow teeth and shifted his cheroot from one side of his wide mouth to the other. "It ain't I need your help, but I'm embroiled in a decision here." His chrome and steel right arm prosthesis came up, and he pointed across the room with his index finger. A little red laser dot danced in the center of the high-definition LCD Sony MuralVision television screen. "When we watch the Suns game tomorrow night, we have a choice. The national commentators hate Phoenix and talk trash on us."

I shrugged. "So listen to the local radio coverage."

Sarge shivered, and that sent a sympathetic ripple down my spine. "I would, but it ghosts, you know?"

I nodded and the shiver shook me again. In Lhasa, fighting with the Tigers against the Hans, all our real-time video communication went up to satellites before it bounced back down to us guys on the ground. I remembered eyeballing boys as a sniper splashed them, then getting their RTV call for cover fire over the helmet videovisor. We called that "ghosting" and dreaded it so much we only used RTV for talking to support units well behind the lines.

Ghosting, as far as the game was concerned, led to a curious phenomenon. The pictures on the screen would show a player setting up to take a shot, but Marjerle and Johnson on KSUN would announce the shot had been made before the ball left the player's hands. They managed that trick because their broadcast went over phone lines to the transmitter and made the trip faster than the TV signal going to the satellite and back down. It wasn't nearly as nasty as ghosting had been in the field, but purists who watched the game at the Tigers' Den claimed the paradox spoiled it for them.

Deep down inside I thought they were nuts, but I didn't say anything because commenting would make me seem more antisocial than Hank was afraid I'd become. It also had a chance of making me seem uncaring toward my adopted home, and that could be suicidal in the current atmosphere. The Suns-Sonics series, with Seattle leading 2-1 with the fourth game here in Phoenix, had taken on Apocalyptic importance. While I admit having gotten caught up in the series so far, and was looking forward to meeting Cleveland in the finals, I maintained enough perspective to remember it was only a game.

"I don't know, Sarge. Trash talk or prescient praise." I reached for my scanner again. "Go with the radio, I guess."

My suggestion fell upon deaf ears. And the silence in the bar made me wonder if I'd gone deaf as well. I looked first at Hank, figuring that if he were being quiet, he had to be dead. A chunk of ash dropped from the cigar stub hanging from his thick lips, and exploded into a grey puff when it hit his bulbous stomach. The reddish light in his right eye still burned, but that only told me the batteries were still working. When his jaw dropped, and the stogie dove toward the linoleum, I knew he was alive and surprised, and I'd be hearing how he wasn't surprised at all for the next three years. In fact, I'd hear he hadn't been surprised since before I was born.

I followed Hank's gaze toward the doorway and decided surprise was the appropriate reaction. The man stooped to get through the rounded opening and, as he straightened up, the cut of his impeccably tailored suit somehow made it possible to believe the Den had shrunk. I knew that wasn't true, because the man standing there, according to the official Suns program, was a foot and a half taller than me, and outweighed me by over a hundred pounds. Still, the building's having shrunk seemed, for a moment, a viable explanation for what I was seeing, because there could be no way Christian Bradley had come to the Den.

Bradley surveyed the room—and, as did everyone else on their first visit, found the window into the gym distracting—then started coming in my direction. As he cut through the people seated between us, he adjusted his tie to hide his irritation, but I read it in neon. His smile reminded me of a tiger's warning growl. To his credit, when he got to me, he just looked me in the face and refrained from eying me up and down.

"You're Killian Sloane."

I nodded. "You're the Whirlwind, the Duke of Dunk, the Stuff-o-lith." I saw annoyance flash through his brown eyes as I reeled off his nicknames. I took his reaction as a good sign. A sign at odds with the public image of an egomaniac who luxuriated in his status as the savior of the Phoenix NBA franchise. "Is there something I can do for you?"

"I sent for you."

"You did? I didn't know I was listed in any fax-order catalogs."

His nostrils flared for a second, then he ran a long-fingered hand over his shaved ebon head. "I asked for you to meet with me. I have a job for you."

I shrugged. "I'm not looking for employment."

"You know what I mean."

"I do?"

Anger came as quickly as it had before, but he caught it and discarded it instantly. "Okay, I see your point. I did this wrong. I have something I need for you to do for me. That's why I wanted you to come see me."

"I have a rule, Mr. Bradley, that a man asking for favors comes to the person from whom he wants the favors."

The tall man's eyes half shut. "So I heard. That's why I'm here, Mr. Sloane."

I watched him, intending to let the silence build a wall between us, but Hank blasted through it. "He is here, Kill, right here, in my bar, in the Den." Hank wiped his chrome hand off on his stained apron and extended the squeaky metal appendage toward Bradley. "Hank Winchester. You can call me Sarge."

Bradley nodded in acknowledgment, but made no move to take Hank's mechanical hand. "Pleased, but I'm not putting my shooting hand in your vise."

Hank glanced at his hand as if it had betrayed him, then nodded. "Sure, need you whole for tomorrow night, right? Gonna stomp them Sonics, right?"

"That's the plan."

"Great. Can I get you something? On the house?"

I got up off my stool. "We just need a place to talk, Hank. We'll be over there. If we need anything else, we'll let you know."

"But, Kill . . ."

I shot Hank an easy smile. "I'm sure Mr. Bradley will sign a picture for you later or something."

"Sure thing, Sarge, my man."

"Great." Hank pulled the ScanReader from the bar and set it back by the cash register. "If you need anything, let me know."

"Right." I steered Bradley to a small booth near the massive window overlooking the other enterprise Hank ran out of the Den. The glass wall gave us a perfect view of the huge warehouse-like structure which had been carved down into Camelback Mountain. Honeycombed stacks of small stalls rose from ground to ceiling. On the bottom two levels the stark white rooms had martial arts enthusiasts who were fitted with Virtual Reality helmets and who wore Kinsense suits beneath their gis. Most of them worked through simple katas, though a couple appeared engaged in sparring matches with opponents in neighboring battlehexes.

Just above them the fighters were using an array of

weapons that ran from historical to the sort of ridiculous things scriptwriters dreamed up for VRTV series. From the moves made by a half dozen people, I assumed the latest upgrade of PredatorDuel had arrived, and most of them were losing their fights with an imaginary extraterrestrial. Still, one guy did manage a victory and danced around exuberantly in his little slice of honeycomb.

The top level, which stood even with the floor of the bar, had double-sized battlehexes which were open on both sides. Within the hexes fighters actually sparred against each other, without the benefit of VR helmets or Kinsense suits. While a KS suit could leave a bruise as the result of an enemy's strike, the shots the fighters were taking on the top row had a chance of breaking bones and rupturing organs. Each one of those fighters had been chromed so his reflexes were neuroelectrically enhanced, and his expertise in martial arts came from whatever software he happened to have wafered at the time.

Beyond the top hexes stood a large open area with green mats. In it a black belt was leading a group of thirty individuals through a training exercise. The students were a mixed bag, from young kids to a couple of senior citizens. They all seemed quite earnest, though some of the teens had a tendency to swagger and abbreviate their bows.

Bradley tapped the window before he dropped into the booth. "I used to do that stuff."

"I know."

"Yeah? I wouldn't have figured you for the fan type."

"I'm not really. I read stuff as self-defense. Tip sheet on you says that you have a black belt in keupso chirigi. That's wrong, though."

Bradley's head came back around so he watched me instead of the fighters in the hexes. "How do you know?"

I shrugged. "You don't have the right moves. That style involves a lot of strikes at vital points, which the PR guys like to suggest you have, in a tactical sense, on the court. Fact is, you look like you studied yu-sool or judo for the way you get inside on the boards."

"Yu-sool it was, while my father had his church in Seoul."

"But you're not here to have me evaluate your expertise in the martial arts, are you?"

The tall man shook his head. "I have a problem. I need you to fix it. See, when I came over here to college . . ."

I held a hand up. "Give it to me in the short form." As with every other citizen of Phoenix, I had heard Bradley's life story recounted more times than I wanted to remember. Eldest son of a Baptist preacher from Mississippi on a mission in Korea, he'd grown tall and developed a lot of skill playing basketball. Eleven years ago he came to America and gave Michigan State another god in their basketball pantheon. Right around that time, back in Asia, the Chinese empire started to come apart, sparking wars in Korea, Indochina, Mongolia, Chinese Turkistan and Tibet. So, while he came across the Pacific to glory, guys like Hank and me went the other way to play policeman to the world.

Apparently Bradley's return to the land of his birth had not been all sweetness and light. The same affirmative action legislation that drafted whites preferentially over minorities—atoning for Vietnam—sparked a racist backlash in the States. Bradley hadn't been faced with the problems of growing up African-American in the States, so the prejudice and hatred hit him hard. He earned a reputation for speaking his mind. The fact that he became a poster child for the Islamic Nation of Purity didn't help calm things down, either.

As he started to talk I could tell, from his pauses, that he was carefully choosing words that were less incendiary than he might have otherwise used. "When things went to hell in Korea, my folks moved back here. We're a close family and I've always involved them with my career. My parents, both when I was with Philly and now here in Phoenix, handle my fan mail. There's always folks who don't like me, so they've gotten used to that, but recently something came through that bugged them."

He pulled a folded slip of paper from inside his jacket and slid it across the table to me. I detected a slight tremble to his fingers, which surprised me. I took the paper and opened it, then found myself amazed by how mild the message on it really was.

Dear Mr. Bradley,
We love uppity niggers and we make them pay. We have money on the Seattle game on the 14th. When you win, we win. Or did we pick you to lose?
In appreciation of your efforts on our behalf,
[signed] World Aryan Resistance

"I guess the Suns really are bringing this community together."

"I'd just as soon the bottom feeders not come into the alliance."

I shrugged. "Cosmic Balance. You've allied yourself with the Islamic Nation of Purity, so WAR decides to work you, too. Sounds like a personal problem to me, Whirlwind. Reaping what you sow."

"I'm not allied with the Nation."

I raised an eyebrow. "Unless you're on the court, I see Lester Farouk grafted to you." I looked around the Den.

108

"In fact, I'm surprised he's not here right now."

Bradley frowned heavily. "I didn't tell him I was coming here. He's not my keeper, though there are times he thinks he is."

Again the break between the real man and the public image caused me to stop pushing him away. "Okay, these white-outs say they're betting on you. Or against you. Maybe. Bottom line: they're tampering with the game. Turn them over to the NBA."

"Can't, man. Ever since the Jordan debacle, the NBA has been paranoid about gambling. Remember, old man Colangelo was on the Committee that expelled half the '97 Bulls from the NBA. If I come forward with this and we lose, he'll fire me personally. If we win, I can still be disciplined and these idiots get rich."

"And you will win tomorrow night, right?" Phoenix had won the first game in Seattle, but then dropped the next one to the Sonics and had lost the first home game to them as well. They had to even the series up because, as good as they were, they weren't the '92–'93 Suns. "Have to and will. And WAR will win, too."

"Unless they bet against you."

"They could be that stupid. I suppose." Bradley leaned back and laid his hands flat on the table. "So, I'm coming to you. I know you've got no love for white supremacists 'cuz of the Temple thing . . ."

"Don't start with that. WAR is not the Disciples of Jesus Fuhrer, and the murders got personal." I gave myself a second to tamp back down my anger. "WAR may have gotten personal with you, but not me."

"Look, I'll make it worth your while, Sloane, really."

The plea in Bradley's voice died as silence again settled over the Den and a hand descended on my shoulder.

109

"Chris, man, you shouldn't be asking this blank for help. I told you that."

I looked up at the slender man standing between us. Lighter-skinned than Bradley and the two men standing behind him, Lester Farouk bore a striking resemblance to Malcolm X. I knew the similarity had been the result of a surgeon's art, but everyone, save athletes like Bradley or the utterly destitute, had been modified in some way. To heighten the link with Malcolm, Farouk wore glasses—an artifact that marked him as different in a day when an hour at a LaserDoc kiosk could take care of vision problems.

I let him keep his hand on my shoulder because I could tell he wanted me to knock it off. The two goons behind him, arrayed in black fatigues, with dark sunglasses and black berets, were ready to react in a split second if I made a move. The confident grins on their faces told me they had to be sporting the latest in martial arts flexware wafers. I figured them for KataPerfect 4.2, or maybe the new CarnageMaster 3000. They'd have just loved to pulp me— the last Great White Hope—here in the Den.

I drummed my fingers on the table, beating out the rhythm of a lullaby I'd learned during my time in-country with the Tibet Tigers.

Bradley broke the silence. "Lester, I appreciate your concern for me in this situation, but I can handle it."

Farouk shook his head and withdrew his hand from my shoulder. "Brother Christian, you say you can handle it, then you come to this blank, this ghostman, to handle your problems. You are buying into the power structure that says only the white devil can solve our problems."

I smiled. "Set a devil to catch a devil."

"That sort of glibness will not save you when you face

Allah's judgment for the way you have oppressed us, Killian Sloane."

"I've not done any oppressing, Farouk."

The Islamic Nation of Purity leader shook his head slowly. "You, Sloane, are heir to centuries of white oppression of people of color. You ice people are incapable of feeling compassion, and you cannot understand how people of color can take such joy in life. You have to keep us down because we will overwhelm you otherwise."

My green eyes narrowed. "Seems to me, Farouk, that plenty of us 'ice people' fought and died in Tibet trying to prevent people of color from killing other people of color."

"Ah, but the Han imperialists in Tibet and elsewhere were brainwashed by the philosophy created and promulgated by white Europeans."

"Mao Zedong was a white European?"

"Droll, Sloane. Marx was white and under the influence of Jewish cabals."

I nodded thoughtfully. "Ah, the other shoe drops."

Farouk's nostrils flared. "What is that supposed to mean?"

"So you'll handle this situation for Bradley here, will you? What'll you do, get together with WAR and discuss this over a crackling synagogue fire?"

Farouk reacted as if he'd been slapped. "You have a reputation for being very tough, Sloane, but don't imagine yourself tough enough to accuse us of trafficking with WAR and get away with it."

"Forgive my mistake," I apologized. The bodyguard nearest me developed a tic around his right eye. "Must have been ice people logic. I thought birds of a feather flocked together."

Farouk raised his right hand and pointed at me. As the

man with the tic started toward me, I wove my right hand through a series of finger-forms akin to sign language, but which would have been gibberish to Aslan readers in the room. The bodyguard suddenly convulsed. His limbs snapped out tight and his back bowed as every muscle contracted. In a heartbeat his entire body slackened and he fell to the floor in a puddle of twitching muscle and bone.

The other bodyguard started forward, but a red laser dot appeared on Farouk's glasses. Farouk stopped the man and nodded toward the bar, where Hank held a sawed-off quill gun rock-steady in his right hand. The light didn't go out, but shifted down to Farouk's throat, accompanied by the squeak of Hank's elbow.

"That little dot is ice people for 'it's time you left.' " I glanced down at the man on the floor. "Aspirin and a lot of fluids for a couple of days."

As the ambulatory bodyguard dragged the other toward the door, Farouk pointed at me. "Remember, ice man, Phoenix can be very hot."

I ignored him and turned back to Bradley. "Okay, Farouk and his boys are too incompetent to count on for handling this. Why me?"

Bradley looked down at the floor, then back at me. "What did you do to him?"

I waited for the Muslims to clear the room, then spoke in a soft voice. "The fighters behind you, for the most part, aren't as muscle-bound as Farouk's bodyguards. The bodyguards are lifters, but they came in here, a place where martial artists gather, and were ready to take a piece out of me. That meant they were running hot brawlware. That type of software sizes up the foe, picks a response based on what he's doing, and executes it. The man who went down was running KataPerfect 4.2 with Norris Utilities on the side."

"How did you know?" Bradley's eyes narrowed and he answered his own question. "The tic?"

"The drumming on the table I did got picked up by his ears and the software translated it into a version check, which caused the tic."

"And your hand signals, those were a system interrupt?"

I nodded. "Very good. KataPerfect's main software engineer is from Tibet."

"And did you a favor."

"She and a bunch of her countrymen are under the mistaken impression they owe me a debt they can never repay." I leaned forward on the table. "Unlike them, I know I owe you nothing, so why am I going to tangle with WAR for you?"

"He told me to tell you it was 'a favor for a friend.' "

Damn, those are the ones that hurt. I frowned. "He would do that."

Bradley smiled. "I met him up in Seattle, before the first game. Despite living there, he's rooting for the Suns, mainly because you live here. He said you wouldn't like it, but you'd help me. He said you were the only man who could help me—not because you're his friend, but because you're a friend of humanity. High praise from the Dalai Lama."

I winced. "He's just a kid."

"You impressed him."

"Seven-year-olds impress easily."

"He's not seven anymore," Bradley shook his head. "And he even has a good jump shot from outside. Says you taught him."

"He exaggerates things," I growled, because you can't say the Dalai Lama lies, after all. "Enough. I'd rather the Chinese had me again than go through more of this."

Bradley nodded carefully. "I understand. So you'll do it?"

"Yeah, I've got an idea or two that might work." I thought for a second and added, "You handle the Nation and win the game and I'll tackle WAR."

"Deal." Bradley slid from the booth and offered me his hand. "I really appreciate this."

My hand disappeared in his. "Let's hope you mean that when this is all over."

The trick to figuring out how to stop hatemongers from profiting from Phoenix's win was to think like them. This was painful and painfully simple. White supremacists, and all racists, for that matter, operate from a basis of willful ignorance and malicious suspension of disbelief. Bad things happen because conspiracies make them happen, and the general population doesn't believe in conspiracies because they have been duped.

It's a vicious cycle that functions with its own twisted logic. The fact that there is no evidence of conspiracy proves not only that the conspiracy exists, but exists with such sophistication that it leaves no clues. Of course, the fact that all the conspiracies are run by people who are genetically inferior to the average Aryan means that the average Aryan can pick up clues to the conspiracy's existence, even though the average Aryan is stupid enough to believe a 157-year-old Hitler is plotting in Argentina.

The World Aryan Resistance was typical of the majority of hate groups. Foster Gench headed the organization and his two sons, Grendel and Wolfgang, served as his lieutenants. Foster had been a colonel in the Lhasa Leopards—the other American unit serving in Tibet. The Tigers used to call them the Lhasa Apsos because they never left the capital. Foster apparently did some weird stuff while on-station, and some of the boat people who escaped with the kid and me told the government all about it. That resulted in a court-martial and his dishonorable discharge that freed him up for his new career as a hatemonger.

Grendel—despite being a shaggy, bearded giant—controlled a cadre of skinheads who had caused trouble at various times in Phoenix, though nothing beyond some felonious assaults and an arson-bombing of a synagogue up in Scottsdale. He saw me as the prime mover behind his father's disgrace—despite the fact that I wasn't even called to give evidence in the trial—and had long vowed to get me. His trouble was that he'd not found a flexsoft package that could beat me, so he did a lot of growling but no actual biting.

Wolfgang functioned as the group's disinformation officer. He authored and edited two newsletters and countless tracts that WAR sent worldwide to similarly-minded groups. Wolfgang could be counted on to provide good face for the group in TV and radio debates about racial purity and superiority, and he had issued any number of challenges to Lester Farouk to face him in an intellectual discussion. Wolfgang also used the radio to castigate me for the Disciple thing, but he was easier to ignore than his bigger, dumber brother.

It struck me that WAR was trying to kill at least two birds with one stone by sending the notes to Bradley. If they had bet on a win and Phoenix won, they made money and it would gnaw away at Bradley's conscience. If Phoenix lost, they could always claim that Bradley, as one of the mud races, was unable to stand up to the pressure being placed on his shoulders. If Bradley were subsequently investigated for gambling and expelled from basketball, they could have an even larger PR coup.

Of course, the only way they could have a really big victory was if they actually bet on Phoenix to lose and then got Bradley exposed as having dumped the game so they would win their bet. It would be perfect for them and absolutely destroy Bradley. It was just the sort of double-think their little brains would be capable of, and the note they had sent might have been enough to make Bradley have an off-game even under the best of circumstances.

If that were the plan, and it seemed viable to me, the next thing I had to do was to locate the agency with which the bet had been placed. While it was possible that one of the Genches had gone to Las Vegas or Reno to make the bet, I decided to check more local sources. After all, with every Indian tribe in North America living off gambling proceeds, WAR could get another bird by having non-whites pay out on their bet.

I placed a call to Jerry Begay over at the Kachina Casino and Sports book. Jerry had been a Tiger and the one to suggest—one cold Tibetan night—that we all move to Arizona with him after the war. His tour in Lhasa ended when a Han booby trap took his left leg off at the knee, so he came back early and served as a magnet for the rest of us. I explained the situation to him, cutting out Bradley's role and letting him think I was interested in WAR because of the Disciples. He ran a computer check and called me back to confirm that they had some heavy betting against Phoenix that had been laid down—before the series had begun.

"Kill, looks like those blank-bastards will pull in about half a million if the Suns tank it."

"That's not pocket change, Jerry."

"Nope, it'll buy lots of crosses and gasoline. WAR has affiliates up in Seattle, too, so we're cross-checking with the casinos on the Makah and Quinault Reservations. We worked too hard in the nineties to get these casinos to let some whiteouts screw us now. We'll cancel the bets, of course."

"That'll just leave WAR its nest egg. I'd rather hurt them bad, wouldn't you?"

"Sure. You have a plan?"

"I think so. Remember in Lhasa you told me about a stash your grandfather had . . ."

"Christ, Killian, don't mention that. I had to have been drunk."

"Actually, at the time, we were both thinking up plans for shafting the government that had us freezing our nuts off in Tibet."

"I remember."

"Yeah, well, a shaft that was good enough for Uncle Sam ought to be more than sufficient for his half-wit kids, you think?"

I knew timing would be crucial in the whole operation. I called Bradley to tell him I thought I had things under control. I could hear the relief in his voice and I hoped he'd have a great game. As much as my plan counted on it, he had to have a great game.

I met Jerry at the Den about an hour before game time. He did not look pleased with me, but handed me the briefcase nonetheless. "You better know what you're doing, Sloane." He took a hard look at the clothes I was wearing and swore. "Shit, you're not wearing body armor and you don't have a gun. Are you nuts?"

"You know I'm nuts, Jerry." I gave him a lopsided grin. "I'm just going to see some of my white brothers. What do I need weapons for?"

Jerry tapped the silver, dime-sized disk behind his right ear. "You got a Looney-Tune program running, bro? These guys may not be the stone-killers that the Disciples were, but they're not nice people. They'll bust you up if they get a chance."

"Don't have much of a choice, Jerry." I sighed. "If I go in like I expect trouble, they'll think something is up." I jerked a thumb at the glass wall. "Even if Grendel is running the latest spatsoft, I can beat him."

"Yeah? I heard you almost lost to a KataPerfect puppet the other day."

"Not even close, but that package is fast."

"Well, CarnageMaster 3000 is faster and there's a beta of it on the street. I heard a rumor that Grendel pissed his brother off because he used WAR cash to score the beta instead of putting it down on the game."

That made me stop for a second. In the army all of us had been "tweaked" so we could run various MOSware—military occupational specialty software—so we could fill a number of roles in the force structure. We all learned very quickly that our performance at an MOS depended upon the quality of the software, and with government contracts going to the lowest bidder, a lot of soldiers ended up getting splashed because some programmer dropped lines of code when his wife left him. If you ran into a situation that called for a subroutine that didn't exist, you could freeze or freak or flee.

A lot of us did without anything more complicated than a language package, preferring to trust grey-RAM more than Nintendo Rambo-wafers.

Commercial software packages had a higher quality control level, but were still full of problems; As with game programs, once you learned what the computer would use to counter a particular move, you could trick it. Of course, the tricks and traps would only work if you were quick enough, and a lot of packages recovered fast. KataPerfect, for example, was almost fast enough to beat me. The earlier versions of the CarnageMaster line had caused me some trouble, and the word on CM3K had been impressive.

"I'll have to take a chance on it, I guess. Did they solve the compression problem for the beta version?" Because flexsofts interpret motion in terms of attacks, all brawlware has to be consciously invoked or a user will be attacking anyone and everything in sight. The amount of time the software takes to become operational provides a sucker punch window.

"I don't think so, but it only takes a half-second to decompress."

"Then I'll have to take that half-second to coldcock Grendel, won't I?"

Jerry shook his head and donned a Suns baseball cap. "I won't bet against you. After all, the odds of you getting the kid out of China were, what, a billion to one against? Good luck."

"Save your luck for the Suns."

Driving across town I came to realize just how much the Suns might have needed Jerry's luck. We started out playing very sluggishly and Bradley seemed off to one of his worst starts of the year. At the end of the first quarter he, according to Marjerle's play-by-play, got hacked while scrapping for a rebound. When no foul was called, he cursed out a ref, earning himself a technical foul that resulted in Seattle being ahead by twelve at the quarter. The second quarter went better—as usual the technical settled Bradley down—and I used a little ear-cuff radio to keep track of the game while I walked to WAR's bunker.

I'd parked my beat-up Ford Atlas 4x4 a block from the old U.S. West building on Indian School that WAR had chosen as its headquarters. The old brick building was the closest thing to a brownstone still existing in Phoenix. Aside from a sign painted in black, red and white beside the door, the building looked rather unassuming—presumably to make it less of a target for drive-by spray-ups.

Two skinheads frisked me before conducting me to the executive office suite. They looked disdainfully at the little radio I wore in my right ear—less because it was cheap than because it was made by Mitsubishi—but they pronounced me clean. The one following me up the stairs prodded me with his pump action quill gun when I paused for Marjerle's description of Bradley cutting through the lane and putting the ball through the hoop in a reverse layup. That put Phoenix up by five at the half, which strengthened my chances of success.

Describing the office to which I was taken as a suite makes it sound a lot more elegant than it was, because, though the room was more than ample for the three desks and plethora of bookshelves, all the furnishings looked worse than my Atlas. Everything had been painted grey. I guessed it was with paint left over from doing the walls—which made the television, Nazi flag and portrait of Hitler the most colorful items in the room.

That included the Genches themselves. Foster looked drawn and half-dead, which fit with rumors I'd heard about his liver getting cancerous. Grendel dressed in black from throat to Doc Marten's boots, and his beard and mane of hair made him look positively leonine. Wolfgang appeared to be a younger, slender version of his father, only his hair's retreat from his forehead marred the strong image he sought to project.

Foster half roused himself in his chair and croaked at me. "Killian Sloane, if I'm not mistaken."

I nodded. "I have a deal to offer you."

Wolfgang pointed a remote control at the 47-inch Curtis Mathis SparkFresco monitor, muting the halftime commentary on the game. "Beware quislings bearing gifts."

Grendel laughed at that remark, sounding much like a grizzly trying to cough up a steel wool hairball. He had risen to his feet when I came in and hovered just on the other side of his father's line of vision from me. He reached up and tapped his head behind his right ear, letting me know he had flexsofts screwed in and ready to handle me, giving me a warning I didn't need, but one I appreciated nonetheless.

I pretended I was ignoring Grendel. "You put some bets down against the Suns in this game. You placed them at the Kachina over a period of five days, using seven different people to place them. If the Suns lose, you stand to make five hundred thousand dollars. In the briefcase I have two hundred fifty thousand—your bet and a hefty profit—to exchange for the betting slips."

Wolfgang shook his head. "We are forty minutes from winning five hundred thousand. Why should we exchange it for what you have?"

I looked down at Foster. "Are your boys really that stupid? You've screamed about conspiracies all your life, and you don't see what's happening here?"

Foster's lids just half closed, so I pushed on and focused myself on Wolfgang. "This is a professional sporting event, Wolfie. The adverts there are going for a half a mil for thirty seconds." I tapped the radio in my ear. "Local radio is going for ten K for a minute. They'll make what you'll win in this one broadcast alone. When you figure this game is being broadcast all over the world, the amount of money being generated here is incredible."

"And so we're getting our piece of it." He thrust his lower lip out at me defiantly, but I saw doubt clouding his eyes.

"But you're going to lose the bet. What makes more money, a five-game series or a six-game series?"

Wolfgang narrowed his eyes suspiciously. "What are you saying?"

"I'm saying the fix is in. Seattle drops this one here. Everyone knows that. How in hell do you think the Navajos allowed you to make these bets? They knew what was going to happen even before the playoffs began. You were suckered."

Grendel nodded solemnly. "The Jews do control the media."

I let that remark pass. "You were screwed before you left the casino. I'm offering you a chance to bail out."

"Why?" Foster's head came up. "You have no love for us."

"It doesn't matter what my reasons are."

"But I have to know them or no deal."

I hesitated and Wolfgang brought the sound back up on the TV. "Second half is starting. You're in the way, Sloane."

I shrugged and turned toward the door. "You want to lose, go ahead. See if I care."

Foster raised a hand. "I believe you, and I will take your money. I just want to know what makes a man like you come to us."

I took a deep breath, then exhaled slowly. "The guy who authorized the accepting of your bets is going to run for Tribal President against Jerry Begay, a buddy of mine from the Tigers. Evidence that he did a deal with WAR will torpedo his campaign."

"Loyalty." Foster smiled slowly. "Pity you are not more loyal to your own race, Sloane."

"Loyalty to my species overrides that. You going to do the deal?"

Foster nodded. "Wolfgang, the slips." Wolfgang produced them from a drawer in his father's desk. I set the briefcase down and he opened it, then passed the slips to me. Wolfgang riffled one packet of twenty-dollar bills, counted the rest, then nodded as I backed to my original position. "It's all here, Father."

"Good doing business with you, Mr. Sloane."

I glanced over at the television as the Sonics took the ball out to start the second half. "Bradley is supposed to have the game of his life in the second half."

"He better," Wolfgang snarled. "As goes the nigger, so go the Suns."

As he spoke, a shot went up and missed. Bradley dragged down the rebound and caught an elbow in the ribs from a Sonics player. A ref whistled the play dead and the TV shifted to a full-court shot for Phoenix to inbound the ball. Even as the basketball went to the sidelines, the picture began to shift again and I reacted.

Whirling around, I launched myself in a spinkick that planted my left heel on Grendel's right temple. Spittle flew as his head snapped around. The giant stumbled backward, his arms flailing uncontrollably. He slammed into the TV screen hard enough to shake the room. Grendel's body supplanted Bradley's screen image so it looked as if the ref were giving Grendel his second technical foul, tossing him from the game.

Grendel bounced back from the TV and smacked into the floor facedown.

As I landed, the two skinheads who had been my escort

went for me. I sidestepped the first and tossed him back over my right hip. He flew above Foster and across the desk to harpoon Wolfgang with his head. The briefcase toppled down over both of them, launching packets of bills into the air like obese confetti.

The second skinhead clubbed his quill gun and swung it at my head. I blocked it on my left forearm, then shot my right hand forward. Stiffened fingers caught him in the stomach and sent him down retching and thrashing. A quick kick to the head stopped him.

Appropriating the quill gun, I covered Foster as I backed to where Grendel lay. "A deal is a deal, Colonel." I turned Grendel's head to the right and popped open the wafer-hole behind his ear. Beneath the Mein Kampfwafer I saw what looked like it could have been the CarnageMaster 3000 beta. If the radio's ghostly reportage of the technical foul had not given me the time to react, I might well have been left finding out how good CM3K really was.

Foster stared dully down at me. "Why are you working for the nigger in this?"

"I said it before, species loyalty." I slipped the wafer into my pocket with the betting slips and stood. "That, and if anyone's going to clean up the messes my race makes, I'd just as soon it be me."

Behind him, Wolfgang and the other skinhead started forward, but Foster's raised hand and my raised gun stopped them. "A deal is a deal, Mr. Sloane. We have your money, you have our slips. And a promise we will deal with you in the future."

Take a number, I thought. I left the building and checked my back trail both on the way to my Atlas and then when I drove away. When I finally felt confident I didn't have a tail, I stopped, made two quick phone calls, then drove down to the Arena to wait for the game to end.

I walked into the arena down through the loading docks and one of the security guys took me through the tall corridor around to the south where Christian Bradley waited in the practice court. I stepped through the glass door and walked down the stairs to the hardwood floor. Neither one of us said anything at first, so the cavernous room just echoed with the thunder of a ball being dribbled, then the *koosh* of its hitting nothing but string.

Bradley palmed the ball, then tucked it under his arm. He still wore his game uniform and a scowl of titanic proportions. "Did it work out?"

I nodded. "I gave them two hundred fifty thousand and I have the slips. They'll go to a friend I have in the Navajo nation, and the original wagers will be turned over to the Thurgood Marshall Scholarship Fund. The Navajos owe you one."

Bradley shook his head. "No, they owe you one."

"No," I said, keeping my voice low, "*you* owe me. And it may be more than one." I pointed up at the auxiliary scoreboard that showed the final score as a twenty-point Phoenix loss. "Why the second technical? You almost got me taken apart, you know. All you had to do was win, I was doing the hard stuff. What was the deal?"

Bradley bounced the ball over to me. "I did what I had to do, man. My end of the bargain."

"How's that? Flying off the handle at an elbow wasn't part of our bargain."

He shook his head. "Not that. I handled the Nation. At the half, Lester told me he'd fixed the whiteouts. Beat them at their own game. He'd gone out and dropped a bundle of the Nation's money on us to win. He promised he'd use the profits to destroy WAR."

I spun the ball around, feeling the dry leather flash across my left palm. "You don't like the Nation's rhetoric any more than I like WAR's, do you?"

"Sloane, my father's a Baptist preacher. I grew up believing in Jesus and I still do. By the same token, blacks are still a minority, and one that needs an identity all its own. I can try to stand for things, but people just see me as a basketball player, and want to make the same money I do. The Nation isn't perfect, but it provides another place for a kid to get some self-esteem. I can support that, but I'm not going to finance the Nation going to war with some Nazi trash."

I slowly nodded. "I can understand that. I can even respect it."

"Sorry if that hung you out, man."

I shrugged. "No blood, no foul." I tossed him back the ball. He bounced it once, hard. "I am still pissed those whiteouts have two hundred fifty thousand dollars."

"Don't be. About fifteen minutes ago the Genches were arrested by Treasury agents. They had two hundred fifty thousand in bogus twenties and hundreds in their headquarters and are trying to explain how they traded winning betting slips worth twice that much for it."

Bradley raised an eyebrow. "You bought the slips with counterfeit money? How did you . . . do I want to know?"

"Probably not, but say, hypothetically, that you're a sovereign nation subject to the laws of an invader, and agents of the invader are not letting you make a living—for example, they're blocking the gambling establishments you are setting up."

"As states did on the reservations back around the turn of the century."

I nodded. "And say you decided, if they weren't going to

let you make money, that you'd just print some up to wage covert war against the invader. But, they relent, you get your casinos . . ."

"And you save your secret weapon in case things change."

"Hypothetically speaking, of course."

"Of course."

Bradley smiled. "Nice, Sloane, very nice."

"It was nothing." I turned to walk away.

"Hey, wait, what do I owe you?"

"Me?" I turned back and frowned. "You don't owe me anything. This was a favor for a friend, remember?"

"But don't you want something?"

I smiled. "Tell you what, just win the next three straight, then beat Cleveland."

"I'll be doing that for me and you and everyone else in the Valley. Don't you want something special?"

"That will be special." I nodded to him and mounted the stairs. "I have a friend in Seattle who's a big Suns fan. Win it all. Consider it a favor for a friend."

"Absolutely Charming" was born during a conversation with Dennis L. McKiernan. He and I had both just had novels come out that were a bit slow to start. Dennis said, "It's too bad we couldn't do something that would make the readers just follow the story all the way through." The idea for this story immediately flashed through my head.

Absolutely Charming

I felt excited tremors of anticipation ripple through me as the postman took the folded slip of paper from my hand. The bored look of indifference in his flat eyes died beneath the wave of lustful hunger surging onto his face. His mouth hung open as his eyes devoured each word and his lips faithfully echoed them a second later. His eyes flicked from word to word, faster and faster as he neared the end of the paper, then he flipped it over, greedily looking for more.

When he saw he had read it all, he reread it quickly, and would have started on it a third time, but my hand closed on the paper. He tried to pull away, but I folded the sheet, hiding the writing from him, and he snapped out of it. Reluctantly he let me pluck the paper from his hand.

"My God, that's great!" He wiped his brow with a yellowed handkerchief. "Is there any more? There's got to be more. I mean, that's the best thing I've ever read. My God, you're a genius!"

I smiled in a kindly fashion. "Thank you, Carter. It's just a little thing I tossed off this morning."

The mailman gave me a low whistle. "Boy, I thought you gave up writing five years ago, after that guy rejected your book. I mean, you know, I've not read your book, but if it's anything like this, that editor was a fool."

I forced my ire away at the mention of HIM and maintained the cordial façade on my face. "Yes, well, editors are known for momentary lapses in judgment. Perhaps he will see the error of his ways. Thank you, Carter, for your encouragement."

"Yessir, Mr. Daye." He pointed a trembling finger at the note in my hand. "When you get that published, let me know where. I'm gonna buy bunches of copies."

I contained my mirth until I'd shut the door and shot the bolts, then let it ring loudly within the confines of my dingy domicile. I crumpled the slip of paper in my left hand, then carelessly tossed it into the corner. I had succeeded! After five years of research, trial and testing, I had done it. I had discovered the secret, and now that I knew it, I would have my revenge.

I stooped and recovered the ball of paper, then smoothed it out against the cover of The Grand Albert. A simple, slender piece of ruled paper, it was unremarkable. It was actually less than that, this collection of words that imbecile Carter had seen as a great work of literature. Feeling the power surge through me, I started reading it aloud, "Clorox, assort. soup, rice-1 lb., toilet paper," but my oration was subsumed by laughter.

The words meant nothing and would have been nothing if not for the device I had painstakingly inscribed at the head of the sheet and now hid beneath the ball of my thumb. This was what had taken five years of delving into arcane tomes. Elusive and deceptive, I tracked it through aged parchments that had not been touched in centuries. I waded through witchhunter diaries and forbidden books of lore in languages long thought dead but pulsing with power. A hint here, a clue there, led me on my quest for a symbol of power, a symbol because of which men and women had perished in legions.

Ultimately, my quest was frustrated because all trace of the sigil I sought had been destroyed. Those who knew its power had learned to fear it, so they caused all representations of it to be destroyed. However, other sigils that had adopted bits and pieces of it to steal some of its power still remained. Like an archaeologist or a geneticist, I tracked back to this Eve of arcane symbols. I stole a piece from the Key of Solomon here and the Enochian alphabet there. Little by slowly, methodically and scientifically, I synthesized the device I had so long hunted.

I brought it back from extinction.

I recreated the Siren Sigil, and I knew it was good.

Carter had proved it. Carter, my simpleton lab rat, had endured countless lists of nonsense as I tried out variations on him. Some provided curious and amusing reactions, but none, until this morning, had given me what I wanted. Carter, under the Siren Sigil's influence, gobbled up my grocery list like some tawdry thriller and could not put it down. He wanted more and, when there was none, read again what I had written. From that fragment he deduced I was a literary genius.

If it had worked on Carter, certainly it would work on HIM.

I crossed through the musty stacks of books piled like stalagmites on the floor of my front room and into the bedroom. Feeling invincible, I reached up and pulled the framed letter from its place above my bed. My spur, the thorn in my side, the driving force in my quest, this letter had haunted me since Carter had borne it to my door. Over the years, when despair had sapped me of strength and will, I'd reread it to fill me again with rage. Now, with victory in my grasp, I allowed myself the luxury of again reading of my humiliation.

Dear Mr. Daye,

    Under normal circumstances, as a common courtesy, I undertake to thank writers for sending their work here to Mountain Books. However, in your submission I find nothing that motivates me to do this. I do appreciate, in both your cover letter and Chapter 3, your expressing your opinion of the "substandard and puerile" work we have produced in our various lines. Repetition of that criticism in Chapters 7, 12, and 127 might be viewed as excessive, no doubt motivated by your belief that our "moronic editors" would be "incapable of recognizing subtlety if it jumped up and shot them with a nuclear particle accellerator [sic]."

    I must agree with your assertion that your work is difficult to bracket, though, not as you suggest, "because literature, as a concept, is really too limited to encompass [your] work."

    You are not Dostoevsky.

    You are not Dickens.

    You are not literate.

    The novel you have submitted to us is useful only as a dictionary of mercilessly overworked clichés. I would call your characters cardboard, but I am not of a mind to insult cardboard. Elizabeth Taylor's entire wardrobe is less purple than your prose. The suspension of disbelief necessary to accept your tale is only exceeded by that which is required to believe we would actually consider publishing this work. If 50,000 chimps banging away on typewriters for years could produce Shakespeare, I would guess that 50,000 Hyram Dayes banging away on typewriters could produce an almost publishable CumQuik novel.

I truly hope this is the only novel you have attempted. If not, I fear your home could be classed a toxic waste dump by the EPA. You should be reported to a Civil Rights Commission for sending this work out without a warning label, and were the Nuremburg court still in session I would report you for human rights violations for producing this work.

If, by some twisted piece of logic (of which you are most assuredly capable), you do not understand that I suggest you cease and desist all writing, please do not consider Mountain Books a possible market for your work. The same goes for any and all relatives you have.

> *Wishing you were dead,*
> *Gordon Cobb*
> *Editor in Chief*

I flung the frame from me and it smashed against the wall. Chuckling to myself, I reached up on my highest shelf and pulled down the box containing my manuscript. Lovingly I blew the half-decade's accumulation of dust from its lid. Setting the box down on the bed, I opened it and pulled the 600-page manuscript forth. Clutching it to my breast, I headed back out to my worktable.

Love's Chainsaw Caress would finally see print!

I resisted the temptation to paint the Siren Sigil on the cover page. That page was superfluous and likely would not be copied were the manuscript duplicated within the printing company. Also, I assumed that were the sigil to exert its influence in the mail room, it would take forever for my manuscript to reach HIS hand. I turned to the first page and, in the wasted white space at the head of the Preface, I set to work.

Dipping my narrow brush in the bottle of black ink, I started to draw the Siren Sigil. With serpentine forms I created the lozenge device that encompassed the whole of the design and empowered it. Near the top I then added the triskell vortex that would draw the reader down into the work. Light shading and twists through the lines hinted at seductive feminine curves and the womb-warmth we all distantly remember and crave. This urged the reader on and reassured him that no matter what he read, nothing could be more right or perfect.

Strong, quick tentacles laced down from that and intertwined in a morass of Celtic knotwork. This firmly placed my work as part of reality and rewarded the reader with the knowledge that he was truly capable of adjudicating what was art and what was not. Clearly, in the reader's mind, my work deserved exaltation as the highest form of human endeavor in the world of literature and in all of art.

Finished, I resisted the trap of wanting to admire my own work. I had slipped an index card over the first half of the design as I worked on the second. I knew, had I allowed myself to succumb to temptation, I would have read through my book, and again and again, until I fainted from starvation or someone physically tore me away from the manuscript. Three days of reading and rereading the *TV Guide* on which I'd idly doodled the sigil convinced me not to make that same mistake twice.

I returned the title page to its place, then put the cover letter I'd prepared earlier in the week on top of it. This time I refrained from giving HIM the benefit of my wisdom. In fact, other than a strongly worded suggestion to include the "design" on page one of the manuscript on the first page of the novel, my letter was perhaps the most banal thing I had ever written. I smiled because I knew there would be time enough for other letters with yet other sigils that would show HIM the error of his ways.

Carefully packaging up the manuscript, I hauled it down to the Post Office. I resisted the temptation to send it express, and relied on Priority Mail to get it to New York inside two days. Revenge should be savored, I reminded myself, and an expressed manuscript would instantly send up a red flag. This would not do. I wanted HIM taken utterly unaware.

The next week was one of exquisite agony. I started and stopped a dozen different novels featuring Clint Kerage, the hero of **Love's Chainsaw Caress**. Countless were the times I'd picked up the phone to call Mountain Books, but I always hung up before HE could be put on the line. No. No! I would not tip my hand. The time to gloat would come later, when **Caress** had made me a fortune and I had HIM groveling at my feet at my hideaway on the Cote d'Azur. Begging for my next novel, HE would be, and I'd tease him and lead him on, then deny him, lashing out with those words of his, the words I'd long since had burned into my brain.

Toward the end of the week I had resolved to buy, with the huge advance they would offer me, a video camera. I realized that the real money would be made with the movie version of **Caress** and I felt fairly certain the sigil would function, with some changes, in a film or video format. For a half-second I felt a chill as it occurred to me that some television executives might already know of my secret and have been using it for years. My sense of horror almost overwhelmed me, but I rose above it and vowed not to let others exploit my secret.

Then, on Saturday, Carter appeared at my door. I signed for the Express Mail package he had for me, then shut the door on his simpering whine for another look at what he had read before. When I told him I had destroyed it as unworthy, he wilted and began to moan. As I tore the package open, the sound of his pitiful voice faded from my consciousness.

The letter was from HIM.

Obsequious is a delicious word that feels perfect in the mouth for spitting out with derision. To describe his letter with it, however, would be describing the sun as a photon or an ocean as a molecule. I read the letter as avidly as had Carter my grocery list.

"Brilliant . . . unparalleled work of a scope and vision unimagined before . . . gritty and realistic, yet fantastic and allegorical . . . a genius for description, characterization and plotting . . . a masterwork from a Grandmaster of the English language. "

Yes, yes, he said everything I expected and more. He had been shattered, broken on the anvil of his own ego. I'd sunk the hook in and gotten him. He said he was rushing the book into production and assumed I would find the enclosed contracts satisfactory. *"Sign both, put them in the SASE, send them and we'll be in business. "*

He closed with, *"Until I read your book, I had been an atheist. Reading your work has convinced me that God does exist and he has smiled upon you. "*

My own laughter ringing in my ears, I sat at my desk to look at the contracts. "The author warrants . . ." Yes, standard boilerplate. I hitched as I came to the clause in which Mountain Books retained all serial rights to the work, but I let that slide. I could not allow a magazine to use my sigil on a portion of the book, lest millions of zombies be left rereading the excerpt without ever getting the full book. No, that would not do.

On I read, faster and faster. The legalese flew past, seeking to entangle me in copious clauses, but I sorted them through. Then I hit another rough spot: no advance for the book! And another: royalties of .0001 percent of cover, due once a century, on the 29th of February! What was the meaning of this?

Further and further I raced through the contract. Outrage upon outrage was heaped upon me and my novel. Mountain Books retained all rights to foreign editions and book club editions, and had to pay me nothing! They demanded exclusivity from me, with a novel coming every three months, for as long as I lived. I would move to New York and live in their building and write for them; then, whenever I perished, they wanted the right to farm my work out to any hack willing to work beneath my name!

My jaw dropped in utter disbelief. Here Gordon Cobb— HE—had proclaimed my work akin to that of something penned by God, yet some grasping flunkie in his legal department sought to deprive me of my due. Some little, empire-building munchkin with a sheepskin from South Bayou College of Law and Cosmetology, no doubt. Well, he would learn to rue the day he dared draft this mandate of involuntary servitude. When I got through with HIM, HE would be through with this moron!

In a fury I flipped to the last page of the contract and stopped cold. Gordon Cobb had already signed the contract. How could he have allowed this travesty to go out over his signature? Did he not know with whom he was dealing? Could he not see he was cutting off his nose to spite his face?

Then, down toward the bottom of the page, I saw it. I

recognized the gentle shape of its triangular outline. The tendrils flaring off like black flames began to writhe as though fanned by an unfelt breeze. The uneven scales at its heart righted themselves as I tilted my head to study it. Its shape, its simplicity, its invitation to join the fold. It all made sense.

The Thrall's Sigil.

I picked up my pen.

"The Parker Panic" is a story written in the universe of the Deadlands® role playing game, designed by Shane Lacy Hensley. Since I do a lot of work in universes owned by others, I thought having one story of that type in here would be appropriate. The goal of such stories is to use fiction to explore the world and yet have a tale that no one needs to have studied the game to understand. All you need to know about Deadlands is that it's set in a very weird version of the wild West, where magic exists, but most folks ignore it, and to cast a spell a huckster astrally projects himself to a plane where he wrestles a spirit into giving him the power to make the spell work. The main character, Nevan Kilbane, and his background is what I came up with when creating a character to be run in a Deadlands game.

The Parker Panic

The train had barely left the station, its wheels squealing and engine puffing, when I heard the sound of cards being shuffled. I could have feigned disinterest on account of having watched two of the men there play three-handed poker with a greenhorn who got skinned on the El Paso to Tucson leg of the trip. They were bad poker players, but the greenhorn had been worse—and the cardsharps had seen fit to cheat outright on the few hands where luck hadn't abandoned their victim.

A new man had joined them in Tucson, though, and I didn't want to see him skinned.

I tipped my Stetson back and glanced across the car toward where the three men sat. The dealer, a young and plump fellow, was a hawker for some outfit from Chicago that wanted to "out-Smith & Robards" Smith & Robards. Menomony Wilson was the name of the company. I mention it because I reckon no one else ever will again, if management can be judged by its hires. It also explains what I call him since I never did get his name. His traveling case sat across his knees and served as their poker table.

I stretched lazily, then got up and swayed my way with the train on over to them. "This just three-hand?"

Wilson looked up with a big smile on his face and perspiration at his temples. "Howdy, pardner. Sit on down."

I ignored his attempt to turn his flat Midwest accent into something western. I offered him my right hand, which I wore a black glove on, and he took it without seeming to find it a slight. I guess if you're a salesman, you have to accept all types. "Name's Nevan Kilbane."

Wilson didn't recognize my name right off, but one of the other two did. Wilson's partner in crime introduced himself as Anderson Quilt, late of St. Louis, a lawyer. The new man, all tall and rail-thin, wearing clothes black enough to make him an undertaker or Old Testament preacher, said he was Mitchell Johns. He didn't say where he was from, but his voice had that southern lilt that always set me a bit ill at ease, even here in Confederate territory.

Quilt, whose hair had enough white and his middle enough girth to suggest he was pushing forty, gave me an easy smile. "Your name, it's the same as the guy who writes them dime novels. The Doctor Sterling books."

"That would be because I write them." I gave him an easy smile. "The good Doctor frowns on the writing, but he hopes stories of his adventures will keep folks from straying outside the law."

Wilson blinked his piggy eyes in my direction. "You're that Nevan Kilbane? I just read *The Parker Panic*. That was a corker of a tale. That Doctor Sterling—or do I call him Lord Uxbridge? He's someone I'd not mind meeting some day. Think I will?"

"Possible, but not likely, unless you've got more hidden in that case than I'm guessing you do."

Johns leaned away from me and rested himself up against the carriage wall. "*The Parker Panic*? Forgive me, but I'm not familiar with that much of your work, sir."

Wilson's eyes brightened and his hands stilled the manipulation of the deck he'd been shuffling. "Oh, it's a great story. It starts in Parker, Arizona, up northwest of here. I mean, is it okay if I tell it, Mr. Kilbane? It being your story and all?"

I gave him a nod and let him tell it. Given that he'd never meet Reginald Sterling, I was thinking I might as well let him have some enjoyment in life.

As Wilson started to drone on, I recollected as how things in Parker had unfolded in a way I'd not have guessed they would. I left my horse at the livery and moseyed on up to The Grand Hotel in Parker, which wasn't very grand and was called a hotel because "kennel" ain't the right term for a place where people live. By the bunch of keys dangling on the wall past the front desk I determined getting a room would be possible, so I signed the guest registry.

The scarecrow of a man clerking turned the register around, blew on the ink, then traced the lettering of my name with an inkstained finger. "Are you that Nevan Kilbane?"

I nodded, then pressed a finger to my lips. He looked one side, then the other—just his eyes moving, not his head, and them eyes didn't always move together. His voice sank into a hoarse whisper that still could rattle panes in the window. "Coming to see for Dr. Sterling about the Lividians?"

"Nope. Down from Nevada."

He gave me a conspiratorial nod. "Say no more, I understand. Shall I be saving the Presidential Suite for the Doctor, then?"

Again I pressed a finger to my lips, then winked.

He palmed the key to the suite, then gave me the key to

room 214. "Upstairs, fronts on the street. It'll let you see the ghost stampede."

I found "ghost stampede" a fascinating idea, but decided not to let myself be dissuaded from my original plan concerning Parker. What I intended was to let my horse and me get a couple days' rest, then continue on down to Quartzite. From there I'd see if I could pick up von Kreiger's trail and keep after him. The Confederate territory on the continent was huge, but he'd run out of hiding places eventually.

You may not know about von Kreiger, but those of us who were guests of his at Colton, the prison camp just outside Sparta, Georgia, will never forget him. The Rebels kept Colton as a prison for "special" prisoners: mainly those of us who had escaped other places. Von Kreiger kept us in line by starving us and doing things that were, well, were not quite playing by Hoyle. Kind of unnerving to have the area outside the camp being patrolled by the reanimated corpses of friends.

After that big escape at Colton, von Kreiger was disgraced. The folks in Sparta saw what he'd been doing to the prisoners and ran him out of town on a rail. He vanished and I returned back north with my Lieutenant, Augustus Henry Adams. I vowed von Kreiger would pay for his crimes and set about training myself to be ready to deal with him.

So, years later, being a fair mite bigger than when last von Kreiger would have seen me, I traveled the West looking for him. I kept running into odd things and would send August letters about my adventures. He went and wrote one up as a story about Dr. Reginald Sterling, this British peer who adventured through the West with his loyal aide, me, searching after things dark and devilish. He got an editor whose son had escaped with us from Colton to publish the thing, and the piece was popular. The money coming in from the stories didn't hurt.

I'd protested early on that chronicling my adventures would let von Kreiger know I was looking for him, but August had disagreed. He said von Kreiger probably didn't know who I was anyway, and even if he did, he'd dismiss me since these adventures were all so improbable. More important, even if von Kreiger did decide I was a problem, he'd look to be killing Sterling—in the camp he always struck at the head of any protest group—and since Sterling didn't exist, von Kreiger, in his frustration, would not be looking in the direction I'd be coming from.

August and I knew Dr. Sterling didn't exist, but not so thousands of readers like Wilson and Quilt. Sterling got lots of mail at the publisher. Folks asked him to find lost items, look for kin who vanished in the war and other more odd things. Sterling was known to be a man of science, always at war with superstition, and he always managed to explain how something seemingly supernatural was really a trick of some foul villain.

August added those parts. Not that he don't know how the world works, but because he knows enough to know others don't want to know. There are times, I'll admit, when I read Sterling's adventures and wish his logic were something I could load into my six-gun.

There in Parker, in room 214, I set down some notes on my experience up in Nevada, near the Groom Mine, and the strange goings-on there, for to send on to August. I reckoned he'd call it something on the order of the "Gruesome Gauntlet of Groom." I'd just gone to turn the wick up on the lamp there, when the thunder of hooves started in the distance. I set my pen down, then opened a window and poked my head out, looking toward the east, not being sure what I'd see coming my way.

Parker, it's laid out on one main street which is dirt where it's not mud, running east to west, with west pointing down toward the Colorado River. At that west end of town is the church—Congregationalist, I think, but in the tale we said it was Methodist since the Congregationalists write too many angry letters to the publisher. From there in, on the north side of the street, was the General Store, the Golden Rule Saloon, and Maud's Rooming House and Restaurant. On the south side, between the church and the Grand Hotel, was the Municipal Building, which housed a school, library, and the sheriff's office. On the east side was a red building known locally as Friendly House, which, near as I could make out as I came into town, was a rooming house for women. It had a big parlor for entertaining menfolk guests, and them women must have had good senses of humor because I heard giggling a lot from over there. Past them, at the edge of the street, was the smithy and stable. Back beyond the main buildings were small clusters of houses, and there were ranches ranging out all over the surrounding area.

Night had fallen, and the few weak gaslights on the street just made sure gloom covered Parker. Out of the east that sound of thundering hooves grew, then coming past the stable I saw them. The very sight sent a shiver through me and dropped my left hand to the six-gun riding on my left hip.

Buffalo, hundreds of them. Their eyes glowed with a pus-green light and their approach sent a tremor through the hotel. A huge white buffalo led the herd, and I knew it was a symbol of powerful magic among the Indians. Behind it came a flood of hide and hooves, horns and muscle wide enough to scrape chairs and barrels off the boardwalk in front of the saloon and send the women of Friendly House backing away from the edge of their porch.

As the buffalo came abreast of me, I climbed out of my window, onto the roof covering the hotel's porch, and ran to the edge. I drew my pistol and fanned it, blasting bullet after bullet into the brown meat avalanche. I knew it was futile, but I also knew I had to try it. A pistol cartridge wouldn't have brought one of them beasts down if all were normal, and it weren't. I didn't know if they'd been hexed so no shots would hit them, but they might as well have been for all the good my shots were doing.

Still, using a pistol to stop them was easier than trying to do it the other way.

As I said, things weren't normal with these buffalo. Even in the dim night light I could see bones poking through holes in hide, and places where the hide had been sliced clean through. I suspected these buffalo had been some of the thousands that had been slaughtered for the amusement of Easterners out for a visit, most having been shot from moving trains. A few had their tongues taken, other delicacies cut out, but most had just been killed for sport. They'd been reanimated and made to do someone's bidding, and that bidding looked like it was bent on driving them like a spear through the Church.

I sighed and dropped my gloved hand into the pocket of my vest. Despite the Church being of the Congregationalist denomination, I felt a bit of an obligation to save it. Not that I had any ties to that particular brand of Christianity, mind you, but something in me found it just plumb rude to run zombie-buffalo through a House of Worship.

I closed my eyes and concentrated for a moment, flashing on an image of the Hunting Grounds. To me that place almost made Parker into Paris, France in terms of desirable, and I don't really take to the French all that powerful. Shadowy figures, some big and spiky, others small and slithery, moved through the Grounds. I latched me on to one of them and we wrestled a bit, but he saw things my way.

Back in Parker I glanced at the deck of cards I pulled from my pocket and saw I'd thumbed a half-dozen and one cards off the deck, from which I had a straight. I melted into the shadows of the hotel and appeared again out by the school house. I'd tried for the shadow of the Church but hadn't been good enough with the hex. Instead of being in front of the stampede, I was just parallel with the white monster leading it.

Though a touch winded, I needed to use another hex. In the Hunting Grounds I grabbed hold of the tail of the manitou I'd used an eyeblink before and tied him up in knots all good and tight. His outrage poured down through me and the full house of cards I'd drawn. From my left palm poured out a bolt of ethereal energy that landed beneath the white buffalo's feet, then exploded like twenty sticks of TNT, casting his body up into the air and breaking it into little bits. The blast also gouged a huge hole in the ground and scattered the lead buffalo it didn't kill.

The rest of them kept on coming, of course, but passed around the crater, leaping over their re-dead brethren. Without the white buffalo to lead them, they remained split, never forming back up again, leastways, not until they got past the Church. I was hoping that if they did keep running, they'd run straight into the river and get washed on down Mexico way.

That was a concern for later, though. I slumped back against the Municipal Building's wall and let the exertion of casting hexes claim me. I did manage to get my cards back

in my pocket before I closed my eyes, but only just barely
and that didn't work out as badly as it might have.

Wilson pulled a grey handkerchief from his pocket and
mopped sweat from his brow. "I will say, sir, that I was
pure-D-amazed at how quick-thinking that Doctor Sterling
is. I mean, being there in the Methodist Church, saying his
devotionals, and hearing the hooves. He comes out and sees
that big, white automaton buffalo charging straight at the
Church. I would have fainted dead away."

Quilt nodded in agreement. "But Doc Sterling, he just
slipped back inside the door, takes the oil lamp there, and
throws it so precisely at the buffalo that the machine ex-
plodes, just busting it apart into pieces."

Wilson held his hands up. "And I don't take it as none of
a disgrace, Mr. Kilbane, that you'd slunk off away from that
mechanical terror. I woulda done that myself."

"And it was you who happened to see where they had
come from, after all." Quilt gave me a favorable nod. "You
see, Mr. Johns, after Doctor Sterling sent that buffalo
flying, he got to thinking and found out a lot about the secrets being harbored in Parker. And then there comes the
part I liked best."

"Yes," Wilson smiled broadly, "Miss Jezebel Knox."

I was awakened quickly enough by some of the citizens
of Parker who were afraid I had been hurt in the stampede.
I assured them that I was fine, just that I'd caught a lung
full of the dust the beasts were raising. I coughed all weak-
like to make that point. Several of the women were sympathetic, but most of the men looked at me as if I'd declared
myself delicate. That might have rankled but if it kept them
away from me, at least for the moment, it meant there was

less of a chance they'd discover I was a disciple of the Great Hoyle.

I didn't take it, from the nature of the conversation about the stampede, that the folks in Parker were too partial to those who could work arcana. It weren't that they were all Hellfire and angry about the obvious magic that had just pounded down their main street. Instead, they talked about the stampede as if it were normal. In their minds they'd already transformed it into a stampede of cattle, and talk quickly ran toward a debate about fencing off the ranges and why or why not that might be the death of freedom on the continent.

The people of Parker clearly wanted to remain ignorant of what powers were at work here, and in that way they were nigh onto normal for most folks. They'd immediately picked up on one fact that had nested in the back of my brain, which was almost as odd as the fact of the buffalo being undead. The fact was that buffalo come from the plains, and Arizona is a desert. It was possible someone marched them down from wherever they'd been killed, but that would take a lot of power and time. The payoff for that sort of investment had to be huge, and, looking at Parker, there just wasn't enough there to make it make sense.

I dusted myself off and headed back to the Grand Hotel. The desk clerk, who I took to calling Scrub in my mind for a variety of reasons, beckoned me over in a method guaranteed to attract major attention while supposedly doing just the opposite. I sidled over, letting urgency paint my face, and tipped my hat in his direction.

"You seen the stampede, did ya?"

"Is that what it was?"

"Yep, but different, this time." He leaned closer to me, his breath as sour as the miasma from an old spittoon. "Before they was just ghosts, but this time, they was real."

I nodded. "I saw that."

Scrub eyed me slyly. "What does Doctor Sterling think? He on the trail already?"

"He's on the trail, and he wanted me to enlist your help." I lowered my voice. "Who would you guess is behind this?"

He thought for a moment, though I knew he had an answer on the tip of his tongue from the start. "The Lividians. They's behind it."

"Lividians. You mentioned them early on. Who are they?"

"Perhaps," came a female voice from behind me, "you should ask someone who can answer the question."

I turned and, standing there, in the hotel lobby, was one of the most beautiful women I'd ever seen in my life. She wore her long, black hair simply plaited and hadn't a touch of warpaint on her face. The dress she wore wouldn't have been called more than plain by anyone who had any sense about clothes. No rings, no necklace, no bonnet nor gloves; she didn't have none of those things and still she would have been the toast of London or Paris or New York or Boston.

I immediately removed my hat. "It has been a long time, Miss Knox."

"It has, Mr. Kilbane, the hardships of which are forgotten upon seeing you again." Her blue eyes raked me up and down, prompting a blush, which made her smile. "You've not changed that much."

"No, I reckon not." I waved her toward the chairs in the lobby. "Shall we talk?"

She glanced past me at Scrub, then wrinkled her nose. "What I have to say is for your ears, not the town's. Your room, perhaps?"

"After you."

Scrub scurried out as we mounted the stairs, but I was too aware of Jeze to pay him much mind. She lifted her skirts enough to expose dainty feet and a well-turned pair of ankles as she ascended. I knew I'd seen those boots before and I recollected where, which took me back years, years before Colton.

In the war men go and do things about which they are not proud. After the Battle of the Dead River, in which both sides had been broken, and broken badly, I had been cut off and lost my way, heading south when I should have gone any other direction. I found myself in the root cellar of a burned-out plantation house and hid there, when Jezebel, her two sisters Lilith and Salome, and her pappy, Leviticus Knox, came down to join me.

Leviticus Knox was a General in the Reb army, but the battle that had broken my unit had crushed his command, too. The man had always been powerful built, with a flowing mane of thick hair and a big black beard. He looked enough like John Brown for men to call him John Black, and he was famous for his towering rages and fiery speeches to his troops. We used to call him Lividicus Knox, given that he'd get red in the face, or so we were told.

At Dead River, so Jeze told me, her father had seen things that put the fear of God into him. He knew he was involved with things that weren't right and it had "fatigued" him. The man I saw was more than tired—he was haunted. He knew things I'd not know until Colton. His mind might not have been broken yet, but it was hurt bad.

Knox just kept mumbling Bible quotes—lots from Revelations, which ain't the sort of thing you want to be hearing in a dark cellar with troops roaming about. I knew that if the Rebs caught me, I'd be a prisoner, and Jeze was afeared of her father being shot for a deserter. I doubted they'd do that since he was one of their better generals. His experience as an engineer before the war, and the staff he'd assembled, gave him a good tactical sense for battles. When you faced the 3rd Georgia Volunteers, you knew it was on a battlefield that would be to their benefit, not yours.

Jezebel didn't say anything as we walked down the hallway to my room. I opened the door for her and closed it behind us, but wasn't prepared for her to turn and hang her arms around my neck. She kissed me once, hard, with an urgency that melted the years away. I slipped my arms around her and held her close, kissing her back, hoping the years since we'd last kissed would somehow be kept at bay.

Finally our mouths parted and she rested her head against my shoulder. "Thank God, you have come. I wrote that letter to your publisher months ago. I wrote it in code, but I knew you'd see through the ruse and know it was me. And you came."

I didn't know of any letter, and I wasn't sure August would have seen through any code she'd used. He knew of Jeze, but didn't know who she'd really been. We'd remained hidden in the cellar for days, then someone had to go get water. I volunteered, having stripped out of my uniform so the Rebs wouldn't shoot me on sight. In the interim, though, the Union had taken the area and the First Massachusetts Regiment, my old unit, was camped around us.

I found August, my lieutenant, and assured him I'd not deserted. I presented to him the Knox family, calling them the Whites, and said Leviticus was a preacher who had been treated poorly. August arranged for safe passage for all of them out of the area and that was the last I'd seen of Jeze until Parker.

"I need to know more than you could put in your letter.

In that time things must have changed."

She nodded solemnly, wisps of her hair tickling my throat. "They have. They've gotten worse. I'll tell you all about it. In the morning."

"Morning is a fair piece off, Miss Knox."

"I know, Mr. Kilbane." She pulled away from me, but took my hands in hers and drew me deeper into the room. "I never had a chance to thank you for saving my father, my sisters and me. I'd not have you thinking me ungrateful."

She gave me a smile that set my heart to flame, and that fire spread through my body. Jezebel Knox let go of my hands for a moment, just long enough to turn down the wick on the lamp, then we passed the time in a room just about as dark as the cellar had been, but a lot more inviting.

Wilson swiped more sweat from his brow. "For Doc Sterling to meet the one woman who had broken his heart all those years ago, then to gallantly stand guard as she slept in his bed and got her rest, well, sir, that's the kind of honorable man Doctor Sterling is."

Quilt toed my left boot. "If you hadn't a run off in your terror, you could have stood guard outside their door and let them have some privacy."

Johns sniffed. "It sounds as if Doctor Sterling wouldn't have taken advantage of the woman had such an opportunity arisen. No gentleman would."

"Then don't paint me a gentleman!" Wilson's laugh shook his jowls fiercely.

Quilt gave his seat companion half of a wall-eyed stare. "I don't think you'd have been the sort who could have saved Jezebel and her family from the Bengali uprising in Lahore—that was before you were with Doctor Sterling, wasn't it?"

I nodded. "It was. A harrowing time, I hear tell."

"It might have been scary, but what Doctor Sterling ran into out there at Resurrection Farms . . ." Quilt shivered as if he found himself naked in a block of ice. "I won't be forgetting that any time soon."

From the road, Resurrection Farms seemed almost a mirror of the plantation lands the Knoxes had left behind in the Deep South. A dirt track wriggled its way up a hill toward the big house. I reckoned as how that house must have cost a fortune to build, given that the lumber would have had to be trekked in from Flagstaff or thereabouts. The two-story structure had glass in the windows, two chimneys at each end of the building and huge, tall pillars supporting a portico. It was as impressive a structure I'd seen since torching plantations in the South years past.

I also noticed, like with the buffalo, someone had gone to a lot of work to put something big where it ought not to have been.

Jeze brought her horse close enough to mine that our knees touched. "Father calls the house the Holy Sepulcher."

I frowned. "That's where the Lord rested until his resurrection, ain't it?"

She nodded slowly, and I could sense the dread in her. "After we were out here for a bit, I was required to go back to Georgia and deal with certain business matters. My father and sisters remained here. In the three months I was gone, things changed. The mansion was raised and the other things came into being."

The other things she mentioned became visible as we came up on the top of the hill and could see past the mansion, down toward the Colorado River in the distance. The illusion of a southern plantation had been wounded because of the saguaro cacti and dusty red rocks everywhere. The squatter's camp of shacks beyond the mansion dealt that illusion a *coup de grace*. Little ramshackle buildings, half-constructed out of mud bricks, with mismatched wooden slats and gaping roofs, spread out down the back side of the hill. They were squatter shacks, no doubt about it, similar to the things I'd seen near the silver mines in Nevada, though thrown up more hastily. Beyond them were some terraces built up for farming, but the plants looked stunted and shriveled in the hot sun.

More disturbing than all that was the population of people shambling their way up the hill toward the rear of the big house. They wore threadbare and plain garments, akin to the dress Jeze wore, but none of them looked nearly as good as she did. Probably that was because their flesh had an ashen hue to it that matched their filthy clothes. They looked listless, akin to folks found at the collision of hangover and dawn rising. Kids stumbled after parents, and if my reading of the groupings was right, polygamy wasn't unknown among the Lividians.

Scrub's comments, especially the vehemence of them, came back to me. "You were gone and this cult sprang up?"

Jeze nodded as the people wandered into the big house's basement through a cellar door. "My father, you remember how he was fatigued, don't you? How he took refuge in the Bible?"

"Seemed concerned with Revelations a mite."

"While I was gone he said he found a code in the Bible. It confirmed for him that Parker was the place Jesus Christ would return to the world, and His coming is soon, very soon." She reined her horse up in front of the big house. "He started preaching to the people here and followers

158

came to the farms. "They give everything to the Church of Leviticus, live by his Rules, do his bidding, and prepare for the Return."

I dismounted, then came around and helped Jeze alight. "And your father believes all this?"

She came out of the saddle and hugged me. "I don't know, Nevan. Since my return I've never seen him alone. My sisters, they care for him. They won't let me near him. I get to hear him when . . . come on, you'll see."

She took me by the hand and led me into the mansion. Whereas it was impressive on the outside, the inside looked pretty much gutted. Walls were half-plastered and furniture was scattered about without worry about grouping like with like. I reckoned that the best of Parker's furnishings were ending up here. What I seen coming into the place told me as much about Parker's distance from civilization as it did the devotion of folks who gave everything up to Leviticus Knox's dream.

I followed Jeze down some stairs to the basement, bringing us out midway in this big rectangular room. It got cooler down there, but it wasn't just because of the dark and dank. The basement was one big room, a meeting hall of some sort, fitted out with long tables of crude manufacture. Grey people filled them and lifted wooden bowls to servers. The servers wheeled around big pots full of some steaming mush that made me nostalgic for the rations served at Colton. Portions were dished up with a big plop and folks started eating right away—many ignoring spoons for fingers and sucking spills off stained shirt-fronts.

Things remained shadowed and grey 'cepting at the north end of the room. There they'd built up a little bit of a stage and had centered a gilded throne on it. Red velvet covered the cushions on the back and sea-serpents and dragons and other Biblical nasties twined over the wooden parts, ending with a dragon's head and a serpent's head, suitably crushed, being the footrest.

Flanking it either side were Jeze's sisters, Lilith and Salome, hanging all loose and languid to the throne. They wore white gowns that looked to be of silk. They clung to the women's bodies the way ivy hugs a building, letting a man appreciate the underlying architecture. Their eyes were the same blue as Jeze's, but colder somehow, and their hair had taken on a reddish hue that I didn't recollect from having seen them before.

The figure seated in the throne, though, he commanded my full attention as he stood. He wore a Reb general's uniform, but it was cut of cloth so white that it almost hurt my eyes to look at him. Gold braid trimmed it appropriately, and a gilded plume rode in his hat. He wore white gloves and tugged at the hem of them as his daughters smoothed the sleeves and back of his jacket. The white mask he wore ran from hairline to jaw, but opened enough to reveal his mouth and the black shock of beard on his chin. The mask's eyes had been cut on a slant, which combined with the gold-embroidered circle of sixes on the forehead to give him a diabolical cast to his features.

I felt a chill run down my spine. The way his daughters stroked his arms was a bit more familiar than I would have expected, and that set me to feeling uneasy. Leviticus Knox drew his hands around behind his back and his daughters went to their knees at his side. They faced him and bowed their heads, as if they were unworthy of looking upon such a countenance. The Greys in the room likewise looked down. I was feeling contrary and kept my head up.

Leviticus began to speak and the bass tones of his voice were mesmerizing. "Brothers and sisters, the time is near.

You have been saved from Perdition by your faithful adherence here to our work. You make the world ready for the coming Armageddon. You await a sign and should know that such a sign was seen in Parker last night. A stampede of Hellbeasts raced through Main Street and would have shattered the Church there, but God, in his infinite mercy and wisdom, had placed me there. While those who have not joined us are confused, God would not abandon them. He placed me there and I turned the beasts, sending them on into the river where they were swept back to Hell where they belong."

Murmurs of ascent washed over the room in waves, and heads bobbed as if floating. I felt a spark of hope in my heart as Leviticus spoke. In the back of my mind I knew something was off, something was wrong, but I couldn't figure what it was. Leviticus' words assured me I needn't ought to think, and the gentle nodding from Jeze confirmed this notion.

"Brothers and sisters, the time comes of our elevation and exaltation. Those among us who have died will rise again to join our Lord. They are the lucky ones, they are the fortunate, for through their deaths they have already been cleansed of sin and are prepared for Paradise."

Leviticus raised a hand and touched the triple-six design on his forehead. "You ask yourselves why I wear the mark of the Beast? It is because I acknowledge myself to be a sinner. I know I harbor evil and it will be through my death that I am purged of inequity and shriven of my sins. For us, for the Chosen, death holds no fear, for it is only the portal to eternal paradise."

An *amen* or two rose from the assembly. I felt my lips forming the word, too; and panic sparked in me. I was not one of the Chosen. I was not one of those who would be saved with Leviticus through his work. I wasn't under his brand and when the great roundup came; I would be abandoned. I didn't want that and knew I had to find a way to prove to him that I was worthy of being saved.

Jeze had said that the people here had given everything to the Church. I remembered her saying that. I knew that was the key to my salvation. I looked to be offering him my greatest possession, to prove I was part of his herd. My left hand slipped into my jacket pocket and I grabbed the deck of cards therein. I thumbed off seven, preparing to flash them at Leviticus, just to let him know how powerful a gift it was I'd be giving.

The room vanished for a moment, having the Hunting Grounds slip into place for it. I found a manitou tangled in my fingers. It was only a scrawny one, barely worth catching a hold of, but tussling with it was enough to mule-kick me into sensibility. Leviticus had been using a hex to maintain influence over his people, I seen that straightaway. Since they believed him, that made it easier for him to fool them. His grip on me had been weaker, and easily busted up by my Hunting trip.

But knowing what he'd been doing wasn't the same as undoing it. I tightened my grip on the manitou and wrung power out of it. I melted back into the real world and flashed the cards in my hand. I only had a measly pair of fours, but that was enough to suit me.

The dazzlingly colorful display they made only affected two people, since only two of them were looking in my direction. Jeze raised a hand to cover her eyes, gasping at the display. Leviticus blinked twice, then took a step toward me. His daughters' heads snapped around, their eyes blazing at Jeze and me.

"There they are, infidels! They are demonic minions, my

faithful." His hands emerged from behind his back and clawed toward the sky. "Rise and destroy them!"

Bidden by the sound of his voice, the mass of Greys rose as one, and scrambled toward us.

Wilson produced a silver flask and took a long pull on it. He wiped away a bead of amber liquid from his thick lips with the back of his hand, then shook his head. "That Doctor Sterling, figuring out that Leviticus had ether flowing in the basement there to weaken the minds of the Greys; that was genius, pure genius."

Quilt frowned as Wilson hid the flask away again. "Anyone could have figured that out, even Mr. Kilbane here. It said in the story he was thinking on it, but . . ."

Wilson gave me a nod. "He was, but he didn't have the background to know what it was. And it took Doctor Sterling to strike those matches to burn away the gas around him and Miss Knox. Then he dragged the two of them, Mr. Kilbane and Miss Knox, to safety."

Johns looked over at me from the corner of the seat. "It would seem you are more a hindrance to your master than a help. Or does modesty prevent you from fully describing your contributions to things?"

I shifted my shoulders uneasily. "I do what I can. My efforts pale in light of Doctor Sterling's."

Wilson smiled at me. "You do all right."

Johns raised an eyebrow. "Few men would enjoy hiding in the shadows of a greater man. It must chafe."

Quilt answered for me. "Not when you're working for a man like Doctor Sterling. He's saved Mr. Kilbane's life more times than can be counted, isn't that true? What kind of man would our friend be here if he didn't show gratitude for that kind of thing?"

Johns smiled. "Normal?"

"I'm just old-fashioned." I gave Johns an easy smile. "I give credit where due, take what I can get and carry out my orders. It's a simple life, but it's mine."

Wilson laughed. "You call that simple? Maybe then you've forgotten what happened in Parker, there at Resurrection Farms!"

The Greys came for us, men and women jostling to be first, with little ones snarling from between legs and behind skirts. I shoved Jeze up the stairs behind us, then I followed. I jammed my cards away and drew my six-gun. I pointed it at the Greys and cocked it, then thought about triggering a warning shot. They didn't blanche at the sight or sound of the gun, so I knew flame and lead that wasn't directed toward them wasn't going to turn them.

A .45 Peacemaker spits out a hunk of metal big enough to wipe the smile off anyone's face. Now these Greys, they wasn't smiling none, but the slugs about wiped everything off their faces. In fact, it made it so their faces had to be wiped off other folks' faces, which I would have thought would slow them down a piece. They *did* drag the bodies back away but kept coming.

As I came around the turn in the stairs I saw Jeze's skirt disappearing up the next flight. With her out of sight, I shifted the pistol to my right hand and went for my cards again. I dealt myself a pair into the spell I'd used on the lead buffalo. It splashed a Grey man all over the stairs, leaving him dripping down the walls slow as molasses. Better yet, it blew apart the landing and the lower half of the flight I was on. A half-dozen greys stumbled into the abyss below, screaming as they went.

I dashed up the stairs, opening my pistol and letting the

spent shells tinkle their way back down in my wake. I reached the main floor and knew I had to get out of the house quickly. The Greys had entered the basement through an exterior entrance, so their being stopped by the damage to the stairs would only be temporary. I looked around for Jeze, but couldn't see her.

Then I heard a scream from above. I took stairs two at a time, my spurs jingling as I went. At the top of the stairs I found a number of closed doors. I went from one to another, but it wasn't until the master suite that I found Jeze. She stood in the middle of the room, which was huge. It had a big fireplace set into the interior wall, two small vanity tables with big mirrors and wardrobes crammed full of clothes on either side of the massive canopied bed.

She hugged her arms around herself and shivered. "It can't be, it can't be."

I slipped bullet after bullet back into my pistol, then snapped it shut. "No doubt about it, there's something wrong here."

Jeze turned to face me, her complexion whiter than that of a consumptive. "Those vanities, these two wardrobes, they belong to my sisters."

I nodded and followed her gaze to the third wardrobe, the one full of her father's uniforms. The presence of the clothes and only one bed suggested some unsavory things that matched up with how the devoted daughters were acting in the basement. My mouth soured immediately, but I knew I didn't have time to sort out all that appeared to be going on.

I reholstered my pistol and grabbed Jeze by the shoulders. "When I said there was something wrong here, that wasn't what I meant." I nodded toward the fireplace. "That's the problem."

She frowned. "What are you talking about?"

"No chimney for it—I seen that riding in. It's hiding something." I crossed to the hearth and squatted in front of it. I reached up inside and found a simple catch that I flipped. The back part of the hearth retreated, exposing a wooden ladder leading down. "I reckon I found it."

"I don't understand. What's going on, Nevan?"

"I don't reckon I know either, Jezebel, but I aim to find out. Down this hole I will."

"I'm coming, too."

I shook my head. "No, I want you to get out of here. It's important that you do." I explained to her how the only thing that could stop me was her being used against me, and I explained a few other things, too.

She gave me a hug and a kiss, neither of which lasted long enough as far as I was concerned. I winked at her, then descended the ladder. The wood felt rough to my left hand, and three-quarters of the way down an unlit torch in a sconce drew a soot line up my spine, but otherwise I reached the bottom of the pit without incident.

I had to walk along a short tunnel before I emerged into a cavern. It might have once been natural, but a lot of work had been put into it by people. Up beyond the crevasse, to the west, I saw another tunnel I reckoned came out near the river. It occurred to me that the excavations had provided the dirt for the gardens. It was my guess that the Lividians had done the work, 'specially because I could see some broken bodies down in a sharp crevasse that slanted off to the south, in the bottom of the cavern. They'd fallen in and likely been smashed up beyond saving by the time they reached the bottom.

That put them one step closer to Hell, which was fine by my thinking.

Above the crevasse, clinging to a ledge on the north side all spiderlike, a stout wooden scaffold had been erected. It resembled the deck of a heaving ship, only because it was slanted down at an angle pointing it toward the crevasse. Mounted on it was a cannon, the type of which I'd seen hundreds in the war. Despite its not being very remarkable to sight, I got the feeling something was odd about it, so I dealt myself into a hex that would give me the gospel on any magic worked on the cannon.

I got a fun house full of information on the thing. Enough magic had been worked on it to turn it into a talisman, and from what I knew of the Hoylist arts, that wasn't an easy thing to do. First one had to get an item with some significance to work with, then weave magic into the item through a long ritual. It all worked best if the item and the magic being worked were akin to each other—traveling the same trail. Since a cannon is meant for destruction, I wasn't thinking this was a good omen at all.

Leviticus appeared on the scaffold above me with a lit torch in his hand. "So you've found it. Pity you didn't find the secret exit from the ladder tunnel. It was at the torch. Then you would be here and have a chance of stopping me. As it is, you can't."

He patted the cannon with his empty, gloved hand. "In case you were wondering what sort of significance a cannon could hold, this is the one that fired the first shot at Fort Sumter. This started the War of Southern Liberation and I will use it to birth a new nation."

He touched the torch to the fuse. It sputtered and sparked, then began to burn. "Farewell. Your effort to stop me was just too little, too late." He shoved the torch into a wall sconce there, banishing shadows, then ran back to the ladder tunnel.

167

I stood there, torn. I almost ran to the tunnel and fired six shots up into the darkness, but killing him wouldn't stop his cannon. I couldn't climb up there fast enough, and even walking through shadows to get up there might not work since I'd have to emerge too far from the cannon to pinch off the fuse.

I even thought about trying to shoot the fuse from the gun. I thought I could hit it, was pretty sure I could, but the bullet itself might keep it burning. *And what if I miss?*

I hesitated for a second, then I knew what I had to do. I drew the cards and sprinted toward the crevasse. I cut them one-handed quick, then thumbed off a set of seven. In the Hunting Grounds I found me a manitou that was kind flat and even soft, if you ignored claws and teeth around the edges. It seemed intent on wrapping itself around me, and I let it. Then I grabbed its eyestalks and tied them into a painful knot, letting it know that I was having a lend of its power.

In the cavern I leaped up as the cannon went off, putting me between firing cannon and hole in the ground.

I know it sounds foolish, what I was doing, and I'd rightly have been rewarded by having a hole blowed in me as big as a politician's sense of self-importance. Truth to tell, I wasn't certain that what I was going to do would work, but I didn't really reckon on as how I had much choice in the matter. The hex I wrapped around myself was the same one I figured have been warp and weft of the buffaloes—something to make shots taken at them miss. Now, strictly speaking, that cannon weren't aimed at me until I put myself in front of its muzzle. Had there been some lawyerly hex worked on that cannon, I'd be guessing I'd have been the first creature entombed at the bottom of Parker Bay, but that wasn't the way turned out.

The cannonball, as near as I can figure, had been worked with a powerful hex on account of being fired from the Sumter cannon. The hex is known to some as *earthwrack* and can set the ground to shaking a little or a lot. Given that California already had a serious dose of the shakes, I could imagine what would have happened had the shell hit its intended target. As it was, it missed, slamming into the crevasse lip, then ricocheting up and around.

Now, while I was happy that the Lividian plan had been thwarted, I did find myself in something of a mix-up. There with a hexed cannonball bouncing around inside a cavern, setting off little earthquakes whenever or wherever it hit. On top of that it kept blasting pieces of the scaffold into splinters, many of which were as long as my arm and a mite worrisome if they struck home. On top of all that, all the hexing I'd done had me plumb worn out.

I do remember diving for cover in the tunnel and thinking that I wasn't really sure anything could protect me from an earthquake anyway. I'm sure that thought would have niggled and nagged me to distraction but as luck would have it—bad luck, mind you—a piece of rock spanged off my think box, and I slumbered through what would have been a most harrowing time.

"You see," said Quilt rather solemnly, "It takes a man of Doctor Sterling's noble spirit and sharp mental faculties to be able to come up with a solution to so dire a problem. Only he could have figured out how to use a stick of TNT to blow out a single scaffold support that would allow the cannon to rotate around and shoot its projectile back up toward the mansion. And then to drag you, Mr. Kilbane, to the one place the scaffold would save you from the falling rocks, impressive. Such quick thinking, and sound application of scientific principles."

Wilson scrubbed his handkerchief under his nose. "But what about the cost to Doctor Sterling? It must have crushed him."

Johns frowned. "What happened?"

Quilt's voice grew quietly respectful. "The cannon shell ripped up into the house and exploded. The central beams were broken and the whole house collapsed in on itself. Oil lamps caught on fire. Leviticus Knox, his daughters and, alas, Jezebel, were trapped in the house. A note she left on Doctor Sterling's saddle said she had to go back to try to save her sisters. They were all in the house when it was destroyed. All dead."

Wilson nodded. "Serves Knox right for trying to blast a hole into Hell, to free the demons so Jesus would have to return."

"You could take it as that, surely." I nodded solemnly. "The Knoxes, they all died when the house went down. Jezebel, too. The Doctor, he . . . searched all he could, but the fire . . ." I swallowed hard against the lump in my throat. "I guess it brought him some comfort that she died trying to save her family. So, for all intents and purposes, the Parker Panic is over."

Wilson gave me a jowl-lifting smile. "It was a corker of a tale, still is. You going to do another?"

I shrugged. "As the Doctor dictates, I guess." I stood. "If you gentlemen will excuse me, I think I'll get some fresh air."

I retreated through the car and slipped out the door to the small platform at the rear of the car. I shut the door behind me and sat down on the steps. I leaned my spine against the car's weathered wood and let the click-clack vibrations of wheels on track loosen the muscles in my back. I closed my eyes for a moment, then didn't bother to open them when I heard the sound of the door latch.

"Mr. Kilbane, if you don't mind, a question."

"Ask away, Mr. Johns."

His voice grew louder as he squatted at my left shoulder. "Doctor Sterling, being a man of science, he couldn't have imagined that Knox was truly intent on blasting an opening into Hell, could he? I mean, such an explanation is at odds with the engineering brilliance it took to put together the automaton buffaloes and that Hell-cannon. That's not truly what he thinks, is it?"

I shrugged, then opened my eyes slowly. "I don't always know his mind, but you might could be right there, Mr. Johns. See, after we dragged ourselves from the cave down there we actually found Jezebel and her father alive, outside the burning house."

"They lived?"

"They did, though Salome and Lilith didn't. Perished in the fire." I gave him a slow smile. "See, it turns out that while Jezebel was in Georgia, one of her father's old army aides, Dalton Jeffries, came to Parker. He'd been a bright engineer, which is why he was part of Knox's staff in the war. Dalton, though, he started dealing with things dark and dangerous. The Doctor reckons that Jeffries usurped Knox's place after the old man broke down. He took up with Knox's daughters and used his sorcerous ways to make slaves of the Lividians. He took all of their lands, which comprised most of Parker, and was intent in splitting off California, to make the ocean come right to Parker. It would become the new San Francisco and he'd own it all."

Johns smiled and slowly stood. "A brilliant plan."

I nodded. "I guess it's true then, what you said. You chafed at having to serve under another man, even to

171

having him take credit for your madness. Isn't that right, Jeffries?"

Johns started, then sank his hands into the pockets of his long coat. "You're not surprised I'm here?"

"Quartzite is another town on the fault that runs through Parker." I leaned back, letting the train car tip my Stetson up so I could see his eyes. "And there was that theft of the first American cannon to fire in the Revolutionary War from Boston last month. We figured you'd be making a move."

"I guess, then, we'd best end this now."

"I guess, because 'The Quartzite Quandary' will just make for a lousy title." I gestured with my gloved right hand and saw Jeffries' eyes widen. Being a Hoylist himself, he knew a talisman when he saw one. His right hand twitched within his pocket, thumbing cards into a hand. I don't know if he was trying to see what the hex on the glove was, or was doing something to defend himself, but it really didn't matter.

He'd run afoul of the best tool a magician ever had: misdirection.

In this case, he paid attention to the right hand of a left-handed gunslinger.

I only put three bullets into him, which was probably one more than I needed, but that first shot to his right knee likely misdirected him even more than my glove. The second one blew out his heart and took a chunk of spine with it. The last ventilated his brain pan, then I grabbed a lapel of his jacket and pitched him out into the night.

I reholstered my pistol and returned to the two cardsharpers.

Wilson looked up. "Did I hear shots?"

I nodded. "Thought I saw coyotes out there." I slipped

into my seat opposite them. "Gonna play?"

Quilt frowned. "Shouldn't we wait for Mr. Johns?"

I cast a little hex that drained their memories of Mr. Johns. I didn't think much of the manitou I grabbed to do the job, but he proved up to the job. And then some, judging by the blank stares I got from the two of them.

"Evening, gentlemen," I said, tugging on the brim of my Stetson. "Name's Nevan Kilbane."

Quilt's eyes brightened. "Your name, it's the same as the guy who writes them dime novels. The Doctor Sterling books."

"That's because I write them." I smiled. "Perhaps you've read the latest. It was called **The Parker Panic**, and what was in the book was only half the story."

"Wind Tiger" is the oldest story in this collection. It was originally written in 1983, back when I assumed my career would be built on Marek and Rais stories. In 1992 I rewrote it for inclusion in *Mage's Blood and Old Bones*, an anthology I edited along with Elizabeth Danforth for Flying Buffalo. All the game companies were doing fiction then, and we were not going to be left out. The story's plot is the same as it was when I wrote it in '83, just much better written.

Wind Tiger

"Are you well? You've been injured."

Her soulmate replied with enough levity to drive the worry from her mind. "I will live. We are safe now. The storm can no longer hurt us."

She paused. "Yes, but we are trapped. We can never go home again."

"What matter, if we are secure?" came the gentle reply. "Rest easy, this will now be our home. Be at peace, I will protect you. I promise we will be together and safe . . . Forever . . ."

"Let me see . . . smoked quail, Devorkian's best white wine, some bread, Khalarian brandy and a copy of Hessoch's *Verses for Lovers*." The scar-faced thief surveyed the contents of the large wicker basket sitting in the middle of the table. "That should suffice, unless . . ." His left hand strayed to stroke his coal-black goatee as he thought. "Marek, do you think a sharp Klessa or a mild Shlor would be a better cheese choice to go with the wine?"

Marek, seated with his feet up on the table, barely heard the question. Without tipping the slouch-brimmed hat back to reveal his eyes, he stretched and yawned. "That sounds fine, Rais. Whatever you think is best."

"Marek, this is important." Before sleep could reclaim him, Rais slapped his open hand against the table. Sharp insistence in his voice, he offered in explanation, "How are we to make the correct impressions on our ladies if you do not care about the selection of the cheese? Everything must be perfect."

In one easy, fluid motion, the long, lean thief swung his feet off the table, doffed his hat and leaned forward. "Listen, Rais, you're the one who wants to impress these ladies. You're the one who approached Lady Mariette, not me. I'm only going along on this little outing because she refused to go with you unless you could find someone to accompany her country cousin, Lady Natica."

Letting a wounded expression steal slyly over his face, Rais stared down at his partner. "Here I attempt to share some culture with you, and you make it sound as if I'm asking you to cut off your swordarm." Dressed in a black velvet jacket over white shirt and black velvet trousers tucked into the tops of knee-high riding boots, Rais looked very much the picture of cultured citizens living in Gull. "Surely you cannot object to being paired with Lady Natica."

"Not having met her, I don't know." Marek yawned again and threatened to pluck the peacock feather from the band of his hat. "That, however, is beside the point. You asked me to secure us a wagon and some blankets. I have and they are waiting for us at the stables near Northgate. I've done my part. It is up to you to worry about cuisine. Now give me one of those apples."

Grumbling an oath, the smaller thief swept all four of the apples from beneath his partner's grasp and deposited them in the wicker basket. Marek rose quickly, slammed the basket shut and scooped it up under his arm. Without breaking stride he dashed toward the Black Dragon Tavern's door, then stopped as he realized Rais was not giving chase. He turned and shook his head. "Grab my sword and cloak. Let's go, we've wasted enough time already."

Rais fastened his own black cloak around his throat with a silver ram's-head clasp before flinging Marek's green cloak over his arm. He checked his rapier to see that it hung correctly at his left hip, then adjusted the dagger riding in his right boot to a more comfortable position. On top of Marek's cloak he piled his brown-haired partner's swept-hilt rapier and both cloth-wrapped packages of cheese.

"When no clear choice can be made, the best choice is both."

Holding the door open, Marek laughed lightly. "Why didn't you make that decision earlier?"

"Because, my friend," Rais smiled, "you'd not yet volunteered to carry the basket to Northgate."

The distance to the stables was not particularly far, but no easy, direct route led from the Black Dragon to their destination. In a city crisscrossed with canals, all transit takes place either in a slender route-runner, on foot through alleys or pedestrian byways or in carriages on the more major thoroughfares. Land travel necessitates the use of bridges which, when carrying a heavy, blocky basket, can be an annoyance.

"Sure you don't want to carry this basket a while, Rais?"

"Quite certain, my friend."

Marek shifted it from his left hand to his right and pulled Rais away from an urchin selling half-dead flowers. "No. You don't need flowers. Where we're going there will be plenty of them and you and Lady Mariette can pick them to your heart's content."

The dark-eyed thief scowled. "You have no romance in your soul."

"Ha!" Marek's emerald eyes flashed impishly. "This from the man whose great romances have the survival rate of a gold Imperial dropped on the street."

"Those other women were not like Lady Mariette." Rais' eyes grew distant, signaling a change in his mood that Marek had come to dread in the past two weeks. "She is different. She is alive. She understands . . ."

"She's intrigued with being wooed by one of the most notorious thieves in Gull." Before Rais could utter a protest, Marek stopped short and pointed across the cobblestone courtyard. "There you go, our wagon!" He beamed proudly.

Rais swallowed hard. "You should have let me buy the flowers."

"No need." Marek dumped the basket on the back of the wagon's flat bed. "There's a few left in here from when I stole it."

The black wagon, though it lacked the squared-off black canvas canopy that normally covered the back, was unmistakable. The matched black stallions that came with it were magnificent animals, and the lacquered woodwork positively glowed with polishing, but the evil omens of using that wagon could not be dismissed.

"You stole a hearse, Marek."

The younger man climbed up into the driver's seat. "How many other wagons are you going to find with two seats and a fine pair of horses like this?"

"But a hearse?" Rais placed the cheese in the basket, then draped Marek's cloak over it. He studied the flatbed anxiously and frowned. "A hearse?"

"Rais, it has extra-heavy suspension and is guaranteed to

provide a smooth ride on those roads you've got us traveling." He watched his friend look beneath the bed. "And, no, I did not hide a body. I took it after it delivered the body to the cemetery. Satisfied?"

Rais climbed up onto the bench beside him. "I suppose it could have been worse."

"I do have some sense, you know. Just because I'm not overly eager to go romancing these highborn ladies doesn't mean I want to spoil your chances of becoming a kept man." A light breeze blew his collar-length brown hair back from his shoulders and a broad grin stole over his clean-shaven face. "I do wish, however, I had not allowed you to talk me into wearing these clothes."

"What's wrong with them?" Rais gave Marek's attire a critical glance. "My tailor was painstakingly exact when he measured you, despite your antics. That green satin in your tunic and breeches came all the way from Knor. The cobbler who made your boots is the best in the city, and the seamstress who embroidered your cloak with that silver thread said it took her twelve hours to finish it."

Marek recognized the tone in Rais' voice that told him his plans for ditching the cloak had best be abandoned. "I'm not complaining, mind you, about the clothes or being forced to dress-up like the Prince's own forester."

"You look good in those clothes." Rais gave him a conspiratorial grin. "You cut quite a handsome figure in that suit. One I'm sure Lady Natica will find very, ah, attractive."

Marek gave the traces a twitch, starting the horses out of the stableyard and toward Northgate. "I have no trouble with that prospect, but you know what happens whenever I wear fancy clothes like these. I've not had a set of fine clothing last me the day I put it on."

"I don't think Lady Natica will find you that attractive." Rais raked fingers back through his black widow's-peak hair. "I cannot foresee anything we are going to do that would ruin your clothes. We're only going to a cove up the coast for a short outing."

"If it's so short, why did you pack enough food for a month?"

Rais' eyes narrowed to obsidian slits. "You left your hat back at the Black Dragon."

"I guess I did, didn't I?" Marek clucked. "Pity, I was just getting used to the feather, too."

The ride to the estate Lady Mariette considered her spring home passed quickly and quite uneventfully. Rais checked and straightened his jacket as Marek guided the wagon up the horseshoe-shaped carriageway at the front of the manor house. A uniformed valet stepped from a small guardhouse and accepted the reins while the two thieves lighted from the wagon. The man clearly did not like their presence, but he said nothing as Marek belted on his rapier and fastened his cloak in place.

Rais strode boldly to the front door and banged a huge bronze knocker twice. In slightly less time than Marek figured it would have taken him to pick the locks and enter the mansion unbidden, a wigged servant opened the door slowly. "Yes?" he asked slowly, the disgusted tone in his voice matching his sneer perfectly.

"We are here to call upon the Ladies Mariette and Natica." Rais' face sharpened. "Surely your superiors would have informed you to expect our arrival."

Though Marek tried to warn him off with a shake of his head, the servant stiffened. "I have no superiors among the staff in this household."

"Which explains why you cannot find work in the city."

Rais took a step forward. "Unless you've not heard out here in this backwater, the custom is for gentlemen callers to await their ladies inside." Rais' icy voice and the sharp looking-over he gave the butler had its expected effect.

"Indeed, come in and wait." The man moved from the doorway, then snapped an order at a maid that sent her scurrying up the curving marble stairway to the second floor. While he backed far enough onto the white and black marble foyer floor to let them enter, he blocked their pathway further into the house. Behind him a cook's helper and a wine steward took up other positions to keep the thieves trapped.

Marek smiled. "We were expected, it seems."

Rais returned the grin. "And our reputations have preceded us."

Any decision to test the strength of the household's defenses were forestalled as the women the thieves had come to see appeared at the top of the stairs.

In an instant Marek saw that Rais' fortnight of mooning over Lady Mariette had not been without good cause. Of average height and slightly slender build, she carried herself with a self-confidence guaranteed to attract notice. Her raven hair fell in waves to the middle of her back and gleamed with blue highlights. Her well-sculpted features and blue eyes formed a portrait of classic beauty that she accentuated with the judicious application of cosmetics. As she descended, she let a subtle smile play across her face. She established—then shyly broke—eye-contact with Rais as if embarrassed and flattered by his attention.

Rais smiled joyfully. "She is a flame and I am a moth."

Marek choked back bile. "She's a net and you're a fish." He allowed himself a secret smile, knowing his friend had fallen hard for Mariette. He didn't think the relationship would last very long, but if it made his normally cynical friend happy, that was good enough for him.

The second woman descended and presented quite a contrast to the first. Taller than her cousin, Lady Natica was also more of a full-figured woman. Her face had a bit more roundness to it than she might have liked, but Marek found that roundness reflected elsewhere on her, in places where it could be appreciated. Her blond hair had been cut shorter than Mariette's and had been pulled back into a ponytail. Though a paler shade than those of her cousin, Lady Natica's blue eyes seemed to have just as much life in them.

She stared at Marek a moment, then caught her heel on the last step. She stumbled, but kept herself upright with one hand on the banister and Marek's help. "Thank you," she mumbled. Color flooded her cheeks and she refused to look up at him.

Both women had chosen to attire themselves in nearly identical riding outfits. Lady Mariette wore a black velvet jacket cut short enough to accentuate her nearly invisible waist. Beneath the jacket she wore a white, off-the-shoulder blouse designed to show off her bosom. Loose-legged riding pants extended just beyond her knees to complete her outfit, but they had not been tucked into the tops of her boots. The boots themselves hugged her shapely legs like a second skin and had been fitted with silver toecaps.

Lady Natica's outfit differed in slight but substantial ways. Her green velvet jacket had been cut to a more modest length to accentuate her height. While she wore a white blouse, it covered her to the throat. Her riding breeches matched her jacket in color and fabric. Both they and the boots she wore revealed legs a bit thicker—but no less attractive—than those of her cousin.

Lady Mariette offered her hand to Rais. "I trust we have

not kept you waiting."

Rais bowed curtly and lightly kissed her knuckles. "Not at all, my Lady, not at all. We only just arrived."

Like an angry cat, Lady Mariette turned on the butler and hissed at him. "Rene, why have you not taken their cloaks and offered them some wine?"

The butler met her stare with one of defiance. "The list of supplies your father left to be used in his absence did not include wine for sundry travelers. I would not wish to incur your father's wrath, my Lady."

Before Mariette could respond to that, Marek intervened on the butler's behalf. "My Lady, Rais and I had hoped to travel quickly—before the tide can wash away the little place we have chosen for this excursion. I am certain your Rene understood this and did not wish to delay us any longer than absolutely necessary."

Rene's almost imperceptible nod accompanied Marek's suggestion. Mollified without being fooled, Mariette let the matter drop. She smiled at the taller thief. "Marek, allow me to present to you my cousin, the Lady Natica ni-Aelas. She is from the northern barony of Sollern."

Marek accepted her hand and raised it to his lips. "My pleasure, Lady Natica."

She smiled and blushed again, but said nothing.

Before her silence could become embarrassing, Mariette filled it. "Rene, we will return later. I trust you will be able to employ yourself and the others in some useful service to the household." Her tone left no doubts that harsh punishments would follow her being defied.

"I shall see to it, my Lady." Rene's tone left no doubt in Marek's mind that he found her implied threats to have the substance of fog.

Once outside, Rais helped Lady Mariette into the

wagon. She seated herself squarely in the middle of the back bench. Rais climbed up beside her and she slipped her right hand through the crook of his left arm.

Likewise Marek waited to assist Lady Natica into the front bench of the hearse. Oblivious to his intentions, she vaulted up without his help and grabbed the reins with practiced ease. Marek swung himself onto the bench and waited for her to move over. "My Lady," he coughed lightly as he reached for the reins, "I think it would be best if I drive. I know the route."

Again her cheeks flushed scarlet. "Forgive me, I'm sorry, I . . ."

"You can talk!" Marek smiled. She looked down, but Marek gave her hands a squeeze as he plucked the reins from her grasp. "Forgive me. As Rais will tell you, one of the reasons I had to become good with a sword is because my mouth tends to get me into trouble." He flicked the traces and started the horses forward. "Being from Gull, I've not had much practice with horses and wagons. If things start getting difficult, I'll turn the reins over to you."

Imitating his dark-eyed partner, Marek offered Natica his right elbow. She didn't notice his gesture until he was about to withdraw it, so his elbow retreated as her hand advanced. As soon as Marek realized what had happened, he extended his elbow again, and her hand withdrew. Laughing lightly, he kept his elbow out. "It will not bite, honestly."

Lady Natica smiled nervously and placed her left hand gently inside his elbow.

The wagon rolled from the estate and headed back down the road toward Gull. Before the seaside city could come into sight, Marek turned the wagon off on a pair of wheel-ruts that eventually intersected with an old coast road. They took that back toward the west and north, then cut off on another little-used road when the main route cut back toward the eastern estates.

Marek could feel Lady Natica's nervousness through her hand. To ease her tension, he started a travelogue and spoke loud enough to drown-out the whispers and giggles from behind them. "The place we are going to visit was once a smuggler's cove. Years ago ships could get into it, but a storm about a hundred years ago dredged up tons of sand from the sea bottom and dumped it there."

He pointed at the twin moons hovering near the horizon. "With both of the moons together, the tide will be very low and we might see some things normally hidden by the water." Marek frowned, trying to remember what else Rais had used to convince him the trip would be diverting. "Maybe we'll find some hidden treasure or something."

Natica turned and looked at, then beyond him. She took in the ocean and the twin moons with a concentration Marek recognized from times he studied the glittering fruits of his labors. She was lost in the beauty of the vista and, to Marek, that conferred upon her some of the beauty she drank in.

As the wagon left the main road, it dipped to the left and she crashed into Marek before she could catch herself.

"Are you all right?"

"Yes," she whispered in a small voice. She straightened herself and moved down on the bench. She reluctantly took his elbow when he offered it, but her hand remained woodenly hooked through his arm for the rest of the trip. She nodded when he spoke to her, but her nervousness prevented her from making even the most shallow of conversation.

At trail's end, Marek tugged back on the reins, stopping

the wagon as closely as possible to the sandy, downhill track to the beach. "Rais, escort the ladies to the cove. I will hobble the horses over there in the grass."

"My pleasure . . ." Rais began, but Natica cut him off.

"I'll help Marek." She pointed to the basket. "You two just get the food down there."

She clambered down from the front seat and began to unhitch one of the stallions. Her strong fingers made short work of the buckles. Marek, working on the other horse, admired how quickly she freed her horse. He caught Rais' reproving glance, but shrugged as the other thief and Mariette departed with the basket and two woolen blankets.

Marek led his horse over to the grass. Natica had pulled up a great handful of grass and was using it to rub down her horse, something the beast clearly liked. Marek slipped around to her side and held his hand out. "You should let me do that. It's not a job for one such as you."

Eyebrow arched over a blue eye, she turned on him. "One what?"

"A noble." Marek swallowed hard beneath her harsh gaze. "I mean, I cannot imagine seeing your cousin doing this."

"Me neither." Natica laughed aloud and Marek heard most of her nervousness bleeding out.

"Nice laugh."

"Thank you." She smiled at him, then resumed rubbing the horse down. "I do this all the time at home. Sollern may be a barony, but it is not overly genteel so I'm used to doing things for myself."

She sighed heavily. "I hope you won't think poorly of me, but I'm very uneasy in this situation. You and your friend are much more well-mannered than the men I know. City life is so much different than it is in the north. I'm very uneasy here and, well, acting so formally is very unnatural to me. If it weren't for my cousin's sake, I'd not be along on this trip."

Marek's eyes narrowed. "Do you want to explain that part about 'for your cousin's sake?' "

"Ah," Natica stammered, then looked Marek straight in the eye. "I don't want to hurt your feelings or anything, but Mariette said Rais would not go with her unless she found a companion for you. She said you can never find women yourself and she wanted to help you." She looked him over sharply, making Marek feel like a horse at auction. "You seem nice, so you must really be odd."

A low growl rumbled from Marek's throat. "That's almost exactly what I was told about you. Did your cousin dream up your half of our matching outfits?"

"Yes. Rais did yours?"

"He's going to die." Marek looked back toward the trail down to the cove. "I've half a mind to hitch the horses back up to the wagon and leave the two of them for the tide."

"No, you can't." She tossed the grass down angrily. "It wouldn't be fair to the horses. Besides, I think Mariette wanted to have chaperones along, in case my uncle found out who had called upon her while he was away." She grabbed her horse's halter and led the animal over to a small bush centered in a stand of grass. "There are probably some lead lines in the box under the second bench."

Marek entrusted his horse to her and returned to the wagon. In the box, as she had suggested, he found two slender pieces of rope. Returning, he gave one to her, then tied one through his horse's halter. They both used the lines to tie the horses to the bush.

"I suppose, my Lady, you are correct about Lady Mariette."

"Please, Marek, call me Ti. I can't stand titles, and Ti is what my friends know me as."

"Well, Ti, what do you say we make the best out of this?" Marek removed his cloak and tossed it into the back of the wagon. He offered her his elbow and she took it immediately. "There ought to be tidal pools or other things to explore down there, which will be interesting for us, and give our compatriots time enough alone to get to know each other."

Both of them suppressed laughter as they marched down the cliffside path to the beach. Below, lounging on a blanket spread across white sand, Rais and Mariette looked like a couple straight from a romantic comic opera of the sort currently the rage in Gull. A cutting board lay between them, with cheese—cut from both blocks, Marek noticed—and the sliced remnants of two of the apples arrayed in a sunburst pattern. They sipped the white wine and laughed the cultured little laughs of two people who dearly believe they are supposed to be having fun.

"Marek, Lady Natica, come, join us."

Marek thought he detected a note of urgency in his friend's voice, but he chose to ignore it. "Sorry, Rais, but we want to explore the area for tidal pools or smugglers' treasure." Marek squatted beside the basket and reached in to pull out the remaining two green apples. Without looking back he lofted one to Ti, then shined the other on his satin shirt.

Rais' look would have killed him, or at least maimed him, but Marek bounded up again and moved quickly from its range. Neatly skirting the edge of the water, he headed deeper into the natural harbor and the cul-de-sac formed by the cliff at its end.

Ti shocked her cousin by deftly plucking the thrown

apple from the air and sinking her white teeth into it. With a sharp pop she tore a chunk of flesh from the piece of fruit, then quickly caught up with Marek. Both of them looked back over their shoulders as Rais and Mariette consoled each other with silent expressions of outrage and sympathy.

Satisfied his account with Rais had at least partially been settled, Marek slipped his right arm around Ti's waist and walked with her along the beach. "This channel was once deep enough for an ocean-going vessel to draft it free and clear. The level of the ocean has risen since then, and the cove has filled with sand, so smugglers don't find it very useful anymore."

Ti pointed out a small archway at the base of the cliff. "Did the smugglers store goods in caves?"

"I think so." He looked at her. "Do you want to explore?"

"Yes, definitely." Ti ran over to the entrance and dropped to knees. Apple firmly clutched between her teeth, she crawled on in. After several seconds of hearing nothing but water on the beach and Ti shuffling through the sand, Marek her Ti's voice echoing back from the hole "I feel a bit of a breeze coming through this cave. And there's some light."

"I'm coming in." Marek headed in after her, letting his left hand brush across the top of the short tunnel. He awkwardly squat-waddled forward, but easily felt the breeze she'd mentioned.

"Don't stand up immediately," she cautioned. "The ceiling gets high, but not fast, and you could bump your head."

"Thank you for the warning." He didn't feel it was necessary to tell her the placement of his left hand was an occupational trick he'd learned to prevent such mishaps.

Looking her direction he saw her form dimly silhouetted by light coming from a passage deeper in the cave. As he stood, he could see the low tunnel opened into a small antechamber that definitely showed signs of having been worked by the hand of man.

The opening in which Ti stood was no larger than a normal doorway and faced inland. As he approached her, he saw a soft, green glow on her face. The light cast shadows that etched her puzzlement onto her features. She took a couple steps forward, as if entranced by whatever she saw. When he reached out and touched her arm, she started, then turned to face him.

"What is it, Ti?"

She shrugged and moved out of the way. Beyond her, in a huge cavern, Marek saw a waveless ocean reflecting the green light. He also saw the source of the green light and suddenly understood the questioning look on Ti's face.

Shaking himself, he turned to her. "Go get Rais. Tell him to get the rest of the rope and the lantern from the box in the wagon."

She turned to leave, but he caught her hand. "And, Ti, tell him to bring his sword."

Marek knew the look on Rais' face very well. "What do you think, Rais?"

"I see it, but I cannot really believe it is there." Rais stroked his goatee, barely aware that Lady Mariette hung on his left shoulder, using his body as a shield against the thing beyond the small opening.

The massive cavern looked to Marek easily large enough to encompass the whole of the Prince's palace were it to be transplanted from the highest hill in Gull. Its size, and even the fact that it was filled with water, did not so much surprise him because he had heard of such things before. What surprised him, and clearly baffled Rais, was the ship floating on the subterranean sea. The rigging on the large ship glowed with a mossy luminescence, providing the green illumination.

Rais squinted at the ship, then shook his head. "It's definitely the *Wind Tiger*. Even if the name was not painted on the hull, those malachite eyes riding up front would be enough proof for me."

Rais' mention of the ship's name freed an involuntary gasp from Lady Mariette's lips. She tightened her grip on Rais' shoulder and moved so only her eyes peered over his shoulder. Without looking back at her, Rais patted her hand.

Ti took advantage of the opening to look at the ship again. "So, what was the *Wind Tiger*?"

Marek seated himself on a wave-worn rock just inside the large cavern. "The *Wind Tiger* was the ship used by a pirate who sailed these waters about a century ago. The captain of the ship, Solana ni-Jian, was a warrior-woman of legendary skill. Her abilities with magic were also impressive, which made her unique and quite deadly. There's more than one story about her using sorcery to destroy or elude forces chasing her."

Rais nodded in agreement. "There's more fact to those legends than fiction. Her conquests, on the high seas and in the beds of kings and emperors, made her a whole host of friends and enemies. It is said most leaders pursued her more to possess her than to end her bloody reign of the Range Sea. Even the Rangers, the pirates who normally control the waters around Gull and the island of Phoron, could not capture her. It is said she even found and dared attack their island headquarters. Each raid was more daring than the last, and each haul was more valuable.

"Then, suddenly, she passed into legend. It was said the Rangers had cornered her, but the storm that sealed this cove also scattered their war-fleet and allowed her to escape. She was never caught, just never seen again. Stories varied from her being killed outright by a rival wizard to her being dragged to the Sea's floor to become the consort of the Sea god, Nadon."

Marek pitched a small stone into the inland sea and watched the ripples spread out. "Solana became a blood-drinking witch who would come and take all the bad children in Gull away on the *Wind Tiger* to grow them into coral or jellyfish. Some folks really believe those stories."

Mariette shrunk even further behind Rais.

Rais dropped to one knee and pointed back at the wall of the cavern nearest the cove. "Before the storm there must have been an opening large enough to allow the *Wind Tiger* to get into this cavern. On that night, the *Wind Tiger* must have run in there for cover. The storm dumped enough sand into the cove to trap the ship. They stayed here and died."

Ti rested balled fists on her hips. "Died? Wouldn't they have left this place through this cave?"

Rais sucked air in through clenched teeth. "Perhaps not. There was a story that said Solanna and her crew were married to the ship, or bound to it through some ritual. It's been said the *Wind Tiger* was more than a ship. For them, abandoning the ship might have been like leaving a lover behind."

"For them it might never have even seemed an option." As Marek spoke, he could imagine hearing his words echoed by the ship's ghostly crew.

Ti pointed toward the shoreline nearest the *Wind Tiger*.

"Looks like a ledge that rises up to deck level. I bet we could find an old gangplank or use the rope to get ourselves aboard."

Marek stood up and brushed sand from the seat of his pants. "The wood might be rotten, but there is no telling what might be riding in the hold."

"True, indeed." The broad grin on Rais' face narrowed as he felt trembling hands pressed against his back. He turned and took Mariette's hands in his own. "Come on, it will be exciting. It will be an adventure. There is nothing for you to worry about."

She seemed childlike in her terror. "Do you promise nothing will go wrong?"

"Of course, I'm not going to let you get hurt."

Mariette nestled herself in beneath his arm as Rais drew his cloak about her shoulders.

The quartet, with Marek and Ti in the lead, worked their way along the shoreline to the ledge Ti had noticed earlier. From the ledge, Marek leaped to the *Wind Tiger*'s deck, then used the rope Rais tossed to him to secure the ship to a stalagmite. Ti jumped to Marek's side, then Rais helped Lady Mariette onto the deck.

Marek pointed to the deckhouse where a skeleton could be seen manning the wheel. "It appears at least one of them refused to abandon ship."

"I wonder if he remained behind to pilot the ship into its next incarnation?" Rais watched the skeleton, as if expecting an answer. When none came, the dark-haired rogue smiled to try to reassure the shivering Mariette.

Marek gingerly worked his way across the deck. "Looks like hatch cover to the hold has fallen through." With one step he discovered a board that tipped up and almost caught Rais in the chin.

Crouched down on one knee, Ti ran her hand across the planking. "This is very strange. If this is the *Wind Tiger*, and it was lost a century ago, the wood should be rotted through."

Marek tested one rung of the ladder leading down into the hold. "Seems solid enough to me." He started to descend, but the green shadows from above created more shadows than were good for his very active imagination. "If you want to light the lantern and bring it down, Ti, I think it would be most helpful." Swallowing his terror, he continued his blind descent, both pleased and unnerved to hear no rats.

At the bottom of the ladder he found things solid and fairly dry. Above him Ti mounted the ladder and worked her way down, with the lantern in hand. When she got halfway down, a scream from above stopped her. Marek dropped a hand to the hilt of his rapier, but Rais appeared at the hold and held his hands out to calm both of them.

"It's nothing." Rais stopped as Marek heard some whimpering. "All right, it's not nothing, but it is not significant." Rais looked down into the hold. "Lady Mariette thought she saw something pulse out green light near the prow. Since we've boarded the ship, we've disturbed the water and the reflections make for all sorts of illusions."

Marek steadied Ti with his hands around her waist as she reached the foot of the ladder. Above, Rais and Mariette started their own climb to the hold, but Marek and Ti chose not to wait for them before conducting their survey of the hold. Ti turned from the ladder and let her lantern's light play over the cargo.

Boxes and crates were scattered haphazardly throughout the hold. Wooden barrels and casks had been crushed, boxes had burst open and cloth sacks had mildewed to nothingness. Their contents were strewn around the hold chaotically, carpeting it with a sparkling cloak of gold and jewels.

"Rais, it looks as if the *Wind Tiger* took damage as it ran from the Rangers and the storm." He stooped and picked up a shiny gold coin. Holding it up so Ti would play the lantern-light over it, he commented, "Minted over a hundred years ago and it still looks absolutely new."

"There has to be a fortune here," she breathed reverently.

He pitched the coin back on the pile. "Several fortunes, by the looks of it. Some of these are Imperial coins. Solana and the *Wind Tiger* really roamed the seas and raided at will."

"Shine the lantern over here, please." On the other side of the ladder, Rais knelt beside a chest that lacked a top. The light swung around and burned bloody life into a string of seven rubies set in a silver necklace. "Looks as though the crew sorted their treasure before stowing it." He lofted the necklace to Marek.

Holding it close to Ti's lantern, Marek gently fingered the piece of jewelry. "Superior workmanship and gorgeous gems. It has got to be from the continent. Beautiful." The thief moved from the light and looped the necklace around Ti's throat. "And it looks even more beautiful there."

Not to be outdone, Rais pulled a sapphire-encrusted bracelet of gold from the shattered chest and snapped it around Lady Mariette's left wrist. They crossed to the light and all four admired Mariette's latest acquisition.

Mariette, moving the bracelet through the light so it flashed and glittered, became almost as radiant as the bracelet itself. She reached up and caressed Rais' cheek with her unencumbered hand. "Oh, Rais, it is wonderful."

She kissed her fingers and pressed them to his lips.

"I hoped you would like it." Rais smiled, but Marek could tell his friend would have preferred a kiss transferred to his lips by a more direct means.

Lady Mariette looked thoughtful for a moment, then laughed. "I see it all now. You and Marek arranged all this for Natica and me, did you not? You had someone build all of this special for us, correct?" A smile lit her features and the nervous tremor in her voice all but vanished.

"Of course they did, cousin." Ti clapped her hands and stared hard at Marek. "How clever of you to figure it out. They just wanted to give each of us a bit of a scare to make these gifts more memorable."

Taking his cue from Ti, Marek sighed and shook his head. "I told you she would figure it out, Rais. We should have known better than to try to fool her."

"You were right. I'm sorry I doubted you." Rais gently brushed his hand down Mariette's spine. "I should have known."

"Yes, you should have," Mariette scolded him lightly. With each statement she brightened and became more of herself.

Suddenly the ship lurched as if it had been rammed. Rais crashed into the treasure chest, twisting just enough to catch Lady Mariette as she fell. Ti's feet flew out from under her, dumping her on the carpet of gold coins, but she managed to keep the lantern from smashing on the hard deck. Marek flew across the hold, but managed to grab the ladder to the deck before he went down.

Marek shot a glance at his partner. "What in the seven hells was that?"

"I don't know." Rais gently eased Lady Mariette from his lap. "We'd best get topside and find out!"

198

"Your tricks won't work anymore," she smiled knowingly.

Marek scrambled up the ladder like a monkey being chased by a leopard. Like the leopard, Rais followed him quickly. Reaching the deck, Marek stopped and drew his rapier. "We have trouble, my friend."

Rais' head cleared the hatchway. "Big trouble."

The hatch leading back to the crew's quarters stood open. Skeletal sailors with an unholy green light festering in empty eye sockets shuffled onto the deck. Patches of skin still clung to the skulls or arms of some while moth-eaten remnants of clothing covered others. The most dangerous looking ones had hooks mounted where hands should have been while the unmaimed undead just flexed bony fingers.

Once Rais reached the deck, the sailors oriented on the thieves. "Damn, magic! Solana must have placed a curse on this ship."

"The glow is in their heads. Maybe . . ." Marek dashed forward and slashed at one of the skeletons. The overhand blow sliced off the bowl of the sailor's skull. The pulsing green mist therein clutched at the sword with thready tendrils, then evaporated. The skeleton collapsed in a pile of bones and clothes dust.

"Good." Rais backed toward the place where the party had first boarded the *Wind Tiger*. "I'll hold them off. You get the ladies over here and we'll escape."

"OOH, scary monsters and fighting!" Lady Mariette cooed as she stepped from the hold. "Natica, come look at this. They look so brave."

Ti reached the deck right behind her, and Marek could tell from the expression on her face that she reached a different conclusion than her cousin. "Mare, take the lantern here." Ti ran to the mainmast and armed herself with a belaying pin. "Cousin, come, this way to the shore."

Two of the crew moved to surround Marek, and the thief found himself facing foes who moved with more intelligence than he would have imagined in the undead. He parried the hook-slash by one of them, but knew the sailor at his back had a clean shot at him. He whirled and brought his rapier up in a windmill parry, but braced himself against its ivory talons ripping through his flesh.

The blow he expected never came. The deck plank between the skeleton's legs shot up, pulverizing its pelvis into bone splinters and dust. The sailor's torso fell to the deck and Marek leaped up above its slashing arms, then snap-kicked its skull toward the deckhouse. He tossed a wink at Ti, whose foot had been applied to the far end of the plank to save his life, then whirled and slashed his way free of the encirclement the skeletal crew had attempted.

Ducking, dodging, and whittling at his foes, Marek moved toward the wheeldeck to get the ship's superstructure at his back. The battle struck him as bizarre because against living foes his attacks would have been more precise and conservative. When fighting against flesh and blood, a well-placed thrust could pierce a vital organ or open an artery. Pain and fear often made even minor wounds sufficient to force a foe from the field of combat.

Against the skeletons, however, even the most savage of assaults did not stop them. He could slash off a hand, but it would continue to inch like a spider across the deck after him, and the skeleton would have two sharpened bones to poke at him. As he felt the stairs to the wheeldeck at his back, Marek knew it was only a matter of time before the skeletons overwhelmed Rais and him.

"Look out, Marek," Lady Mariette called to him.

Her voice had all the conviction of a play-goer yelling a

warning to a character on stage, but he availed himself of it. He lay flat back against the stairs as skeletal claws raked through where his head had been. Reaching up, he entangled the fingers of his left hand in the skeleton's ribs and heaved them at the boneyard of sailors tearing at his boots. The sailor's impact fragmented several of its allies, buying Marek enough time to scramble up to the wheeldeck and survey the battlefield.

Below, Rais swore sharply at the bone sailors pressing him in his defense of the escape route. He swept the shins from one skeleton that ventured too close, but it continued to crawl forward as two others rushed him from the sides. As the first grabbed at his boots, another trio surged forward. As Marek watched in horror, Rais went down beneath an ivory avalanche.

Before Marek could act, Rais rose from amid his foes like a whale rising to crush the puny whaling boats tormenting it. Both hands wrapped firmly around the hilt of his sword, he slashed right and left. Roaring a wordless challenge he shook himself, scattering fingerbones enmeshed in his clothing. Chopping and stomping without any regard to finesse or style, Rais let his fury guide his scything blade. Kicking his way free of the crippled skeleton at his feet, he carried his attack forward and the battered skeletons retreated.

"Mariette, Natica, move. Get to the shore now!" Rais' growled command befitted the man who had cleared the pathway to safety. His jacket had been shredded enough to reveal the shirt beneath. The shirt itself had grown spotty with blood. His cloak hung in tatters from his shoulders and his boots were a patchwork of long scratches and bite marks.

Hypnotized by the spectacle of his friend's rise and fall,

Marek almost failed to notice the clicking approach of the dagger-wielding skeleton attempting to sneak up behind him. With a grin, the thief reached out and grabbed a line hanging down from the mast. Laughing aloud, he swung from the wheeldeck, across the maindeck, to the foredeck. Alighting easily on the railing, the thief turned and sent the rope back to his waiting skeletal foe.

The ossified swashbuckler's bony fingers wrapped themselves around the rope as it returned. With a heave back and lunge forward, the undead pirate clenched his dagger in his teeth and launched himself through the air. As he flew, the wind tore away the last threads of his clothing, leaving him clad in dried boots and a stiff belt. Drawing closer to Marek, the green light in his eyes pulsed with a hunger.

Seconds before the skeleton reached the foredeck, Marek jumped out and down to the maindeck, slashing his rapier through the rope in the same motion. The skeleton, flying fast and dropping a foot as the rope parted, slammed full force into the foredeck railing. Powdered bone dusted the railing itself as a spray of bone chips skittered across the foredeck. Chunks of shattered bone likewise showered down upon Marek's head and clattered on the maindeck.

Shaking bone flakes from his hair, he crossed to where Rais stood holding the skeletons at bay. He helped Ti get Mariette up onto the ledge, then started to assist her evacuation of the ship, but a guttercurse from Rais stopped him.

"Damn, Marek, we're in serious trouble."

"This hasn't been serious enough?" Marek's surprised expression melted into one that mirrored Rais' look of despair. "Yeah, serious."

Solana had appeared before the wheeldeck.

The pulsating green light that had shone in the eyes of the crew surrounded, suffused and defined her skeletal form. The translucent glow layered flesh onto her bones and gave them a tantalizing glimpse of the beauty she had once known. Naked in the illusion, her taut, slender body triggered a flash of desire in both men.

The expression on her exquisite face killed it again.

Solana's ghostly form surveyed the damage, and disbelief of what she saw locked her face into a deathmask of fury and outrage. Her crew, scattered and broken, limped and crawled toward her as if scraps of iron drawn to a lodestone. Hands raised in supplication and jaws clicking out pleas for forgiveness, the crew wordlessly begged for protection and revenge.

Even as the green light sought to recreate her, it was not enough to fully mask the horror she had become. Bare bones could be seen through her emerald flesh. Unruly wisps of brittle, once-black hair escaped the magical aura enfolding her. No sounds issued from her mouth even though her jaw worked up and down. Her green lips formed words that Marek and Rais could only guess at, but their purpose went unquestioned.

Where the crew's skill at arms had failed to destroy the intruders, her sorcery would succeed.

Marek knew with an unquestionable certainty that they were going to die if he didn't do something. He wanted to act, but just looking at Solana seemed to sap his will from him. He shot a sidelong glance at his partner and hoped he was not wearing the same slack-jawed expression on his face.

Stepping up beside him, Ti screwed her left eye shut and let fly with the belaying pin. It shot in at the revenant captain and clearly had sufficient force to blast her bones apart. Marek felt his heart leap, but as the wooden pin reached the nimbus surrounding the witch, it whirled around her. With a life of its own, the belaying pin sailed across the deck and replaced itself in the rack.

"Sorry, Marek," she whispered as she stooped to arm herself with a femur.

The spell broken by her action, Marek shook himself. "At least you tried." He reached down and stroked her hair. "I have a question for you, Ti."

"Yes?"

"What do you want to be in your next life?"

"Wiser." As she touched the femur, the bone twitched. It glowed green and twisted itself free of her grasp. As a tendril of green light from the witch touched it, the bone rolled and thump-bumped across the deck toward Solana.

Ti clutched her hand to her breast. "Cold."

Clouds of green mist drifted away from the sorceress and coalesced into tiny whirlwinds that gathered the scattered and broken pieces of bone from where they lay on the deck. The small tornadoes rattled and clattered about as they bore their treasures back to Solana. Rais hissed and nearly collapsed as one mistdevil swirled about him and snatched up the remains of his fallen victims. "Evil." He sank to his knees, wrapping his arms around his chest.

Only vaguely aware of his friend's plight, Marek again found his gaze drawn to Solana. "By the gods!" His rapier clattered to the deck as what he saw took his breath away. Unconsciously he reached out for Ti and tried to shield her with his own body.

"We're done," she whispered in his ear.

The whirlwinds of green mist returned to Solana, but did not slow or stop their spinning. Instead they combined into one giant cyclone that stripped away all of the bones below her neck. The pulsing light in her eyes grew in intensity as the emerald and ivory storm shrieked around her.

The light's brightness threatened to obscure the heart of the storm, but then it cleared and let the interlopers see everything.

Solana and her sorcery were rebuilding herself and her crew.

Five pirate skulls surrounded Solana's skull like a grim collar. Vertebrae, formed of smaller bones fused together like half-melted lumps of iron, stacked themselves into a bonewhite snake that joined to the back of her skull and extended for another foot above it. Femurs, warped and reshaped by magic, lined up to form a new ribcage. With grinding clicks they locked into place along the spine. Two pairs of shoulders, one a foot above the other, linked into the spine above the ribs and prepared themselves to receive arms. Six upper arm bones, braided by sorcery, slid into place in the shoulder girdles, while shin bones were pressed into service to provide the creature's forearms. Bone chips and heel bones served as wristbones while forearm bones dropped into place to create the creature's paws. Ribs— some broken, others whole—capped the fingers with a nasty quartet of claws.

Marek noticed the creature had no thumbs and he knew that was because it was not designed to grab anything.

A magically melted bone plaster congealed into the graveyard beast's pelvis. With a thundercrack the spine mated itself to the broad, bony bowl. Woven thigh and shin bones served the creature as they had served the individual pirates. Bits of fractured skulls served as kneecaps, while kneecaps and the knobby ends of long bones condensed into the monster's ankles. The pattern of formation for the upper paws repeated themselves in the lower, with the rib-claws shorter but no less deadly.

A tail of fused vertebrae steadied the creature, while

shoulderblades ran like sharkfins from one end of the spine to the other.

Life pulsed from the center of the monster outward. The green light in Solana's eyes dimmed, then flared malevolently in the eye sockets of the skulls that surrounded her. The verdant glow then seeped from them and poured over the skeleton through arterial pathways. With power caressing its ivory form, the creature flexed its paws and took its first tentative step forward.

Rais blanched as he looked up from where he knelt. Ti, her eyes wide with terror, reached behind to steady herself against the ship's railing. Marek, unable to tear his eyes away from the horror shambling toward him, stooped and felt around for his sword. Only Lady Mariette, safe on the shore and wrapped in her mad fantasy, seemed unaffected by the monster's appearance or threat. She clapped her hands and laughed politely at the sight of the creature.

"Ti, get ready to throw the lantern at it." Rais slowly stood. "Marek and I will distract it."

"Make your aim true," Marek whispered as he moved to the left.

"One problem with that plan, Rais." Ti's voice could barely be heard above her cousin's giggling. "Mariette has the lantern."

Marek's clear voice drowned out Rais' groan. "Lady Mariette, this is your chance to be a heroine. Throw the lantern at the monster." He tried to make his voice sound as light and carefree as possible, but his growing panic threaded a note of command into it.

He dove low and to the left, avoiding the slashing pair of paws on the monster's right side. Ti dashed back behind Rais, circling around the beast's left side. Rais shifted his sword to his left hand and pulled his boot-knife. Balancing its tip between thumb and forefinger, he whipped it forward.

Spinning swiftly, the blade slipped between two ribs and cracked one of the heart-skulls. Marek noted the pulse of power to the left leg had been dimmed as green energy played along the length of the dagger. "Good toss. We can hurt it."

The creature reoriented itself on Rais, clearly finding him the most obvious threat to its continued existence. The scar-faced thief tightened his grip on his sword as the creature moved it, its four arms held wide for a deadly, crushing hug. "Come on, witch, my life for my friends is a fair trade."

In the sepulchral tones Rais used, Marek sensed his friend's decision to sell his life dearly. "Quick, Ti, get its tail!" Sheathing his sword in the creature's pelvis, Marek grabbed the tail. Ignoring the burning cold washing over their hands in successive waves, both Marek and Ti hauled back on the creature's tail, unbalancing it.

"Now, Mariette, throw the lantern!" Ti screamed.

Mariette's laughter greeted the command with disbelief.

Rais broke to the creature's left as the skeletal beast spun to its right. The tail jerked Marek from his feet and bowled Ti over. She rolled from beneath it and levered herself up to her feet, while Rais rushed forward. His sword raised hilt first over his head, he stabbed down with both hands, driving the blade through the creature's tail and deep into the deck.

Whirling, he thrust both clutching hands back at Mariette. "Dammit, you frivolous bitch, throw the lantern!"

Mariette's laughter ended as if Rais had strangled her from afar. "How dare you!" she shrieked. Fire in her eyes, she threw the lantern at him.

Her aim was good.

That she'd ignored the monster in front of Rais was better.

The lantern, still half full of oil, exploded as it hit the monster's left leg. Oily, black smoke wreathed the beast, blackening its ivory skeleton. Flames greedily licked at it and spread over the deck in a growing pool of fire.

"Mariette, run for the cove." Marek hoped she heard his shout above the crackle of the conflagration raging amidships. "Ti, can you swim?"

"Like a fish."

"Over the side, then." He watched her dive cleanly into the water, then followed her. As he broke the surface of the dark sea, he looked back to see Rais dive from the railing. Behind him, bones black within the golden firelight, the monster swiped helplessly at the fleeing thieves.

Swimming as fast as they could, the trio reached the entrance to the cavern just as Mariette completed her roundabout circuit of the trapped sea. She stared past them as they dragged themselves dripping to the shore. "No game?"

"No game," Ti assured her.

"The eyes." Mariette's face grew slack as she pointed back toward the ship. "The eyes."

The green malachite eyes had become radiant enough to rival the fire shooting up the mainmast. The mooring line with which they'd tied the *Wind Tiger* to the shore parted with a thunderous snap that echoed throughout the cavern. Decks, rigging and masts ablaze, the ship drove at them.

Marek felt sheer terror jolt energy through him. "To the tunnel. Get out, now!"

"Can't, the tide's come in—the passage is underwater." Frustration underscored Ti's words. "Mariette refuses to swim."

"Force her," Rais snarled. The cavern brightened around him as the *Wind Tiger* approached. Water curled high and foaming from the ship, and the wind muffled the roar of the flames gnawing into the ship's back.

Mariette's scream of outrage died with a gurgle as Ti dragged her beneath the water. Marek and Rais crowed into the small antechamber. Water splashed up as they ran through the knee-high depths, then plunged forward into the safety of the water.

Sparks streaked through the small chamber and ricocheted off the stone walls as the *Wind Tiger* rammed its prow into the mouth of the small cave. Planks splintered and snapped. The keel cracked and yawned open like a long bone split for the marrow. Burning fragments of the ship hissed as they extinguished themselves in the water.

Sitting up, Marek let the arm with which he'd shielded his face slowly fall. He glanced back at the *Wind Tiger* and saw one of its eyes glaring at him. He'd seen that look before, in the eyes of a dying man watching his killer walk away. Shaken and subdued, the thief ducked beneath the water and left the ship to die alone.

My promise, my promise! The *Wind Tiger*'s anguish silently filled the cave as it watched the last of the murderers disappear out the tunnel. Despair flooded it like the water gushing into its shattered hold. *How could mere mortals do what nature and empires could not? How? Why?*

Its anger burned hotter than the fires raging over its decks. It tried to hold on to its fury, but as the fire consumed it, its reason for wanting to cling to life also burned. With the shattering of its promise, the *Wind Tiger*'s tenacious grip on immortality slackened.

Life drained from the malachite eye that stared after the

thieves. The eye blackened and tightened as if to prevent the escape of the coppery tear forming in its corner. The tear hung poised, then, as life fled from the ship, the tear scorched a furrow down the hull of the ship. It flowed onto a small ledge above the waterline, safe . . .

Forever.

"Blood Duty" was one of those tiny stories that appears in the brain fully formed. I was at Indian School and 16th Street when it hit me. I drove home and wrote it. It collected a few rejection slips; then nine years later Roger Zelazny bought it for his anthology, ***Warriors of Blood and Dream***.

Blood Duty

The night was as black as blindness. I only saw him because he was blacker than that black. He was dark and cold, an obsidian statue moving through the night, padding silently across the tiled roof overhanging the courtyard. He was as black as the death he carried in him.

He paused as the wind changed, waiting for it to carry to him a scent, a sound, a clue to the identity of the one who waited for him. He knew someone was there, someone had to be here. Lord Kusunoki would not be unprotected. He would slay the one who waited, then slay the Lord. Then his treachery would be complete.

He crouched and moved to the roof's edge. Another would have lost him without the night sky to offer contrast, but I did not. I knew where to look. I knew where he would move. I knew him better than he knew himself.

He jumped down to the courtyard floor. Soft leather tabi allowed his toes to grip the stones while his powerful legs absorbed the impact of the drop. His left hand reached out and touched the ground to balance him. His right hand bore a fire-blackened katana. Again he searched the courtyard for the guardian.

I let him see me. I did not move from the shadows or

draw my weapon. I made no sound to challenge him. I just let him see me.

He gave no outward evidence of the shock—shock at having missed the guardian before; shock at learning who it was. He rose to his full height and bowed to me. "The others honor me by setting you out for my capture." His tone mocked me.

I returned his bow. He thought I could not read his face, hidden as it was by the cloth mask. He believed he was closed to me, but I read his eyes and his stance, even his breathing. He was surprised, pleased and confident.

I narrowed my eyes. "The others decided you would not dare approach this way and are waiting for you by the south wall."

His mask tightened across his face, revealing a hidden smile. More confidence and now contempt. "Woman, you are old. Leave and I will spare your life." His words were reassuring, offering me an escape. It was the silence between the hisses of a snake.

I shook my head. "Leave, and dishonor my clan as you have? I would sooner slit my belly. You owe a debt to me and my clan. I will collect it." I saw his smile fade. "I will collect it now."

His eyes tightened, a conscious effort to fight his true feelings. Disbelief filled them, backed by memories. Then the coldness, the black void of his life, sucked all but hatred from his eyes. "Can you collect that debt, woman? It is not too much for you to bear?"

I refused to join his game of pettiness, of blaming others for acts he had committed, fully cognizant of the consequences for him and for me. "The debt is vast. My husband's life, taken by his own hand. The same of Lord Kusunoki refusing me the same surcease. The dishonor my clan has felt since your betrayal. It is a great debt, one that must be collected before you build upon it. But it is not for me to carry. It is yours to bear."

His smile returned and power shook his frame. "I will kill you, woman, and you cannot kill me. You know that."

I felt my stomach writhe. "We love each other . . ."

"You love me. I have no more love . . . none for you, in any event."

"Your lack of love is obvious, by your actions here and in the past." I concentrated on my breathing, centering myself and purging myself of fury and hurt. "If you had love, you would kill yourself now to repair some of the damage you have done." I calmed myself more. My action was of love and therefore could have no anger or hatred in it. "Would you take tea with me first?"

His body shook with the laughter he could not voice. "I have wasted enough time. Come and I will kill you."

I stepped from the shadow and faced him. We were similarly attired, from tabi and hakama up to quilted jacket, gloves and hooded mask. Our clothing was black. My katana, like his, had been blackened over a sooty flame. Our blades were invisible in the darkness.

We bowed to each other, his bow a fraction deeper than mine, but not out of respect, only out of habit. His mind rebelled, but his body performed as it had many times before. We straightened, five paces apart, and each struck a guard.

Both hands on my sword's hilt, I had the weapon cocked high by my right ear. My stance was low and wide. My left leg was nearest him: my left side lay open.

His blade almost vanished within his body's silhouette. His stance was good, his legs wide enough apart and tensed to spring. He held his sword before him, hilt to tip, protecting him groin to eyes.

We waited.

An eternity passed without notice. We were both alive and dead. An attack would take centuries to reach the opponent, but the counterstrike would take less than a heartbeat. It was a game of waiting where time could not be noticed, for if time entered the mind, impatience would come with it.

In the game of waiting, impatience is death.

Stars shot through the heavens, omens to be read by monks and soothsayers. That one might be my death, or his. Were the gods mocking us with skysparks like those that would fly when our blades met?

If our blades met.

In an instant, an infinite moment, it began and was finished. In our black clothing, surrounded by darkness, wielding razor-edged steel that could not be seen, we were shadow within shadow. Like tendrils of oily smoke we drew together, twisted about each other, passed through each other. In that instant, as it had been before, we were one.

This time there was a difference. Before, life and creation was our concern. Now death and corruption was the fruit of our labors.

Beyond him I turned, and likewise he turned. Then he stopped turning. His knees buckled, his sword flew. His hands fell to his stomach and tried to stem the tide of entrails abandoning him. He stared at me, eyes now wide. His body, his eyes, said he was afraid.

He did not voice his fear. Like his laughter, it was for no one but himself.

I watched him die, the man I'd killed. The man who had betrayed my clan and wished to assassinate my Lord. I watched him with remorse and grief, for when love dies that is all there can be.

And when he was dead, I buried my son.

"When You're Dead . . ." was written for the anthology *Historical Hauntings*, edited by Jean Rabe. I'd agreed to do a ghost story even though I don't write horror. I wasn't certain *what* I was going to write until a trip to Las Vegas. I emerged from a casino into the bright sunshine and just saw the escape from a dark, dim underground. From there the rest was easy.

When You're Dead . . .

I felt dead, and it was all Lancaster Dean's fault.

Pain pulsed through my skull. I was pretty sure it was cracked, but at least it wasn't crushed like the hard-hat that had protected it for a short while anyway. I saw the remains of it flattened beneath a broken concrete beam, with a twisted piece of rebar stabbed straight down through it. Something about that prompted me to smile and I felt the blood coating the right side of my face crack.

Despite having my brains feel like someone had used an in-the-egg-scrambler on them, the cracking of the blood registered and sent a jolt through me. I'd been out long enough for the blood to clot and dry. That wasn't good, because I didn't hear any sounds of digging. *And if they aren't digging . . .*

I did a quick inventory of body parts and found all of them still attached—many things bruised, but nothing busted. I snorted once, blowing out a bubble of bloody mucus that I cleared away with a hand, then, for lack of anything better, I wiped it on a pant leg. If I was going to get out of here, neatness points wouldn't count for much. Then I laughed, knowing my mom would be happy to know I had clean underwear on for when they took me to the hospital later.

One solid knock on your head, and your thinking takes on a distinctly non-linear nature.

I forced myself to think past the fog of pain, and began a search for my cell phone. The only light I had came from a few of those battery-powered emergency lights, and the other ones that Lancaster Dean—"the Elusive Dean of Magic"—had placed around for his TV special. As near as I could tell that was the *only* favor he'd done me; and it wasn't close to enough as far as I was concerned.

For a half second I considered that it might not all be his fault. The Scottsdale Galleria was this pink monstrosity of a building that had been erected in downtown Scottsdale as an upscale mall. It had failed miserably in that job, being more of a ghost town than a commercial center. It went bust, then got used as a set in a couple of movies. *Tank Girl* was the most notable of these, giving you an idea of how bad things were. Then it housed a traveling Smithsonian display for a bit, but only after it failed to become a sports bar complex and, after that, failed to become a corporate center.

The building was so snakebit, I don't think they could have made it work as a homeless shelter.

Some genius at City Hall decided it had to go, and what better way to attract attention to Scottsdale than to have the building blown up on a magician's made-for-TV special? Lance Burton and David Copperfield passed on the project—they're just too classy. I guess it's good Siegfried and Roy also passed or I'd have been trapped with big cats who were pissed off. I'm sure other modern Houdinis turned the city down, then they got to Lancaster Dean.

I don't know magicians from a hole in the ground—just those I see billed on signs in Vegas—but folks made a big deal about getting Dean. The usual press kiss-up went on, so all the local news outlets told of his background. You know local TV—all press releases, all the time.

According to the legend he died when he was eight—a cub scout pal of his still swears he had no pulse after a fall—and he said he escaped from death and came back. Having accomplished that greatest escape, he launched a career as an escape artist. None of the newsies described his career as "modest" but they used all the words they use when they wished they *could* say modest.

All I know is that for me, he was a pain in the ass. I'd gone into the Galleria to make the final check on the explosives, just to make sure things were wired up perfectly, that the right pillars would be blown, so the building would come down folding in on itself, and not take out the other buildings nearby. Controlled implosion it's called, and we'd set up to do it right. Dean made the inspection a pain by having his set dressing scattered around and insisting he'd do a final inspection after mine, "just to make sure things were all set."

If everything that clown knew about explosives was C-4, it wouldn't have been enough to blow his toupee an inch off his scalp.

And certainly all the C-4 we had in the Galleria couldn't have cracked his ego.

I only found pieces of the cell phone. My Walkman survived fine, stayed clipped to my belt and everything. I'd not been listening to it while making my inspection. I'd just taken to wearing it when having to deal with Dean, putting it on and cranking up tunes when I couldn't stand listening to him tell me how to do my job anymore.

I tuned it into the local talk station and got confirmation of what I already knew. "Welcome back to 620 Talk Radio.

We have with us Lancaster Dean. Mr. Dean, just to recap . . ."

I could see Dean preening as he spoke—not caring that it was radio—and it set my teeth on edge. "We have one man down in there. A very brave man, very brave. He was doing an inspection of the explosives and . . . I should have been in there with him, but he's a trained professional."

"Now, pending notification of next of kin, they've not released his name, but we know he's thirty-five, a demolitions engineer . . ."

"Right and, well, Tom, if by some miracle you can hear my voice, you have to know we're coming for you. I swear to you, Pat, and all your listeners, that I'm not going to let Tom die down in there. I've been talking with the rescue team and when we go in . . ."

"Did you say 'we'?"

"He's in there because of me. How could I not . . . ?" Dean's voice broke, then returned thick with emotion and subdued. "The team is working on some initial problems, but I'm in constant consultation with them, and I'm sure we'll be moving fast."

I turned the Walkman off and hugged my knees to my chest. The reason there was no digging, and no rescue team coming in yet was the same reason I'd survived. Something had set off *some* of the charges, not all of them. Static electricity could have, but that was unlikely. Thunderstorms blow up quickly in the desert, but it wasn't the season and I'd have been called if that looked possible. Could have been some idiot ran a truck into a power pole or substation and caused a huge arc; but whatever it was, it blew some of the charges, leaving an unstable building sown with explosives for the rescue crew to try to figure out.

This building was a danger for them, and that meant it was a tomb for me.

"There you are. C'mon, let's go. You don't have much time."

I whipped my head around, which was *not* the thing to do with a concussion. The world kind of sizzled, as if a sparkler had been pressed up close to each eyeball, then things came back into focus. I saw this little guy, little ball of muscles, wearing a white shirt and tuxedo pants standing there. His sleeves were rolled up to the elbow and his dark eyes half-glowed. Grim determination settled over his face, and he impatiently waved me onward.

I got up to follow, with about a billion questions lining up in my brain, but the world began to defocus again, scattering them. I reached up and touched a low ceiling, steadying myself. "How did you . . . ?"

He glanced back at me from within a narrow crack in a wall. "We've got to get out of here. It's not going to be easy, but given what it took to get this far, the rest will not be that hard."

I shook my head, which is also not recommended with a concussion. "Can't get out." I tapped the earphones. "Radio says the building is unstable."

"Radio? Where?"

I shifted to show him the unit on my hip. "It made it through better than I did. We're stuck."

"So that's it, you're just going to give up?"

"Don't have a choice, do I?" I slowly lowered myself to my knees. "They'll think of a way to get us out."

"The only person getting you out is you." He came back into the small chamber where I knelt and towered over me. "Let me tell you something, son. Life is a grand adventure, and you don't live it by waiting. If you're right, that you're dead, and you do nothing, then you'll stay here and faint from thirst and die. *Or,* even if you *are* right, you can be out of this place. You can be farther along, working your way out. You might still die, but they'll see you didn't lie down and die. You kept fighting to the end. It might be that you're going to be remembered as the guy who died here, but better to be remembered as the guy who died trying to get out, not trapped."

Then he winked at me. "And, if I'm right, this will be the greatest escape this town has ever seen."

It wasn't like he hypnotized me or anything, but something in his words just thundered through me. I struggled to my feet, and he made no attempt to help me. He let me do it on my own, reinforcing what he'd said. I smiled— cracking blood be damned—and followed him as he melted through the hole in the wall.

Being a bit bigger than he was, I got a little scraped up going through. I had to shift my butt around and tore a pocket on my jeans. I reached out with my right hand, hoping he'd take it, but found a good piece of rebar and pulled myself along. I slipped free and leaned against a half-collapsed slab to catch my breath.

My partner stood there, arms crossed over his chest. "That's the first step, let's go."

"Give me a second here, will you?"

"You have the remainder of your life to rest."

"Which is likely to be fifteen minutes if you don't let me catch my breath."

"Less. You don't have fifteen minutes." He frowned at me. "Are you really that out of shape?"

I straightened up and grabbed a double-handful of beer belly. "Everyone gets a little thick around the middle as they get older."

The man slapped his own flat stomach. "Only if they don't have discipline." He flopped down on his back and tapped a dark, triangular hole in the wall. "In through here."

"You're crazy."

"It will work. Drops to the left halfway through, then up for a while. Don't go left, go up." He wriggled his way into it and was gone.

I walked over to the hole, but couldn't even hear him scrabbling along. I debated for a second not following and didn't like the silence. I pulled the headphones on and heard just enough of Dean's voice to decide the silence was better. I did a quick check for size, realized the Walkman would hang me up, so I left it behind. That didn't get rid of Dean, though, because in my mind I could hear him some time in the future talking about how they found my Walkman and how he hoped his words of encouragement had given me solace in my final moments.

I wanted to puke and I was pretty sure it wasn't because of my concussion.

The little tunnel *was* a tight squeeze. I pulled myself along, reaching up with my hands, pushing off as I was able with my feet. Things raked my flanks, tugged at my belt and clawed at my gut. In the pitch black it was easy to imagine them to be the talons of strange creatures, which made me wonder about rats that might be lurking, or snakes or scorpions or black widows. I decided even the tiniest of God's creatures had sense enough to be leaving the vicinity, but that didn't stop me from shivering whenever something brushed my face.

Halfway through my left leg did dangle into space, but things were so cramped I couldn't look down. I kept on moving, even though without left leg purchase it was harder. My fingers started tingling and hurting from pulling myself along. The fact that I felt air flowing up past me helped me to keep going, aided and abetted by determination that I'd *not* be found wedged in some cement tube like a hot dog in a fat man's throat.

Finally I wiggled my way free, swaying this side and that like one of those time-lapse photography images of a seedling stalk emerging from the earth. I plopped onto my back and lay there for a moment, sweat stinging my eyes. I was breathing hard and had started wheezing a bit. I figured that was from the dust.

My partner stood over me, looking down disgustedly, his fists planted on his hips. He had that commanding presence, sort of like Rudolf Valentino. Very dramatic, very forceful and clearly not pleased with my performance so far.

I shrugged. "Sorry."

"Sorry for whom? Your wife? Your kids?"

"No kids. I want them but my wife, she has her career— she's a lawyer. She's probably soon to be my ex-wife, and is probably out dancing on the cemetery plot that's soon to be mine." I slowly rolled onto my belly, then worked myself up onto my knees. "You got kids?"

He shook his head. "Bess and I . . . it's one of my regrets."

I gave him a gentle nod, then sighed. "Sorry I'm not making this getting-out-thing easy."

He cracked a smile. "You couldn't make it easy. Easier, perhaps, but not easy. If it were easy, it wouldn't be worth doing because anyone could do it."

"Yeah, but if Dean were trapped in here . . ."

The man waved that idea away dismissively. "Better a thousand of you than one of him. C'mon, let's go. One more ordeal and you're out of here."

I stumbled to my feet and shambled after him. We picked our way along a corridor that had survived the collapse pretty well, which suggested to me that some undetonated explosive lurked nearby. My best guess is that I'd awakened on the second subground parking level and was moving up through the first. Then we rounded a corner and I stopped dead in my tracks.

A chunk of the mall courtyard had collapsed and dropped down, forming an archipelago of tiled islands linked by twisted threads of rebar. They floated above a black chasm in which dimly burned a couple of emergency lights. The darkness made it hard to judge how far down they were, but they illuminated jagged hunks of broken concrete. No matter how shallow the drop, the landing would be painful.

My companion walked to the edge of the chasm and squatted down. He pointed off toward a triangular island. "That one is the key. Once you get there, it's a simple walk out."

I closed my eyes for a second, then opened them again, but the islands had not shifted. "Um, getting to that one will be the tough thing. There are those three there, which get smaller and smaller, and a good eight feet up and over to our goal."

"Easily done. Watch." He backed up past me, got a six-foot running start, then leaped out to the first little island. He landed square in the heart of that oval, skipped high in the air and landed on the next one, six feet along. Another step and his powerful legs launched to the smallest island. He landed in a crouch, then shot up and off again, flipping through the air like a gymnast, sticking the landing on the higher island.

He held his hands up as if waiting for applause, but only

the reboant click-clacking of debris falling into the blackened pit echoed through the ruins. He turned slowly, his face lit by a glorious smile, his eyes shining, then he nodded to me.

"You can do this, Tom. Come on, you can do it."

I shook my head slowly. The throbbing pain built until I was pretty sure the top of my skull was going to explode clean off. "I can't do that."

"You can." His voice hardened. "You *must!*"

"I *must?* Who the hell do you think you are?" With my head pounding, I straightened up to my full height. "It might be that they find me here, or they find me down there, but they find me where I decide I'm going to be. There is no *must* about this."

"But there is, Tom, there is." He crouched and pointed out toward where I felt certain the rescuers would be waiting. "If you don't do this, Lancaster Dean wins."

"He wins?"

"Yes, he wins." The man shook his head. "I've seen his kind hundreds of times, thousands. They have no real talent, save for marketing themselves. Now I know something about that, I really do, but when you market something, you have to have something there, something real. He's done nothing but use the ideas of others forever. If you don't do this, you know what will happen. He'll dedicate a performance to you, maybe a tour. You'll become a friend he lost, a momentary pause in his show when he can't go on. Your death will be what humbles a great man before his audience, and that will make him greater in their eyes still.

"Do you want to do that? Do you want to make the man who placed you here into a hero for shedding a crocodile tear in your memory?"

I growled. "Yeah, so I try and fail and then folks know

how horribly I died. I know this media crap, I see it all the time, right? I'm not stupid. How I die will be forgotten fast enough, and he'll still win. He's Lancaster Dean. He's a star. He's the man who escaped death!"

"HA!" The man shot to his feet and gave me a glare that drove me back a step. "Don't tell me you believe that nonsense. He never died. It was a trick."

"How do you know that? Were you there?"

"No, but I *know*." His voice grew a bit softer. "When you die, it puts things in perspective. Winning the applause of millions doesn't matter. You learn what's important in life. He's clearly not learned that lesson."

I nodded slowly. "Maybe you don't have to die to get an angle on those things." Not being a very deep guy, and having been whacked on the head, what was important to me in that moment was some sunshine, a smile from my wife, a cold beer, a barbecued burger and, maybe, just maybe, a chance to poke Lancaster Dean in the nose.

I backed up to where he'd started his run, then took off. I made the leap to the first island easily, perhaps too easily. I didn't get as much of a push-off as I wanted, but still made the second island. I got a spare step there, then launched myself at the third. It hung there like a tiny speck of land in a black ocean, but I was on target. All I had to do was crouch there, then spring up again just as he'd done . . .

Yeah, then flip through the air like some little girl gymnast . . .

That thought, and the impossibility of my duplicating his action, isn't exactly what doomed me. My friend, being smaller and lighter than me, hadn't impacted the islands the same way I had. He was a little Velociraptor, whereas I was a Jurassic Park Tyrannosaurus Rex, setting everything to shaking and quivering as I bounced along.

My target shook on my landing, listing hard to the left. A

tile crumbled beneath my foot and I went down. I landed on my right hip and started to slide. I could feel my feet flailing in the air, my rump sliding off the edge. I grabbed at the island, tearing the nails off my right hand as I clawed for any hold at all. I still was slipping then, all of a sudden, I jerked to a halt.

My legs dangled and pain shot up from my left hip. I felt around and found a hooked piece of rebar had caught my belt back by my right cheek. I started to tip forward, but my right foot hit a long piece of rebar below, steadying me. Shivering, I clung to my little piece of rock.

"You're okay. You're okay." I heard his voice from the triangle, which hung above me. "Are you okay?"

"Oh, hell yeah, for someone caught on a rock in the middle of the goddamned air. Sure, I'm just ducky." I growled again, then looked up. "Don't even think of coming down here. Even if you could free me, there's not enough room and you couldn't get back up. Go on without me."

"I'm not leaving you here." His voice took on the edge again. "You *will* get free, you *must*."

"No shit, Sherlock, I'm the one dangling here."

"You can do it, Tom."

"Will you shut up? I need to think here for a moment."

"Yes, of course."

His voice softened, and I knew he wasn't going to stop talking. I almost told him to shut up again, but since I couldn't see him, hearing his voice meant I wasn't alone. Where I was at the time, not being alone took on a lot of importance in my life—which, all things considered, was looking pretty close to being over at that point.

"Want to know how he did it, Tom?"

"Did what?"

"Faked his death?"

"Um, sure." I reached down and began to unlace my left workboot. I hooked my little finger through the laces so it couldn't fall off as I loosened it. Very carefully I worked it off and brought it up to my island as my companion explained Dean's trick.

"It's a pretty common thing, Tom. Fakirs in India used to do it. You get a hard little ball of rubber and place it up near your armpit. As you squeeze your arm down against your chest, you shut off the flow of blood to the artery there in your wrist. Dean's friend checked his wrist, found no pulse and ran off for help."

"You don't say! Why that son of a bitch, been lying all this time." I smiled and shifted around enough to grab an unseen piece of rebar with my toes and then bring my right foot up to where I could unlace that boot. "I guess that's why you said he had no real talent."

"Part of it, yes. And, Tom, I trust you will keep that secret to yourself."

"Dean's secret?"

"The secret of the ball. It's frowned upon to reveal such things."

"Your secret is safe with me." I brought the right boot up on the tile-land by its mate and unlaced both of them, down to the last three eyes on each boot. This gave me a good four feet of doubled-lace between them. Using my teeth and left hand I knotted them together good and tight, giving me two boots linked by over a yard of laces.

I glanced up at the triangle island and could make out a rebar fringe. "Okay, look, get back from the edge. Hang on to something up there. I have only one choice here and I don't want it killing the both of us."

"Don't give it a second thought, son, just do what you have to do."

"Okay, here goes nothing." With the boots dangling from my left hand, strung together the way sneaker pairs are when hung from high power lines, I started my small island bouncing. I know that sounds insane, but I really had no other choice. My weight had lowered my island to the point where I couldn't reach the triangle. Only by using the springiness of the rebar, could I get up high enough.

The rocking motion did nothing good for my head, other than to sync the throbbing with my movement. As I rose I made the first cast with the boots, but they missed. I rocked more and harder, but bounced the boots off the rebar. I could hear chunks of rock pitching down below, clattering around, and knew the whole network might give way.

I gave it one last solid heave, and timed it beautifully. The right boot arced over a metal stake and wrapped around twice. With my right hand I jerked my belt buckle back, loosening my belt and letting the rebar that had held me up slip free. The little island did batter my right leg as it descended, then just quivered below, with the shaking rebar webwork angrily chattering at me.

I stripped my belt off as I hung there, doubled it and hooked it over another piece of rebar. I held on tight, and started to pull myself up. I let go of the laces and grabbed more metal, then shortened my grip on the belt. My left foot found another long strand of rebar and latched onto it with toes.

"Now just hook your chin on the top here. Handhold to the right." He stayed on the high side of the triangle, nodding and pointing.

It was that nod, that acknowledgment that I was on the right track, showing his confidence, that got me up on the triangle. Being able to chin myself like that and haul myself up, I'm sure adrenaline gave me some help there, but his nod told me I'd make it. Not disappointing him seemed somehow as important to me as getting out alive.

I crawled up onto the triangle, then reached back down for my boots.

"Leave them, we've not much time."

"No. They saved my life." I smiled over my shoulder at him. "Besides, you know how long it takes to break in a good pair of boots?"

He laughed and nimbly moved to a long strip of tile. Looping my boots around my neck by the laces, I followed carefully and we quickly reached a solid portion of the flooring. I turned to look back and saw the islands bobbing, bits and pieces of them beginning to crumble. From higher up pieces of debris fell cometlike, trailing dust. One large chunk pulverized the island where I'd hung.

I shivered. "Another minute."

"Another minute you don't have, Tom." He pointed to a tunnel that sloped up and, at the top, I could see the artificial glare of klieg lights. "Get going."

I started to scramble up and got past a tough point. I turned back to give him a hand, but he hadn't moved. He just stood there at the opening. "C'mon, we're safe, we made it."

"You're safe, Tom. You've made it." He gave me a salute and a smile. "I have to go back for my mother."

At the time those words made no sense to me, mainly because of the thunderous crack of concrete breaking and riding over them. Major chunks of what had remained standing chose that moment to collapse. Situated where I was in the tunnel, well, I was pretty much a BB in the barrel of an air rifle. A heavy gust of dust and air slammed into me, hurling me up and out of the ruins. I arced through the artificially lit night, an ill omen for Lancaster Dean, but feeling very lucky indeed.

Because of all the media coverage and cameras, I've been able to watch my flight many times, from many different angles. The landing is always the best part because there he was, Lancaster Dean, sitting at a makeshift desk, being interviewed, when I came down. He and the anchor had turned toward the building with the crack. The newsie fell one way, Dean another and his toupee yet a third, with me smashing Dean through the table.

The doctors, they told me that I was pretty much out of it because of a concussion and loss of blood. They even had a shrink come in and explain to me that my traveling companion, about whom I kept asking, never existed. "It's normal, in a time of stress, for some people to imagine another person being there, so they won't be alone. Don't worry about it."

Sure, don't worry about it, but take these pills until you stop talking nonsense. I stopped talking nonsense pretty quickly, especially after someone leaked my story to a tabloid and I found myself in print saying an angel had helped me escape. But even though I stopped talking, I knew I wasn't wrong. I had proof.

And that little red ball of proof was great for draining the blood from the face of first-year medical students taking a pulse—and not finding one.

Kim, my wife, brought me the ball. My almost being dead helped her reorient what she thought was important in life, too, which meant our paths merged again. She was the one who discovered that the power unit that had shorted, triggering the explosives, had shorted when Lancaster Dean plugged a nose-hair trimmer into an overloaded socket in his trailer.

And it looked like the settlement would more than cover

the cost of the new house we were going to need, being as how the kids would want their own rooms as they grew up. The settlement with the tabloids for misquoting me was what would get them through college.

About the time my bruises had healed up enough for me to be photogenic, Lancaster Dean arranged to meet me at the Doubletree Resort for dinner. It was a photo-op, pure and simple. We were being billed as the two men who had cheated death, and the photographers loved it when I suggested they get a shot of Dean taking my pulse.

The expression on his face when he doesn't find any is priceless. Pity those shots never get into his publicity packet.

But it wasn't until three weeks later, when I was watching one of those tabloid TV shows while working out at the gym that the last little bit of things put themselves together for me. It was right after the segment where Dean announced he was retiring from performing. They did a little piece on me and my escape, comparing it with the best escapes of famous magicians. And that was when I saw my companion again.

The only footage of him they had was black and white, but the smile and the eyes, the eyes especially, came through in the stills. In reviewing his career, to tie things all together, they said my escape was better than any escape he'd ever performed.

Of course, they were wrong. Harry Houdini's greatest escape was passing over that gulf that separates life from death. He plucked a reluctant volunteer from the audience, brought him along and got him out. And, true to himself, only Harry would believe he could make the trip twice, the next time to bring back his mother.

And, you know, I don't doubt he's done it.

"It's the Thought That Counts" was written for one of the *Whatdunit* anthologies edited by Mike Resnick. Mike offered each author a choice of two scenarios, and we were to write a mystery SF story to fulfill those conditions. I had two false starts before I came up with this tale, which was supposed to be about a man who had murdered his wife and a telepath had to prove it. Things got a bit twisted around, but it's a fun story anyway.

It's the Thought That Counts

She walked into my office on legs long enough to be stilts. Gams like that usually only come out of a vat, but she looked baby-factory original to me. The black sweater-dress hugged her tight, but the wide black belt, pearls, and the veiled hat told me she wasn't stalking a swain. She wanted something else and she figured I could deliver.

She looked up at me, flashing green eyes from a fox face. I felt something jolt through me. I checked to see that the Datamaster 301 desk hadn't shorted again, then I gave her a smile. She returned it, with interest, then clasped her gloved hands over her purse and held it against her flat stomach.

"Mr. Martel? Your secretary said I could come right in." She glanced down at the wooden chair in front of my desk. "May I?"

I nodded. A woman like her looks totally out of place in an office like mine. I keep it dark so I can't see how dingy it really is. The microwave over on the file cabinet has the stains of a million cups of nuked coffee in it. Optical data disks spill over the shelves; even their rainbow surfaces can't reflect the weak light. The couch is covered with old printouts from old cases.

It struck me, all of a sudden, that all my cases were *old,* just like my suit. Bad run of luck, but maybe it was changing. I nodded to myself and she took it as a signal to start. I could have told her different, but I didn't.

"I am recently widowed. My husband, Ken Cogshill, took his own life."

I'd heard it all before. Actually, I read it all before, straight from her mind. About a second before she spoke, the words appeared in her head and I had them. She impressed me—deliberate and direct. Most women don't have a quarter of that lag-time.

She blinked her big eyes, but made no move to brush away the single tear painting mascara down her right cheek. "I loved my husband, Mr. Martel, but he became involved with Richard Hybern. I thought it was just this Neo-men's movement, but Kenny, he became part of Hybern's inner circle. Ken gave him everything, then went out and killed himself. I have nothing."

I wouldn't have said she had nothing, but what she had wouldn't pay the rent or power. I watched her without saying a word. Most of my clients take this as tough-guy silence or stupid-guy silence. Okay, it could be either, but it gives me a chance to see if they're holding anything back as they assume I assume they are. If they are, it comes out, then I wait a bit more to see if they will spill it or think about yet more stuff they think I'd want to know.

She was holding a hole card but she didn't want to play it. "I talked to some friends and they said Hamilton Martel was the best private investigator around." I saw the face of Mortimer Phibbs flash through her mind. I still had scars from that divorce case. "Mr. Martel, you have to help me."

"Ham. You can call me Ham." Sure, it's a dumb nickname, but it saved my life in the Steinberg cannibal case, so

I stick with it. "I'll help you if you answer me one question, Mrs. Cogshill."

"Louise. Please, what is it?" She took off her hat and let a cascade of fiery red hair spill over her shoulders. "I want to be very open with you."

"Did you ever tell your husband that you went to see Hybern and ended up doing the horizontal tango with him?"

"How did you know?" Her cheeks reddened just a shade darker than her hair. She tore her gaze away from mine. "I guess you *are* the man I need."

She didn't know the half of it, but I let that slide. "You think Hybern confronted your husband with that news, and that's what drove him over the edge, isn't it?"

I knew the truth before she answered. "Yes, no, I . . ." Purse opened and a handkerchief came out in time to catch the tears tooling down the mascara motorway. "Ken and I had been through a lot and we loved each other. He had strayed once, with his secretary, and I forgave him. I never assumed that meant I could . . . I knew we could have worked through it, but I felt dirty and ashamed. I felt *used.*"

Everything registered true on my built-in horse-pucky meter. "Okay, Louise, I can help you. You want me to find out if Hybern told your husband about your tryst and you want me to see if I can get you the family assets back, right?" I phrased that question that way on purpose. It made me seem altruistic and that's the priority she'd put on things anyway.

"Yes, yes, you understand."

I gave her my "I have it under control" smile. "I get five K a day, plus expenses." I sensed her shock because she knew, in the Phibbs case, I'd gotten twice that *and* stuck Phibbs for my new kidney in the process. What she didn't know is that I scale my prices in accordance with client-based eye-strain.

She nodded and reached her hands up to her neck. They came back down with the pearls dangling between them. "This is all I have to pay you."

I shrugged. "Let's go see my secretary. She can make the arrangements." I trusted Louise Cogshill, and she *believed* the pearls were cultured, not synthed. I'd made a living proving that guilty husbands will say anything to wives, but I didn't want to tell her that Kenny might have pulled another fast one on her.

I let her precede me out to the reception area of my office. It was polite. It was also a joy to watch her walk. "Dolores, this is Louise Cogshill. She's our new client. We're billing her four large a day, plus expenses." When both of them looked at me in surprise, I shrugged. "She's a widow." With a walk.

Dol would have raised a questioning eyebrow at me if she had one. She's a platinum blond—real platinum, too. I rescued her from a blind date with a big magnet and used the data on a Prom hidden away in her to bring her former boss's house of disks tumbling down. She's been with me since, the loyalty and infatuation programs built into her working overtime since I turned out to be her white knight.

The pearls clacked gently in Dol's open right palm. She pulled them close to her face and a little red beam shot out of her right pupil. The laser scanned two or three of the pearls then clicked off. She looked up at me with electric Big Blue eyes and blinked them once. The pearls were genuine.

I guided Louise to the door, letting my hand rest on the small of her back. "I will contact you when I have something."

"Do you want my number?"

I winked reassuringly at her as I memorized the number floating in her mind. "I'll find it."

"It's unlisted." She doubted me.

"I have my resources, Louise." I made a note of her private line as well. "That's why I'm the detective."

She gave me a smile that made me forget what she was thinking. "They said you were the best. Good luck."

Luck is what you need when playing cards. I don't. I cheat. Every gamble for me is a sure thing. It may be immoral to bet on a sure thing, but I figured what Hybern had done to her and her husband was immoral. Fighting fire with fire.

Live by the sword, Hybern, and you can die by it, too.

I shut the door after her and turned to look at Dol sitting all prim and proper at her desk. She held her hands poised as if over a keyboard, but there wasn't one there. Her fingers worked phantom keys. Some folks call it a virtual keyboard. I call it a way to burn out those expensive little servomotors in her hands.

"Ham, I've sent the scan on the pearls down to Bronco. I have him on the phone now. He says he'll go fourteen on them, but we're bargaining. He wants to know if they're loaners or his for resale."

Even though I couldn't read her, I knew what she was thinking. She wanted me to sell the things outright and that way I couldn't make a gallant gesture to the widow Cogshill by returning them. "Loaner for now. They may be the only thing of her husband's she has left."

Dol nodded her head the way she always does. She says she has my best interest in her power supply. Says I'm a stalled car on the railroad crossing of love, but she's always there to pick up the pieces after the crash. "Yes, Mr. Martel."

"Dol, not this time. I'm all for you, you know that."

Her fingers stopped working. "Yes, Mr. Martel," she repeated, letting her voxsynther raise the pitch of her words for ironic effect. "With the sixteen-five I just talked out of Bronco, we're nine to the good over all our triple-notice bills."

I grunted, thinking. "Good. Look, I need you to run down everything on Richard Hybern. Ditto a file on Cogshill, too." I reached for my hat and shrugged my trenchcoat on. "I'm heading out for lunch. Tell the Weasel I'm at Mickey's."

"How come you never take me anyplace, Ham?"

I knew where this conversation was going as well as if I were reading a script. I glanced over in the corner behind her desk at the silver pretzel the landlord's reps had made of her legs the last time I went overdue. "How much?"

She's got that innocent blink down pat. "Five."

"Do it." I smiled at her and opened the door. "Do it and I'll take you dancing."

Us telepaths are about as rare as honest politicians. I'm not sure why, but I have my suspicions. The Feds making insider trading a capital offense dusted some of us while I figure the spooks and Bureau picked up most of the rest. The Mob's got some interesting tests for telepathy, but the prize for passing is small, lead and moves fast, so I stay clear of them.

I slid into my booth at Mickey's and scanned Arnie's mind for what was good to order. That drew a blank, so I checked for least toxic. "Burger, fries and some joe."

"Sure, bud," he snapped around a well-gnawed cigar. "Burn a cow and oil-boil some roots," he shouted at the Elvis working the cookstove.

Coffee flowed like 10-W-40 oil into my cup. It would be

a race to see if I could drink it before it etched the porce-
lain, but I gave it a head start. Letting it cool would make it
harder to chew, but poaching my tongue wasn't on my list
of things to do today.

The Weasel slid into the booth across from me, the
cracked naugahyde tearing at his polyester double-knits like
newshounds at a scandal. He flashed me a big smile, hoping
to provoke a reaction, but I shut him down. "How it be,
man?"

I shrugged. The Weasel is a low-grade psychic. If I'm the
Major Leagues, he's strictly T-ball. Reads emotions like
greed or lust and works cons off them. I don't even know if
he's aware he has that ability. I know he does because I can
feel him tickling around, trying to get a read.

"Got a new case. You've worked some of the Neo-men's
stuff, right?"

"Bly Institute lectures? Yeah." He gave me another grin.
"All these suits ready to shed their synthskin and get back
to basics. I got some connections and sell them 'Navajo'
cast-offs so they can be proper for their pow-wows."

His brain wrapped smugness around a label reading,
"Made in Moldova." "Nice scam."

"I even get their Halstons in trade. Resale on those is
pure profit."

"Ever run into Richard Hybern?"

Arnie set my plate down and the Weasel recoiled like it
was a traffic accident. Might have been the food. Burger
looked like it had been forged, then shellacked. The fries
. . . well, smothering them with ketchup was a public service. Besides, I needed a vegetable with the meal.

"Never him, but I've seen some of his recruiters. Colder
than Marxism's promise, those dudes. They hang at
Blyathons and pull the elite with them to meet Hybern."

245

The Weasel frowned. "Never take any of my customers."

"You're working different tiers of the food chain, babe." I broke a piece off my burger, forced it back to my strong teeth, and tossed some java down to lube its passage. "You've never worked a Hybern meeting?"

"Compared to Hybern, the Masons are a public gathering. Tight group. Members direct other members to check out a Bly lecture, then the Hybern recruiters go to work." The Weasel visualized me wearing a bullet-riddled dunce cap. "You're not going after Hybern, are you?"

"You know something I don't?"

He thought so, but by that time it wasn't true. "Folks join his group for *life,* my man." He didn't mean a long time, either.

When I got back in the office I saw a repair-meck kneeling behind Dol's desk. I might have thought something kinky was going on, but repair-mecks don't have the right tools. Two of his arms held her left leg braced while another pair slowly straightened it out. The last two, the dinky ones meant for fine work, were soldering connections on her stumps.

Her head swiveled all the way around to look at me. "I'll be an inch taller!"

Tossing my hat on the rack, I winked at her. "Files are on my desktop?"

"Yes, Mr. Martel."

I draped my trenchcoat over my couch and slid in behind the Datamaster 301. It wasn't the latest model, but it worked. The big, flat LCD display looked like a cartoon desktop and three folders sat stacked in living color on it. I touched the first one with my right hand and slid it down into place. Hitting the corner, it opened and I started reading.

Hybern started with the Bly Institute and looked, for a bit, to be the logical successor to the old man himself. Then the Wolf-Warrior schism hit the movement and the Blyers were reduced to running "Play Nice" seminars at pre-schools. Hybern looked like he'd jump to head up the Wolf-Warriors, but he balked and disappeared for a while.

The Wolf-Warriors were a curious outgrowth of the men's movement. They rejected the logical fallacy of embracing the "warrior within," while abandoning the violence and hostility that came with that role. Like most misguided movements, they went overboard in the other direction, assailing Christianity and Buddhism as religions for "wussies." Embracing the Sadlerite Gospel of Casca the Eternal Warrior, they went to Guatemala to take over and form their own Militocracy.

The world quickly learned that NOW *did* have the bomb and the Wolf-Warriors did a fast atomic fade. The Bly Institute used their example as positive reinforcement about the folly of violence and jumpstarted the movement again. Hybern re-emerged as a leader who helped men realize their full potential. When his list of successful clients became long enough, he split and set up his own group: Hybern Organization for Male Motivational Existentialism.

As I dug deeper into the clips I saw the reason the Weasel had reacted so violently to my mentioning Hybern. HOMME had an unfortunate list of client suicides and accidents. The first couple of times HOMME was listed among the victim's affiliations, but after that all mention of HOMME was quashed. Touching the screen over the little ✓ icon on the scanned clips showed me how Dol'd cross-correlated obits with other articles and pictures to make up the list of dead folks tied to HOMME.

Other articles Dol had found suggested a couple more

people had found themselves in Louise's position. I saw two mentions of lawsuits to get money back from HOMME that the deceased had given before his death. One was settled out of court. Another obit told me the disposition of the second case.

The Cogshill file made for a quick read. Ken had been a fast-track executive with Mutual of Prudential-Tokugawa Insurance. He and Louise had been playing house for seven years, married for four of them. No kids. Ken's grandfather traded shrapnel for a Congressional Medal of Honor in Panama in '89. His father got a pass into West Point because of it. He resigned his commission in '32 to join the Ronald Reagan Brigade of the Tibet Tigers in the Sino-Tibet War. Ken was born six months before his father caught a fatal bullet in the fighting outside Lhasa in '33.

Kenny looked primed for Bly and Hybern. His father and grandfather were heroes, but had paid for it in blood. Kenny opted away from military life. Not following them, he needed some sort of reassurance he was a real man. For me, waking up with Miss Bedroom-Eyes '49 every morning would have been plenty. Kenny wanted more and was willing to pay Hybern to get it.

And pay he did. According to the Cogshill account summary Dol had included in the file, Kenny transferred his entire savings to HOMME. HOMME was also listed as the beneficiary on an insurance policy he had. Hybern wouldn't get the insurance because Kenny had done himself—house edge for the company. The fund transfer, on the other hand, had been for over ten mondo, which was enough to buy anyone a dacha on the Black Sea and the government stability to keep it.

My mind revving high, I wandered out to the front. "Dol, how does this bank transfer thing work? How does the bank know Cogshill actually made the transfer to HOMME?"

She let out the closest thing to a sigh her chip could produce. It sounded like the wrong-answer buzzer on a vidgame show. "I've explained this to you before, Ham."

"Humor me. I've still got bugs in my wetware."

"Widows, more like."

I winced. "Can the Eliza emulation, Dol, unless you don't want me to help you put those tin pins through the Foxtrot."

She blinked once, giving me her full attention. "The bank supplies each customer with an account number and an access code. The first is supposed to be common knowledge and the second a deep, dark secret. Some banks even give good customers emergency codes so a transaction can be traced and stopped while appearing to go through. Prevents extortion."

"Huh. I never got one of those."

She stared at me to emphasize the adjective *good*. If my average balance were a thermometer reading, they'd have to recalibrate absolute zero. "Of course, folks are encouraged to change their codes often, but they seldom do, or tie it to a number like their birthday."

I made a note to change mine. "So transfers are pretty easy to fake, right?"

Her head swung back and forth. "Banks use one more check. When you go to make a transfer, they feed back a word or phrase for you to type in. The computer checks the response time and typing patterns, then runs that by a file of examples they have from work you've done in the past. If things match, the transfer is authorized. Numbers you can steal. This you can't fake."

"Wouldn't that database be limited for folks who

don't type much?" Like me.

"Chances are people who don't type much don't have much money."

Like me.

"So Cogshill really did authorize the transfer to HOMME."

She nodded. "To the bank's satisfaction, he did. That's good enough for the Feds. If Mrs. Cogshill were to sue, she'd have to find a lawyer who wanted a loser."

"That much of a guarantee for a loss?"

"Not as good as the one you get with the Cybernags you bet on, but close." She extended both her legs and flexed her toes. "Now I'm faster than they are."

"What about the two suits against HOMME?"

"They involved real estate transfers. Different stuff. Brokers mess things up." She reached over on her desk and extended the glass bowl of batteries to the repair-meck. He took a nine-volt, then tipped the top of his head to her. She gave him a tinny giggle. He folded up his arms and stood.

The repair-meck headed for the door. I let him out, then reached for my hat. "I'm heading out."

Dol stood. "Let me come with you."

"I don't think so." Her head slumped forward, disappointed. I crossed to her desk and gave her a peck on the cheek. I ignored the fact that her flesh was colder than a proctologist's tools. "Head out for a trial run on those titanium trotters. Buy yourself a dress. Make it something nice. Real nice. For when we go dancing."

"You promise?"

"You're the Apple of my eye, Dol." I winked at her. "Charge it to my account."

"Okay!" She looked at me with eyes like limpid pools of neon. "Where will you be?"

I gave her a patented "I'll be okay" smile. "I'm going to see Hybern. I want to find out what his thoughts are on this."

I'd had stale sandwiches tougher than the security man working the HOMME front office. A big guy in a maroon blazer, he flexed his pecs as he moved to bar my path. "Where do you think you're going, pipsqueak?"

I stopped, tipped my hat back and looked up into his eyes. His mind had the typical bully feel to it. "I was thinking that spot back there, near the elevator, looked a bit softer for your landing, ace." A little question mark lurked beneath an ocean of laughter in his mind. "You got an ambulance service you prefer here?"

The question mark got a bit bigger. Like all bullies he expected me to be afraid of him, and when I wasn't, he began to wonder. I stepped closer, violating his personal space and bringing him into range for my secret weapon. Our gazes met and I let him have it.

If I work real hard and am in close, I can sometimes project a thought into someone's head. The trick doesn't work with women—reading more than surface thoughts off them might as well be torture, and projecting is impossible. Women think differently than men. They're a lot like cats.

This explains why dogs are a man's best friend.

A long time ago I got the Weasel to dummy up a magazine cover for me. It shows me holding something that looks a lot like a World Championship Belt above my head. The magazine is titled, "Killer Karate Today" and the headline reads, "Minute Martel Hammers the Hulk." I studied that image harder than the IRS does a banker's 1040 form. I planted a comp copy in the bully's brain.

Worked better than planting a fist in his groin. He got all white and kinda sucked himself inward. 'Cept for his eyes—they bugged out.

"Mr. Martel to see Mr. Hybern."

A phone on the wall buzzed and the security man moved off to get it. I breathed a silent sigh of relief. Ever since folks started using T1K Secmecks, that trick hasn't worked too well. Those machines think, or so I'm told, but their artificial intelligence is a marriage between that of Ted Bundy and the average Mako shark. Using a sociopathic Cuisinart to safeguard property might be some folks' idea of wisdom, but not mine. Mecks think in binary. Ones and zeroes. On and Off. If a T1K turns someone Off, even by accident, turning them back On requires microsurgeons with a taste for jigsaw puzzles.

The bully hung the phone up, then walked over to the elevator doors. He pushed the button and the doors opened. "Mr. Hybern will see you now. This elevator will take you to him."

I nodded and headed for the box. The guy touched me on the shoulder to stop me, then jerked his hand back like he'd been snakebit. "Excuse me, sir, Mr. Martel, but . . ."

"Yes?" I opened my coat so he could see that I wasn't heavy.

"No sir, not that." He smiled weakly. "Could I have your autograph?"

The Weasel doesn't work much, but when he does, what he does is good.

The elevator's doors closed behind me. I braced for the ascent, then half-stumbled as it rocketed down. I started to regret not having Dol get me the plans for HOMME's building, but the elevator stopped short. I knew if I was being dropped into some trap, the place wouldn't show on the plans anyway.

The doors opened onto a dark corridor. Walls looked like Lucite blacker than the coffee at Mickey's. The only light came from a dull red strip running along the top of the wall. I could see well enough to walk forward, but not too far. Behind me the doors slid shut silently.

The plush black carpeting smothered my footsteps like a pillow. Thin red stripes cut across the carpet every ten feet. They bled out from the thicker red strips bordering the walls like the sidelines in some corridor football game.

The corridor took a right-angle turn to the left after fifty feet. Another ten feet and it broadened out into a room. Same decor as the hall, but everything was wider, taller and deeper. The room looked square, but the corridor bled into it at the corner. Funny how they'll pay architects to waste space like that.

Just over halfway into the room a stepped, pyramidal facade of black Lucite backed Hybern's desk. Glowing red lines separated the slabs of the pyramid. Scarlet red light bled from around the edges of the design, giving it a dim halo. A similar red strip, a bit brighter than the facade, ran around the edge of Hybern's ebony desktop.

The desk light and the facade combined to sink Hybern in bloody shadows. Red highlights glowed from his shaved head, and his goatee looked woven from the same shadow they used to make his turtleneck and shirt. A big ruby sat in a gold setting on his left ring finger. He steepled his fingers when he saw me, then he nodded me forward.

"Welcome, Mr. Martel."

"Thanks." I walked forward and hid my surprise as a chair rolled out from behind the pyramid and stopped in front of his desk. "Who did your decorating? Dracula?"

White teeth showed in a grin I'd have figured threatening, but I got nothing from the guy. "Real men are not afraid of the dark."

"Real men don't live in it." I settled myself in the chair

and hooked my hat over the corner. "I'd like to talk to you about someone who used to be in HOMME."

He leaned back in his chair, laying his chin in his right hand with his index finger next to his temple. "Let me guess: Ken Cogshill?"

I nodded. "Very good. Care to show your work?"

"Elementary deduction, really. In the time it has taken for you to get here, I was able to check you out." He patted the polarized top of his Datamaster 9000 desk. "Among fourth-rate detectives you have a following, Mr. Martel. Only Mrs. Cogshill is desperate enough to keep trying to find someone to investigate her husband's death."

"Okay, you're on target there—about her, not me." I narrowed my eyes in an expression that usually puts the subject of my investigation on edge. "She thinks you had something to do with his death. Cops ruled it a suicide, but if she's right, you've gotten away with the perfect crime, haven't you? Now why would she be after you?"

"She wants a scapegoat." The man remained a rock. I'd accused him of being a murderer and he gave me less re-action than the pizza delivery boy when I stiffed him on a tip. "She wants to assuage her guilt over Ken's suicide. She came to me first, accusing me of all sorts of heinous things. She claims we slept together and that my telling her husband about our fling caused him to kill himself. This is non-sense."

In the detective game you learn to see the signs of lying. Scratching the nose is one. Forced levity is another. Refusal to look someone in the eye is a big one. I go by all of those, and follow them up with a mental snapshot from the person talking.

I concentrated on Hybern as I asked, "Why would she say that?" Nothing.

He smiled effortlessly. "The woman is schizophrenic and delusional. She suffers from paranoia. Her inability to deal with the fact that her husband felt trapped in their life and killed himself has made her yet more unstable."

I should have seen it coming, but he misdirected me perfectly. I'd been in the mind of a schizo before. It's like looking at an x-ray movie. Everything is there, but reading Brett Easton Ellis' *The Bride Wore Black and Decker* is easier. Louise Cogshill might have been upset at her husband's death, but if she was crackers, then I was tuned-in to the same channel.

"You're lying!" I snarled and mentally pushed at him. I cracked through his defenses and caught his lie. I saw him showing Ken Cogshill pictures of his wife hugging her legs around someone who wasn't him. I heard Hybern muttering things about a man's honor and pride. Cogshill nodded, his head hanging in resignation, then I looked up at Hybern's face and saw him scratch his nose.

The trap closed on me faster than Broadway's *Tiananmen Square '89, A Musical Review*. I felt an alien presence in my mind. It was everywhere at once, but I couldn't pin it down. I felt like I was wrestling with a shadow. Worse, it was winning.

"You really want to know what happened to Ken Cogshill, Mr. Martel? I will show you." I heard Hybern's laughter ringing in my ears, but it sounded very distant. *"Watch carefully."*

Hybern rummaged through my brain until he found my bank account number and my personal identification code. Across the desk from me, I saw him hit a series of icons on his desktop. He frowned. A vise pressed in on my head.

"Only three thousand dollars in your bank account?" His anger pummeled me.

My fist clenched. *You think you're sore; that means Dol's spent a thousand dollars on a dress!*

"Spare me." Hybern did something that felt like he was taking steel-wool to my brain, then my eyes focused. My interview with Louise played through my mind. Hybern lurked there like a pervert and watched it all. He caught my reaction to Louise's walk and froze my mental image there. *"She is fine, is she not? She was very good."*

Every muscle in my body went rigid. *You bastard. If I get my hands on you!*

Suddenly I felt my hands around my own throat. *"You'll what? Do this?"* They tightened and I made a croaking sound. My thumbs pressed in on my windpipe. I felt the pulse in my neck thud against my fingers. I knew that Hybern could, in an instant, make me break my own neck.

Hybern came around and sat on the front edge of his desk, folding his arms across his chest. *"I could, but I'm more subtle than that. Both you and Mrs. Cogshill are a problem. I should have given Ken the order to kill her when he killed himself, but he wasn't strong enough for that. However, your interest in her suggests a solution to me."* He touched an icon on his desk and I heard a phone dial tone. *"You're calling Louise and telling her to come here."*

Never!

"Never say never, Mr. Martel." He plucked her private number from my brain. He hit an icon on the desk that reversed the view so I could see everything, then punched the number into the dialing pad icon on the desk. The tones played out the first three bars of an old march, then it started ringing. I hoped it was busy, but she picked up and the Datamaster's hidden speakerphone filled the room with her voice.

"Hello?"

"Louise?" I heard myself say. "This is Ham. I'm at Hybern's place over on South King. I've been talking to him and he's interested in some sort of settlement." I tried to make my hands complete the job Hybern started, but he restrained me.

"Do you think it is safe?"

"I wouldn't be calling you if it wasn't. How fast can you get here?"

"Fifteen minutes?"

"Perfect." Hybern made me purr. "See you then."

He touched a button and cut the connection. "*Now you and I need to do some work to prepare for her arrival and your departure.*" He integrated our views so I could see things through his eyes. He punched up his bank account and arranged a transfer into my account. "*I think five hundred thousand looks like a sufficient amount for an operator like you to extort out of me. You manufactured evidence to link me with Ken's death after you and Louise, in the midst of a torrid affair, discovered HOMME had turned Ken into enough of a man to contest the divorce she asked him for.*"

Hybern gave me a devilish smile. "*I'll even use one of my 'extortion' code numbers, so the bank will return the money to me after you're gone.*"

All the pieces of the puzzle started to drop into place for me. "You have to be in the men's movement, because the only folks you can read and control are men."

He didn't like that and punched a white-hot mental poker into my brain. "*No, I am not like you at all. You are a simpering fool who uses a minor talent to accomplish nothing. I detected your weakling effort up at ground level and decided to amuse myself with you. I am, you see, your mental superior. I use my gift to build empires. The corporate masters of this city, of this country, come to me for advice. I pluck their desires from*" *their minds, then present them back to them as goals. I synthesize bold strategies for them by pitting the strong against the weak."*

"Men like Ken Cogshill are only a small part of my empire. His position was more useful than he was. He cleared all the claims for survivor benefits that I got when my useless members had their accidents. He had decided to take his wife's advice and break it off with HOMME, but, like a man, felt he had to come and explain it to me himself. I was forced to make him kill himself."

Not man enough to do it yourself, eh?

His face screwed up into a mask of disgust. *"My will, their hands. Watch, you will be the instrument of your own destruction!"*

Against my direct orders, my hands left my throat and settled themselves on his desktop. He slid the keyboard icon beneath my fingers and forced me to start typing. I vaguely remembered having hit the same series of commands before. The desk tied into an international database. I picked out icons like a puppet with a twitcher on the strings. I ended up with a menu of airlines and flights in front of me.

"Any preference, Mr. Martel? Are you and Louise the sort of traditionalists who want a Costa Rican holiday? The winds won't blow wrong for another three months. Or, ah, I have it, a month at Club Med Antarctica. You'll pack plenty of sunscreen and keep each other very warm. Perfect."

My hands selected Aero Hielo and Flight 4763, non-stop to Tierra Del Fuego. I made reservations for me and Louise Cogshill. I got us confirmed seating. The video was even one I hadn't seen yet.

The machine asked me for preferred method of payment. I got my right hand halfway to my wallet to grab a card before Hybern reasserted control. *"Nice trick, Martel, but using your overdrawn VISA to set up a trace won't work.*"

My hands returned to the keyboard and dutifully typed in my account number and access code. The computer asked me to type in "Rosebud" as a check phrase and I resisted. *No!*

All the agony in the world crushed itself down to the size of a pinhead. It smashed down through the top of my skull, driving bone splinters into my grey matter. It got to the center of my brain and transformed itself into a sphere. It expanded and turned its surface into a razor-studded ball made of doorscreen material. It grew and grew, slicing and straining my mind.

I resisted until it started spinning. *I surrender, I surrender!*

"*Resistance is useless.*" Hybern reached over and lifted my chin up. "*Do it right or I destroy selected portions of your autonomic nervous system and you'll suffocate slowly.*"

I nodded. Folding all my fingers in except for the indexers on each hand, I carefully hunted and pecked out the keyword. I hoped the machine would reject it and send a warning flag out. It didn't. "Have a nice flight," it flashed beneath a smiley-face icon.

"*How will I make you kill her?*" He shrugged as if it were a minor matter. "We can decide that when she gets here. In the meantime, I see, during your sleazy little career, you've learned some nasty things about a lot of interesting people." He caught my thought about Louise. "*Don't expect her or anyone else to rescue you. When they leave the elevator, I'll pick them up, the same way I did with you.*"

He started drilling test holes for a muck-gusher in my brain. I saw bits and pieces of my life whirl past in dizzying confusion. Steinberg's mad face dissolved in blood. Biker-mecks roared on through the puddle, drenching me. I tasted blood and smelled cordite. I felt the cold kiss of a knife and the hot fire of a gunshot. Faces popped up like targets and each one sank back into the obscurity from which Hybern dredged them.

A sidewinder smile twisted his lips. *"And just so you won't think I've forgotten you, I'll see to it that Dictameck in your office gets recycled into tin cans."*

Not Dol! I pushed with my mind as hard as I could. He gave an inch. I tried to take a mile, but lost half an inch in the attempt. He shoved back harder. I felt my mind start to crumble.

Then I saw it. He saw it too, through my eyes. The red laser-dot blossomed on his forehead like a zit on prom night. We both knew what it meant.

"Give it up, Hybern, we have you covered."

His control wavered for the second it took him to identify the voice through my memories, but that was all I needed. Coming up out of the chair I hooked a right fist at his gut. I missed and he tossed me clean across the desk. Twisting, I ended up in his chair, with my feet pointing at the ceiling.

I felt helpless and I fed that along to Hybern as he tried to defend himself.

Dol didn't need my assist. In the past I had cause to doubt whether or not the Secmeck boards the Weasel had sold me for Dol were genuine. Rendered a copper Valkyrie by the lights, she drove at him like he was a Wolf-Warrior holding Girl Scouts hostage. Her left fist landed about where I'd meant my punch to. He doubled over and she dropped him with a right to the side of his head.

Dol vaulted the desk and pulled me upright. "Are you hurt?" Her laser scanned me for a second, then winked off.

I shook my head, but that hurt, so I stopped. "He dribbled my brain around inside my skull, but aside from that,

I'm okay." I sat down in the chair the correct way and massaged my temples.

She cocked her head to the right, then blinked her eyes at me. "I just contacted the police. They say the Feds are sending a couple of Hoovermatics to take him into custody. One of his disciples was a Senator."

"Wow!" I looked at Dol. She had a dark jacket over a red chemise and dark skirt. A black leatherette bag hung on a gold chain from her right shoulder. They matched the black shoes on her feet. I stared at her. "I'm stunned."

"I've called the cops for you hundreds of times before."

"No, the outfit." I swallowed hard. "Wow!"

"Oh, this?" She helped me up out of the chair and we walked toward the elevator. "You told me to get something so we could go dancing."

I nodded and smiled at her. "So how'd you know I was in trouble here?"

Her head waggled back and forth, which is her equivalent of a shrug. "I was buying the purse at the same time you charged the airline tickets."

"You thought I was taking off with Louise Cogshill."

"At first." She fell mum as the elevator doors opened and Bureaumecks rolled down the corridor. "Then you typed in the check code and I knew you were in trouble."

We got into the elevator and it started climbing upward. "How? The bank didn't kick it. I typed the word perfectly."

Her head swiveled toward me. "I know. I know you. You didn't miss a single key."

"Oh." I stepped back and looked at her again. "That outfit cost you a full K?"

"Of course not, silly." The elevator doors opened and I saw a suitbag draped like a shroud over the goon she'd coldcocked on her way in. "We have a date to go dancing. If

I dress up, so do you. We are going, aren't we?"

I looked up and saw Louise enter the HOMME lobby. "Is it over?"

I nodded and felt her relief roll over me like a tidal wave.

"I don't know how I can ever thank you," her lips said, but I saw her mind had some fine ideas about gratitude. "Can we discuss things over dinner? Tonight?"

I looked at her and thought about the plane tickets Hybern had made me book. Thought long. Thought hard. She could do a lot to make long, cold winter nights seem neither.

I shook my head. "Sorry, Louise, but I'm a stalled car on the railroad crossing of love." I shouldered the suitbag and slipped my arm around Dol's waist. "And tonight I'm dancing down the rails with a dame on steel wheels."

"**Asgard Unlimited**" was written for an anthology titled *Lord of the Fantastic*—which were stories all in honor of Roger Zelazny. For a while I'd been toying around with the idea of what would happen if the God of the Old Testament took a look at the last two millennia and decided to take the family firm back from his son, regressing to that old-time religion. In essence, the spiritual reset button would be punched, taking things back to the first century, but with all our tech. This piece was a proof of that concept.

Asgard Unlimited

Aside from the raven-shit on his shoulders, Odin looked pretty good in the Armani suit. The matching blue pinstriping on the eyepatch was a nice touch. Odin had never been a slouch, but even I was impressed at how quickly he was picking up on the ways of this new age.

He looked down on me from a composite video screen taller than he had ever been in life. He wore a smile that I knew was for the benefit of his audience, but the spectators in Valhalla assumed the smile was for them. If it pleased them to think so, I saw no reason to disabuse them of this notion. I was feeling too good to indulge myself.

I stood in the Grand Foyer of Valhalla and smiled at what I had wrought. Massive steel spears were bound together to form pillars and rafters, giving the grand hall the retro-martial look all the architectural journals had raved about. In the old Valhalla the roof had been made of shields, but I had them cast in lexan so they let light in during the day and allowed people permitted into the upper reaches to see the stars at night. Carefully crafted sword-shaped sconces hid halogen lights that provided the lower levels with a constant, timeless glow.

The old, tired wooden benches, moth-eaten tapestries

and well-worn animal skins had been replaced with more modern Scandinavian furnishings. Shields, swords, spears and armor all still figured into the motifs, but that's because they were familiar to people. One of the special aspects of the new Valhalla allowed everyone to see some decorations as those things with which they were most familiar—the Christers spoke in tongues, we provided Icons-for-all.

Valhalla was a beautiful place no one would mind dwelling in for eternity. The Valkyries were certainly striking and one of our better attractions. It took me a while to convince Odin that bringing in men to wear similarly brief outfits would be a good way to offer something to the female market. He finally succumbed after I convinced him that he thought up the name by which the beefcake would be known. "Valiants" were now one of our more popular features.

Then again, Odin had not been the reactionary element among the Aesir. At the very first briefing I gave the others just over a year ago, Odin had already begun to adapt to the changed circumstances. The Perry Ellis ensemble he wore had been a season out of date, but of a conservative enough cut to enhance the patriarchal nobility that had long been his trademark.

The others were a bit slower to adjust, but that was how it always had been. Thor, wearing some urban commando fatigues, began to do a wonderful imitation of a beached fish gasping for oxygen the moment I walked into the room. Tyr noticed my entrance, but returned to studying the bio-mechanical prosthesis replacing his right hand. He opened and closed the fist in rough time with the opening and closing of Thor's mouth.

And Heimdall, well, that venomous glare took me back centuries.

Thor slammed a fist onto the conference room table, pulverizing Formica and particleboard. "What is *he* doing here?" Wood dust rose up in a great cloud and lodged firmly in Thor's red beard. "It's his trickery that has woven these illusions that mask Asgard's true nature."

Odin slowly shook his snow-maned head. "No, Loki is the reason we are all here; hence his place with us."

Little lightning bolts trickled from Thor's eyes as he glanced at me. "It is a trick, Odin Val-father. This is the one who had Baldur slain. It was he who caused the Ragnarok, in which we were slain . . ."

"Is that so, Thunderer?" I smiled and seated myself in the chair at the opposite end of the lozenge table from Odin. "I triggered Ragnarok?"

"Don't seek to deny it." Thor folded his arms over his chest, his bulging muscles sorely testing the resiliency of his jacket's synthetic fibers. "We know this is true. The serpent and I slew each other. Odin died in Fenris' maw and Tyr slew the hell-hound Garm, but was slain by him. Heimdall killed you and you him. This we know."

I allowed myself a little laugh and had Odin not smiled and nodded in my direction, any of my brethren would have gladly torn me apart. "How do you know this, Thor? Do you recall smiting the serpent with Mjolnir? And you, Tyr, do you recall Garm's bite?" My smile died a bit as I regarded Heimdall. "And you, do you recall the twisting agony of my sword in your guts?"

Heimdall's smile revealed a glittering mouthful of golden teeth. "No more than my hands remember twisting your head off."

I shot the cuffs of my shirt to cover the momentary difficulty I had swallowing. "None of us have memories of the events of Ragnarok actually happening. We knew what *would* happen, how the world would end, because of Odin's wisdom and the various oracles that predicted the twilight of the gods, but we did not live through that predicted end."

Tyr's hand snapped shut. "Do not try to tell me Baldur did not die. I feel the pain of his loss still in my heart."

"You are absolutely right, Tyr, he did die, but the events his death presaged did not come to pass. There was no Ragnarok."

"Impossible!" Thor started to pound the table again, but a rare bit of restraint left his fist poised to strike. "Ragnarok must have happened. There has been so much nothing—I must have been dead. I will not believe there was no twilight of the gods."

I gave him my most disarming smile and his fist began to slowly drift down. "There was a twilight, but not the one we expected."

Thor's red eyebrows collided with confusion. "Was there or was there not a Ragnarok?"

"*Our* Ragnarok, no." Odin laid his left hand on Thor's arm. "Allow Loki to explain."

Thor grumbled and glowered at me. "Speak on, Deceiver."

"For forever and a day we have known of other gods and their realms. We have also known that we draw life from the belief of our worshippers in us. Their prayers and invocations, sacrifices and vows sustain us." I opened my hands. "We use the power they give us to grant boons to our favorites, inspiring others to greater belief and sacrifice in the hopes we will favor them, too."

My fellow gods squirmed a bit in their chairs. Though they knew nothing of B. F. Skinner, they had intuitively grasped the fact that random interval reinforcement was truly the most powerful inducement to create and maintain a behavior pattern. Often, in fact, we received credit for things we did not do. If a tree fell on a longhouse during a storm, the enemies of the person so afflicted would offer thanks to me or another god for our smiting of their enemy.

There may be no such thing as a free lunch, but people are much more protective about their food than they are their devotion.

"Well to the south of our Midgard holdings, in the desert crossroads, Jehovah decided to retire."

Heimdall's treasure-trove smile broadened. "Had I created the world in six days, I would have chosen more than one day's rest, too."

We all laughed. While it was true most of us could not remember where we had come from, and therefore made up rather elaborate stories about our antecedents, only Jehovah had come up with the tale of his being the end-all and be-all of existence. While claiming to have killed your own parents wasn't necessarily the most attractive story we could have come up with, it was easier for humans to relate to than a tale of willing oneself into full-blown, egotistical existence.

"I'm certain that had something to do with it, Heimdall. In any event, to facilitate his retirement, he had a fling with a human and she gave birth to a son, Joshua—though he is now more commonly known as Jesus and the Christ. He performed some miracles, gave his people the benefit of his wisdom, then hung from a tree until dead."

Thor frowned. "How long was he on the tree?"

"An afternoon."

The god of Thunder snickered. "An afternoon? That's nothing compared to Odin's nine days, and he was stuck on his own spear at the time."

"Josh may well have heard of the tale, or his followers

did, because there was a spear-sticking involved in the whole incident, too. His disciples bundled him off to a tomb, and after a day and a half, Josh came back to life." I shrugged my shoulders. "Again, a substandard performance, but one that was convincing for his people."

Tyr swept golden locks away from his blue eyes. "I recall hearing of this Christ when some of his followers were slain for spreading his story among my people."

My eyes narrowed. "Would that we had realized the danger of his cult. This Christ demanded two things of his followers. The first he borrowed from his father: they were to have no gods but him before them. This demand of exclusivity is fine when you are a lonely godling ruling over nomads in featureless wastes—there were no other gods who wanted those people."

Odin frowned. "When Jehovah's people were captive in Thothheim and Baalheim, they were no threat to the indigenous gods."

"No, but the Christ's second demand of his believers is what made them malignant." I put an edge into my voice so even Thor could understand what I was saying was important. "The Christ demanded they share their religion with others, who would then become exclusively his and spread the faith further."

Thor shook his head. "I don't believe you. I would remember such a thing."

"You don't remember because the Christ movement took hold in our realm almost overnight. As we concerned ourselves with the coming of Ragnarok, the Christers stole into our lands. Our believers dwindled, then abandoned us. We fell into the sleep of the forgotten."

Heimdall cocked an eyebrow at me. "If this is true, if we all became forgotten, how is it you know this story?"

I pressed my hands together, fingertip to fingertip. "In their zeal to spread Christism, they linked me with Lucifer, the ancient enemy Jehovah spawned and who tormented Joshua. There are those humans who always go against the prevailing sentiment of society, and worshipping me became a viable alternative for them."

Tyr reached up with his mechanical hand and tried to pluck a fly out of the air. "If these Christers hold sway, how are we here, now?"

My smile broadened. "Christism did become quite widespread and certainly became the dominant religion in the world, but it is based on tolerance and pacifism. As a result, some evils in the world go unchecked. I believe it was the slaughter of Jehovah's core constituency in Central Europe that first alarmed Jehovah. He took a look at what the Christ had done with the family firm and initiated a hostile takeover of the enterprise. He forced Joshua out and returned things to the way they had been. Joshua immediately struck out on his own, but his people had become fragmented and his doctrine muddled. At the same time Christism became seen by any number of people as theological imperialism, so they rejected it and returned to the old ways.

"Our ways."

"I cannot believe it." Thor frowned mightily. "You say this Christ was a pacifist who preached tolerance."

"Exactly."

"No fighting? No warrior tradition?"

"No, he was a pacifist. He completely eschewed violence."

Thor's lower lip quivered for a moment. "If he was a pacifist, how were we defeated?"

I smiled. "He offered people something they wanted. He

promised them life after death."

"So did we."

Odin pressed his hands to the tabletop. "This brings us to the point of this meeting. The return of people to the old faiths has given us another chance at life, but these people are not the people we knew of old. Things are different, now, and we must avail ourselves of the means we have today to guarantee we do not go away again."

Thor shook his head. "I don't understand. We are the gods. We do not change. People worship us for what we are, what we offer them."

"And there is the problem." I frowned. "Quite frankly, the Aesir are a public relations nightmare. All of us here have our warrior aspects, but war just isn't in vogue anymore."

Thor's eyes blazed. "War is the most noble and lofty pursuit to which a man can aspire. This is why the boldest and most brave warriors are plucked by the Valkyries from the fields of the dead and brought to Valhalla. Odin himself ordered warriors to be buried with their arms and armor so they would be prepared to join us in the last days, fighting against our foes at Ragnarok!"

I sighed. "Look, we really need to rethink this Ragnarok thing. The Christers pretty much own the idea of a grand battle to usher in the end of the world, so our Ragnarok just comes across as a pale imitation of their Armageddon. And this warriors-only thing, that's got to go, too."

The god of thunder's voice boomed. "What? You want to admit other than warriors to Valhalla?"

"Thor, what you would recognize as warriors in this era carry weapons that can kill a man at over a mile. Most of the wars now are called police actions, which means people far away use weapons that hit with the force of Mjolnir to shatter their enemy's cities. The heroic nature of combat you recall so fondly is no more."

Thor's florid face drained of color. "There are no more humans who bravely venture out, risking life and limb, to defeat their enemies and reap riches for themselves?"

"There are, but they battle away in commercial wars."

"Merchants?"

"Think of them as captains of industry."

"You want to admit *merchants* to Valhalla?" Thor shook his head. "Next you will want to allow women into that hallowed hall."

I winced. "Actually, I *did* want to bring women in, but several of the mother-goddess cults have combined with feminism to really block our inroads there. Face it, while all of your wives were wonderful, they're not as inspiring as the Mediterranean goddesses. Still, focusing on men gives us a potential market of roughly half the world's population, and that half controls the majority of the wealth in the world."

"Wealth?" Tyr frowned. "I agree with Thor. We want nobility and courage."

"No, we want *believers*. To attract them, we have to give them something the Christers won't." I smiled. "One of the Christ's pronouncements is that it will be easier for a camel to pass through the eye of a needle than it will for a rich man to enter Paradise. We've got a longstanding tradition of having a person buried with his material possessions so he can have them in the afterlife. We'll build on that tradition and have people flocking in."

I leaned forward. "Welcome to Asgard Unlimited. We're in the religion business. Our slogan is this: Asgard Unlimited—you *can* take it with you."

Heimdall's visage darkened. "The people you speak of attracting sound less like worshippers than pillagers and scavengers, coming to us to see what we can give them."

"You have to understand, all of you, that the human of today is less a worshipper than a fan. They don't so much believe in anyone or anything as much as they believe in and worship the myth surrounding a phenomena. Being gods is certainly impressive, but we need to become more, something that allows everyone to participate in our mystique."

I nodded toward the head of the table. "The three of you will form a trinity—the Christers made that popular and we can use the pattern. Odin will be the head of things and preside over Valhalla. His job will be to dispense wisdom and help our people prosper in their endeavors.

"We'll remake Valhalla into something new and sophisticated. As we have in the past, we'll thin the line between the living and the dead, bringing in dead celebrities to meet and greet folks. This will prove our claims of the afterlife— something the Christers never do. We also want Valhalla to be a fun place—with family entertainment as well as more adult pursuits."

"Adult pursuits?"

I looked at Tyr. "You've not forgotten Odin's taste for hot and cold running Valkyries, have you? One part of Valhalla will be the Hooters of the Gods. Another section will be devoted to weekend warriors—people who always wanted to fight but never had the chance. Add in a casino, an amusement park, a 'Warfare of the Ages' exhibit area, and we have pretty much everything covered. Since Valhalla has five hundred and forty doors, we'll franchise them out to the major population centers of the world, meaning the site stays centralized, but people can get together instantly. That will greatly boost our commercial bookings—conventions everywhere will be coming to us."

I pointed at Tyr. "Your role is going to be that of the divine Princeling. Royalty has gotten a bad name of late, but Tyr, you're the one who can bring nobility back to it. Tragically wounded while saving the rest of the gods, you're already a heroic figure. You're also favored by sportsmen, and sports is big business. You're a natural for skiing and other winter sports at the more exclusive hideaways in the world. If you can pick up golf, cricket, and yachting, you'll be pitching straight to our core market."

Tyr slowly smiled. "All I have to do is spend my time involved in sport, associating with the rich and beautiful?"

"That's it."

"I'm willing to listen more."

I turned to Heimdall. "Though I ridiculed you in the past for the job of being the Aesir's watchman, now is a time we need your keen eyes and ears to safeguard our enterprise. Before you listened for enemies approaching Bifrost on their way to Asgard. Now we will have many more bridges, and each of them will bear watching."

The smile that had begun to blossom on Heimdall's face with my initial remarks froze. "I may be a god, but I cannot monitor the whole world without help."

"And help you shall have." From my pocket I fished a remote control and pointed it at the wall to my right. Hitting a button, I brought a dancing picture to life. "This is television. In our Valhalla you will be able to watch hundreds of such monitors, seeing what they see, hearing the sounds they hear. There is no corner of Midgard that you will not be able to see immediately. When you see danger, you get on the horn—ah, the telephone, not Gjallarhorn— and warn us what is going on.

"It is a grave responsibility," I said, handing him the remote, "but no one else can handle it."

Heimdall brandished the plastic box as if it were Hofud, his sword. "I shall be ever vigilant."

Thor thrust his lower lip out in a pout. "You say war is revered no more. There is nothing for me in your Asgard Unlimited."

"Ah, but there is—a very special role indeed." I gave him a genuine smile. "Among humans there is a need for idols. Many of them come out of sports, and Tyr will cover them, but others come from the entertainment industry. James Dean, Marilyn Monroe, Bruce Lee, Elvis—each of them has attained a near divinity because of how they entertained people."

"But I am a warrior! There is no entertainment for which I am suited."

"You're so wrong, my friend. There is a form of entertainment here that was made for you." I rubbed my hands together. "It's called professional wrestling."

Gunnar, my aide, cleared his throat and brought me back to the present. "If you have a moment, Divinity."

"Always." I reached back and rubbed at the sore spot on my spine. "What do you have?"

"We got our shipment of the new summer-color eye patches in and they're set to go on sale in our boutiques this afternoon. This includes the ones that allow you to tan beneath them."

"Good. What about the Odin jackets?"

Gunnar frowned. "The supplier says the sub-contractor they've got making the ravens has really done a poor job. They're able to join the ravens to the jacket's shoulders and they stand up, but they lose feathers and the eyes fall out."

"You tell them more than their eyes will fall out if they don't fix the problem." I glanced at the video screen behind me and then at my watch. "When is Odin due back?"

"Not for a couple of hours. He's just begun speaking in Tokyo and won't come through from our doorway there for at least another three hours." Gunnar smiled. "By the way, we got the fax this morning: ***The One-eyed God's Business Wisdom*** is going to start at number one on the *Times* list. It's bumping Jesus' ***Business Beatitudes: Charity Before Profit*** from the top spot. Herakles' ***Twelve Labors' Lessons*** will be out in two weeks, but pre-orders are soft, so we'll remain at number one for a while. We'll be selling a lot of books. And Letterman wants Odin in to help host a segment of 'Stupid Demi-God Tricks.' "

"Tell Letterman's people it's a deal, but questions about CBS are off-limits." Struck by the symbology of the network's logo, Odin bought it and didn't take well to criticism from his employees. I sighed, anticipating another long lecture from the Val-father about my making bookings for him. In the end I knew he'd see reason, but enduring the discussion would be torture.

Still, it was all in service to a worthy cause.

"Anything else?"

"Yes, Divinity." He looked down at the personal digital assistant he carried, then grinned. "Ticket sales are way up for the Great Battles of History Symposium series. The Rommel/Patton debate really got people juiced to hear more."

"Who is up next?"

"Hannibal and the two Scipios, Elder and Younger. Nike is going to underwrite part of the cost."

"Right, they have those Air Hannibal hiking books." I nodded. "Very good. Make sure we have plenty of them stocked in our gift shops before and after that debate. I take it Tyr's still in court?"

Gunnar nodded. "Case should go to the jury in two

277

weeks. We anticipate a victory. The other side has good lawyers, but ours are devilishly clever and even the most stone-hearted troll would side with Tyr against a tabloid."

"Good. Keep on top of these things and keep me informed." I gave Gunnar a pat on the shoulder. "I'm going to go see my daughter, but I should be back in an hour or so."

I felt the shudder run through him, but I ignored it and wended my way through the crowd waiting in line to get into the Thor memorial. I was tempted to shift my shape into that of my lost comrade, just to give them a thrill, but the chances of starting a riot weren't worth it. I passed through them unnoticed, smiling as every third or fourth person remarked on what a pity his death had been.

I thought it was more tragic—grandly tragic at that. Thor had taken to professional wrestling like a fly to carrion. He knew there was no one who could best him in a fight, and the audience knew that as well. Every night, every bout, it was a morality play. It was a reenactment of the classic solar hero struggle to overcome the forces of evil and return to a new day and dawn. The bouts would start even; then Thor's foe would use some underhanded trick to gain a temporary advantage. Thor would take a beating and while his foe danced around the arena, exultant and triumphant, Thor would crawl to his corner and pull on his belt of might and gloves of iron.

I used to thrill to it. His enemy—some steroided mutant man or odd demi-god from pantheons best left to their obscurity—would remain innocently unaware of his danger. The crowd would begin to pound their feet in a thunderous cadence and Thor would draw power from it. Their desire to see him win, their belief in his invincibility, fueled him.

He would slam his gloves together, letting their peal spread through the crowd, then he would turn and vanquish his foe.

The end came when he fought Louis the Serpent. Louis was yet another in a line of forgettable foes to face Thor, but we'd arranged for a worldwide satellite hook-up. Thor's fame and popularity was peaking—ninety-five percent of the people on the planet could identify him. This bout would solidify his place in the minds of all humanity. Thor had known from the first moment of sentience that he was meant to fight a great serpent, and Louis became it.

And Louis killed him.

After three rounds of battering each other silly, Louis picked him up in a big bear hug and snapped his spine. He cast Thor aside and laughed at his fallen foe. Then he laughed at Thor's fans, called them weak and stupid. He said they were pathetic for having believed in him and that they were losers because their god was dead.

Thor's death was a crushing blow for us, but not for long. Little by slowly, stories began to filter in about Thor having been seen here and there. There was no mistaking him, of course. He helped people out of difficult situations, averted disasters and made the impossible happen for them. To each and every one of his worshippers these stories were proof that he lived and that their faith was anything but false.

In death Thor became bigger than he ever was in life. Caps, shirts, the Craftsman line of Mjolnir tools, the comics, videos and action figures all went through the roof in sales. While Odin was doing very well with his books and motivational speaking engagements, and Tyr added a layer of respectability to Asgard Unlimited, Thor was the backbone of its popularity.

Past the memorial I stepped up to a door few could see and fewer could open. I could and did, passing through and petting Garm as I did so. The hell-hound would have gladly taken my hand off at the shoulder, but he feared my son Fenris, so I was safe. Past him I headed down the spiral stairs that took me to Niflhel, my daughter Hel's domain. I tossed a quick salute to Baldur—making as if I was going to flick my mistletoe boutonniere at him. He flinched and I laughed.

Compared to Valhalla, the mist-shrouded depths of Niflhel were cold and claustrophobic, but I found it bracing and cozy at the same time. The vaporous veils softened the light and dulled sound, though I was certain my laughter had penetrated into the depths.

Confirmation of that fact came from the rising and incoherent growl on my left. Through the mists a huge, shadowed form lunged at me. Its eyes blazed and its teeth flashed; then the length of chain binding it to the heart of the underworld ran out of slack. It tightened, jerking the collar and creature back. It landed with a heavy thud, shaking the ground, then lay there with sobs wracking its chest.

I squatted down at the very edge of its range. "Will you never learn, Thor?"

"This chain *will* break."

I shook my head. "I think not. If you will recall, the chain forged to restrain Fenris resisted the efforts of any of the gods to break it, yourself included. That chain was made from the meow of a cat, the beard of a woman, the roots of a mountain, the tendons of a bear, the breath of a fish and the spittle of a bird. For you I alloyed in yet other things, both tangible and intangible. There's Nixon's belief in his own innocence, the true identity of the man on the grassy knoll and not a little bit of Kevlar. The same goes for the collar. You are here until I decide you are to be released."

Thor pulled himself up into a sitting position. "I know how you did it. You invited me in for a celebratory drink before my match and drugged me, then took my shape and were killed by the serpent."

"Very good—you've been using your head for something more than a helm-filler."

"You won't get away with it. Heimdall has to have seen what you did, and what you have been doing. He knows you have been masquerading as me. He will expose you."

"Ha!" I stood and looked down upon him. "Heimdall spends every hour of every day watching the programming on over five hundred television stations. Even a god cannot escape transformation into a drooling vidiot when subjected to that much television. He's so mesmerized he couldn't blow his nose, much less blow his horn."

"Why?"

"Why what? Why fake your death?" I shook my head. "How often do I have to go over this with you? Every human idol must pass through the mystery of death. Death absolves you of guilt and hides your blemishes. You're more perfect in death than you ever were in life, just like Elvis and Marilyn, Bruce Lee and Kurt Cobain. From the start I knew I needed someone to die, and you were it. Odin had already done it and hadn't had very good results, and death is just too inelegant for Tyr. That left you—Mr. Big, Dumb and Vulnerable."

"*That* I understand." Electricity sparked in Thor's eyes. "I want to know why the deceptions? Why do I appear everywhere? Why build up my army of believers?"

"Because they aren't *your* believers." I snorted derisively

at him. "If all those people who worship Thor were worshipping you, this chain would be like a spider-web to you.
You could tear it and me apart. You can't because they
don't worship you. They worship the *image* of you—the ro-
manticized image of you that *I* project."

I smiled. "My friend Louis and I, after having been so
long linked and vilified by the Christers, realized we could
never be transformed into the noble and hunky sort of god
that people would accept. Lucifer had a constituency—he-
donists, anarchists, selfish, venial people and impotent
people who wanted a shortcut to power. As Louis the Serpent he fed all those 'get it now and easy' fantasies. In
showing contempt for your believers, he earned the respect
of those who hated your image, and he earned quite a bit of
hatred from your people. That was his payoff."

I pressed my hands to my chest. "And I became the
Thor I helped create through the media. What you sowed, I
reap."

Thor hung his head. "When you said we needed to rethink Ragnarok . . .'"

"I wanted it rethought because the way it was scripted
before, I *lost*. No more. Odin is distracted by his writing and
speaking and running his network. Tyr has his diversions—
and I do like that Diana; she looks very good on the arm of
a god. He spends most of his time suing tabloids for stories
they print about him, attending parties and running that
football team he bought. Neither of them is a threat to me.
Odin's star will fade soon enough—seldom does a business
guru survive more than a dozen years before being completely eclipsed, and there's nothing more boring than yes-
terday's financial genius. As for Tyr, a sportsman gigolo
who bumps indolently from one resort to another becomes
pitiful rather quickly. He'll get a talk show, it will be can-

celed, then he can join George Hamilton on the beach."

"And you win."

"At least the preliminary round."

Thor raised his head. "Why keep me around? Is it pity or contempt you have for me?"

"Neither, my friend." I squatted again and tugged at the fringe of his beard. "I only have the utmost of respect for you. You, I need."

"What?"

"As I said, I win the preliminary round, which means I'm going up against other gods. The Meso-Americans appear to be consolidating their pantheons. I expect the war between the Buddhists and Maoists in China will soon be resolved. Jehovah is holding his own and appears to be usurping Allah's position. The Christ is still strong. And then there's the serpent of Eden."

I saw the lightning again spark in Thor's eyes. "Yes, Thor, war might not be in vogue in this world right now, but I think the gods will change that. There's going to be a new Ragnarok, a bigger, nastier one, and in it, my friend, you will get your crack at a serpent."

His hunger was such that I could taste its bitterness. "Promise?"

"You have my solemn oath on it." I smiled, then stood and let the mist hide him from me. "The *true* twilight of the gods fast approaches and this time, I mean to survive to the dawn."

"Shepherd" is a Talion short story, featuring Nolan, the hero of *Talion: Revenant*. The story was written after the first draft of the novel, but already had Nolan leaning in the direction of the character he became when I rewrote the novel. (The first draft of that novel was disposed of in a Dumpster late one night after I realized how dreadful it was.)

Shepherd

I swung down out of the saddle and tied Wolf's reins to a maple tree. I patted his neck, watched and listened. Wolf was smart for a horse and remained silent while I studied the meadow beyond the woods' edge. We were almost alone.

Argent sunlight reflected from long, green summer grasses. Gold stalks of wild wheat waved in the breeze while bluebells and pine branches danced at the wind's urging. Bees darted unerringly between flowers while butterflies, brilliantly lit in shades of yellow or orange, floated from plant to plant. Off to my left, hidden amid the forest of tall cattails, a small stream gurgled through the meadow.

If not for the flies, it would have been perfect. Black specks buzzed without end. They circled and landed, so small yet so demanding of attention. Their bodies were the color of oily bubbles: the vibrant false color that fades to dull black when subjected to harsh scrutiny. For the barest of moments, though I understood their part and purpose in life, I hated the clouds of them hanging over her.

She had been young—barely fourteen or fifteen. Her hair, what little of the curly locks that remained unmatted with blood, was white blond. Her eyes, staring blindly up at the sun, were blue. Her face had none of the elfin beauty they'd described to me. Her body was broken and twisted.

I dropped to one knee beside her. Flies rose, angrily hummed and landed on me until I scattered them with a shake of my head. Then they hovered over or landed on nearby plants, waiting for me to leave. I shook my head again. They would feast on her no more.

I could only study her body for a minute because the villagers from Grifmont were following close behind me. I knew just from looking at her that she'd been beaten to death and mutilated thereafter. Though her throat had been cut, there was little blood, which meant she was dead before her body was slashed. She was not a pretty sight and it was clear the knifeman had enjoyed his work.

I reached over and gently closed her eyes.

I nodded to myself and stood. I knew the identity of her killer. I untied Wolf's reins and led the bay stallion back from the meadow down the woods' trail. I met the villagers coming around the first corner I reached.

Her mother and father clung to each other and walked three steps behind the village headman. "Did you find her?" the headman demanded of me.

I nodded. I looked away from him and directly into her mother's eyes. She and her daughter shared the same color eyes and, staring into those deep blue depths, I faltered. "Kara died painlessly. I would guess she was led away from Grifmont willingly, then knocked out. She felt nothing."

She clenched her jaw to stop it from trembling. Her husband hugged her and whispered in her ear, but she did not hear him. Her fist tightened and twisted more of his tunic. She stared at me, fury burning all weakness from her. "Do you speak the truth?"

The headman whirled on her. "Quiet woman, he tells

the truth. He's a Talion isn't he? He cannot lie!" The headman turned his white-haired head to me and smiled. "No offense meant to you, my Lord Talion, but she's distraught."

No one there so much as breathed. All the townsfolk stared at me and willed me to forgive her. I was a Talion, worse yet a Justice. I was one of the lonely folk enforcing laws of an empire that collapsed in disorder and civil war a thousand years ago. My word was law, and my sentence was death.

All of them knew that. They believed I would strike her dead for heated words spoken in anger. I knew the words were not directed at me as much as they were directed at the gods or demons that must have conspired to take her daughter away from her. She wanted to believe I was right, that Kara had felt nothing, but any pain her daughter could have suffered was her pain as well.

No Justice, no matter how inhumanly cold-hearted, could take offense at her words.

I breathed out slowly. "Kara felt no pain."

Macinne, the headman, sighed audibly. "You being a Justice, you'll be wanting to go after him, eh?"

"That is my intention. His day of judgment is long overdue." I balled my right hand into a fist. Despite the noon warmth, my palm was ice cold. The headman glanced at my fist and shuddered. He'd seen the death's-head tattoo on it earlier, and spotted me as a Justice immediately.

Some of the other villagers grumbled a bit, but the headman shook his head. "Well, we figgered it would come to this. No one will get in your way. He may have been good to us in the past, but no more. You'll find him up in the castle's crypt, or so the legends say."

I frowned. "What castle? You can't be talking about the

girl's killer. Hasan ra Kas has never been good to anyone, and, to the best of my knowledge, he's never even been in Leth before this."

The headman returned my frown. "I don't know who this Hasan is. She was cut, eh, like a lamb being slaughtered?" At that, Kara's mother broke and cried out, but it didn't stop Macinne for a second. "It was the Duke what did it to her, Talion. He's been awake again recent. Killed a dog and some sheep in Elmford and a calf in Clayton on the same night a week or so ago. Makes sense he'd take something from Grifmont."

Neighbors led the girl's parents back down the mountainside while a group of men climbed further up to retrieve the girl's body. I snorted and snarled, "That's impossible, those towns are twenty miles apart—thirty by the road. It couldn't be done. No man, even with a fast horse, could do it in one night."

The old man narrowed his brown eyes. "The Duke, Griff ra Leth, can do it."

The second he said the name I recognized it. Another Talion, an Elite from Leth, used to tell stories of his homeland. His favorite tales, best told around a roaring campfire when the world ceases to exist outside the fire's dome of light, were of Griff, the Demon Duke of Leth. "Nolan, have you heard this one?" he'd ask, then launch into a grisly tale of murder and necromancy. I remembered the stories all too well; just hearing the Duke's name sent shivers scurrying down my spine.

The old man seated himself on a fallen log. "Aye, Talion, Duke Griff could do it. You don't know the tales of the old days like I do. I've lived in Grifmont, in the shadow of Castel Griffin, for all my life. My family's been here for ten generations. My grandfather died at Duke Griff's hands, and he came back and killed my grandmother. We ended up burning both of them so they'd be free of the Duke."

My eyes narrowed. Pieces of Erlan's stories came back. "I know of the Duke. A friend of mine, a Talion, told me of him."

The old man snorted. "Sure, and he'd be knowing the Duke better than I? No, Talion, you don't know the Duke. You and your friend have not lived here and heard the beasts of the forest scream when he takes them. A rogue bear, a human bandit, those he and his legion of wolves take when they can. When he can't . . ." He nodded uphill toward the meadow.

I shook my head. "Doesn't sound like the Duke Griff I was told about. A noble who experimented with demons; a man who killed his vassals to find an elixir of immortality. He died three centuries ago. You've nothing to fear from him, he's a tale to scare children. Besides, Hasan ra Kas killed the girl."

The old man stabbed a bony finger at me. "You've been fooled like all the rest, Talion. They don't remember the terror from before, like it's been told from father to son in my family. He's real, Talion, and it'll take the like of you to destroy him." He rubbed his chin and looked far away. "Going to lay a witching line around the village tonight, that's certain," he mumbled.

The old man's superstitious fear infuriated me. "That may well work to keep a vampire at bay, old man, but my mission is to destroy Hasan ra Kas, and a witching line won't even slow him down. He murdered the girl and he probably had two of his men kill the animals on the same night in Elmford and Clayton just to make you think the Duke was real and haunting these woods. You'd be better off seeing to it that no one strays from Grifmont until I return with Hasan's head."

The old man didn't hear my explanation. I could not tell him that I was certain Hasan lurked nearby because a shipment of gold from Memkar—meant to pay off debts in Imperiana—was to travel through the area in a day or two. It was a caravan Hasan meant to rob. The headman was lost in his belief that a man three centuries dead was responsible for the girl's death. Compromising the caravan's security would do nothing to sway him.

The old man hawked and spat to the side. "I'll not be the man to call a Justice a fool. I hope you're right, Talion, because a runner from Clayton arrived in Grifmont after you went out hunting. The Duke took a girl, name of Rori, from there last night." The headman looked beyond me and pointed up at the ruined Castel atop Griffin Mountain. "There's your answer, Talion. Up there, that's the key."

I let the headman vanish down the trail, leading the men who carried the blanket upon which they laid the girl's remains. Another blanket covered her and one of the men picked bluebells and laid them on her chest. I nodded solemnly to the bearers, then crossed in their wake, unhitched Wolf from a tree and mounted up.

I waited for the old man to leave because I was bound for Castel Griffin. The ruins squatted on the mountaintop like an obscenely obese grey toad. The rubble from crumbling walls lay in piles around the castle's base as if rolls of fatty flesh flowed down to obliterate any outline of the castle's true structure. It did not look inviting, but I refused to think of it as haunted by Duke Griff or anything else. This, despite the fact the only reason it remained there at all was because no one in the area dared steal stones from it for their own homes.

The old man had been right in one respect, the castle was the key. From Castel Griffin I'd be able to see the whole of the surrounding territory, from Elmford to Clayton and down into the valley where the road ran through Grifmont. I knew Hasan and the men he had with him were very cautious, but there was a chance they might light a small fire visible from the mountain, and that was a chance I had to take to narrow down my search area.

It took me the better part of the afternoon to reach the mountain's summit. Higher western peaks nibbled on the sun and shrouded the castle in deep shadows. I tied Wolf to a tree and let him graze on the summer grass while I climbed the last hundred yards to the castle's shattered front gate and walked into the rubble-strewn courtyard.

At the first sound I crouched and held my right hand out to the right in case I had to summon my *tsincaat*. Other Justices were far better at that trick than I—the ability to call our swords to the death's-head tattoo in our right palms—but even I knew it was swifter to summon the blade than to draw it manually. But my cautionary reaction was not needed because the creature that made the sound poked its head through a gap in the rocks and bleated softly at me. It was a sheep.

I stood slowly with a grin on my face. The sheep backed and turned away when I stepped forward. The overgrown courtyard held a flock of thirty or forty sheep. Across the courtyard from me, the shepherd appeared in a doorway leading into the manor's ruins. He stared at me for a second, then smiled and bowed his head in my direction.

"Welcome. You are a Talion, are you not?" His voice was rich and his words courteous. He spoke haltingly, as if he was not used to speaking with people.

I bowed my head in return and relaxed. "Yes, I am a Talion. I did not expect to find anyone up here. Grifmont's headman said . . ."

The shepherd tossed his head back and laughed, cutting me off. "He said his grandfather slew his grandmother under the Duke's influence. The headmen in Elmford and Clayton would tell you the same thing if you spoke to them. I think they are all cousins. You expected to meet Duke Griff?"

I shook my head and smiled broadly. Perhaps it was my expectation of finding something sinister here and being presented with nothing more harmful than a shepherd, but whatever the reason, I felt quite at ease. The shepherd stood just above average height, which made him somewhat smaller than me, and was rather lean and hard. His hair was brown and touched with grey at the temples. Crow's-feet lined his face at the corners of his eyes and his hands looked calloused from hard work. His clothing was decently made of brown and grey wool, but had been patched several times.

I chuckled. "Grifmont's headman would have me believing the Duke was still up here, but I don't believe it. Actually I was half expecting to find a bandit scout in these ruins." I looked back out the gateway and toward the wooded hillsides looming over the nearly invisible roadway. "Out there, somewhere, is a motley bunch of land pirates." I turned back. "They've killed one girl already, have abducted another, and murdered livestock in a couple of places such that the villagers believe the Duke is back prowling."

The shepherd nodded grimly. "And you thought you'd wait up here until dark and spot their fire."

I nodded.

He waved me to a rock and seated himself on another one facing it. "Even though the mountains have swallowed the sun, it'll be a bit before it's dark enough to spot a fire. You're welcome to wait here until then. I don't often get company . . ."

I sat. "So, why aren't you afraid of the Duke?"

My question shocked him. He looked up, frowned for a moment, then shrugged his shoulders. "I don't know. He's really a tragic figure, you know . . ."

I raised an eyebrow. "How is he tragic? As I understand it he did horrid things to the people around here. I can't see anything romantic or tragic in his crimes."

The shepherd shook his head. "Of course you can't. You're a Justice. You have a purpose to your life. You have a goal. You'll go out and destroy these bandits and you'll be lauded for it. Because you're a Talion you only look at the result of the crime, you don't have to look at the root causes of it."

I frowned and wiped my forehead on my left sleeve. "I'm not willing to fully concede that point to you, but I will agree that by the time I am sent out after someone, that person has such a catalog of crimes to his name that he is often considered mad. But how could the Duke's motive excuse his crimes?"

"I never said he was innocent, I said he was tragic," the shepherd countered. "The Duke was a man so terrified of dying that he did anything he could, things that horrified him and made him sick, to forestall the inescapable."

"Yes, but I understand he even slew his newly born son in his mad search for immortality."

"Certainly, Talion, but can you imagine how that had to have torn him up? Can't you see that at the end of his quest he would finally beg for an end to the hideous existence he now called life? Could anyone want to live forever when that life means slaying anyone and anything dear to you?" The shepherd fell silent, then continued with some effort. "Some of the minstrels try to deal with that by suggesting the Duke rises to watch over those he used to abuse, but no one ever pays attention to those stories. No one thinks about the depth of pain that must drive someone to try and make amends like that." The shepherd shook his head slowly and looked down at his feet.

I said nothing. I sensed a need in him to talk and perhaps justify his own existence in the light of his discussion of the Duke. I knew there were no words I could voice that would help him or encourage him.

Finally he looked up with a pain-shot expression on his face. "I know what it is to be an outcast. I know how it feels to have everyone fear and loathe you. Imagine that for eternity, Talion, and then decide if there is any crime worth that punishment."

I pursed my lips and studied the silhouette of the tumbled castle walls before answering him. His statement told me more about him than he could ever imagine. He was like a thousand other men hiding throughout the Shattered Empire. At some point in his life he made a mistake and fled. He was not truly evil and could never join the outlaw bands that roamed the countryside, like Hasan and his men. He found solace in solitude, and worked on earning his own forgiveness. It would be a long time in coming, but it would make him a better man than any number of years in a prison or slave mine.

I nodded slowly. "No, I think you are correct. There is no crime worthy of an eternity of hatred." I forced a smile to break the tension. "So I take it that you and the Duke have worked out an arrangement to share his castle?" I waved my hand to take in the ruins about us and to suggest the accommodations were fantastic.

This brought a smile back to his face. "Well, Talion, you must understand that the Duke is supposed to be a vampire lurking in the crypts deep below this castle. If the legends are true it means he wakes once every two or three weeks and comes out to feed." He smiled and pointed to his sheep. "On those occasions he takes one of my sheep, though he is quite clever about it . . ."

"Oh," I asked. "Clever, is he?"

The shepherd nodded confidently. "He always makes it look as if one of his wolf legion took it."

I laughed aloud. "Crafty, these ancient vampires, eh?"

The shepherd joined me. "Very crafty, Talion."

In the complete darkness Hasan's fire winked like a lighthouse beacon to draw me in. I spotted the fire instantly from the mountaintop and the shepherd pointed me to a trail that would cut my time reaching the fire by at least an hour. I strapped my *tsincaat* across my back, let my daggerlike *ryqril* ride in its sheath at the small of my back and hung a pouch with four poisoned throwing darts at my right hip.

I silently approached the bandit camp on foot. I left Wolf back up at the castle under the shepherd's care. He promised to watch over the horse despite his name, and it pleased Wolf to have a spot out of the wind. By the time I reached the crest of the hill overlooking the bandit camp, the Wolf moon—big and full—rode high in the sky and bathed the forest in silver light.

Hasan posted sentries in positions that gave them a command of the surrounding area in daylight, but were useless at night. The first guard I saw silhouetted himself against the moon. Careless and cold, he stamped his feet loudly enough to enable me to sneak up on him and knock him out before he could shout for help. I tied and gagged him, then moved in closer.

Further along I discovered that the bandit camp was set up on a stretch of dry, sandy river bottom. Around it grew scrubby bushes that made any silent approach a difficult problem. While I had enough cover to conceal myself, it was so dense, and full of thorns, that my original plan—sneak into the camp, free the girl, and then take Hasan—was obviously not going to work. Before I could decide on a secondary course of action, though, Hasan took all my choices away from me.

"Talion, you might as well come in. We know you are out there. We have the girl and your friend." Hasan laughed in his deep bass voice, and Rori screamed.

"Talion, stay out. They don't know where you are . . ." The shepherd's shout ended abruptly, and the sound of flesh striking flesh punctuated it. The girl screamed again.

That was enough for me. "Fine, Hasan, you have won. I'm coming in." I cut through the brush and reached a narrow path leading through to the camp. I trotted along it and formulated a quick plan which I would decide whether or not to put into action when I reached the clearing.

I broke through the brush, took a quick look around, and made my decision immediately. Rori was bound by her wrists to a deadwood log set upright in the sand on this side of the bonfire. Her tattered clothing hung open and firelight caressed her pale flesh. Her brown hair was matted and tangled, and her dark eyes were rimmed with red from crying. She slumped at the base of the post and her chest heaved with silent sobs.

The shepherd was down on the sand. A man I recognized from Grifmont—which explained how Hasan knew I was out there—stood over him with his fists balled. The shepherd was bleeding from a split lip, but other than that looked uninjured.

Two other men stood with Hasan on the far side of the camp. One was the sentry I'd taken down and the other was someone who probably had been sent out to relieve him or had followed me to Castel Griffin, captured the shepherd and then followed me back to the camp.

Eight bandits stood in the camp. Two were armed with crossbows and they had them pointed at me. The other men had swords, but only two had them drawn. Everyone looked somewhat at ease, or drunk, hence my swift decision.

Instead of slowing to surrender, as anticipated, I increased my speed. I swerved to run at an angle to both crossbowmen. Each man triggered his weapon, but hitting a running figure at night is not an easy task and the bolts whistled wide of their intended mark—for which I was grateful.

I flicked my right hand in one bowman's direction and threw a dart at him. The six-inch long needle tip jabbed into his left shoulder. It opened only a small wound, but the toxin dropped the man to his knees and flat onto his back in a matter of seconds.

I summoned my *tsincaat* to hand and engaged the first bandit even as the shepherd kicked up and smashed his shin into his assailant's groin. The shepherd thrust his falling foe aside as if the man was but a child, and rolled to his feet. My foe blocked further sight of the shepherd.

I parried the bandit's overhand blow and whipped my *tsincaat* down and across his chest. He caught the first half of my slash on his left forearm, which laid it open to the bone, but the second half of the slash hit home. I cut him just below the ribs on his right side and he reeled away trying to staunch the flow of blood.

A second bandit sailed in at me and slashed the air before him with tremendous scimitar cuts. In an instant I measured his timing and lunged as he drew his sword back for another blow. I ducked below the cut, stabbed him through the chest and he sagged to the sand. The momentum of his fruitless blow twisted his dead body all awry.

I shifted the *tsincaat* to my left hand and threw another dart. This one hit the bandit rushing at the shepherd's unprotected back. The bandit spun and arched his back as his hands vainly clawed at the dart quivering dead center. The shepherd backhanded the bandit he was fighting and that man bounced backward and flopped to the ground. I heard the sound of the blow and could tell, just from the way he collapsed, the shepherd had broken the bandit's neck.

I looked up and time slowed to a nightmare dream-pace where each second took an hour and though I knew exactly what was to happen, I could do nothing but play my part and watch the bloody tragedy blossom before me.

Hasan—dark haired, fully bearded, and dressed in studded leather armor—pointed at the girl and commanded the second crossbowman, who had nocked another bolt by then, to shoot her. She screamed and the shepherd dove toward her. The crossbowman shot and I arced a dart at him. My dart hit his neck even as the crossbow bolt struck the shepherd and flipped him over onto his back. My last dart was a second too late and sliced through open air as Hasan ducked and broke into the woods.

I ran to the shepherd and skidded to a stop in the sand on my knees. Rori screamed and stared wide-eyed at the bubbling scarlet ruin of the shepherd's stomach. The bolt twitched as he breathed and blood welled up around the wound. I shuddered because I knew there was nothing I could do for him.

The girl continued to scream. I whirled and shouted at her. "Be quiet, Rori!" I showed her the death's-head on my right palm. She looked from me to the shepherd in utter, mindless terror and fainted.

"Talion," the shepherd whispered with blood rising to his lips, "take the bolt out."

I shook my head. "It won't help, shepherd. It'll be bad for you. It'll be more pain."

He grabbed my right hand with incredible strength and dragged it over to the bolt. "Pull it, Talion." Pain seared his features into an inhuman mask. "I cannot die like this!"

I wrapped my hand around the bolt's shaft. I pulled but it was stuck. I couldn't see clearly but I was sure the head was lodged in his spine. "It's in solid, too solid. It will tear you up. I can't hurt you like that!" I trembled with rage at my inability to save him.

Again I felt his hand, weaker this time, on my own hand. "Talion, I am beyond hurt. I would not die like this . . ."

His voice reached inside me and said there was a way to ease his pain. Perhaps there would be more physical pain— for a moment that might feel like a century—but there would be no emotional anguish. I looked down at him and nodded.

I took firm hold of the bolt and ripped it free. He screamed in agonies I hope never to know, then fell silent.

I stood, blood streaming from my hands, and screamed at the Wolf moon. "Now, Hasan, I come for you!"

I summoned my *tsincaat* and ran into the woods. Around me I heard the howl of wolves echo through the moonlit forest, but I felt none of the fear or dread I would have normally expected. I ran in a effortless lope—a stride that conformed to my mental image of a wolf running for miles and miles—and ate up ground greedily.

Though it was dark, Hasan's pathway might as well have been lit by torches. Trees held shreds of cloth out for my inspection. Pine needles and dead leaves parted to show me where Hasan had run. Broken sticks fell and pointed out the bandit's path, and a muddy stretch of ground showed where a root had tripped him and left him sprawled out. It was as though every plant in the forest was outraged at the murders within its demesne and wanted to reveal the murderer to me.

Finally I knew I was getting close. Hasan had run around the perimeter of his camp, found, then took flight along one of the trails his sentries blazed through the woods. This strategy made him easier to follow, but it also gave him greater speed through the woods. I assumed he was heading for wherever his group had hobbled their mounts. The second this thought occurred to me I heard more wolves howl and the frightened neighing of horses. I turned toward the sound and cut through the brush.

That was a mistake. While it slashed distance from the chase, it also left me running through the woods without the safety of the trail. Thorn bushes tore at me and tree branches slashed at my face. Still, none of these natural hazards could stop me, and none of them did. I fell prey to Hasan's planning and a trap his men had set out days ago.

Suddenly a loop closed about my right foot and whipped it up behind me. My body pivoted and my face slammed into the loam. The snare pulled me up and back. I smashed into a tree and stars exploded before my eyes. Pain burst through my head, back and ankle a second before I blacked out completely.

I came back out of it only a moment or two later, but by

that time I was lost. My *tsincaat* was gone. I could not see it, and with the agony shooting through my head I could not concentrate enough to summon it. I felt behind me for my *ryqril* but it, too, had vanished in the dark carpet of leaves and ferns below me. I hung there limply, spinning slowly. The world swam in and out of focus. I felt blood running from the back of my head and heard it drip on the ferns below me like wine from a loose cask spigot.

A stick snapped to my right. I could do nothing but wait until I turned in that direction. I reached out and touched the tree enough to stop me and upside-down Hasan came into focus.

"So, you came for me, eh, Talion?" He laughed mercilessly. "I'll kill you with your own sword." Hasan brandished my *tsincaat*. "Will that make you happy?"

Before I could even attempt an answer, a chorus of wolf-howls shattered Hasan's confidence. He looked nervously around the woods and raised the sword when he saw the titanic wolf-shape backlit by the moon crouched on the crest of a small hill facing me. Slowly and horribly hundreds of other wolves flanked that figure. Though I could only see in one direction, I knew we were surrounded. The Duke's Legion had found us.

The first wolf we'd seen trotted forward but by the time he reached the level area where Hasan stood he had changed. Halfway down the hill he took to running on his hind feet alone, and by the time he reached us he was fully human.

Fear gathered like a thunderhead in my stomach. Duke Griff stood there before me! A massive hooded cloak shrouded him and was black enough to have been cut from shadow itself. I could not see his features, but his eyes sparkled with red highlights. He raised one arm and pointed a shadow-sheathed finger at Hasan.

"You have killed in our forest!" His voice rasped like dry dead leaves skittering wind-driven across cobblestones. "You have done abominable things accounted to us. We do not tolerate that." The Duke took a step forward and the wolves growled as one.

Hasan took a step back, then held my *tsincaat* forward. " 'Ware, vampire. This blade is enchanted. With it I can kill you." Confidence crept into Hasan's voice as the Duke hesitated for a moment. "Be gone and leave this Talion to me."

Anger flashed through me, and terror crept in as rage evaporated. I was powerless. Hanging there like a carcass in a butcher's bazaar stall, I could do nothing to either combatant. Who to wish victory upon? If Hasan won—and my *tsincaat* made that a distinct possibility—he'd cut my throat and might have time to gather more men to take the caravan. If the Duke won, a human monster would be slain, but an inhuman monster would be left to roam free. Just because he didn't murder Kara, and the shepherd felt he was tragic, there was no reason for me to believe he wasn't capable of repeating the crimes he'd performed in his lifetime.

Hasan took a half-step forward and brandished the *tsincaat* more confidently. "Back, vampire, I've given you fair warning!"

The Duke laughed. His voice echoed within itself, as if he laughed within a closed hall. "Hasan ra Kas, you do not scare me. Nothing, not even a magic sword, will stop me from slaying you."

The vampire darted forward in a swirl of cloak and raked Hasan's chest with his right hand. I heard Hasan's shirt tear and the gasp driven from him by the stinging pain of the wounds scored across his torso. Still, the bandit rose up on his toes and arched his body so the blow would not disembowel him and brought my *tsincaat* down on the vampire's back. Hasan spun away from the blow and the vampire crumpled as he passed his victim.

The wolves howled and started down the hillside, but the vampire raised a hand and they stopped. The vampire staggered as he gathered his feet beneath himself and stood again. He weaved unsteadily and I could see the pain-fired stiffness in his posture.

Hasan probed his wounds with his left hand, and grinned when he realized they were trivial. "Come, vampire, you and all your wolves, too. Tonight there will be a new Duke in these forests!" taunted Hasan. He struck a guard position and waved the Duke forward with his left hand. "Come and die, ancient one. Your time is ended."

I saw the vampire drop into a crouch and I knew, as much as I feared and loathed him, I had to act. I forced all pain from my head, reached out with my mind, and summoned my *tsincaat*. But before I felt its hilt safe in my palm, the world swam and pain swallowed me whole.

Dawn came and with it my senses returned. I awoke at the base of the tree. A noose still encircled my ankle, and had attached to it about a dozen feet of rope. The end had been gnawed through. Beside me Rori lay sleeping.

I looked up and saw an old, grey wolf rise to his paws. He looked at me and I nodded at him. He raised his head back, let loose with a howl, then turned and trotted off up the hill. All around us other wolves, six or so, also rose and ambled after him. I was awake so their task was done.

I worked the snare-line off my ankle and stood. My ankle was tender so I hopped back away from the tree. A flash of red caught my eye. I looked up, started and fell down.

305

I suppose the fact that I'd awakened at all should have told me how the fight turned out, but until that moment I'd not thought about the victor's identity. When I looked up and stared into Hasan's dead eyes, the night's black horror flooded back.

The vampire had ripped Hasan's head from his body and jammed it on a branch above where I'd hung. The insane look on Hasan's face was one I am not likely to forget, ever.

I woke Rori up and sent her off to see if the bandits' horses were still nearby before I knocked Hasan's head off the tree and tossed it away where she would not see it. She yelled that the horses were still there and when I followed her I was only slightly surprised to see Wolf munching grass right alongside the bandits' mounts.

I led the horses back to Grifmont and left four of them with the family that lost Kara. I knew the animals could in no way replace a member of the family—nor did I intend them to—but I did know they could replace the money the girl might have earned over the next few years. The other horses I sent to the people who'd lost livestock to Hasan and his men while they roamed the area.

I stayed in Grifmont two days, both to recover and wait for the gold caravan. A witchwife managed to clean my scalp wound and sewed it up so it healed without a scar. While I waited I took one trip out to the bandit camp. I found nothing there but lots of wolf tracks and the four darts I'd used on bandits. There were no bodies.

I left Grifmont with the caravan.

A fortnight later a cold mist seeped from a stone coffin deep within the heart of Castel Griffin. It was thinner than the white smoke produced by sacrificial incense, yet it was thicker than a seafog. It hung in the air for a moment, gathering and roiling like a stormcloud, then it drifted into the form of a man. Slowly it became opaque and took on color.

I shifted, let my blanket drop from my shoulders and stood. "I wanted to thank you, my lord, for saving my life, but I don't know the proper way to thank a vampire."

The vampire studied me with cold, red eyes, then he smiled. "And I should thank you, Talion, for saving my life. Twice, in fact." His smile once again brought life to the shepherd's face. "If you had not pulled the quarrel from my chest I would have died."

I bowed slightly in his direction. "Why didn't you tell me who you were and why you wanted the bolt pulled from you? Now it all makes sense—your strength and the fact wood would kill you. Had I known, I would have yanked the quarrel free immediately."

The shepherd regarded me wordlessly. "I think now, perhaps, you would have freed me of it, but at that moment I could not risk it. You were so certain the Duke was an evil worthy of no pity, I could not take the chance you would have let me die right then and there had you known who I was."

I thought for a moment, bit my lower lip, then nodded. "I cannot honestly say I would have helped you had I known the truth."

The shepherd smiled again, this time quite warmly. "You helped me when you had the chance, Talion, when you knew what I was. I read the fear in your body as you hung there. You were not scared for yourself at my coming; you feared for the girl, and Grifmont, and the shepherd. Yet you decided to help me. I think it was because you realized what you and the shepherd had talked about was true."

He seated himself on his bier. "One night I rose from my slumbers here and actually saw the ruins surrounding me.

In an instant I realized that everything I had ever wanted faded and died because of my wanting it. In that mote of time the Duke died. Since then there has only been the simple shepherd you first met."

I shook my head. "You should let the people around here know who and what you have become."

The shepherd laughed painfully. "Their hatred and fear has been bred into them for centuries. I did that to them. There is no way to change them. Their fear is my eternal punishment."

I stayed and spoke with the shepherd for the rest of that night, then, as the morning sun splashed green and gold over the sides of Griffin Mountain, I rode down into Grifmont. I reined Wolf to a stop in front of the headman's hovel.

Macinne came out, squinted against the sun, and raised a liver-spotted hand to shade his eyes. "Come to mock me, Talion? Just because you were right this time don't mean the Duke won't take someone another time."

My jaw muscles twitched and I narrowed my eyes. A crowd slowly gathered around us. They waited to see what I would do to this man who had been so insolent. I'd not struck Kara's mother down for her actions before, but Macinne had no excuse for his words. My right hand tightened into a fist and Macinne's knees shook.

I waited.

I waited until Macinne's terror seeped out of him and bled into the others. Sweat formed on his brow and rolled down from his temples. His lips parted and his lower lip trembled. Other villagers glanced nervously at him and moved so they'd be out of the way when I butchered him.

"No, old man, I've not come to mock you." I hunched

forward in my saddle and stared into his eyes. "I've come to tell you that last night I opened the Duke's crypt and I drove a wooden stake through his heart." I sat back and swept my gaze over the others. "He will trouble you no more."

The story of Duke Griff's death reached Elmford and the surrounding countryside before I could ride from the county. Within a year I even heard a minstrel sing of the Talion who entered the Duke's den and slew him. And soon enough even that song of Duke Griff faded from memory.

And the shepherd discovered that eternity is not without end.

"**The Final Gift**" is a fourth Wise Man story. I figure every writer, especially Catholics, has one of those in him, the same way we all have a vampire and a werewolf story in us. I'd been invited to a Christmas party by Scott Wareing's fiancée, Sabrina. She was active in theater and I was told that everyone at the party would "perform" something as part of the entertainment. I sat down and wrote this story—which is not terribly Christmassy when you come down to it. Even so, it's pretty powerful. It was printed in *Amazing Stories* magazine after Dennis L. McKiernan prompted the editor to ask me to send it to him.

The Final Gift

The youth cleared his voice as he waited in the doorway. He'd learned well not to speak until I gave him leave. I suppressed a smile as I narrowed my old, tired eyes, squinted one last time at the stars and reconfirmed the story I'd read there countless times before. I made the last few notes on the wax tablet with my stylus, then I turned to face him.

I saw nothing but a clean-limbed outline silhouetted against the light from below. He waited anxiously to tell me what I'd heard taking place down in the courtyard. He fairly burst with excitement but, mature beyond his seven years, he restrained himself. *Not one of my students, not even Balthazar, has shown such self-control,* I thought to myself, *and none have ever needed so much of it before him.*

I let a thin wisp of smile twist my lips just enough for him to notice, then I nodded. "They have finally come?"

The boy nodded enthusiastically. "Yes, Master, they have arrived. The one from the Orient brought you tea and I have it brewing."

He stepped forward to help guide me down the stairs, but I waved him back. "Go, see to their needs. Serve them the tea, then leave them. I will address them alone."

He smiled. "Do you wish me to prepare your things for the journey?"

Smart lad, I laughed to myself. I shook my head slowly. "There is no need."

He'd half-turned back toward the stairs and the yellow tallow light flickered shadows across his puzzled face. "But they said you would go with them."

"Go do what I told you, and think no more of it." I turned and looked up at that star, the one burning like a torch at midnight. Just as strongly as it beckoned them on, it pinned me in my place. *Terrible Star!* I cursed, *I wish your light would not shine so brightly.*

Even without the youth's help, I climbed down the worn stairs without mishap. Thoughtfully, the boy'd left lamps burning so their light allowed me passage from one illuminated sphere to the next, but he should have known better than to waste the oil. I'd lived my entire life within these walls. My senses would not fail me, and the building itself would never betray me. No, to fall and die, that would be too easy an escape.

They stood, the three of them, when I entered the room and were kind enough to mouth lies about how hale and hearty I looked. They were resplendent in their robes of silk and cloth-of-gold. Though each of them had grown and aged, I could still see in them the children I'd trained so long ago. Instantly they dropped to their knees in a rustle of cloth even I could hear, but I held a hand out to forestall any further contradictions about my condition, or any efforts to touch what little vanity I had left in me.

"Please, my Kings, please return to your chairs. We have much to discuss." I paused while they reseated themselves and adjusted their clothing. "It is good to see the three of you again, for this final time. I will not be going with you."

Surprise widened their eyes and emotion rode on faces unaccustomed to showing it. At court any of these men would have been an implacable instrument of wisdom, compassion or justice without revealing anything to those they judged; but here, with me, they became half-trained scholars wrestling with minor problems as if they were titanic monsters, as they had done here years ago.

Jasper, the youngest and furthest traveled, here from far Tarshish, could not contain himself. "Why? Why will you not join us in this thing you have prepared us for?" Betrayal seeped into his voice and told me the hot-blooded passions of his nation had nibbled away at my training.

Even before I spoke I knew Balthazar and Melchior anticipated my answer. I smiled at them and bowed my head in a silent salute. Jasper, impulsive but not a dullard, suddenly understood and blushed.

"Could you imagine, Jasper, having asked that question when you left me so long ago?" I shook my head in a mild rebuke. "Use what I gave you, use the training and pierce the mystery of my refusal." I looked to the others and wordlessly invited them to help their companion. "Share what you know with the others, and perhaps you will see why I cannot go."

Jasper swallowed thickly, then bowed his head to me and began to speak. "As I was bidden, I have studied the one we seek and delved into his ancestry. He is noble born, to be sure, for his mother comes from the House of David and he will be every bit a King in blood as any of us are." The King of Tarshish glanced up, and I recognized the look of confusion on his face from long ago.

Melchior, the dark Nubian, likewise caught Jasper's hesitation. "You say nothing of his father."

Jasper shook his head. "The stars confuse me. They tell

315

me he has two fathers. Of one I see nothing, as if the stars cannot contain his story. The other, the one I see guiding his early days, is a good man, also of the House of David. I would take this as a good omen, a fulfillment of the stories, but I fear this man is not his true father."

Melchior would have offered a solution to the mystery, but I shook my head almost imperceptibly and he acceded to my unvoiced request. "What did you bring him as a gift?" I asked, encouraging Jasper to forget his paradox.

Jasper's face brightened. "I have brought him gold, Master."

"Practical as always, Jasper," laughed Balthazar.

Jasper's face flushed again, but he rose to the challenge. "I selected that gift as suitable for a babe of his blood, and because gold is pure and incorruptible. This is the sort of man I sense coming from so noble a beginning, hence an appropriate gift."

He looked to me for agreement and praise. I gave him both in a solemn nod, but turned toward Melchior to forestall Jaspar's demand for the reasons behind my decision not to accompany them. "Melchior, tell what you have learned."

The Nubian smiled and flashed bright eyes and white teeth at me. "As I was asked, I have followed the stars' telling of his childhood." Melchior nodded toward Jasper. "You are right, oh King of Tarshish, for this will be a remarkable man. As a child he is extraordinary in his abilities and devotion to studies. I saw no duality as far as his father was concerned. I saw a boy who loves his parents and who, after helping his father and brothers in the carpentry shop, turns to studies of things ancient and holy. By the time his people count him a man, he will possess the wisdom of an elder. I would guess he becomes a great teacher."

Melchior fixed me with an ebon-eyed stare, for I was to study the man's adult life, but I ignored his demand to have his speculation confirmed. "And what do you offer this miracle child, Melchior of Nubia?"

Frustration bunched muscles at his jaws, but he banished it and once again acknowledged me his master. "I bring him frankincense. Useful in sacrifice, it can also be burned to banish evil demons and the sweet scent encourages studious behavior." The Nubian smiled wryly and looked at Balthazar. "And, as the King of Chaldea would note, it is valued and could be traded for supplies needed to further his studies."

Balthazar accepted without prompting his part in the discussion. My eldest pupil, his hair and beard were nearly bone-white, but aside from that he had not changed. He was still the practical, calculating man; as cynical a soul as ever born to woman. He stood as he had done to lecture the others so long ago, and explained his studies.

"As the master charged me, I studied his legacy and puzzled out what his life will mean to the world." Balthazar smiled slyly and turned to me. "You asked me to study the effects of his life because, had one of the others said what I will say, I would never have believed it."

I nodded and he turned back to the others. "This man is mortal, in one sense, and will die. But he will not stay dead; he will rise from the tomb and return to confirm the veracity of his teachings. He will be a god then, and his disciples will spread throughout the world. They will topple old empires and create new ones. They will do good things in his name, and they will do evil defending him, but those who are true to his life and message, they will make the world into a paradise."

Jasper and Melchior stared at Balthazar, for what he was

saying horrified them. *Could this man,* they wondered, *this man we have studied defeat death and have so much power?* Balthazar confirmed their fears with a slow nod, then turned back to me. "And what did I bring him for a gift, Master? I brought myrrh so they can anoint his body when he dies."

Jasper laughed. "Hardly practical, your gift, Balthazar, for you yourself say he will not remain dead. He returns a god."

Balthazar narrowed his eyes until they appeared bare slivers of grey. "I give him myrrh for its scent will stay with him in the grave, and will remind him, when he returns, he was once a man."

I levered myself up out of my chair and smiled at my students. "You have seen correctly, and chosen your gifts well. Now you must proceed with your journey so you will arrive in time."

Jasper stood but showed no intention of leaving. "Master, you have not told us why you will not join us."

Balthazar bowed and passed between me and the King of Tarshish. He gently took Jasper's arm and steered him toward the door. "He has told us, Jasper; you did not hear." He looked back at me and swallowed past a lump in his throat that told me he'd studied more than he should have. "He cannot come because his gift for this child is not ready yet."

Jasper thought to protest, but my curt nod and Balthazar's grip on his elbow deterred him. He bowed his head to me, as did Melchior, and the three kings left my home.

The boy found me once again on the roof staring at the stars. Each time I looked at them, half hoping my creeping blindness would swallow one that would change the story they told, I only read again the tale of pain and suffering that sapped my strength and eroded my will. But, just as I'd read his story in the stars, I had read of my pupils and of myself.

Bless you, Balthazar, for making your attempt to accept my burden.

I snorted and shivered, then turned to the boy. "Yes, what is it?"

Mist trailed from his mouth as he replied. "The eldest, King Balthazar, said you would want to speak with me."

The weight of eternity forced me to sit on the roof's edge. "Yes, he is correct. Come here." I pointed to a spot at my feet and forced a smile on my face so I would betray nothing. It was finally time to prepare my gift.

The boy looked up at me, his face innocent and guileless. So trusting, so smart. My gift, the gift that binds all the others.

"One day you will travel from here and meet a man. You will find, Judas, he is a very special man and he will call you friend . . ."

"Kid Binary and the Two-bit Gang" was a story written for the *Highwaymen, Robbers, and Rogues* anthology edited by Jennifer Roberson. Jennifer invited me into the anthology and originally wanted me to write a story set in Japan. Then she had another writer who wanted to write in Japan, so she asked me to do something about a Highwayman on the information superhighway. Kid Binary was born, and sparked a bunch of ideas for other stories that I've just not gotten around to writing.

Kid Binary and the Two-bit Gang

I crashed into his domain though a back door, leaking data as I went. I quick slapped a patch on the hole in my side, but that still left golden letters and symbols hanging in the air. I glanced at it fast, making sure it was ascii and not hex. As nearly as I could tell I'd taken the hit through a trolling ascii buffer—I'd have to go back out and recover the data at some point, but it wasn't important and the damage was far from serious.

I stood up slowly and dusted my avatar off. If I'd walked into the Bitter Root saloon in the real world, I'd have called it seedy. Here in OutLAW territory, the grunge just meant the proprietor hadn't upgraded his graphics package recently. It wasn't bad, probably only a couple of revs old.

I tipped my hat to the man behind the bar. "Howdy, partner. Sorry about hacking in this way, but I was in something of a hurry." I flipped him a gold Ike and he snapped the icon out of the air in his right hand. It represented a keycode to a discreet deposit on a Swiss cyberbank and would more than pay for the damage I'd done to his domain.

"Obliged." The man's avatar had golden eyes, which were novel the first hundred times I'd seen the same on others, but his were a bit close-set. "You hunting or hiding?"

"I was one; now I'm the other, I guess." I looked around the domain. It looked pretty small, but had a stairway leading up to some doorways off a corridor, and I imagined there were hidden rooms beyond them. Through the windows I saw more buildings outside, but no other avatars wandering the streets. If it weren't for the age of the graphics, I would have figured his domain for a new start-up—a start-up that was going to fall to bits fairly soon. "Get much traffic out here?"

"Not really." He flashed my Ike. "Don't need much if folks pay well enough."

I fished another of the coin icons from my pocket. "I pay well. Set me up."

"Bourbon or beer?"

"Bourbon. I'll need the hard stuff."

The bartender's avatar arched an eyebrow at me. "Bad men must be coming after you."

"Yeah. Kid Binary and the Two-bit Gang."

"Oh," he said, "you'll be wanting doubles."

Time had once been that ranging out on the information superhighway hadn't required fortification, but that was back in the early days before governments decided the nets couldn't be allowed to go unregulated. Regulations were set in place all over the world creating Licensed Access Wards, or LAWs, in which behavior was proscribed and the average user was well protected. Corporations sponsored many of the early LAWs, with things like DisneyLAW and Six-FlaggedLAW still proving very popular.

To make the regulations and enforcement workable, the governments looked to software providers to create environments that could be controlled. Microsoft immediately released its Iconographic Domain Format products, setting a standard for LAWs everywhere. With IDF software, every user could create a graphic avatar through which he would interface with the LAW environment. Microsoft's first release featured a Wild West graphics package and that quickly became the standard for much of the western world. While some corporations and some nations created their own proprietary images, pretty much everyone built on Microsoft's IDF architecture, so MS icons could find their way into any LAW.

The main problem with the LAWs was the fact that the environments were perfectly safe because government E-rangers went everywhere and looked into everything. If a corporation wanted to conclude a deal of questionable legality, or wanted to transfer data of a proprietary nature between sites, doing so through an environment that lent itself to scrutiny wasn't wise.

OutLAW territory was born. Anyone with access to an IDF package, a computer and a landline or cell-modem could create his own Personal Access Domain. PADs took the place of web pages pretty quickly. Many folks maintained them like a hobby: having one was like having an aquarium through which all sorts of odd things could swim. Provide access to interesting data files, create shortcuts to other PADs or LAWs, do on-the-fly icon modifications and your PAD would become popular. In some cases the PADs became popular enough that a prop could make enough money collecting Ikes to pay for the upkeep of the domain.

The PAD I'd crashed into wasn't really that unusual, except that it seemed a lot more quiet than most others. I actually found that to be something of a relief since Microsoft had recently released Circus Maxx 3.2—a circus-based IDF—and I was sick and tired of running into clowns everywhere. But, the fact was that if this place didn't have a lot of traffic and the prop was running it as a commercial enterprise, he had to be providing services that folks were willing to pay for.

My avatar consumed the bourbon. I couldn't taste it, of course, and didn't get a buzz off it—though there were software patches that did allow for sensory disorientation. The bourbon here acted as temporary armor against shots taken by my enemies. Each ounce of the bourbon formed a data-buffer through which another avatar's hunter-killer programs would have to chew before they got to vital data.

Most folks learned early on that if they're going to run through OutLAW territories, they'd best be working on a dedicated machine and keep nothing on it they weren't ready to lose. Combat in the cyberwest boiled down to sending modified virus programs out to trash the other avatar's system. When Microsoft released the Wild West IDF it included guns and bullets—the latter being viruses that just logged a user off when she was hit too many times. Guns were the virus launchers and limited the number and size of the bullets any user could have ready to fire at any one time.

Of course that sort of Marquis de Queensberry combat lasted about as long as it took for the first hacker to pirate a copy of the IDF software. Now bullets varied in caliber and impact. A derringer might shoot something that logged a user off, or added donkey ears to his avatar, while a Sharps 5.6 Buffalo Gun would head-crash a drive or cause a power surge that would burn out a scanning laser on a CD-ROM.

The bartender looked at my avatar carefully. "You've been around a while. You should know better than to be going after Kid Binary."

"Oh?" I gave him a smile. "You know something about him?"

"I might."

"Like?"

"Like the reason they call him Kid Binary." The bartender mimed drawing a gun. "When he's *on,* you're *off.*"

I laughed. "Heard it before, but I've always liked it. What else do you know?"

"Something."

"You gonna be telling, or selling?"

The bartender winked at me. "A story told is just a story, but a story *sold* has facts in it."

I fished into my pocket and pulled out a big gold double-eagle Ike. I had them minted especially for me at my bank. The bartender immediately recognized how rare the icon was. I slid it across the bar to him and it disappeared. "Give me the full Geraldo on this guy."

The bartender poured me another bourbon. "Kid Binary is a coach-poacher who works the badlands. I don't get a lot of newsgroups out here, but word has it that he was once an E-ranger from the States who found out that some of the alphabet agencies were running black data through covert channels layered into LAWs. He took off some of their ones-and-zeroes as evidence and they set him up for a big wet-delete. They missed him and he's been working from breaks to stop them and their pals in the military-industrial complex from taking over the world."

"I see." He hadn't told me anything I hadn't heard in slightly altered forms elsewhere. The Badlands were Business Access Domains (local area networks, downloads and security) which were a lot like PADs, but with nasty software packages that could hurt folks who weren't meant to be interfacing with them. To transfer data between badlands sites, corps would "coach" them: layer them with shells of protective software that made them as appealing to deal with as a Bengal tiger crossed with a porcupine. Picking them off wasn't easy and the list of Kid Binary's successful targets read like the Fortune 500.

The fact that Kid Binary worked from breaks explained how he had lasted so long, and could easily be seen as confirmation of an assassination attempt in the real world. While programs could disco a user or trash a system, data hijacked on the net had real world uses. Some corps, if they had a line on a user's true identity, would try to disconnect him from life, which tended to hurt a lot, and was usually very messy.

Breaks were cracks in the system that allowed covert entry. Every LAW and PAD required a basic address—the minimum being the phone number through which it connected to a server that provided access to the net. Going in through a break meant Kid Binary either hardwired access into a net or hacked his way into the phone company and gave himself temporary access points through numbers that were, thanks to his work, unlisted and untraceable.

"What's the story with the Two-bit Gang?"

"Smalltime data-sifters and code-pokers mostly." The bartender shrugged. "They mostly prey on nubes who leave the LAWs and go ranging. A couple of them—Doc and Hurrikane—are vets of the Samurai Invasion, but the rest aren't very good codeslingers."

I took another look at the saloon. "You get hit in the invasion?"

"Not hard—I had protection."

"Right. Doc and Hurrikane?"

"Right."

I winced. "I think Doc is the one that got a piece of me."

The bartender nodded. "Like as not. Learned good during the invasion, that one did."

Of that I had no doubt. Executives in Kotei Software's Tokyo headquarters decided to dispute Microsoft's domination of the net about five revs back. They launched their Shogun IDF with an invasion. Ninja hackers infiltrated PADs and unleashed viruses that redrew the icons in the IDF software. A suit became a kimono, a ten-gallon hat became a helmet and bourbon bottles became sake flasks. The Chicago Stockyards LAW became a fish market in nanoseconds. The assault came as a complete surprise, as did the strength of the reaction from the States.

Most of the folks in the States couldn't have cared less about Microsoft and their domination of the IDF market, but they resented the hell out of Kotei launching this invasion on December 7th. Nubes and vets flooded the Out-LAW territories and made up for with enthusiasm what they lacked in skill and software. The world's phone system locked up tight and would have melted down, except some cybergenius unloaded a virus called "Fat Man" on the Kotei mainframe and the scent of melting silicon could be smelled across the ocean.

I held my hands up. "I don't want to cause you any trouble, but the Two-bit Gang has gone and done something they shouldn't have."

"No surprise. They just use my place as a dead-drop for information, so they don't really mean that much to me. They long ago burned the goodwill they earned keeping them samurai out of here." The bartender smiled carefully and leaned forward. "If you want, I have some arcs on them. I'll let you have them cheap."

I nearly went for what he was offering because archived files about the Two-bit Gang would be useful, and any data on Kid Binary might help me sort fact from fiction concerning what was out there. The problem was that to download the files, I'd have to lower my guard and accept data into my system. If I did that, I'd leave myself open to a virus attack or a sneak shot. "You tempt me, friend, but I'll pass."

"I understand." The bartender nodded and poured me another bourbon. "So, you an E-ranger or something?"

"Could be." I narrowed my avatar's malachite eyes. "You hear anything about their hitting a coach containing a code key?"

"Maybe." The bartender didn't meet my stare. "What was it for?"

"Scientists at a research lab in Kolwezi completed the DNA sequencing of the Ebola-Zaire B virus. They encrypted the genetic code and sent that to AMRID, with the code key to follow. Without the key, AMRID's people can't use the sequence."

The bartender shook his head. "Have the researchers send the code key again."

"Can't. Katangese guerrillas hit the lab because they thought the researchers were part of a government program to spread the epidemic, which they think the government has used to wipe their people out. The truck-bomb disco took out the lab and two city blocks around it."

The bartender poured himself a bourbon and tossed it off quickly. "Sounds like this code key could be really valuable."

"A reasonable offer might be made for its recovery."

"Pair it with the virus code and you'd have quite a package."

My avatar nodded. Doing a DNA sequence on a virus was a great help in finding a cure for it, but advances in sequencing meant the technology became cheaper and more abundant. For next to nothing a dissident force could manufacture a vial of some hideous plague and introduce it into a major metropolitan water system. Chechens were have rumored to have done that to cause the Winter Fever that killed 250,000 people in Moscow during the winter of '07. That had been a genegineered version of the Marburg virus, and the harsh winter kept folks indoors, limiting the spread. Had it been summer or a mild winter and Chechnya would have had its independence.

"I can't let that happen." I shook my head. "From everything I'd heard of Kid Binary, I didn't see him pulling that sort of job off. I always thought he was kind of a Robin Hood."

The bartender shrugged. "Maybe they didn't know what it was they were getting, or maybe Kid Binary decided to get something for himself. Times a man gets tired of just making do."

"Anything's possible."

The bartender nodded toward the bat's-wing doors at the front of the saloon. "They're incoming. Doc may be inclined to be reasonable. Watch out for Tenniel. He's just crazy mean."

"Thanks." I checked the two six-guns I wore, one to a hip. I had more bullets in my pockets and on my belt. I began to wish I had brought my Winchester .44 because it was more accurate at range, but its lack meant I was faster. That was the tradeoff with avatars—the more software options and armor you packed, the slower your processing time. Granted, running on a fast system could give you an edge, but in the Territories, you could only see an appreciable difference when going up against some Nintendo Cowboy thinking he's Dooming in God Mode.

My Colts would suit, I figured. Walking over to the doors, I noticed that the floorboard creaked and the doors themselves needed oiling. Even a tumbleweed skitter-click-clacked along the boardwalk and a dust-devil hissed as it sprayed sand against the saloon's windows. I smiled. What this domain lacked in graphics it more than made up for in sound.

Down toward the far end of the small town setting that defined the rest of the domain, the Two-bit Gang arrayed itself and waited for me. Doc was almost pure MSWest: tall, slender, black jeans, duster, hat, handlebar moustache, pointy boots, with a six gun on his right hip and a shotgun cradled in his arms. The only variation that separated him from every nube was the pair of samurai swords whose hilts peeked up over his left shoulder. The blades weren't particularly powerful weapons in cyberspace, but wearing them openly was a death warrant since many Japanese wanted to win them back. The fact that he had them meant he was good.

Next to him stood Hurrikane. The basic avatar had come from one of the fantasy IDFs that were popular with kids. Hurrikane had dressed a huge, hulking troll up in samurai armor, all of which meant he was armored through and through. He'd be slow, but he'd take a lot of codecracking before he logged. The weapon he carried was a flamethrower—it made up in punch what it lacked in precision and elegance. Once it started burning code, you could lose a lot of protection fast.

I assumed the next person was Tenniel. He was pretty much stock MSWest, wiry and cocky enough to only carry one gun. Boots, jeans, a red-checked shirt, buckskin jacket and brown hat completed his outfit. It didn't look like he was carrying much more protection than I was, so he was relying on speed, too, to keep him safe.

The guy next to him looked like a riverboat gambler and I pegged him as Webster. He usually caused trouble by going into PADs that allowed wagering and cheating the nubes out of Ikes. At best he sported a derringer. He was probably the least of my worries, but I knew better than to dismiss him.

The last member of the gang looked, from moccasins and beaded loincloth to the feathers in her hair, to be every inch a Native American Princess. Betty.Drivekiller started with a DisneyLAW Pocahontas avatar, swapped sex appeal for modesty, and had slapped digitized butterflies on the halter top that strained to contain her sex appeal. She sported a knife and a tomahawk on her belt, carried a Winchester and had a bandoleer of shells for the rifle looped over her right shoulder.

I'd have been impressed and even intrigued, but the way Betty kept checking out her reflection in the general store's window, I figured that behind that avatar was some adolescent boy who was correctly thinking that this was as close as he'd ever get to a pair of tits. His reflexes might be quick, but he was outfitted more for show than action. It struck me that Betty was really some whizzer nube they'd picked up to help them crack the coach with the code.

I nodded toward them and swept my jacket back to show both of my pistols. "Where's Kid Binary?"

Doc took a half step forward. "I'm here. You deal with me."

"Fine. You've got something I want, and something you really don't want to be keeping. Hand it over and I'll see to it that you don't get hurt."

"You think I was digitized last rev? I've been around." Doc jerked a thumb at the swords. "I've learned that information is power and power is always a seller's market. You want the code key we got? A million double-eagle Ikes will get it for you."

"A million for each of us," Betty added.

Doc shot Betty a frown, then turned back toward me. "You give me the money, Kid Binary gives you the code."

I shook my head. "Be reasonable. That code key gets into the wrong hands and a lot of people end up dead—really dead, not bit-dead."

"Then take up a collection among them and pay us."

"Not enough time." I smiled. "I guess some bits are going to be flipped before we resolve this."

Doc looked down the line of his compatriots. "You'd go against us, all of us?"

"So many targets, I can hardly miss." My hands dropped to my guns as Doc's shotgun started to come up. I cleared leather and sent my first three shots at him. The first bullet under the hammer in each pistol was a dum-dum—meant to hit hard, which they did. The general effect was to engage Doc's armor and chew up some processing time as his software tried to blunt the trauma. The third bullet was a stinger. It punched through the crumbling armor and exploded into a hail of tiny viruses that immediately ate into Doc's face. His avatar's surprised expression evaporated into a cloud of golden hexadecimal gobbledygook, then his body flopped down on the dusty street with a delicious meaty thwack.

The prop really did have good sound files.

And the rest of the Two-bit Gang gave them a good workout. Hurrikane's flamethrower roared as a stream of burning fluid jetted out toward me. I dove to my right, away from the saloon and beneath a wagon parked in front of the hardware store. I found my flight aided by a tug on my left hip, but I had no time to examine the wound because Hurrikane torched the wagon.

Hoping the fire and black cloud of data would cover me, I rolled to my feet and sprinted as best I could across the boardwalk and through the hardware store's plate glass window. It sounded better than it looked when it broke, and it had been coded with safety glass, so I didn't get sliced to ribbons going through it. I got up and started toward the back of the store, but the limp I'd developed slowed me down.

I hunkered down behind the counter and took a moment to look at where I'd been shot. I was leaking mostly ascii, but I caught some hex strings in the output. I was able to patch the wound on the fly, but what I'd seen told me who'd shot me and why he'd been so confident. Tenniel was using viper rounds. They get their name from an acronym for Virtual Intelligence Program ERaser. They seek out the little bits of virtually intelligent code that allow avatars to do extraordinary things. Viper rounds became very popular after the first comic book company released an IDF package based on their superhero universe. Various VI code packages were popular in the territories and I suspected Tenniel was loaded with code that, at the very least, increased his speed and helped his aim.

The hardware store's interior brightened as the snapping growl of the troll's flamethrower grew louder. With one twitch of his trigger finger he could turn the building into an inferno. A viper round might have helped take Hurrikane down, but since I hadn't been expecting to hunt superhumans, I'd not packed any code-kryptonite. Instead I rotated the cylinder on my right-hand gun to the fourth round, popped up as Hurrikane framed himself in the broken window, and shot him point blank with a parvo round.

Parvo is one of the nastier anti-avatar viruses available, and was big enough that I only carried one round with me at a time. The name is another acronym: Programmed Asymmetric Recursion/Variable Operation. It's also known as a palsy round because what it does is pump different values to the paired variables that make an avatar work, and puts the avatar through rapid repeats of operations. It wouldn't kill him, but it would take him out of the fight for a while.

As Hurrikane did a flaming Macarena out into the street, I ran for the back of the hardware store and jerked the door open. I glanced out, saw nothing, then came out running. Further up the alley running behind the buildings I saw Webster. I started to draw a bead on him, when a bullet smashed me flat and left me to crawl to the cover of some discarded crates and a watering trough behind the jail.

The bullet had hit me in the back and punched out through my flank. It was only an ascii wound and the bullet had been a simple ripper round. It was a little more sophisticated than a dum-dum, but not as elegant as a stinger. I knew Betty.Drivekiller had to have put it in me, but I didn't know where she was, and that was trouble.

The crates and water trough offered me rather weak cover. They were basically icons—not as sophisticated as an avatar, but made up of the same sorts of ones and zeros. A virus would have to chew through them before it could get to me, but most of the atmosphere icons in a domain wouldn't slow down the sort of viruses we were slinging around. All they really did was to hide targets, which was exactly what I didn't want.

I glanced out past my crates to see if I could catch a glimpse of Webster, but he was less of a gambling man than

I thought and didn't show himself. I swore and decided to reload, when I heard a heavy footfall behind me. I whirled back and leveled both of my pistols at the avatar behind me, but didn't fire.

A blonde little girl whose hair fell in curls over the shoulders of her red dress looked at me with concern. "Are you hurt, Mister?"

"Get away from here, little girl. This is not a place you want to be in."

She held a hand out toward me as she inched closer. "I can help you."

"Look, I don't want to be rude, but beat it." I holstered my left gun and dug into my jacket pocket. "Will you go if I give you something? Would you like some candy, little girl?"

Her eyes brightened as my left hand came out with a red gummy bear in it. The candy was an icon just like the coins I'd given the bartender and in the real world could be exchanged for a coupon that would buy the users the candy they got on the net. Corporations had pioneered this sort of thing and I kept candy with me because some netheads always remained in character no matter where they ended up.

"Cherry. My favorite," she giggled.

"Your lucky day." I flipped the gummy bear to her and she plucked it out of the air with a certain amount of élan. Her proud smile dissolved into shock as the gummy bear's upper body grew to life-size proportions. Its arms reached out, pulling her close, then it snapped her head off with one bite.

I winked at her as her head floated down through the bear's jellied insides. "That, Tenniel, is why you shouldn't take candy from strangers." The girl's body collapsed and the gummy bear melted over her.

Tenniel had been running a Proteus VIP that allowed him to shift to a new icon. If I'd let little Alice help me with my injury, I'd have been letting her in past my defenses to mess with my core code. She made the mistake I wouldn't by accepting the candy from me, and paid the price I'd have been charged for her help.

Tenniel had been good, though. His only mistake had been in being lazy. His Proteus program swapped bit-maps, but didn't change sound files. While he looked like all sugar-and-spice, he had the heavy tramp of a codeslinger's booted feet.

I took a moment to reload my guns, slipping stingers into the empty chambers. It occurred to me that my biggest threat, at the moment, was Betty.Drivekiller and she'd been armed with a Winchester. That was a good launcher, especially if the user didn't want to get close to his target—the size of the launcher reflected the complexity of the code used to acquire its target. The kid wearing the avatar was using nube ammo, so I chose to assume he was using nube strategy, too.

That put her on top of the general store, hidden behind the lip of the roof. I rolled to my feet and stood behind the crates. "You're mine, Webster," I shouted and fired a shot at several stacked crates further down the alley, back behind the general store.

Two things happened at once. Webster danced out from behind the crate I'd shot at and fired at me with his derringer. The slug took me in the right shoulder and scored hex. His shot ruined the second one I took in his direction, but I'd corrected my aim by the third shot and nailed him with a stinger right over his heart. He pitched backward, strings of hex spurting up into the air as if the avatar's holed heart was pumping alphabet soup.

Betty.Drivekiller popped up on the General Store's roof and triggered a shot at me. One of the crates at my feet exploded into golden alphanumerics. My first return shot went high, causing Betty to duck down behind cover, assuming out of sight was out of danger.

Big mistake.

Firing my pistols in tandem, I peppered the roof lip with stingers. They blew great honking holes in the clapboard siding, spraying data-lethal splinters everywhere. Betty jumped up and tried to backpedal away from the bullets, but a stinger caught her in the left leg. The avatar spun around, then tumbled from the roof and landed hard, accompanied by a broken-bone cacophony.

I jogged over to where she lay and kicked the Winchester from her hand. "You weren't bad, kid, just not good enough. You need experience."

"I've had plenty of experience," she snarled at me.

"Okay, my mistake. No hard feelings." I dug into my pocket. "Here, have a piece of candy."

Betty smiled at me. She caught the candy in her left hand as her right hand was going for the knife she wore. It didn't help her.

I think she found it a *new* experience.

I limped back toward the hardware store, reloading as I went. I knew I had to deal with Hurrikane, so I pulled out the nastiest bullet I had and loaded it into my left-hand pistol. I spun the cylinder to put the Aphid round next in line to be shot. Like the parvo round I'd pumped into him earlier, it wasn't really designed to be a killer, but Hurrikane had set himself up to be particularly vulnerable to it.

Dozens of little bonfires burned in the street in front of the hardware store. The hotel and restaurant next to the saloon was already fully engaged in a blaze. Golden symbols floated on the domain's ether to land on the smithy and stable's roofs, starting them to smolder. In no time the whole domain would go up and replacing the graphics files would cost someone money or a lot of time.

Being a civically-minded individual, I decided to fight the fire. With fire.

Hurrikane had finally beaten the Parvo. The avatar rested on one knee at the far end of the street while his user was undoubtedly working furiously to reset his variables. I closed my right eye, aimed the gun at him, cocked the hammer and pulled the trigger.

The Aphid round is an Armor-Piercing, Heuristic Interface Disrupter. As avatars perform tasks, the VIPs driving them accumulate experience—they literally amass trial-and-error data that gets factored in with user input to make the avatar function to the best of its abilities. Because of this limited learning capability, an experienced avatar in the hands of even a nube can be very effective.

The Aphid round effectively cuts the avatar off from its accumulated experience and kicks the heuristic portions of the program into problem-solving overdrive. The program quickly cycles through all sorts of behaviors, though it will not do anything self-destructive. All avatars carry that self-preservation coding.

Hurrikane's flamethrower did not. The Aphid round hit it and immediately started its tiny VIP running through problem-solving situations. Pretty quickly it explored the consequences of a simultaneous detonation of all the fuel it had left in the twin tanks. The resulting supernova immediately reduced the south end of the domain to twitching characters dancing like water droplets on a hot skittle.

Of the Two-bit Gang and everything from the general

store back there was no trace.

In the aftermath of the blast's tremendous thunder, I heard the sharp click of a double-barreled shotgun's twin hammers being drawn back. I dropped my guns and slowly raised my hands. "Kid Binary, I presume?"

"Right the first time out." The voice came strong and rich. "Turn around slow."

I limped around in a circle and found myself staring at an avatar I'd seen thousands of times before. It was stock MSWest, the Avatar with No Name. From the stubby cheroot to trademark squint and serape, it was one of the more popular avatars roaming around. The shotgun wasn't standard equipment, but it didn't add many gigs to the package, so this wasn't the first time I'd seen ANN hauling one around.

"So that's your secret, Kid? You choose a dead common avatar so you're hard to track?"

Kid Binary nodded.

I winced. "Wrong answer."

"What?"

"I know Kid Binary." I shook my head. "You're no Kid Binary."

"Yeah?" The shotgun's barrels came up at my face. "Process this."

He pulled the triggers and the hammers fell. Two flags shot from the ends of the barrels and unfurled to reveal the message, "Bang!" The sound file that played was a raspberry, which seemed somehow serendipitously appropriate.

I hooked a toe beneath one of my pistols and kicked it up into the air, then snatched it with my left hand. "As I said, you're no Kid Binary."

ANN's face slackened and the cheroot fell to the ground. "You really know Kid Binary?"

"Yup. All my life." I smiled. "And the secret to my success is not picking one common avatar, but to change common avatars the way other folks change clothes." I gestured with the pistol. "And I believe you're wearing one of my hand-me-downs."

The avatar snapped its fingers and the ANN facade puddled at his feet like a silk gown. "I found it. I didn't know what it was or how to use it until Betty.Drivekiller started checking out some of the coach-cracking code you had there."

"That's kind of what I figured." In taking off a datacoach a couple of revs ago, I got hit with a tracer round. I stayed online long enough to pull the coach's data onto an opdat disk, then crude-coded an evasion VIP for my avatar. I let it run while I did a hard-disco—I literally yanked the cable from wall—before agency apes could find me and peel me like a banana.

The bartender kept his hands up. "How'd you gimmick the shotgun? You never touched it."

"Nope, but you took a double-eagle from me. I like to guarantee that those who take my money aren't going to be taking shots at me." I nodded toward his saloon. "I assumed you were the one using my old avatar when you started drinking, and confirmed that guess when Doc started asking for double-eagle Ikes, which he shouldn't have known I was carrying. Next time you communicate covertly with him, remember he can't keep a secret."

"Right."

"So, where did you find this thing?" I kicked the sloughed-off avatar onto the burning remains of the wagon and watched it melt.

"It was here. I was going to be out of touch for a while, so I set up a bunch of Guardian programs to keep hackers out. When I came back I found there had been many attempts to get in, but only one had succeeded. It was your avatar. He was here in my saloon, downing bourbon after bourbon."

"No surprise. Self-preservation programming had taken over."

"That's some great code you've got if an abandoned avatar can survive being hunted."

"I like to think it's good." I frowned. "What disturbs me is that the avatar had a destruct timer. He should have been nothing more than a corpse when you found him."

The bartender smiled and leaned back, hooking a heel over the bar rail. "I put the Guardians in the perimeter and street here, but null-timed the building interiors so I wouldn't have to repair the entropic decay when I got back."

"I guess that's it, then."

The man waved a hand at me. "Come back any time you want."

"I think you're forgetting something." I held my right hand out. "The code key." As he started to slip behind the bar I added, "Just set in on the bar and move away from it."

Pain washed over the bartender's face as he set the glowing green cylinder next to the bourbon bottle. "Look, at least give me some of the money you'll get for it. How about ten percent?"

"You already have it."

"How's that?"

I shrugged and reached for the key. "Ten percent of nothing is nothing."

"But it's going to take forever to repair the damage out there." The bartender shook his head. "With money I could get a new IDF package."

"It was your people who blitzed your bits, not me." I frowned. "You gonna still let them log-in here if you fix the place up?"

"They're friends." The bartender shrugged. "What can I do?"

"Give them a place where they'll fit in."

Poaching a Circus Maxx 3.2 demo-coach wasn't that tough, and kluging it together with what was left of Bitter Root worked fairly well. It took a while to debug things, but pretty soon The Two-bit Circus and Wild West Extravaganza became a popular PAD. I thought it was kind of cute, the prop liked the business and the Two-bit Gang, well, they protested at first but after a couple of revs, those clowns felt right at home.

"**The Greenhorn**" is a cowboy poem. Sure, what's someone who grew up in Vermont doing writing a cowboy poem? It's not my living in Arizona that did it. A good friend of mine, Kassie Klaybourne, read me some of her favorite cowboy poetry—including wonderful stuff by Baxter Black. I got inspired and wrote "**The Greenhorn**" and then, at Kassie's urging, sent it out to see if someone would publish it. *The Tucumcari Review* was the first place I submitted it and they printed it, much to my surprise.

The Greenhorn

There he sat, the greenhorn,
On his horse too proud.
From boots and spurs to ten-gallon hat,
His clothin' was so loud.

Ol' Pete would have laughed,
laughed hard and long.
Never before had he seen a man,
who just looked so damn wrong.

Come for round-up had he,
From back East, Maryland.
Come to the West with a fringy vest,
a sorry-lookin' hand.

Pete figgered teacher or
Clerk or some other.
What he knew was that this man was the
boss' cousin's brother.

Pete had drawn the short straw,
His luck was quite snake-bit.

347

The greenhorn became his companion.
Pete's life had gone to shit.

What is this? What is that?
Questions came unending.
The greenhorn went on and on and on,
Apologizin' for offendin'.

Pete did endure it manfully,
'til ears and throat were sore.
Then he fed the man, got him all bed down.
God, how the man could snore!

Away from camp Pete wandered,
Quiet was his goal.
Ridin' herd on the greenhorn wore him out.
He's feelin' downright old.

Into the night the cowboy went,
On and on he walked.
On 'til the snores were strangled
and around him coy-dogs stalked.

A feral pack, they paced him
down a little hill
Growls and barks, snaps and yowls,
closing for a kill.

Now Pete, he weren't a coward,
and hoped he weren't a fool.
He knew some day he'd end up dyin' but,
This killin' would be cruel.

His gun it lay back in camp,

The Greenhorn

Stoopin' he grabbed a stone.
He snarled at the dogs, flashed some fang.
Not likin' dyin' alone.
Pete brained the first one coming,
Kicked another out the air.
Bit and clawed and snapped and tore,
Pete gave 'em quite a scare.

But a pack of dogs,
stalkin' one man only,
though he gives as good as he gets,
quick makes him feel powerful lonely.

Cussin', fightin' and prayin',
Pete gave it all his best,
but fangs that bite and bites that tear,
bring a man his eternal rest.

So it was, as Pete went down,
A miracle was born,
Up on that hill, eclipsing moon and stars,
Standing tall was Pete's greenhorn.

Into that fray without delay,
sailed the man from the East.
Shoutin' sharp and hissin', the greenhorn
Gave quarter to no beast.

Pete knew they both were dead men,
the dogs would have a feast.
Despite their bold, valiant efforts,
they both would need a priest.

Then the dogs they broke,

yelpin' as they ran.
Growls meltin' into whimpers, dogs fleein',
from the silly little man.

Without a word he helped Pete
limp back to camp and fire.
Pete told his tale all fair and true,
He almost felt a liar.

He looked up at the greenhorn,
then down to burnin' logs.
"I'd like to ask you, partner, how you
dared to fight them dogs."

The greenhorn he just smiled a bit,
fire flashin' from brand new spurs.
"Well, see, its cuz of what I do, I've
got no fear of curs."

"Everyday you're out here,
In this land so pretty.
Whereas my job is drab and dull,
and keeps me in the city."

"It has its dangers though,
Not that different from yers,
I walk a route, I'm a postman, you see,
and I know biting curs."

So into that fight he'd gone,
armed with pepper spray.
It weren't made by Colonel Colt,
but it kept them dogs away.

The Greenhorn

Pete he went and laughed a mite,
laughs spread round the camp.
And the hands recall he who licked the curs,
whene'er they lick a stamp.

"Peer Review" is a superhero story. The main character, Revenant, was someone I designed to be a cross between Batman® and The Shadow® but a bit nastier than either. In trying to write a story for the *Superheroes* anthology, edited by John Varley and Ricia Mainhardt, I had two other tales that were false starts—just not good enough. I had tried to make the tales dark and hard and nasty. To give myself a brand new perspective, I turned all the elements of what I thought made up a Revenant story inside out, upside down and swapped black for white, which resulted in a tale that is a lot of fun.

In 2003, in his *PS 238* comic book, my friend Aaron Williams introduced Revenant as a continuing character mentoring one of the children at PS 238.

Peer Review

Dan Rather smiled for a second before composing his face into the solemn mask he affected when imparting distressful news to the people of America. "The tumultuous kidnap and assault case involving Maria Hopkins, a desperately ill young woman, her little brother, Nathan, and the masked vigilante Revenant took a couple of odd twists today. After the American Justice Committee—a group of superheroes united to uphold the laws of the United States—announced they would hold a hearing on Revenant's actions, news organizations filed suit in Federal court to force the AJC to open their hearing to the public. Lawyers for the networks pointed out that the Federal and States' Attorneys in both Vermont and New Hampshire had refrained from filing charges against Revenant pending the outcome of the AJC hearing.

"The Advocate, charter member of the AJC and their legal advisor, noted that as a legally constituted and privately held Delaware Corporation they were not required to open their meetings. Federal Appeals court Judge Elizabeth Kerin agreed with her argument and refused to issue an order opening the meeting. All indications from the High Court are that they will refuse to hear arguments in the case."

Dan let a hint of surprise lighten his expression. "In the most bizarre turn-around in the case, Revenant—who was believed to be in hiding outside the United States—has agreed to attend the AJC hearing, despite his not being a member of the organization. His agreement was deemed unlikely in light of the AJC's involvement with the case and their active opposition to his actions. Nemesis, founder of the AJC and its current president, gave Revenant a personal guarantee of safety and said the hearing would be fair. Revenant, a shadowy figure who has the distinction of being the only 'superhero' ever to make it to the FBI's Ten Most Wanted list, cited that guarantee as the primary reason for his decision.

"*Quis custodiet ipsos custodies,* the Romans used to ask: Who will guard the Guardians? Now we'll have to ask: Who will guard the guardians while they are guarding themselves?"

The desiccating desert heat surrendered reluctantly as Revenant descended the ramp leading into the American Justice Committee headquarters. Built beneath the Arizona Center—the hole for it being carved out of the caliche by Nemesis and Glacier—the marble-lined walls made him more mindful of a mausoleum than a place meant to be the center for the fight by good against evil. Having holographic images of fallen AJC members built into the walls did not help improve the impression.

The floor leveled out into a small lobby, but the information and ticket booth off to the left was dark and the tour schedule had a big "canceled" sign taped over it. Continuing on ahead, Revenant passed between two twenty-foot high statues of Justice done in bronze and into a narrow corridor with a ceiling that sloped up toward the surface again. At the end of it he entered a huge chamber with red-rock flooring and copper trim everywhere.

Seven members of the AJC waited to render judgment on his actions. Seated behind a high bench, Nemesis occupied the primary position. On his right sat Aranatrix, Hummingbird and Hammersnake; on his left Glacier, Caracal and Thylacine. Each of them wore their costumes and none had deigned to let him see their bare faces.

As he had no intention of doing that either, he did not take their remaining masked as an insult. His midnight blue hood hid his face completely except for his eyes, and his cape shrouded the rest of him. As he walked to the defense table to the left of the central aisle, he refrained from throwing his cloak open quickly—he knew Glacier, Hammersnake and Colonel Constitution would love nothing more than to have an excuse to pound on him. Reaching the table, he gently flipped the cape back behind his shoulders, then carefully drew and laid his dart gun and shock-rod on the table.

He remained standing, taking his cue from The Advocate and Colonel Constitution at the prosecution table. He bowed his head to Nemesis. "I'm sorry to keep you waiting, but parking is at a premium around here." He glanced over at the superhero wearing red, white and blue. "I hope you validate stubs."

Colonel Constitution snarled immediately. "I'll validate your stubby little . . ."

"Enough." Nemesis rose from his chair, muscles bulging. Though born on a planet in a far distant galaxy and sent to Earth as a child, he did not seem alien to Revenant. His uniform had green sleeves and leggings, with white stripes at the shoulders and waist. The blue of the torso matched the hue of Nemesis' domino mask and was not that much lighter than the color of Revenant's uniform. Unlike the Nightmare Detective, Nemesis did not wear gloves or a cape and his long, blond hair touched his broad shoulders.

"I wish to thank you, Revenant, for taking part in this hearing. It is less to ascertain innocence or guilt than it is for us to decide if we will establish a policy concerning you. Your participation in the Hopkins abduction has been the subject of debate here." From the way Nemesis looked around and various members nodded, Revenant guessed the debate had been acrimonious. "It is my hope that we can resolve this situation. Agreed?"

Revenant nodded. "Agreed, though, for the record, I would like to point out that I do not recognize your authority over me, nor do I consider myself bound by any verdict that might be reached here."

A suppressed growl from Colonel Constitution echoed through the cavernous hall. The Advocate, in her trademark double-breasted black suit, black fedora, black mask and black gloves, held Constitution in check, but did not spare Revenant an evil glare. Nemesis nodded affirmatively, then seated himself again. "That is understood."

The AJC leader looked at The Advocate. "Please proceed."

"If it would please the . . . ah, you, my esteemed colleagues, let me remind you of the situation two weeks ago that led to the catalog of crimes pending indictment on Revenant. Fearing for the safety of her six-year-old son Nathan, Jeanette Hopkins—in defiance of a custodial order to the contrary—sought refuge near Groveton Springs, New Hampshire. She said her husband and her daughter were members of a Satanic cult who wanted to sacrifice Nathan in a foul ceremony. Reverend Bert Sunnington took her in and housed her at his Blessed Haven estate near Groveton Springs, then retained legal counsel for her and immediately appealed the Vermont Court's divorce and custody decrees. Her ex-husband, Martin, was enjoined not to do anything to interfere with her temporary custody of Nathan and, in response to a request by the judge who made that ruling, Colonel Constitution led Strike Team Alpha up to New Hampshire to see that the child stayed with his mother.

"That restraining order in place, Revenant entered into a criminal conspiracy with Martin Hopkins to violate that order and commit numerous felonies."

Martin Hopkins never would have described himself as a brave man. A brave man, he told himself, would be able to fight his own battles. He could not, and he acknowledged that fact right along with his failure in any of a number of other areas of his life. Even this appeal might fail, but he was desperate to do anything that might save Maria. Desperate enough to overcome his fear of anything that even remotely looked outside the law and especially anything that had to do with Revenant.

Martin Hopkins in no way looked the part of a hero and certainly didn't feel it, even though a friend he told about the meeting said he had to have balls the size of planets to actually *want* to meet with Revenant. Short and stout, with a pencil-thin moustache and a double chin that rested on the top of his barrel chest, Martin crept into the warehouse Revenant had designated for their meeting as if he were the lead in a very, very bad spy movie. The belt barely kept an old trenchcoat closed and the requisite fedora had given way to a Yankees baseball cap.

Revenant cleared his throat and Martin spun, clutching

at his chest as he saw the shadowed outline of a man. "You wanted to see *me?*"

"Whoa, jeez, don't do that." Martin caught his breath, then doffed his cap and wiped his forehead with his sleeve. "I'm sorry, sir, I mean . . ." Frustration and fatigue wove their way through the man's voice, bringing it to the edge of cracking. "Look, I don't have any money. It's all tied up in the operation."

Revenant slipped from the shadows that had hidden him. "You are getting ahead of yourself. You are Martin Hopkins, forty-one, divorced, two children. Maria is nineteen and Nathan is six. You are the manager of Northwoods Lumber." Revenant's voice, calm and even, drained away some of the panic causing Martin's heart to jackhammer in his chest. "Your ex-wife has your son in a religious commune in New Hampshire."

Martin's brown eyes grew wide. "Good, that's good, that you know that stuff, I mean. That's good."

Revenant inclined his head toward the shorter man. "And why would that be good?"

Martin swallowed with difficulty, his tongue thick in a dry mouth. "Look, my daughter, Maria, she's in the Medical Center Hospital of Vermont over in Burlington. She has leukemia and is going to die. The doctors say she needs marrow for a transplant and I'm not a good donor. Nathan is, but Jeanette . . ."

A lump in his throat choked off the rest of his words. He opened his hands toward Revenant and sniffed.

Revenant's head came up and Hopkins felt the man's green-eyed gaze pierce his soul. "Your wife is aware of Maria's condition and will not allow the donation?"

Martin nodded. "I know Nathan would be willing. He loves his sister." Martin swiped at his nose with his sleeve.

"Reverend Sunnington—I called him to beg, I really did—said Maria's illness is God's retribution for her sins."

Revenant folded his arms and his eyes narrowed perceptibly. Martin felt a chill run down his spine and could see how the man before him had earned the nickname of the Nightmare Detective. Had he been there just for himself, Martin would have run when he first saw Revenant, and if Revenant were ever after him, he knew he'd just die.

"I don't know that I can help you, Mr. Hopkins. While I sympathize with your plight," Revenant shrugged uneasily, "I am only a normal man with a few tricks and a cape. This is the type of case better handled by people like the American Justice Committee."

Martin sagged to his knees. "I tried them. Colonel Constitution says the order is legal and it's a Second Amendment issue. I can't fight them." He opened his mouth, then closed it again. Swallowing the lump down, he croaked, "Please?"

The Nightmare Detective remained silent and motionless for what felt like hours to Martin. Finally he nodded. "How long does your daughter have?"

"Maybe a month. The sooner the better."

"Very well. I will give you details for your part in this. You will have your son as soon as possible."

A charcoal-grey gloved hand extended itself from beneath the blue cape and Martin shook Revenant's hand. Revenant did not seek to crush his hand and Martin drew strength from the firm grip. "One more thing, Mr. Revenant, sir." Martin freed his hand and patted the trenchcoat's pockets until he found what he wanted. He pulled a rabbit's foot from his pocket and handed it to the tall man.

Revenant took it, examined it, then shook his head. "I

appreciate the sentiment, Mr. Hopkins, but I doubt this will help me."

Revenant made to hand it back, but Martin waved him off. "No, look, Nathan is a smart boy and wouldn't go with you unless you can give him a sign that you're bringing him to me. That's his—Jeanette called it Satanic and left it behind when she ran. Give it to him. He'll know."

The Nightmare Detective nodded and the lucky charm disappeared into a pouch on his belt.

Martin smiled and pulled his cap back on. "I can't thank you enough."

"That may be true, Mr. Hopkins, we'll see." Revenant started to withdraw, then stopped. "You can make a start right now, if you will."

Martin stiffened. "Yes?"

"You're not the sort of man to be associating with those who know how to contact me. How did you get the number where you left that message?"

Martin blinked, then thought for a second. "At the hospital, in a Get Well card, someone had put in a note—anonymous. I called."

"Anonymous, interesting." Revenant stepped into the shadows and vanished.

The Advocate turned and pointed at Revenant. "Regardless of the seemingly humanitarian motive of obtaining the marrow needed for a transplant, Revenant mocked the American legal system by planning and executing a series of crimes . . ."

Revenant held a hand up. "Alleged crimes."

Colonel Constitution looked at him, then sank his fingers into the edge of the copper-covered prosecution table. The Advocate bowed her head, her short auburn locks sweeping forward to half hide her face. "Alleged crimes. Revenant did willfully break and enter into the Blessed Haven compound . . ."

"I'll agree to entering, but I did no breaking."

Hummingbird, barely visible behind the microphone that was as big as he was, darted over to within six inches of Nemesis' face, then across to Revenant and back behind his microphone in two seconds. "Mr. President, I have a question."

"Proceed."

"How can you say you did not break, when there was a ten-foot-tall fence with razor wire on the top all around the place? Glacier and I installed it three days before you . . . allegedly entered the Blessed Haven sanctuary." His wings humming, he rose above the microphone, his arms crossed over his chest. "You can't fly, so how did you get in?"

"Trees."

The Advocate frowned. "Trees?"

Revenant nodded. "I climbed a tree, walked out on a branch and went over the fence. The fence later went down when Mr. Force-of-Nature hit it."

The Advocate did her best to speak over Glacier's grumbling. "Regardless, you stole a terrified little boy away from his mother, coerced him into criminal action, then assaulted duly sworn officers of the law in the course of their duty."

Coming across the Blessed Haven compound, Revenant conceded to himself that organized religion did serve a purpose. He chose Wednesday night for his penetration of the commune because he knew the adults would all be at services. He knew, from the handful of articles concerning Reverend Sunnington and Blessed Haven, that all children would be in their rooms studying or praying before lights out at 8:30 P.M.—the commune had its own school, and classes started promptly at 6:30 in the morning, every morning.

Actually locating Nathan Hopkins within the hundred-acre compound had presented a problem, but Revenant managed to narrow down the possibilities. An old map of the compound run in the Manchester *Union Leader* had showed a set of new buildings under construction, and a picture accompanying the same article depicted the construction site as having all the plumbing and electrical fixtures one would need for simple apartment-like housing units. A later map indicated the same buildings were used for "storage," but the article was talking about Sunnington's "Satanic Sacrifice Succor" program. That meant that Jeanette Hopkins and her son would probably be in the new units—labeling them "storage" seemed to be a clearly transparent effort at misdirection.

It did occur to him that the new map, which had only appeared two weeks ago in the *Boston Herald*, might have been planted as part of an elaborate AJC trap. He dismissed that idea because Colonel Constitution was running the AJC operation and "elaborate" became a synonym for "confused" when used in reference to anything he did. The new fence was classic Conny, yet Revenant remained vigilant just in case Constitution had come up with an original idea for once.

Had Blessed Haven maintained a computer listing of its tenants and had Revenant known about it, he could have solved the problem of determining which of the two-dozen apartments in the new complex housed the Hopkins family. As he approached the building, weaving his way through the cars in the church parking lot, he started by eliminating apartments connected to patios or balconies where he saw toys unsuited to a boy or someone of Nathan's age. Crouching in the shadow of the BMW owned by the judge who had signed the restraining order, he also eliminated the dark apartments that looked vacant because they lacked shades on the windows.

Moving on, lest the hiss of the car's quickly flattening tire attract attention, Revenant slipped his knife back into the top of his right boot and worked around to the far side of the complex. Apartment 14 seemed a likely suspect as it had a light on, but no toys on the patio in front of it. He took pride in his deductive ability, then he drew close enough to see a small tag on the door jamb, just above the doorbell, that read "Hopkins, Jeanette" in a small, orderly hand.

He spent his irritation by raking the lock open with his lockpicks in less than five seconds and slipping into the dimly lit apartment. He closed the door behind him, then flipped the flag lock to give himself a second or two extra time to escape if someone were to try to enter. the apartment. He set the heavy pack he had been carrying down in the middle of the living room floor, then crouched and just listened.

The living room and kitchenette were separated by a half-wall. Off to the right a narrow corridor led past a closet to the bathroom—the source of the light in the apartment— and on to two bedrooms. Revenant expected he would find Nathan in one of them, but something didn't feel quite right. He couldn't place it, then he saw a brief flash of light coming from beneath the hall closet door and heard a faint snatch of a hummed tune.

Glancing back out the window and seeing no one, Revenant moved to the closet door. He jiggled the knob, then opened the door. The little light inside snapped off and Revenant recognized the sound of a comic book flapping shut. In the light that slipped from the bathroom into the closet he saw the comic and a flashlight head down into a boot, then a little boy looked up at him.

"Who are you?"

Revenant squatted down. "I'm here to take you to help your sister."

The boy's blue eyes grew wide. "Are you an angel?"

In spite of himself, Revenant laughed. He knew that was the first time and likely the last anyone would ever make that particular mistake about him. "What makes you ask that?"

The boy smiled innocently. "I asked Reverend Sunnington to let me go to help Maria. He said that if Jesus wanted me to help my sister, he would send an angel." The boy reached out and traced the R that made up Revenant's logo on his chest. "You must be Raphael, the helper angel."

"Something like that." Revenant produced the rabbit's foot as if by magic from Nathan's left ear. "I have spoken with your father. He asked me to give this to you."

The boy's face lit up at the mention of his father, then he took the charm and rubbed it in his hands. "If an angel gives this to me, I guess it can't be bad like mommy said."

"Right. Are you ready to go? It will be a little bit of a trip and we can't make much noise."

Nathan nodded solemnly and hitched the rabbit's foot to one of the belt loops in his short pants. He stood up and left the closet, closing it very quietly. On tiptoes he crept out into the living room and stopped beside the pack Revenant had left behind. "I have a pack like this. Mommy had me pack it in case we have to go away. Should I get it?"

Revenant nodded and Nathan ran back to his room. The

Nightmare Detective dropped to one knee by his pack and unzipped one of the pockets. He pulled out two small plastic bottle-shaped items no larger than the rabbit's foot and set them on the ground. Nathan returned, looping a fuzzy bear backpack on, and Revenant pointed to the plastic items.

"Do you know what these are?"

Nathan nodded. "Party favors. Pull the string and they go boom."

"Right. They're for you. Use them only when I tell you to, okay?"

"Okay."

Revenant shouldered his pack, then crossed to the door. He saw no one through the peephole and no one outside the window. "Nathan, when we go out, we're going to keep to the shadows, okay? Follow me and we'll be with your father in no time."

"Okay, Mr. Raphael."

Revenant opened the door and Nathan followed him out into the night. The little boy trotted along as fast as he could, which was not quite fast enough for Revenant's tastes, but the boy said nothing and that earned him points in Revenant's book. They crossed the open area near the apartment complex and got all the way to the church parking lot before stopping. They hunkered down in the shadows of the cars and Nathan began to hum along with the hymn "Nearer My God To Thee."

"Nathan, stop for a second. I have to listen."

The boy clapped his hands over his mouth, then smiled. Revenant looked around but saw nothing out of the ordinary. That did nothing to make him feel any more secure because he knew that his uniform could render him virtually invisible at night and, without the benefit of starlight or infrared vision devices, his chances of spotting someone were very low. He also knew, from experience, that sound would more likely betray a foe at night, but the damned singing would have covered the advance of Hannibal and all his elephants.

Nathan tugged on his cape. "That car over there has a flat tire."

Revenant laughed lightly. "That it does."

A motorcycle's headlight flicked on from the right. "That's not the only thing that's going to be flat around here." Colonel Constitution slammed his right fist into the front of the knight's-shield on his left arm. "I'm going to start with your head and work my way down."

Nemesis nodded as Colonel Constitution finished swearing to tell the truth. "Your witness, Advocate."

The Advocate came around from behind the prosecution table and nodded to Colonel Constitution. "You were present at Blessed Haven with the permission of Reverend Sunnington to enforce the court order protecting Nathan Hopkins, is that correct?"

Constitution nodded, the red threads on his epaulets rocking gently back and forth. "I was in place at Groveton Springs that evening. Nemesis had agreed to my request to let Strike Team Alpha take care of the Hopkins situation. I had Hammersnake, Hummingbird and Glacier patrolling the grounds. I had been watching Jeanette Hopkins in church to prevent any attempt at snatching her. I had a premonition something was wrong, so I left the church and saw the defendant hustling the child away. I hit my Strike Team alert signal to bring the others to me; then I identified myself to the suspect and asked him to comply with the law."

"And his response to that was?"

Colonel Constitution shook his head, his tricorn hat shifting slightly off center. "He responded by violating my civil rights."

Revenant hefted Nathan up and sat him on the roof of the Judge's car, then shucked his pack and set it there. "It's party time, Nathan, and you know what that means. Be ready."

The little boy clutched his party favors and smiled. "Ready."

Revenant stepped away from the vehicle and into the center of the crushed gravel parking lot. "You get one shot, Colonel. Make it good."

Constitution grinned coldly. "I'm going to kick your butt from here to Canada and back, Revenant. You don't stand a ghost of a chance."

"Your puns are cornier than you are." The Nightmare Detective slipped a foot-long silvery tube from the sheath on his right forearm, then shifted it to his right hand. "I bet you call yourself Colonel Constitution because your real name is Bill Wright."

"How did you . . . ?" Constitution snarled furiously and kicked the engine on the motorcycle to life. White stones rooster-tailed out behind the bike as he gunned the motor and the bike reared up. The Premier Patriot wrestled the bike down to the ground and aimed it straight at Revenant. The engine roared as the big Harley bore down on him. Constitution hunkered down behind his shield and Revenant watched as Constitution set himself for a shield punch that would put Revenant down for the count.

At the last second, his cloak a swirling satin cloud, Revenant pivoted on his left foot like a matador dodging a raging bull's charge. He stabbed his shock rod through the spokes of the motorcycle's front tire, then spun away as the shield clipped him on his right shoulder. Moving with the blow, he ended up flat on his back as the shock rod locked against the front wheel's fork. The bike bucked forward and catapulted Constitution through the air.

The Premier Patriot flew like a missile and slammed head first into the grill of a Ford Taurus. Radiator fluid gushed out into the air as the hood crumpled, and in the driver's compartment two airbags exploded from the dashboard and steering wheel. The motorcycle cartwheeled after Constitution, bouncing high on its tires after an initial somersault; then it balanced for a second before falling over to pin Constitution's legs.

Constitution's nostrils flared as he looked over at Revenant. "If it had been an imported car, I would have demolished it and then him. Because it was a domestic, well, I was *hors de combat* for the moment, so I didn't see what happened next."

Nemesis looked over at Revenant. "Have you any questions of this witness?"

The Nightmare Detective shook his head. "None he could answer without grinding his teeth."

"You are excused, then, Colonel." Nemesis stared the man back to his place at the prosecutor's table, then looked at Hummingbird. "I assume, Advocate, you want Hummingbird next?"

"Yes, Your Honor."

Hummingbird zipped from his place to the witness box, then hovered before the microphone, his wings a blur. "On my honor, as a member of the American Justice Committee, I swear to tell the complete truth and labor tirelessly until justice prevails."

The Advocate checked some notes at her table, then looked up. "You were next on the scene, correct?"

"I was."

"Would you describe what happened?"

The Wee Winged Warrior nodded almost imperceptibly. "Not much to tell. He tricked me."

Humming like a furious cicada, Hummingbird's first pass knocked Revenant back to the ground. He'd taken the blow full on his back, so his Kevlar body armor helped absorb some of the shock, but the kinetic energy Hummingbird had built up still blasted him into the gravel. Grabbing the shock rod as he rolled into a crouch, Revenant looked up to see Hummingbird hovering between him and Nathan Hopkins.

"If you want the child, foul one, you must go through me first."

"Have it your way." Revenant slowly stood. "Now, Nathan."

The little boy obediently pulled the lanyard that set off the first party favor. Accompanied by a bright flash and sharp crack, a silvery octopus of fine streamers shot out into the sky. The backdraft and suction from Hummingbird's wings pulled them in, entangling the Wee Winged Warrior before he even knew he was under attack. The streamers enfolded him and the harsh beating of his wings slowed, then stopped, yet before he could fall to the ground, Revenant lunged forward and swirled his shock rod through the trailing tinsel.

His thumb caressed the shock rod's control button for a second and Hummingbird twitched like a spastic marionette, then hung limp from the streamers. Revenant carried him over to the car and set him down, then peeled the tinsel off and flipped the six-inch-tall man over onto his stomach.

"See that, Nathan? He's a small man in a mechanical suit." Revenant pulled the knife from his boot and used the tip of the blade to pry the lid off the little square box between Hummingbird's wings. "These are the batteries he uses to power his wings. If we pop them out, just like that, he won't get into any more trouble."

"If he's trying to stop you, Raphael, he must be a demon."

Revenant shook his head. "Not a demon, just a confused man. It may be a while before you understand it, but there *is* a difference."

Nemesis stared down at Hummingbird. "You say you awoke in the glove box of a Mercedes Benz?"

The tiny superhero shook with indignation. "I'd been stuffed into a tube sock and had a pillow made out of Kleenex."

"That was Nathan's idea," Revenant interjected quickly. "He'd seen cats about in the compound and thought the sock would make a great sleeping bag for you. In the spirit of things, I figured you'd enjoy a suite at the Mercedes hotel."

The Extraterrestrial Titan nodded like Solomon. "I see. Thank you, Hummingbird. Unless Revenant has any questions for you, I think you can be dismissed."

The Nightmare Detective shook his head, then looked up as Hammersnake moved to the witness box. Stretching his right leg up and over the bench, the Elastic Revenger planted it firmly, then let the rest of his body flow down into place like a man-shaped slinky. His right hand snapped up cobra-like and he swore to tell the truth as his two predecessors had.

The Advocate glanced over at Revenant, then smiled and turned to her new witness. "In your encounter with Revenant that evening, you suffered a fate similar to that of two other Strike Team Alpha members, did you not?"

"Yeah."

"But in that encounter you learned something that pertains to his motives for being there, and his methods, correct?"

"Yeah." Hammersnake raked rubbery fingers back through rubbery black hair, the tangled mess making an audible snap as he pulled his fingers free. "Do you want me to tell it now?"

The Advocate nodded. "If you please."

"Yeah, right. I learned Revenant works with the Injustice Cabal . . ."

Revenant and Nathan had hurried along through the night. The Nightmare Detective knew two other members of the AJC's Strike Team Alpha lurked out there somewhere and the only real chance of his defeating them lay in dealing with them separately. "If Hammersnake and Glacier converge . . ."

"Don't worry, Raphael, we have the rabbit's foot."

Revenant smiled and lifted Nathan up in his arms. "Then let's be quick like bunnies and get out of here. Get around there and ride piggyback."

"But rabbits don't do that."

"Angel rabbits have special rules." Revenant shrugged his pack off, then let Nathan settle himself in place. "Ease up on the chokehold there, Nathan."

"Yeah, Nathan, leave something for me."

Revenant whirled and saw an impossibly tall and lean figure silhouetted by the light from the commune buildings.

The man stood with his fists firmly planted on his hips, his chin elongated as it thrust forward. He swayed slightly, like tall grass in a light breeze.

"He looks like a soggy pretzel," Nathan whispered in Revenant's ear, prompting a laugh.

"Yeah, laugh there, Casper, because there ain't nothing you're going to find funny when I'm through with you." Hammersnake jerked a thumb toward himself—deftly done without moving his fist from his hip. "I'm Hammersnake and if you know anything about me at all, you know you better give up now. Don't worry, kid, I'll have you away from him in jig time, then we'll get you signed up with my fan club and get you some action figures and stuff."

Revenant dropped his hand to the holster on his right hip and drew the pistol. Glancing at the selector lever, he switched it over to the second position, then pulled back the cocking lever. He raised the gun to shoulder height, the muzzle pointing toward the stars. "Give it a touch with the foot, Nathan."

As the child happily complied and Revenant drew a bead, Hammersnake laughed aloud. "Shoulda read the press kit on me, Irrelevant. I'm rubber. Bullets bounce off . . . OUCH!" Hammersnake looked down, then plucked a silvery dart from his chest. "A dart. Ha! My metabolism is so special that nothing you could have in there could hurt me. In fact, only the venom of . . .."

"The venom of the Haitian Solenodon can affect you." Revenant pumped two more darts into the Elastic Revenger and the man collapsed into a tangle of garden-hose limbs.

"How did you know? That's a secret!"

"Ever since you got bitten by one when fighting Crimson Carnage outside Port Au Prince, the word's been out on you. The solenodons are being harvested to extinction and the Injustice Cabal's computers list dozens of brokers where you can buy the stuff." Nathan slid from Revenant's back as the Nightmare Detective squatted down and tied Hammersnake's arms and legs around a sapling with a couple of bowlines.

Revenant looked up at the boy. "So, Nathan, you think Hammersnake's a cool hero."

"Not!"

If I ever need a sidekick, Nathan, you're the leading candidate. Revenant took Nathan's hand, recovered his pack and ran off into the darkness before Hammersnake's groans could die away.

"I have a point of clarification, Mr. President."

Nemesis nodded at the woman seated at his right. "Yes, Aranatrix?"

The Mistress of Webs smiled, her silvery costume sharply reflecting the room's muted light. "I have, in spreading my web through the nation's computer systems, come across phantom traces of activity I have attributed to Revenant—though he leaves elusively few clues." She inclined her head toward him and Revenant returned the nod respectfully. "I would note that the information concerning outlets for the purchase of the neurotoxic venom of *Solenodon paradoxus* has been altered and now, as nearly as I can determine, all requests for same are collected and made available to local law enforcement or Federal forces, as appropriate."

Thylacine, down at the end of the bench, smiled beneath his wolfish half-mask. "Mr. President, as you know, Caracal and I pay special attention to crimes in violation of the Endangered Species Act. In Haiti, which is the only place *Solenodon paradoxus* is found, hunting has all but stopped in the past two weeks. I hadn't thought about it until now, mainly because of Haiti and voodoo stories, but rumors of 'The Unholy Ghost' prohibiting poaching and dealing with poachers has destroyed the trade."

Colonel Constitution stabbed a finger at Revenant. "Adding computer crimes and terrorist actions against foreign nationals to your list of crimes now?"

"Alleged crimes." Revenant laughed as Constitution's neck bulged. "And I believe those questions are beyond the scope of your current enquiry."

Nemesis agreed with a nod. "Glacier, you're up next, I think. Thank you, Hammersnake."

Revenant felt the room grow colder as Glacier came around from behind the bench and moved to the witness box. Clad from head to toe in white, Glacier moved with a deliberate slowness. His short-sleeved uniform revealed arms as massively muscled as the rest of him, and icy bracers protected his forearms. His flesh had a bluish tint to it, shades lighter than that used to emblazon the letter G on his chest, but not dark enough to mark him as alien.

After being sworn he stared at Revenant with arctic blue eyes. "Yes, I was the last of our team to face Revenant in the initial encounter. I determined I would not fail to detain him, but I found myself subjected to an unusual form of attack . . ."

Without further interruption, but with a few laughs and giggles, Revenant and Nathan reached the fence the AJC had erected. Revenant dropped his pack to the ground, then upended it. In a nice little bundle a padded chain ladder fell out. Revenant undid the cords holding it together, then lofted it up toward the fence. The thick, canvas padding covered the razor wire while the aluminum rungs provided an easy way to go up and over.

"Okay, Nathan, you go first. Take it easy, and if you see any sharp metal at the top, be careful and don't touch it."

The boy nodded and Revenant tucked the singleton tube sock hanging from the top of the bear pack back inside. "Go for it. I'll be over in a second."

"Halt!" The bellow echoed through the woods like the challenge of a bull moose to a rival. "I arrest you in the name of the American Justice Committee."

"Nuts." Revenant dug into his pack and pulled out a tooled metal device that looked to be the big brother of Nathan's party favors. He looked up at the mountainous man at the crest of the rise they had descended to get to the fence. "That's Glacier."

The boy pulled his remaining favor from his pocket and smiled. "Is it party time again?"

Revenant tousled the boy's light brown hair. "Yeah, but you save that one for later, maybe for when you see your sister, okay? Up and over for you. Wait for me by that big tree over there, okay?"

"Okay."

As Nathan scrambled up the ladder, Revenant stood up and opened his arms wide. "Let me make this easy for you, Sno-Cone, I'm resisting arrest."

"This is ill-advised." Glacier flexed his muscles, eclipsing the moon rising behind him. "I am authorized to use whatever means necessary to detain you."

"Yeah, yeah, you'll put me on ice. There'll be a frost in hell before I walk as a free man. I've heard it all before." Revenant waved Glacier forward. "Do your worst, just don't take all day, okay, Pokey?"

"Tremble where you stand, lawbreaker!" Glacier shook a fist at him as he began to plod forward. "You shall know the inexorable wrath of Glacier!"

Revenant exaggerated a belly laugh. "Oh, that's rich, coming from a guy who went skinny-dipping and sank the Titanic!"

"Aarrgh!" The Chilled Champion lowered his head and started pumping his arms as he charged forward. His legs, which did not look particularly long because of their girth, ate up the hundred yards separating the two men with deceptive quickness. Glacier's body straightened up as he hit his top speed and his fists flexed open and closed as if practicing what they would do to Revenant.

The Nightmare Detective held his ground, crouching slightly, as the behemoth rushed toward him. He could feel the thudding footfalls shake the ground. Glacier's labored breathing echoed like a blast-furnace bellows in the night and the pumping arms reminded him of a locomotive's pistons driving the engine. Twin streams of breath vapor trailed back from either side of Glacier's face and the air took on the bone-numbing cold of an arctic blizzard.

Revenant drew in a breath and held it, waiting until Glacier came within ten feet of him. He raised the metal funnel, then yanked the lanyard. The blank shotgun shell inside the narrow part of the funnel exploded, forcing everything in front of it out the wide end of the device. The waxed cardboard wadding shot out, smacking Glacier squarely in the face, so he never saw the cloud formed by the pound and a half of black pepper that burst out from behind it.

Glacier sucked in pepper like a Dustbuster in overdrive, and immediately choked and coughed back out as much as he could. Then the convulsive sneezing started, with each intake of breath thereafter dragging more and more pepper into his nose and lungs. The tears running from his eyes froze on his face, forming long, Fu-Manchu icicles hanging down from his chin, then a violent sneeze snapped them off as they bashed into his chest.

Revenant, having spun away from the cloud, lowered his cape and saw Glacier stumbling about blindly. He started to reach for his pistol, then decided against it. Walking over to the stricken hero, he spun the man around so his back was to the fence, then planted the heel of his foot on the point of Glacier's chin in a nasty front kick.

Arms and legs flung wide, Glacier flew the remaining half-dozen feet to the fence and sagged into it, like a trapeze artist dropping into a net. A series of high-pitched *twangs* sounded as the cyclone fence abandoned any pretence of holding Glacier up. It tore away from the nearest post first, dragging Glacier off to Revenant's left as the fence contracted.

Nathan peeked out from behind the tree, then whistled as Revenant limped over to him. "He's out cold."

The Nightmare Detective laughed and resisted the temptation to make it tail off into the sinister tones he used when dealing with criminals. "That's good, Nathan. You're a sharp boy. What do you want to be when you grow up?"

Nathan took Revenant's right hand and they started to walk through the woods. "I want to be a hero—not like them, a *real* hero."

"I think you have a chance, Nathan." Revenant gave his hand a squeeze.

"Really?"

"Really. After all, you've already got the dialogue down."

The ice on the witness box banister cracked as Glacier released his grip on it. "That is what I remember."

The Advocate nodded, dismissing Glacier, then turned toward Revenant. "That is the point when you fled to avoid arrest and prosecution. You also conducted the child across state lines, making the kidnapping a Federal offense. Colonel Constitution, if you would be so kind . . ."

Nemesis frowned. "Colonel, if you please, just remain seated at your table. You are still sworn. I know where this is going, so why don't you catch everyone else up."

Constitution cracked his knuckles. "With pleasure."

Nathan stopped when he saw the sleek Corvette waiting in the woods. Dark blue on the top with grey trim along the side panels, the vehicle's nose pointed to a narrow road heading east through the woods. "Wow, God lets you angels have really cool cars."

Revenant winked at him as he disarmed the anti-intruder system. "I got it in trade for my harp and a millennium of payments. Hop in."

Nathan slid into the passenger seat and Revenant closed the door before vaulting the hood and getting in the other side. Nathan had already pulled his pack off over his head and started to fasten the seat belts. Revenant helped him, tucking the pack down in the footwell, and nodded when he was finished. "Next stop your sister's hospital, okay?"

"Okay."

Revenant pulled his own safety harness on, snapping the belts into a stainless clasp over his chest, then fastened the lap belt low and snug. He punched the ignition code in, bringing the engine purring to life. He let Nathan hit the button that turned the lights on, then brought up the onboard navigational computer. "That dot, it's us. We'll use the old Route 110 extension to a covered bridge over the Connecticut River and into Vermont."

"I like covered bridges. Maria does too."

"Good, you can tell her all about this one." The Corvette roared down the woodland track and joined a paved road about a mile further on. Revenant felt apprehensive as he pulled onto the New Hampshire state route, but it was the quickest way he could get to his destination in the car. A more direct route would have continued through the woods, but the Corvette would have bottomed out a number of times and could even have been put out of commission if a tree had fallen in the thirty-six hours since he last scouted that route.

His confidence grew as they blew through Groveton and turned left. The 110 extension had been graded, but maintained only for local residential use. The dark car moved through the rolling New England hills like a panther eluding pursuit and Revenant began to smile as the dot on the computer screen closed with the bridge icon.

"What's that?"

Revenant looked over at what Nathan had pointed out and snarled. "That's trouble." A flickering, bobbing light moved through the woods at a high rate of speed. Revenant lost sight of it for a moment behind a small hillock, then saw it bumping its way across a meadow as he crested the hill for the run down to the bridge.

He hit his high beams as the light slowed—it and the 'vette stopping at the same time. Colonel Constitution extended the motorcycle's kickstand. The front tire peeled apart like a retread shedding its outer skin, leaving behind a D-shaped wheel rim. Revenant blinked as the tire spat out road pebbles and tried to straighten up, but Hammersnake's legs quivered and he sat down hard.

Colonel Constitution ignored his battered companion. "It's over, Revenant. Time to take your medicine." Constitution hit a button on his bike's control panel and two Red Rockets shot out from the launch tubes mounted on either side of the high seat. They arced high into the sky, then arrowed down and slammed into the covered bridge.

The ancient wooden structure had withstood storms and floods in its lifetime, but high explosives were more than a match for it. The twin fireballs blasted the center of the bridge into burning splinters. Cedar shingles flew like autumn leaves through the air and flaming planks sailed out into the river's dark waters. Jagged beam ends burned brightly, marking where the center of the road bed had once stood—memorial flames mourning the gap that separated them.

Constitution rubbed his gloved hands together, then made a big show of punching a button on his belt buckle. "There, I've even gone and summoned the Big Guy so he can use his X-Ray sight to keep track of your bones as I break them. Get out of that car and I'll give you a nightmare it won't take a detective to figure out."

Revenant glanced over at Nathan. "Seatbelts fastened?"

The boy nodded. "Check."

"Rabbit's foot deployed?"

Nathan rubbed it. "Check."

"Let's go!"

Revenant jammed his foot down on the accelerator and worked his way up through the gears smoothly. He finished shifting by the time a surprised Colonel Constitution dove out of the roadway. Keeping both hands locked on the wheel, Revenant came around the last bend in the road and started up the slight incline to the bridge. He watched the digital display continue to add numbers to his speed, but he didn't relax even as it cracked triple digits.

"Here we go, hang on!"

The Corvette shot through the fire at the bridge end, the engine screaming as the wheels met no more resistance. Revenant watched as the car's nose touched Jupiter, holding his breath and praying it would stay pointed in that direction for another second and another after that. Then slowly it began to dip and his first glimpse of flames on the other side seemed to place them just a little more distant than he had hoped they would be.

Nathan shrieked with glee. "We're flying!"

"I guess we are. Brace yourself," Revenant grimaced. "We're landing."

The car touched down hard, sparks shooting everywhere as the vehicle bottomed out on the far side's concrete approach. The impact jammed Revenant down in his seat and he ducked his head so the rebound wouldn't bash him senseless against the roof. He heard metal scream and felt a bump as some of the tailpipe assembly tore away, then a second heavier thump came from the back.

The car immediately started dragging its tail. Revenant saw one of the rear tires whirling off along the road ahead of them. It passed between two cars parked in the darkness on the Vermont side of the 110 extension, but Revenant ignored them as he fought to bring the Corvette to a stop. He spun the wheel to the left to counter the skid, but the car spun and backed into a roadside drainage ditch with a solid bump.

The navigational computer shorted out in a puff of smoke and Nathan's airbag deployed, but it did not muffle his laughter. "That was great. Do it again!"

"Not right now. We have to give your rabbit's foot a rest." Revenant popped his restraining harness open, then freed Nathan. As the two of them left the ruined vehicle, the waiting cars turned on their headlights and a heavy-set man came out of the station wagon.

"Dad!" Nathan, his bear pack swinging wildly in his right hand, ran to his father and hugged the man's legs.

Revenant threw Martin a thumbs-up, then looked at the primly dressed woman getting out of the Infiniti Q45. She pulled a leather briefcase with her and started to open it, but froze when Nathan screamed, "Look out!"

A red, white and blue meteor hurled through the flames burning at river's edge. Propelled like a slingshot pellet by Hammersnake on the far side, Colonel Constitution smashed his shield into Revenant's back, then rolled on down the road until he could bleed off his momentum and regain his feet.

Nathan's warning had enabled Revenant to begin to shift away from the blow. Even so, the shield caught him solidly and smacked him into the side of the Infiniti. Rebounding from metal-sandwiched polymer alloy plating, Revenant landed on his back, momentarily stunned. Feeling flooded back into his arms and legs—pain mostly—but conscious control over his limbs still eluded him.

Colonel Constitution swaggered up into sight at his feet. "Get used to being on your back, because you'll be spending a lot of time in traction." He laughed coldly. "It's party time!"

He raised his shield to bash Revenant with it, but an expanding ball of tinsel shot up from Nathan's last party favor and blinded him. Revenant rolled to his right as Constitution punched his shield down into the road, then swept his leaden left leg back, catching Constitution in the ribs. The Premier Patriot spun away, then clawed the silvery tinsel from his face.

"You've corrupted the minor!"

Revenant rose unsteadily to his feet. "Better that than he grow up like you."

Constitution raised his shield again and closed, but another figure descended from the sky and stopped him in mid-rush by planting a hand in the middle of his chest. "Stop, Colonel." Nemesis looked over at Revenant and held his other hand out to keep them apart. "If you please, Revenant, minimizing the violence would be best for the boy, don't you think?"

The Nightmare Detective nodded. "Just tell that to Captain Collateral Damage over there."

"I'm going to nail your butt!" Constitution's wild gesticulations did not cease even when Nemesis lifted him from the ground. "You're mine. You're under arrest!"

The woman turned from inspecting the dent in her car and pulled a piece of paper from her briefcase. "And you will likewise be under arrest if you continue harassing Revenant, Mr. Hopkins or his son." She slapped the paper against Constitution's stomach. "This is a restraining order compelling you and Strike Team Alpha to stay one thousand meters from Revenant and the Hopkins family."

Nemesis released Constitution. The Premier Patriot unfolded the order, scanned it, then crumpled it up in a ball. "What kind of lily-livered judge would sign that sort of order?"

The woman grabbed a handful of Constitution's tricolored tunic. "*I* signed it, buster. It's got as much force as the order you were upholding over there in New Hampshire, so I suggest you think about that. Then I suggest you start marching off one thousand meters to the east and remember to breathe when you're swimming."

Colonel Constitution looked stricken. "Nemesis?"

The AJC President shrugged his shoulders. "We uphold the law, Colonel. Comply with the order."

Revenant winked at the retreating hero. "Remember that

breathing thing. Pity about the bridge."

Nemesis dropped to his haunches and smiled at Nathan. "So you're the young man who's going to help his sister get better, is that right?"

Revenant looked back at his car and groaned. "Judge, do you mind if I borrow your car for a quick hospital run?"

She shot him a harsh stare. "After I've seen what you did to a 'vette? You sent Mr. Hopkins to me because I'm smart, remember?"

Nemesis straightened up. "I think I can remedy the problem. With your permission, Mr. Hopkins, I'll fly your son to the hospital."

Nathan shook his head. "Let the angel fly me."

Nemesis cocked an eyebrow at Revenant. "Angel?"

"He thinks the R stands for Raphael. Could have been worse; he could have thought I was a turtle." Revenant shook his head at Nathan. "Naw, go with Nemesis. If us angels do everything, guys like Nemesis won't have any reason to be called a hero."

The Advocate opened her hands. "That covers almost everything, I think. Aranatrix has informed me that some tampering was done with Reverend Sunnington's bank account, deducting something in excess of $467,353 from it. This figure is remarkable only in that it is roughly the amount of the bills the Hopkins family ran up in medical and legal fees concerning Maria's illness. This is just one more count of computer crimes—alleged computer crimes—that can be added to the list.

"If it pleases your honor, I rest my case."

Nemesis looked down at Revenant. "You've not questioned any of the witnesses against you. Do you have any witnesses for your defense? The Hopkins family, perhaps?"

"No, I have no witnesses." Revenant stood slowly. "The Hopkins family has more important things to do than to talk here today."

"Do you want to make any comments in your defense?"

Revenant shook his head. "My actions need no defense."

"The hell they don't!" Colonel Constitution shot like a rocket from his chair. "There are guys on Death Row who've broken fewer laws than you have. You trampled all over the very Constitution that I've sworn to defend. You're a lawbreaker—you're worse because you don't even think the laws should apply to you. You offer no defense because there *is* no defense for what you have done!"

"Wrong." Revenant came out from behind his table, shaking his head. "You draw the line at the law. You use the Constitution and the legal framework of this nation like a wall that segregates good from evil. You think and act in a realm of absolutes, rigidly defending the product of a process that you choose to ignore."

"Think." The Nightmare Detective tapped his brow. "Think, dammit. This nation, the tradition of laws you cling to, has undergone multiple changes through the centuries. Why? Because what was once considered just and right is determined, by mutual consent, to be unjust. A thousand years ago it was a man's right—his duty—to beat his wife. In the American South it was once a crime to teach blacks to read. Fifty years ago we imprisoned American citizens just because of the color of their skin and their ancestry. That was unjust, but had you been there, you would have been standing at the gates of internment camps keeping the Japanese in."

The Advocate sniffed. "The Supreme Court upheld the internment order. Extraordinary times demand extraordinary methods."

"Exactly!" Revenant's right hand contracted into a fist. "Extraordinary times require extraordinary methods and yet, fifty years later, reparations were paid to the survivors of internment. We recognized an injustice and made an attempt at making it right again. That's what I did here."

"But the courts were the right place to fight out the battle being waged between Mr. and Mrs. Hopkins."

"No! They were not a good battleground because resolving it there would have taken time—time Maria did not have." Revenant's head came up. "There was an injustice there and it was my duty—the duty of every human being who could recognize it as such—to effect a remedy."

The Nightmare Detective looked at each of the AJC members in turn as he spoke. "I understand why you draw the line at the law, because to move past it is to move into an arena with no restraints, no boundaries. I have chosen, unlike you, to live in that region outside the law because that's where you have to go to hunt down the people who would destroy the world encompassed by the law."

"So," Constitution sneered, "you're admitting you're a criminal."

"No, I admit I am an outlaw, and there *is* a difference. I do have a guide out there: *justice.* Siphoning off money from Reverend Sunnington to cover the operation *was* justice. Forcing Charles Keating to operate one of his resorts for, and act as butler for, the people he bilked, that *would be* justice—perhaps not under the law, but it would be justice none the less." Revenant's hand opened, then disappeared beneath his cape. "I do not hold you in disrespect because of the choice you have made, and I feel no need to defend the choice I made."

Nemesis smiled. "You were eloquent in your non-defense."

The Nightmare Detective nodded. "Colonel Constitution inspires me."

The Extraterrestrial Titan smiled. "I think, then, we can come to a verdict here. You've heard the evidence. Register your votes, please."

Nemesis waited until the last of his compatriots had withdrawn from the chamber before congratulating Revenant on his acquittal. He offered the Nightmare Detective his hand. "I know you don't think it is important, but I appreciated your participation here. There are times when the American Justice Committee needs to remember that while we uphold the law, discretion, latitude and even dissent are part of the system. I have assurances that the Federal Attorney and the State Attorneys in Vermont and New Hampshire will *nol pros* the charges against you."

Revenant shrugged. "Better the indictments never go into the NCIC computer than I have to go in and get them out again." He shook Nemesis' hand, then looked the taller man in the eye. "Close vote."

Nemesis nodded. "Not unexpected, given that we do law, you do justice. I had expected the three members of Strike Team Alpha to vote against you. Your work with the computers and in Haiti swung the other three to your side."

Revenant nodded. "And you cast the deciding vote—which had to go in my favor since you dragged me into this whole affair in the first place."

The big man smiled. "When did you know I was involved?"

"I *suspected* when Martin told me he'd gotten the number he called in an anonymous Get Well card. I'd only given that particular number to a dozen people—including you—and most of them would have been angling for a reward for making the contact, not offering the information anonymously." Revenant shrugged. "*Know,* on the other hand . . ."

"At the river, right? When I flew underneath and gave you the boost to make the jump?"

"Nathan announcing that we were flying was a big clue, yeah." Revenant folded his arms across his chest. "You'll have to be careful there, Nemesis; in doing that, you aided and abetted a fleeing felon."

"Not at all." He clapped Revenant on the shoulders. "I just stopped you from illegally dumping your car in the river."

Revenant laughed. "Gotta know the rules if you're going to play by them."

"Or if you are going to be the exception to them."

"Story of my life."

Nemesis walked with Revenant toward the exit. "So now that the Haitian situation has calmed down and this is over, are you going to take a vacation?"

"I'd love to, but there's always more work to do." The Nightmare Detective shook his head. "I just ran across a couple of IRS agents who have a scam to boost their collection rating. They created a computer program that scans returns to select folks who can't or won't fight an audit. They pounce, the victim settles and the agents are golden boys."

Nemesis nodded thoughtfully. "You could turn the evidence you've collected over to their supervisor and have them dealt with very easily."

"True, but that would be playing the game by *your* rules." Revenant shook his head. "If I did that, the IRS would reprimand them, perhaps put a negative letter in their files and, horror of horrors, ship them to Fairbanks to run the Alaska office. That's not justice for even *one* audit."

"I see." Nemesis frowned. "Then what, by Revenant's

rules, *would* constitute justice in this case?"

"Oh, I have something very special planned. It is guaranteed to fulfill the dictates of justice, and to serve as a deterrent against future crime. I got into their computer and made some changes to their program, directing the selection of their next victim."

"That person being you, I take it?"

"Me? No, that would be too easy." Revenant's sinister laughter echoed through the dark marble corridor. "The next audit on their list is of a guy named Bill Wright."

About the Author

Michael A. Stackpole is an award-winning author, game and computer game designer and poet whose first novel, **Warrior: En Garde** was published in 1988. Since then he has written thirty-six other novels, including eight *New York Times* bestselling novels in the Star Wars® line, of which **X-wing: Rogue Squadron** and **I, Jedi** are the best known. He also writes lots of short stories, as you can tell from this collection.

Mike lives in Arizona and in his spare time spends early mornings at Starbucks, collects toy soldiers and old radio shows, plays indoor soccer, rides his bike and listens to Irish music in the finer pubs in the Phoenix area. His website is www.stormwolf.com.

Additional Copyright Information